PHILO GUBB
Correspondence-School Detective

"IN THE DETECKATIVE LINE NOTHING SOUNDS FOOLISH"
(page 218)

PHILO GUBB

Correspondence-School Detective

BY

ELLIS PARKER BUTLER

WITH ILLUSTRATIONS

Fredonia Books
Amsterdam, The Netherlands

Philo Gubb:
Correspondence-School Detective

by
Ellis Parker Butler

ISBN: 1-4101-0615-2

Copyright © 2004 by Fredonia Books

Reprinted from the 1918 edition

Fredonia Books
Amsterdam, The Netherlands
http://www.fredoniabooks.com

CONTENTS

ILLUSTRATIONS

ILLUSTRATIONS

PHILO GUBB
Correspondence-School Detective

PHILO GUBB
THE CORRESPONDENCE-SCHOOL DETECTIVE

THE HARD-BOILED EGG

WALKING close along the wall, to avoid the creaking floor boards, Philo Gubb, paper-hanger and student of the Rising Sun Detective Agency's Correspondence School of Detecting, tiptoed to the door of the bedroom he shared with the mysterious Mr. Critz. In appearance Mr. Gubb was tall and gaunt, reminding one of a modern Don Quixote or a human flamingo; by nature Mr. Gubb was the gentlest and most simple-minded of men. Now, bending his long, angular body almost double, he placed his eye to a crack in the door panel and stared into the room. Within, just out of the limited area of Mr. Gubb's vision, Roscoe Critz paused in his work and listened carefully. He heard the sharp whistle of Mr. Gubb's breath as it cut against the sharp edge of the crack in the panel, and he knew he was being spied upon. He placed his chubby hands on his knees and smiled at the door, while a red flush of triumph spread over his face.

Through the crack in the door Mr. Gubb could

3

see the top of the washstand beside which Mr. Critz was sitting, but he could not see Mr. Critz. As he stared, however, he saw a plump hand appear and pick up, one by one, the articles lying on the washstand. They were: First, seven or eight half shells of English walnuts; second, a rubber shoe heel out of which a piece had been cut; third, a small rubber ball no larger than a pea; fourth, a paper-bound book; and lastly, a large and glittering brick of yellow gold. As the hand withdrew the golden brick, Mr. Gubb pressed his face closer against the door in his effort to see more, and suddenly the door flew open and Mr. Gubb sprawled on his hands and knees on the worn carpet of the bedroom.

"There, now!" said Mr. Critz. "There, now! Serves you right. Hope you hurt chuself!"

Mr. Gubb arose slowly, like a giraffe, and brushed his knees.

"Why?" he asked.

"Snoopin' an' sneakin' like that!" said Mr. Critz crossly. "Scarin' me to fits, a'most. How'd I know who 't was? If you want to come in, why don't you come right in, 'stead of snoopin' an' sneakin' an' fallin' in that way?"

As he talked, Mr. Critz replaced the shells and the rubber heel and the rubber pea and the gold-brick on the washstand. He was a plump little man with a shiny bald head and a white goatee. As he talked, he bent his head down, so that he might look above the glasses of his spectacles; and in spite of his pre-

tended anger he looked like nothing so much as a
kindly, benevolent old gentleman — the sort of old
gentleman that keeps a small store in a small village
and sells writing-paper that smells of soap, and candy
sticks out of a glass jar with a glass cover.

"How'd I know but what you was a detective?"
he asked, in a gentler tone.

"I am," said Mr. Gubb soberly, seating himself
on one of the two beds. "I'm putty near a deteckative, as you might say."

"Ding it all!" said Mr. Critz. "Now I got to go
and hunt another room. I can't room with no detective."

"Well, now, Mr. Critz," said Mr. Gubb, "I don't
want you should feel that way."

"Knowin' you are a detective makes me all
nervous," complained Mr. Critz; "and a man in my
business has to have a steady hand, don't he?"

"You ain't told me what your business is," said
Mr. Gubb.

"You need n't pretend you don't know," said
Mr. Critz. "Any detective that saw that stuff on
the washstand would know."

"Well, of course," said Mr. Gubb, "I ain't a full
deteckative yet. You can't look for me to guess
things as quick as a full deteckative would. Of
course that brick sort of looks like a gold-brick —"

"It *is* a gold-brick," said Mr. Critz.

"Yes," said Mr. Gubb. "But — I don't mean
no offense, Mr. Critz — from the way you look —

5

I sort of thought — well, that it was a gold-brick you'd bought."

Mr. Critz turned very red.

"Well, what if I did buy it?" he said. "That ain't any reason I can't sell it, is it? Just because a man buys eggs once — or twice — ain't any reason he should n't go into the business of egg-selling, is it? Just because I've bought one or two gold-bricks in my day ain't any reason I should n't go to sellin' 'em, is it?"

Mr. Gubb stared at Mr. Critz with unconcealed surprise.

"You ain't, — you ain't a con' man, are you, Mr. Critz?" he asked.

"If I ain't yet, that's no sign I ain't goin' to be," said Mr. Critz firmly. "One man has as good a right to try his hand at it as another, especially when a man has had my experience in it. Mr. Gubb, there ain't hardly a con' game I ain't been conned with. I been confidenced long enough; from now on I'm goin' to confidence other folks. That's what I'm goin' to do; and I won't be bothered by no detective livin' in the same room with me. Detectives and con' men don't mix noways! No, sir!"

"Well, sir," said Mr. Gubb, "I can see the sense of that. But you don't need to move right away. I don't aim to start in deteckating in earnest for a couple of months yet. I got a couple of jobs of paper-hanging and decorating to finish up, and I can't start in sleuthing until I get my star, anyway.

THE HARD-BOILED EGG

And I don't get my star until I get one more lesson
and learn it, and send in the examination paper, and
five dollars extra for the diploma. Then I'm goin'
at it as a reg'lar business. It's a good business.
Every day there's more crooks — excuse me, I
did n't mean to say that."

"That's all right," said Mr. Critz kindly. "Call
a spade a spade. If I ain't a crook yet, I hope to be
soon."

"I did n't know how you'd feel about it," explained Mr. Gubb. "Tactfulness is strongly advised into the lessons of the Rising Sun Deteckative
Agency Correspondence School of Deteckating —"

"Slocum, Ohio?" asked Mr. Critz quickly. "You
did n't see the ad. in the 'Hearthstone and Farm-
side,' did you?"

"Yes, Slocum, Ohio," said Mr. Gubb, "and that
is the paper I saw the ad. into; 'Big Money in Deteckating. Be a Sleuth. We can make you the equal
of Sherlock Holmes in twelve lessons.' Why?"

"Well, sir," said Mr. Critz, "that's funny. That
ad. was right atop of the one I saw, and I studied
quite considerable before I could make up my mind
whether 't would be best for me to be a detective
and go out and get square with the fellers that sold
me gold-bricks and things by putting them in jail,
or to even things up by sending for this book that
was advertised right under the 'Rising Sun Correspondence School.' How come I settled to do as
I done was that I had a sort of stock to start with,

7

with a fust-class gold-brick, and some green goods
I'd bought; and this book only cost a quatter of a
dollar. And she's a hummer for a quatter of a dollar!
A hummer!"

He pulled the paper-covered book from his pocket
and handed it to Mr. Gubb. The title of the book
was "The Complete Con' Man, by the King of the
Grafters. Price 25 cents."

"That there book," said Mr. Critz proudly, as if
he himself had written it, "tells everything a man
need to know to work every con' game there is.
Once I get it by heart, I won't be afraid to try any
of them. Of course, I got to start in small. I can't
hope to pull off a wire-tapping game right at the
start, because that has to have a gang. You don't
know anybody you could recommend for a gang,
do you?"

"Not right offhand," said Mr. Gubb thoughtfully.

"If you was n't goin' into the detective business,"
said Mr. Critz, "you'd be just the feller for me.
You look sort of honest and not as if you was too
bright, and that counts a lot. Even in this here
simple little shell game I got to have a podner.
I got to have a podner I can trust, so I can let him
look like he was winnin' money off of me. You see,"
he explained, moving to the washstand, "this shell
game is easy enough when you know how. I put
three shells down like this, on a stand, and I put
the little rubber pea on the stand, and then I take
up the three shells like this, two in one hand and

8

"THIS SHELL GAME IS EASY ENOUGH WHEN YOU KNOW
HOW"

one in the other, and I wave 'em around over the pea, and maybe push the pea around a little, and I say, 'Come on! Come on! The hand is quicker than the eye!' And all of a suddent I put the shells down, and you think the pea is under one of them, like that —"

"I don't think the pea is under one of 'em," said Mr. Gubb. "I seen it roll onto the floor."

"It did roll onto the floor that time," said Mr. Critz apologetically. "It most generally does for me, yet. I ain't got it down to perfection yet. This is the way it ought to work — oh, pshaw! there she goes onto the floor again! Went under the bed that time. Here she is! Now, the way she ought to work is — there she goes again!"

"You got to practice that game a lot before you try it onto folks in public, Mr. Critz," said Mr. Gubb seriously.

"Don't I know that?" said Mr. Critz rather impatiently. "Same as you've got to practice snoopin', Mr. Gubb. Maybe you thought I did n't know you was snoopin' after me wherever I went last night."

"Did you?" asked Mr. Gubb, with surprise plainly written on his face.

"I seen you every moment from nine P.M. till eleven!" said Mr. Critz. "I did n't like it, neither."

"I did n't think to annoy you," apologized Mr. Gubb. "I was practicin' Lesson Four. You was n't supposed to know I was there at all."

"Well, I don't like it," said Mr. Critz. "'T was all right last night, for I did n't have nothin' important on hand, but if I'd been workin' up a con' game, the feller I was after would have thought it mighty strange to see a man follerin' me everywhere like that. If you went about it quiet and unobtrusive, I would n't mind; but if I'd had a customer on hand and he'd seen you it would make him nervous. He'd think there was a — a crazy man follerin' us."

"I was just practicin'," apologized Mr. Gubb. "It won't be so bad when I get the hang of it. We all got to be beginners sometime."

"I guess so," said Mr. Critz, rearranging the shells and the little rubber pea. "Well, I put the pea down like this, and I dare you to bet which shell she's goin' to be under, and you don't bet, see? So I put the shells down, and you're willin' to bet you see me put the first shell over the pea like this. So you keep your eye on that shell, and I move the shells around like this —"

"She's under the same shell," said Mr. Gubb.

"Well, yes, she *is*," said Mr. Critz placidly, "but she had n't ought to be. By rights she ought to sort of ooze out from under whilst I'm movin' the shells around, and I'd ought to sort of catch her in between my fingers and hold her there so you don't see her. Then when you say which shell she's under, she ain't under any shell; she's between my fingers. So when you put down your money I tell you to pick up that shell and there ain't anything under it. And before you can pick up the other shells I pick one up, and let the pea fall on the stand like it had been under that shell all the time. That's the game, only up to now I ain't got the hang of it. She won't ooze out from under, and she won't stick between my fingers, and when she does stick, she won't drop at the right time."

"Except for that, you've got her all right, have you?" asked Mr. Gubb.

"Except for that," said Mr. Critz; "and I'd have that, only my fingers are stubby."

"What was it you thought of having me do if I was n't a deteckative?" asked Mr. Gubb.

"The work you'd have to do would be capping work," said Mr. Critz. "Capper — that's the professional name for it. You'd guess which shell the ball was under —"

"That would be easy, the way you do it now," said Mr. Gubb.

"I told you I'd got to learn it better, did n't I?" asked Mr. Critz impatiently. "You'd be capper, and you'd guess which shell the pea was under. No matter which you guessed, I'd leave it under that one, so 'd you'd win, and you'd win ten dollars every time you bet — but not for keeps. That's why I've got to have an honest capper."

"I can see that," said Mr. Gubb; "but what's the use lettin' me win it if I've got to bring it back?"

"That starts the boobs bettin'," said Mr. Critz.

"The boobs see how you look to be winnin', and they want to win too. But they don't. When they bet, I win."

"That ain't a square game," said Mr. Gubb seriously, "is it?"

"A crook ain't expected to be square," said Mr. Critz. "It stands to reason, if a crook wants to be a crook, he's got to be crooked, ain't he?"

"Yes, of course," said Mr. Gubb. "I had n't looked at it that way."

"As far as I can see," said Mr. Critz, "the more I know how a detective acts, the better off I'll be when I start in doin' real business. Ain't that so? I guess, till I get the hang of things better, I'll stay right here."

"I'm glad to hear you say so, Mr. Critz," said Mr. Gubb with relief. "I like you, and I like your looks, and there's no tellin' who I might get for a roommate next time. I might get some one that was n't honest."

So it was agreed, and Mr. Critz stood over the washstand and manipulated the little rubber pea and the three shells, while Mr. Gubb sat on the edge of the bed and studied Lesson Eleven of the "Rising Sun Detective Agency's Correspondence School of Detecting."

When, presently, Mr. Critz learned to work the little pea neatly, he urged Mr. Gubb to take the part of capper, and each time Mr. Gubb won he gave him a five-dollar bill. Then Mr. Gubb posed as a "boob" and Mr. Critz won all the money back again, beaming over his spectacle rims, and chuckling again and again until he burst into a fit of coughing that made him red in the face, and did not cease until he had taken a big drink of water out of the wash-pitcher. Never had he seemed more like a kindly old gentleman from behind the candy counter of a small village. He hung over the washstand, manipulating the little rubber pea as if fascinated.

"Ain't it curyus how a feller catches onto a thing like that all to once?" he said after a while. "If it had n't been that I was so anxious, I might have fooled with that for weeks and weeks and not got anywheres with it. I do wisht you could be my capper a while anyway, until I could get one."

"I need all my time to study," said Mr. Gubb. "It ain't easy to learn deteckating by mail."

"Pshaw, now!" said Mr. Critz. "I'm real sorry! Maybe if I was to pay you for your time and trouble five dollars a night? How say?"

Mr. Gubb considered. "Well, I dunno!" he said slowly. "I sort of hate to take money for doin' a favor like that."

"Now, there ain't no need to feel that way," said Mr. Critz. "Your time's wuth somethin' to me — it's wuth a lot to me to get the hang of this gold-brick game. Once I get the hang of it, it won't be no trouble for me to sell gold-bricks like this one for all the way from a thousand dollars up. I paid fifteen hundred for this one myself, and got it cheap.

That's a good profit, for this brick ain't wuth a cent over one hundred dollars, and I know, for I took it to the bank after I bought it, and that's what they was willin' to pay me for it. So it's easy wuth a few dollars for me to have help whilst I'm learnin'. I can easy afford to pay you a few dollars, and to pay a friend of yours the same."

"Well, now," said Mr. Gubb, "I don't know but what I might as well make a little that way as any other. I got a friend —" He stopped short. "You don't aim to *sell* the gold-brick to him, do you?"

Mr. Critz's eyes opened wide behind their spectacles.

"Land's sakes, no!" he said.

"Well, I got a friend may be willing to help out," said Mr. Gubb. "What'd he have to do?"

"You or him," said Mr. Critz, "would be the 'come-on,' and pretend to buy the brick. And you or him would pretend to help me to sell it. Maybe you better have the brick, because you can look stupid, and the feller that's got the brick has got to look that."

"I can look anyway a'most," said Mr. Gubb with pride.

"Do tell!" said Mr. Critz, and so it was arranged that the first rehearsal of the gold-brick game should take place the next evening, but as Mr. Gubb turned away Mr. Critz deftly slipped something into the student detective's coat pocket.

It was toward noon the next day that Mr. Critz,

peering over his spectacles and avoiding as best he could the pails of paste, entered the parlor of the vacant house where Mr. Gubb was at work.

"I just come around," said Mr. Critz, rather reluctantly, "to say you better not say nothing to your friend. I guess that deal's off."

"Pshaw, now!" said Mr. Gubb. "You don't mean so!"

"I don't mean nothing in the way of aspersions, you mind," said Mr. Critz with reluctance, "but I guess we better call it off. Of course, so far as I know, you are all right—"

"I don't know what you're gettin' at," said Mr. Gubb. "Why don't you say it?"

"Well, I been buncoed so often," said Mr. Critz. "Seem's like any one can get money from me any time and any way, and I got to thinkin' it over. I don't know anything about you, do I? And here I am, going to give you a gold-brick that cost me fifteen hundred dollars, and let you go out and wait until I come for it with your friend, and—well, what's to stop you from just goin' away with that brick and never comin' back?"

Mr. Gubb looked at Mr. Critz blankly.

"I've went and told my friend," he said. "He's all ready to start in."

"I hate it, to have to say it," said Mr. Critz, "but when I come to count over them bills I lent you to cap the shell game with, there was a five-dollar one short."

"I know," said Gubb, turning red. "And if you

go over there to my coat, you'll find it in my pocket, all ready to hand back to you. I don't know how I come to keep it in my pocket. Must ha' missed it, when I handed you back the rest."

"Well, I had a notion it was that way," said Mr. Critz kindly. "You look like you was honest, Mr. Gubb. But a thousand-dollar gold-brick, that any bank will pay a hundred dollars for — I got to get out of this way of trustin' everybody — "

Mr. Critz was evidently distressed.

"If 't was anybody else but you," he said with an effort, "I'd make him put up a hundred dollars to cover the cost of a brick like that whilst he had it. There! I've said it, and I guess you're mad!"

"I ain't mad," protested Mr. Gubb, "'long as you're goin' to pay me and Pete, and it's business; I ain't so set against puttin' up what the brick is worth."

Mr. Critz heaved a deep sigh of relief.

"You don't know how good that makes me feel," he said. "I was almost losin' what faith in mankind I had left."

Mr. Gubb ate his frugal evening meals at the Pie Wagon, on Willow Street, just off Main, where, by day, Pie-Wagon Pete dispensed light viands; and Pie-Wagon Pete was the friend he had invited to share Mr. Critz's generosity. The seal of secrecy had been put on Pie-Wagon Pete's lips before Mr. Gubb offered him the opportunity to accept or decline; and when Mr. Gubb stopped for his evening meal, Pie-Wagon Pete — now off duty — was waiting for him. The story of Mr. Critz and his amateur con' business had amused Pie-Wagon Pete. He could hardly believe such utter innocence existed. Perhaps he did not believe it existed, for he had come from the city, and he had had shady companions before he landed in Riverbank. He was a sharp-eyed, red-headed fellow, with a hard fist, and a scar across his face, and when Mr. Gubb had told him of Mr. Critz and his affairs, he had seen an opportunity to shear a country lamb.

"How goes it for to-night, Philo?" he asked Mr. Gubb, taking the stool next to Mr. Gubb, while the night man drew a cup of coffee.

"Quite well," said Mr. Gubb. "Everything is arranged satisfactory. I'm to be on the old houseboat by the wharf-house on the levee at nine, with *it*." He glanced at the night man's back and lowered his voice. "And Mr. Critz will bring you there."

"Nine, eh?" said Pie-Wagon. "I meet him at your room, do I?"

"You meet him at the Riverbank Hotel at eight-forty-five," said Mr. Gubb. "Like it was the real thing. I'm goin' over to my room now, and give him the money —"

"What money?" asked Pie-Wagon Pete quickly.

"Well, you see," said Mr. Gubb, "he sort of hated to trust the — trust *it* out of his hands without a deposit. It's the only one he has. So I thought I'd put up a hundred dollars. He's all right —"

"Oh, sure!" said Pie-Wagon. "A hundred dollars, eh?"

He looked at Mr. Gubb, who was eating a piece of apple pie hand-to-mouth fashion, and studied him in a new light.

"One hundred dollars, eh?" he repeated thoughtfully. "You give him a hundred-dollar deposit now and he meets you at nine, and me at eight-forty-five, and the train leaves for Chicago at eight-forty-three, halfway between the house-boat and the hotel! Say, Gubby, what does this old guy look like?"

Mr. Gubb, albeit with a tongue unused to description, delineated Mr. Critz as best he could, and as he proceeded, Pie-Wagon Pete became interested.

"Pinkish, and bald? Top of his head like a hard-boiled egg? He ain't got a scar across his face? The dickens he has! Short and plump, and a reg'lar old nice grandpa? Blue eyes? Say, did he have a coughin' spell and choke red in the face? Well, sir, for a brand-new detective, you've done well. Listen, Jim: Gubby's got the Hard-Boiled Egg!"

The night man almost dropped his cup of coffee.

"Go 'way!" he said. "Old Hard-Boiled? Himself?"

"That's right! And caught him with the goods. Say, listen, Gubby!"

For five minutes Pie-Wagon Pete talked, while Mr. Gubb sat with his mouth wide open.

"See?" said Pie-Wagon at last. "And don't you

mention me at all. Don't mention no one. Just say to the Chief: 'And havin' trailed him this far, Mr. Wittaker, and arranged to have him took with the goods, it's up to you?' See? And as soon as you say that, have him send a couple of bulls with you, and if they can do it, they'll nab Old Hard-Boiled just as he takes your cash. And Old Sleuth and Sherlock Holmes won't be in it with you when to-morrow mornin's papers come out. Get it?"

Mr. Gubb got it. When he entered his bedroom, Mr. Critz was waiting for him. It was slightly after eight o'clock; perhaps eight-fifteen. Mr. Critz had what appeared to be the gold-brick neatly wrapped in newspaper, and he looked up with his kindly blue eyes. He had been reading the "Complete Con' Man," and had pushed his spectacles up on his forehead as Mr. Gubb entered.

"I done that brick up for you," he said, indicating it with his hand, "so's it would n't glitter whilst you was goin' through the street. If word got passed around there was a gold-brick in town, folks might sort of get suspicious-like. Nice night for goin' out, ain't it? Got a letter from my wife this aft'noon," he chuckled. "She says she hopes I'm doin' well. Sally'd have a fit if she knew what business I was goin' into. Well, time's gettin' along —"

"I brung the money," said Mr. Gubb, drawing it from his pocket.

"Don't seem hardly necess'ry, does it?" said Mr. Critz mildly. "But I s'pose it's just as well.

Thankee, Mister Gubb. I'll just pile into my coat —"

Mr. Gubb had picked up the gold-brick, and now he let it fall. Once more the door flew open, but this time it opened for three stalwart policemen, whose revolvers pointed unwaveringly at Mr. Critz. The plump little man gave one glance, and put up his hands.

"All right, boys, you've got me," he said in quite another voice, and allowed them to seize his arms. He paid no attention to the police, but at Mr. Gubb, who was tearing the wrapper from what proved to be but a common vitrified paving-brick, he looked long and hard.

"Say," said Mr. Critz to Mr. Gubb, "I'm the goat. You stung *me* all right. You worked me to a finish. I thought I knew all of you from Burns down, but you're a new one to me. Who are you, anyway?"

Mr. Gubb looked up.

"Me?" he said with pride. "Why — why — I'm Gubb, the foremost deteckative of Riverbank, Iowa."

THE PET

On the morning following his capture of the Hard-Boiled Egg, the "Riverbank Eagle" printed two full columns in praise of Detective Gubb and complimented Riverbank on having a superior to Sherlock Holmes in its midst.

"Mr. Philo Gubb," said the "Eagle," "has thus far received only eleven of the twelve lessons from the Rising Sun Detective Agency's Correspondence School of Detecting, and we look for great things from him when he finally receives his diploma and badge. He informed us to-day that he hopes to begin work on the dynamite case soon. With the money he will receive for capturing the Hard-Boiled Egg, Mr. Gubb intends to purchase eighteen complete disguises from the Supply Department of the Rising Sun Detective Agency, Slocum, Ohio. Mr. Gubb wishes us to announce that until the disguises arrive he will continue to do paper-hanging, decorating, and interior painting at reasonable rates."

Unfortunately there were no calls for Mr. Gubb's detective services for some time after he received his disguises and diploma, but while waiting he devoted his spare time to the dynamite mystery, a remarkable case on which many detectives had been working for many weeks. This led only to his being beaten up twice by Joseph Henry, one of the men he shadowed.

The arrival in Riverbank of the World's Monster Combined Shows the day after Mr. Gubb received his diploma seemed to offer an opportunity for his detective talents, as a circus is usually accompanied by crooks, and early in the morning Mr. Gubb donned disguise Number Sixteen, which was catalogued as "Negro Hack-Driver, Complete, $22.00"; but, while looking for crooks while watching the circus unload, his eyes alighted on Syrilla, known as "Half a Ton of Beauty," the Fat Lady of the Side-Show.

As Syrilla descended from the car, aided by the Living Skeleton and the Strong Man, the fair creature wore a low-neck evening gown. Her arms and shoulders were snowy white (except for a peculiar mark on one arm). Not only had Mr. Gubb never seen such white arms and shoulders, but he had never seen so much arm and shoulder on one woman, and from that moment he was deeply and hopelessly in love. Like one hypnotized he followed her to the side-show tent, paid his admission, and stood all day before her platform. He was still there when the tent was taken down that night.

Mr. Gubb was not the only man in Riverbank to fall in love with Syrilla. When the ladies of the Riverbank Social Service League heard that the circus was coming to town they were distressed to think how narrow the intellectual life of the side-

show freaks must be and they instructed their Field
Secretary, Mr. Horace Winterberry, to go to the
side-show and organize the freaks into an Ibsen
Literary and Debating Society. This Mr. Winterberry did and the Tasmanian Wild Man was made
President, but so deeply did Mr. Winterberry fall
in love with Syrilla that he begged Mr. Dorgan, the
manager of the side-show, to let him join the side-
show, and this Mr. Dorgan did, putting him in a
cage as Waw-Waw, the Mexican Hairless Dog-Man,
as Mr. Winterberry was exceedingly bald.

At the very next stop made by the circus a strong,
heavy-fisted woman entered the side-show and
dragged Mr. Winterberry away. This was his wife.
Of this the ladies of the Riverbank Social Service
League knew nothing, however. They believed
Mr. Winterberry had been stolen by the circus and
that he was doubtless being forced to learn to swing
on a trapeze or ride a bareback horse, and they
decided to hire Detective Gubb to find and return
him.

At the very moment when the ladies were deciding to retain Mr. Gubb's services the paper-hanger
detective was on his way to do a job of paper-hanging, thinking of the fair Syrilla he might never see
again, when suddenly he put down the pail of paste
he was carrying and grasped the handle of his paste-
brush more firmly. He stared with amazement and
fright at a remarkable creature that came toward
him from a small thicket near the railway tracks.

23

PHILO GUBB, THE DETECTIVE

Mr. Gubb's first and correct impression was that this was some remarkable creature escaped from the circus. The horrid thing loping toward him was, indeed, the Tasmanian Wild Man!

As the Wild Man approached, Philo Gubb prepared to defend himself. He was prepared to defend himself to his last drop of blood.

When halfway across the field, the Tasmanian Wild Man glanced back over his shoulder and, as if fearing pursuit, increased his speed and came toward Philo Gubb in great leaps and bounds. The Correspondence School detective waved his paste-brush more frantically than ever. The Tasmanian Wild Man stopped short within six feet of him.

Viewed thus closely, the Wild Man was a sight to curdle the blood. Remnants of chains hung from his wrists and ankles; his long hair was matted about his face; and his finger nails were long and claw-like. His face was daubed with ochre and red, with black rings around the eyes, and the circles within the rings were painted white, giving him an air of wildness possessed by but few wild men. His only garments were a pair of very short trunks and the skin of some wild animal, bound about his body with ropes of horse-hair.

Philo Gubb bent to receive the leap he felt the Tasmanian Wild Man was about to make, but to his surprise the Wild Man held up one hand in token of amity, and with the other removed the matted hair from his head, revealing an under-crop of taffy yellow, neatly parted in the middle and smoothed back carefully.

"I say, old chap," he said in a pleasant and well-bred tone, "stop waving that dangerous-looking weapon at me, will you? My intentions are most kindly, I assure you. Can you inform me where a chap can get a pair of trousers hereabout?"

Philo Gubb's experienced eye saw at once that this creature was less wild than he was painted. He lowered the paste-brush.

"Come into this house," said Philo Gubb. "Inside the house we can discuss pants in calmness."

The Tasmanian Wild Man accepted.

"Now, then," said Philo Gubb, when they were safe in the kitchen. He seated himself on a roll of wall-paper, and the Tasmanian Wild Man, whose real name was Waldo Emerson Snooks, told his brief story.

Upon graduating from Harvard, he had sought employment, offering to furnish entertainment by the evening, reading an essay entitled, "The Comparative Mentality of Ibsen and Emerson, with Sidelights on the Effect of Turnip Diet at Brook Farm," but the agency was unable to get him any engagements. They happened, however, to receive a request from Mr. Dorgan, manager of the side-show, asking for a Tasmanian Wild Man, and Mr. Snooks had taken that job. To his own surprise, he made an excellent Wild Man. He was able to rattle his chains, dash up and down the cage, gnaw the iron bars of the cage, eat raw meat, and howl as no other Tasmanian Wild Man had ever done those things, and all would have been well if an interloper had not entered the side-show.

The interloper was Mr. Winterberry, who had introduced the subject of Ibsen's plays, and in a discussion of them the Tasmanian Wild Man and Mr. Hoxie, the Strong Man, had quarreled, and Mr. Hoxie had threatened to tear Mr. Snooks limb from limb.

"And he would have done so," said the Tasmanian Wild Man with emotion, "if I had not fled. I dare not return. I mean to work my way back to Boston and give up Tasmanian Wild Man-ing as a profession. But I cannot without pants."

"I guess you can't," said Philo Gubb. "In any station of Boston life, pants is expected to be worn."

"So the question is, old chap, where am I to be panted?" said Waldo Emerson Snooks.

"I can't pant you," said Philo Gubb, "but I can overall you."

The late Tasmanian Wild Man was most grateful. When he was dressed in the overalls and had wiped the grease-paint from his face on an old rag, no one would have recognized him.

"And as for thanks," said Philo Gubb, "don't mention it. A deteckative gent is obliged to keep up a set of disguises hitherto unsuspected by the mortal world. This Tasmanian Wild Man outfit will do for a hermit disguise. So you don't owe me no thanks."

As Philo Gubb watched Waldo Emerson Snooks start in the direction of Boston — only some thirteen hundred miles away — he had no idea how soon he would have occasion to use the Tasmanian Wild Man disguise, but hardly had the Wild Man departed than a small boy came to summon Mr. Gubb, and it was with a sense of elation and importance that he appeared before the meeting of the Riverbank Ladies' Social Service League.

"And so," said Mrs. Garthwaite, at the close of the interview, "you understand us, Mr. Gubb?"

"Yes, ma'am," said Philo Gubb. "What you want me to do, is to find Mr. Winterberry, ain't it?"

"Exactly," agreed Mrs. Garthwaite.

"And, when found," said Mr. Gubb, "the said stolen goods is to be returned to you?"

"Just so."

"And the fiends in human form that stole him are to be given the full limit of the law?"

"They certainly deserve it, abducting a nice little gentleman like Mr. Winterberry," said Mrs. Garthwaite.

"They do, indeed," said Philo Gubb, "and they shall be. I would only ask how far you want me to arrest. If the manager of the side-show stole him, my natural and professional deteckative instincts would tell me to arrest the manager; and if the whole side-show stole him I would make bold to arrest the whole side-show; but if the whole circus stole him, am I to arrest the whole circus, and if so ought I to include the menagerie? Ought I to arrest the elephants and the camels?"

"Arrest only those in human form," said Mrs. Garthwaite.

Philo Gubb sat straight and put his hands on his knees.

"In referring to human form, ma'am," he asked, "do you include them oorangootangs and apes?"

"I do," said Mrs. Garthwaite. "Association with criminals has probably inclined their poor minds to criminality."

"Yes, ma'am," said Philo Gubb, rising. "I leave on this case by the first train."

Mr. Gubb hastily packed the Tasmanian garment and six other disguises in a suitcase, put the fourteen dollars given him by Mrs. Garthwaite in his pocket, and hurried to catch the train for Bardville, where the World's Monster Combined Shows were to show the next day. With true detective caution Philo Gubb disguised even this simple act.

Having packed his suitcase, Mr. Gubb wrapped it carefully in manila paper and inserted a laundry ticket under the twine. Thus, any one seeing him might well suppose he was returning from the laundry and not going to Bardville. To make this seem the more likely, he donned his Chinese disguise, Number Seventeen, consisting of a pink, skull-like wig with a long pigtail, a blue jumper, and a yellow complexion.

THE PET

Mr. Gubb rubbed his face with crude ochre powder, and his complexion was a little high, being more the hue of a pumpkin than the true Oriental skin tint. Those he met on his way to the station imagined he was in the last stages of yellow fever, and fled from him hastily.

He reached the station just as the train's wheels began to move; and he was springing up the steps onto the platform of the last car when a hand grasped his arm. He turned his head and saw that the man grasping him was Jonas Medderbrook, one of Riverbank's wealthiest men.

"Gubb! I want you!" shouted Mr. Medderbrook energetically, but Philo Gubb shook off the detaining arm.

"Me no savvy Melican talkee," he jabbered, bunting Mr. Medderbrook off the car step.

Bright and early next morning, Philo Gubb gave himself a healthy coat of tan, with rather high color on his cheek-bones. From his collection of beards and mustaches — carefully tagged from "Number One" to "Number Eighteen" in harmony with the types of disguise mentioned in the twelve lessons of the Rising Sun Detective Agency's Correspondence School of Detecting — he selected mustache Number Eight and inserted the spring wires in his nostrils.

Mustache Number Eight was a long, deadly black mustache with up-curled ends, and when Philo Gubb had donned it he had a most sinister appearance, particularly as he failed to remove the string tag which bore the legend, "Number Eight. Gambler or Card Sharp. Manufactured and Sold by the Rising Sun Detective Agency's Correspondence School of Detecting Supply Bureau." Having put on this mustache, Mr. Gubb took a common splint market-basket from under the bed and placed in it the matted hair of the Tasmanian Wild Man, his make-up materials, a small mirror, two towels, a cake of soap, the Tasmanian Wild Man's animal skin robe, the hair rope, and the abbreviated trunks. He covered these with a newspaper.

The sun was just rising when he reached the railway siding, and hardly had Mr. Gubb arrived when the work of unloading the circus began.

Mr. Gubb — searching for the abducted Mr. Winterberry — sped rapidly from place to place, the string tag on his mustache flapping over his shoulder, but he saw no one answering Mrs. Garthwaite's description of Mr. Winterberry. When the tent wagons had departed, the elephants and camels were unloaded, but Mr. Winterberry did not seem to be concealed among them, and the animal cages — which came next — were all tightly closed. There were four or five cars, however, that attracted Philo Gubb's attention, and one in particular made his heart beat rapidly. This car bore the words, "World's Monster Combined Shows Freak Car." And as Mr. Winterberry had gone as a social reform agent to the side-show, Mr. Gubb rightly felt that here if any-

MR. WINTERBERRY DID NOT SEEM TO BE CONCEALED
AMONG THEM

where he would find a clue, and he was doubly agitated since he knew the beautiful Syrilla was doubtless in that car.

Walking around the car, he heard the door at one end open. He crouched under the platform, his ears and eyes on edge. Hardly was he concealed before the head ruffian of the unloading gang approached.

"Mister Dorgan," he said, in quite another tone than he had used to his laborers, "should I fetch that wild man cage to the grounds for you to-day?"

"No," said Dorgan. "What's the use? I don't like an empty cage standing around. Leave it on the car, Jake. Or — hold on! I'll use it. Take it up to the grounds and put it in the side-show as usual. I'll put the Pet in it."

"Are ye foolin'?" asked the loading boss with a grin. "The cage won't know itself, Mister Dorgan, afther holdin' that rip-snortin' Wild Man to be holdin' a cold corpse like the Pet is."

"Never you mind," said Dorgan shortly. "I know my business, Jake. You and I know the Pet is a dead one, but these country yaps don't know it. I might as well make some use of the remains as long as I've got 'em on hand."

"Who you goin' to fool, sweety?" asked a voice, and Mr. Dorgan looked around to see Syrilla, the Fat Lady, standing in the car door.

"Oh, just folks!" said Dorgan, laughing.

"You're goin' to use the Pet," said the Fat Lady

reproachfully, "and I don't think it is nice of you. Say what you will, Mr. Dorgan, a corpse is a corpse, and a respectable side-show ain't no place for it. I wish you would take it out in the lot and bury it, like I wanted you to, or throw it in the river and get rid of it. Won't you, dearie?"

"I will not," said Mr. Dorgan firmly. "A corpse may be a corpse, Syrilla, any place but in a circus, but in a circus it is a feature. He's goin' to be one of the Seven Sleepers."

"One of what?" asked Syrilla.

"One of the Seven Sleepers," said Dorgan. "I'm goin' to put him in the cage the Wild Man was in, and I'm goin' to tell the audiences he's asleep. 'He looks dead,' I'll say, 'but I give my word he's only asleep. We offer five thousand dollars,' I'll say, 'to any man, woman, or child that proves contrary than that we have documents provin' that this human bein' in this cage fell asleep in the year 1837 and has been sleepin' ever since. The longest nap on record,' I'll say. That'll fetch a laugh."

"And you don't care, dearie, that I'll be creepy all through the show, do you?" said Syrilla.

"I won't care a hang," said Dorgan.

Mr. Gubb glided noiselessly from under the car and sped away. He had heard enough to know that deviltry was afoot. There was no doubt in his mind that the Pet was the late Mr. Winterberry, for if ever a man deserved to be called "Pet," Mr. Winterberry — according to Mrs. Garthwaite's description

— was that man. There was no doubt that Mr. Winterberry had been murdered, and that these heartless wretches meant to make capital of his body. The inference was logical. It was a strong clue, and Mr. Gubb hurried to the circus grounds to study the situation.

"No," said Syrilla tearfully, "you *don't* care a hang for the nerves of the lady and gent freaks under your care, Mr. Dorgan. It's nothin' to you if repulsion from that corpse-like Pet drags seventy or eighty pounds of fat off of me, for you well know what my contract is — so much a week and so much for each additional pound of fat, and the less fat I am the less you have to add onto your pay-roll. The day the Pet come to the show first I fainted outright and busted down the platform, but little do you care, Mr. Dorgan."

"Don't you worry; you did n't murder him," said Mr. Dorgan.

"He looks so lifelike!" sobbed Syrilla.

"Oh, Hoxie!" shouted Mr. Dorgan.

"Yes, sir?" said the Strong Man, coming to the car door.

"Take Syrilla in and tell the girls to put ice on her head. She's gettin' hysterics again. And when you've told 'em, you go up to the grounds and tell Blake and Skinny to unpack the Petrified Man. Tell 'em I'm goin' to use him again to-day, and if he's lookin' shop-worn, have one of the men go over his complexion and make him look nice and lifelike."

PHILO GUBB, THE DETECTIVE

Mr. Dorgan swung off from the car step and walked away.

The Petrified Man had been one of his mistakes. In days past petrified men had been important side-show features and Mr. Dorgan had supposed the time had come to re-introduce them, and he had had an excellent petrified man made of concrete, with steel reinforcements in the legs and arms and a body of hollow tile so that it could stand rough travel.

Unfortunately, the features of the Petrified Man had been entrusted to an artist devoted to the making of clothing dummies. Instead of an Aztec or Cave Dweller cast of countenance, he had given the Petrified Man the simpering features of the wax figures seen in cheap clothing stores. The result was that, instead of gazing at the Petrified Man with awe as a wonder of nature, the audiences laughed at him, and the living freaks dubbed him "the Pet," or, still more rudely, "the Corpse," and when the glass case broke at the end of the week, Mr. Dorgan ordered the Pet packed in a box.

Just now, however, the flight of the Tasmanian Wild Man, and the involuntary departure of Mr. Winterberry at the command of his wife after his short appearance as Waw-Waw, the Mexican Hairless Dog-Man, suggested the new use for the Petrified Man.

When Detective Gubb reached the circus grounds the glaring banners had not yet been erected before the side-show tent, but all the tents except the "big top" were up and all hands were at work on that one, or supposed to be. Two were not. Two of the roughest-looking roustabouts, after glancing here and there, glided into the property tent and concealed themselves behind a pile of blue cases, hampers, and canvas bags. One of them immediately drew from under his coat a small but heavy parcel wrapped in an old rag.

"Say, cul," he said in a coarse voice, "you sure have got a head on you. This here stuff will be just as safe in there as in a bank, see? Gimme the screwdriver."

"'Not to be opened until Chicago,'" said the other gleefully, pointing to the words daubed on one of the blue cases. "But I guess it will be — hey, old pal? I guess so!"

Together they removed the lid of the box, and Detective Gubb, seeking the side-show, crawled under the wall of the property tent just in time to see the two ruffians hurriedly jam their parcel into the case and screw the lid in place again. Mr. Gubb's mustache was now in a diagonal position, but little he cared for that. His eyes were fastened on the countenances of the two roustabouts. The men were easy to remember. One was red-headed and pockmarked and the other was dark and the lobes of his ears were slit, as if some one had at some time forcibly removed a pair of rings from them. Very quietly Philo Gubb wiggled backward out of the tent, but as he did so his eyes caught a word painted on the side of the blue case. It was "*Pet*"!

Mr. Gubb proceeded to the next tent. Stooping, he peered inside, and what he saw satisfied him that he had found the side-show. Around the inside of the tent men were erecting a blue platform, and on the far side four men were wheeling a tongueless cage into place. A door at the back of the cage swung open and shut as the men moved the cage, but another in front was securely bolted and barred. Mr. Gubb lowered the tent wall and backed away. It was into this cage that the body of Mr. Winterberry was to be put to make a public holiday for yokels! And the murderer was still at large!

Murderer? Murderers! For who were the two rough characters he had seen tampering with the case containing the remains of the Pet? What had they been putting in the case? If not the murderers, they were surely accomplices. Walking like a wary flamingo, Mr. Gubb circled the tent. He saw Mr. Dorgan and Syrilla enter it. Himself hidden in a clump of bushes, he saw Mr. Lonergan, the Living Skeleton; Mr. Hoxie, the Strong Man; Major Ching, the Chinese Giant; General Thumb, the Dwarf; Princess Zozo, the Serpent Charmer; Maggie, the Circassian Girl; and the rest of the side-show employees enter the tent. Then he removed his Number Eight mustache and put it in his pocket, and balanced his mirror against a twig. Mr. Gubb was changing his disguise.

THE PET

For a while the lady and gentleman freaks stood talking, casting reproachful glances at Mr. Dorgan. Syrilla, with traces of tears on her face, was complaining of the cruel man who insisted that the Pet become part of the show once more and Mr. Dorgan was resisting their reproaches.

"I'm the boss of the show," he said firmly. "I'm goin' to use that cage, and I'm goin' to use the Pet."

"Could n't you put Orlando in it, and get up a spiel about him?" asked Princess Zozo, whose largest serpent was called Orlando. "If you got him a bottle of cold cream from the make-up tent he'd lie for hours with his dear little nose sniffin' it. He's pashnutly fond of cold cream."

"Well, the public ain't pashnutly fond of seein' a snake smell it," said Mr. Dorgan. "The Pet is goin' into that cage — see?"

"Could n't you borry an ape from the menagerie?" asked Mr. Lonergan, the Living Skeleton, who was as passionately fond of Syrilla as Orlando was of cold cream. "And have him be the first man-monkey to speak the human language, orly he's got a cold and can't talk to-day? You did that once."

"And got roasted by the whole crowd! No, sir, Mr. Lonergan. I can't, and I won't. Bring that case right over here," he added, turning to the four roustabouts who were carrying the blue case into the tent. "Got it open? Good! Now —"

He looked toward the cage and stopped short, his mouth open and his eyes staring. Sitting on his

37

haunches, his fore paws, or hands, hanging down like those of a "begging" dog, a Tasmanian Wild Man stared from between the bars of the cage. The matted hair, the bare legs, the animal skin blanket, the streaks of ochre and red on the face, the black circles around the eyes with the white inside the circles, were those of a real Tasmanian Wild Man, but this Tasmanian Wild Man was tall and thin, almost rivaling Mr. Lonergan in that respect. The thin Roman nose and the blinky eyes, together with the manner of holding the head on one side, suggested a bird — a large and dissipated flamingo, for instance.

Mr. Dorgan stared with his mouth open. He stared so steadily that he even took a telegram from the messenger boy who entered the tent, and signed for it without looking at the address. The messenger boy, too, stopped to stare at the Tasmanian flamingo. The men who had brought the blue case set it down and stared. The freaks gathered in front of the cage and stared.

"What is it?" asked Syrilla in a voice trembling with emotion.

"Say! Where in the U.S.A. did *you* come from?" asked Mr. Dorgan suddenly. "What in the dickens are you, anyway?"

"I'm a Tasmanian Wild Man," said Mr. Gubb mildly.

"You a Tasmanian Wild Man?" said Mr. Dorgan. "You don't think you look like a Tas-

manian Wild Man, do you? Why, you look like —
you look like — you look —"

"He looks like an intoxicated pterodactyl," said
Mr. Lonergan, who had some knowledge of pre-
historic animals, — "only hairier."

"He looks like a human turkey with a piebald
face," suggested General Thumb.

"He don't look like nothin'!" said Mr. Dorgan
at last. "That's what he looks like. You get out
of that cage!" he added sternly to Mr. Gubb. "I
don't want nothin' that looks like you nowhere near
this show."

"But, Mr. Dorgan, dearie, think how he'd draw
crowds," said Syrilla.

"Crowds? Of course he'd draw crowds," said
Mr. Dorgan. "But what would I say when I lec-
tured about him? What would I call him? No,
he's got to go. Boys," he said to the four roustabouts, two of whom were those Mr. Gubb had seen
in the property tent, "throw this feller out of the
tent."

"Stop!" said Mr. Gubb, raising one hand. "I will
admit I have tried to deceive you: I am not a Tasmanian Wild Man. I am a deteckative!"

"Detective?" said Mr. Dorgan.

"In disguise," said Mr. Gubb modestly. "In the
deteckative profession the assuming of disguises is
often necessary to the completion of the clarifica-
tion of a mystery plot."

He pointed down at the Pet, whose newly rouged

and powdered face rested smirkingly in the box below the cage.

"I arrest you all," he said, but before he could complete the sentence, the red-headed man and the black-headed man turned and bolted from the tent. Mr. Gubb beat and jerked at the bars of his cage as franctically as Mr. Waldo Emerson Snooks had ever beaten and jerked, but he could not rend them apart.

"Get those two fellers," Mr. Gubb shouted to Mr. Hoxie, and the strong man ran from the tent.

"What's this about arrest?" asked Mr. Dorgan.

"I arrest this whole side-show," said Mr. Gubb, pressing his face between the bars of the cage, "for the murder of that poor, gentle, harmless man now a dead corpse into that blue box there — Mr. Winterberry by name, but called by you by the alias of the 'Pet.'"

"Winterberry?" exclaimed Mr. Dorgan. "That Winterberry? That ain't Winterberry! That's a stone man, a made-to-order concrete man, with hollow tile stomach and reinforced concrete arms and legs. I had him made to order."

"The criminal mind is well equipped with explanations for use in time of stress," said Mr. Gubb. "Lesson Six of the Correspondence School of Deteckating warns the deteckative against explanations of murderers when confronted by the victim. I demand an autopsy onto Mr. Winterberry."

"Autopsy!" exclaimed Mr. Dorgan. "I'll autopsy him for you!"

THE PET

He grasped one of the Pet's hands and wrenched off one concrete arm. He struck the head with a tent stake and shattered it into crumbling concrete. He jerked the Roman tunic from the body and disclosed the hollow tile stomach.

"Hello!" he said, lifting a rag-wrapped parcel from the interior of the Pet. "What's this?"

When unwrapped it proved to be two dozen silver forks and spoons and a good-sized silver trophy cup.

"'Riverbank Country Club, Duffers' Golf Trophy, 1909?'" Mr. Dorgan read. "'Won by Jonas Medderbrook.' How did that get there?"

"Jonas Medderbrook," said Mr. Gubb, "is a man of my own local town."

"He is, is he?" said Mr. Dorgan. "And what's your name?"

"Gubb," said the detective. "Philo Gubb, Esquire, deteckative and paper-hanger, Riverbank, Iowa."

"Then this is for you," said Mr. Dorgan, and he handed the telegram to Mr. Gubb. The detective opened it and read: —

Gubb,
    Care of Circus,
        Bardville, Ia.
My house robbed circus night. Golf cup gone. Game now rotten: never win another. Five hundred dollars reward for return to me.

JONAS MEDDERBROOK

41

PHILO GUBB, THE DETECTIVE

"You did n't actually come here to find Mr. Winterberry, did you?" asked Syrilla.

Mr. Gubb folded the telegram, raised his matted hair, and tucked the telegram between it and his own hair for safe-keeping.

"When a deteckative starts out to detect," he said calmly, "sometimes he detects one thing and sometimes he detects another. That cup is one of the things I deteckated to-day. And now, if all are willing, I 'll step outside and get my pants on. I 'll feel better."

"And you 'll look better," said Mr. Dorgan. "You could n't look worse."

"In the course of the deteckative career," said Mr. Gubb, "a gent has to look a lot of different ways, and I thank you for the compliment. The art of disguising the human physiology is difficult. This disguise is but one of many I am frequently called upon to assume."

"Well, if any more are like this one," said Mr. Dorgan with sincerity, "I 'm glad I 'm not a detective."

Syrilla, however, heaved her several hundred pounds of bosom and cast her eyes toward Mr. Gubb.

"I think detectives are lovely in any disguise," she said, and Mr. Gubb's heart beat wildly.

THE EAGLE'S CLAWS

As Philo Gubb boarded the train for Riverbank after recovering the silver loving-cup from the interior of the petrified man, he cast a regretful glance backward. It was for Syrilla. There was half a ton of her pinky-white beauty, and her placid, cow-like expression touched an echoing chord in Philo Gubb's heart.

Philo felt, however, that his admiration must be hopeless, for Syrilla must earn a salary in keeping with her size, and his income was too irregular and small to keep even a thin wife.

Five hundred dollars was a large reward for a loving-cup that cost not over thirty dollars, it is true, but Mr. Jonas Medderbrook could afford to pay what he chose, and as he was passionately fond of golf and passionately poor at the game, and as this was probably the only golf prize he would ever win, he was justified in paying liberally, especially as this cup was not merely a tankard, but almost large enough to be called a tank.

Detective Gubb hastened to the home of Mr. Medderbrook, but when the door of that palatial house opened, the colored butler told Mr. Gubb that Mr. Medderbrook was at the Golf Club, attending the annual banquet of the Fifty Worst Duffers.

Mr. Gubb started for the Golf Club. As he walked he thought of Syrilla, and he was at the gate of the Golf Club before he knew it.

He walked up the path toward the club-house, but when halfway, he stopped short, all his detective instincts aroused. The windows of the club-house glowed with light, and sounds of merriment issued from them, but the cause of Philo Gubb's sudden pause was a head silhouetted against one of the glowing windows. As Mr. Gubb watched, he saw the head disappear in the gloom below the window only to reappear at another window. Mr. Gubb, following the directions as laid down in Lesson Four of the Correspondence Lessons, dropped to his hands and knees and crept silently toward the "Paul Pry." When within a few feet of him, Mr. Gubb seated himself tailor-fashion on the grass.

As Philo sat on the damp grass, the man at the window turned his head, and Mr. Gubb noted with surprise that the stranger had none of the marks of a sodden criminal. The face was that of a respectably benevolent old German-American gentleman. Kindliness and good-nature beamed from its lines; but at the moment the plump little man seemed in trouble.

"Good-evening," said Mr. Gubb. "I presume you are taking an observation of the dinner-party within the inside of the club."

The old gentleman turned sharply.

"Shess!" he said. "I look at der peoples eading and drinking. Alvays I like to see dot. Und sooch

44

A HEAD SILHOUETTED AGAINST ONE OF THE GLOWING WINDOWS

goot eaders! Dot man mit der black beard, he vos
a schplendid eader!"

Mr. Gubb raised himself to his knees and looked
into the dining-room.

"That," he said, "is the Honorable Mr. Jonas
Medderbrook, the wealthiest rich man in Riverbank."

"Metterbrook? Mettercrook?" said the old
German-American. "Not Chones, eh?"

"Not Jones, to my present personal knowledge
at this time," said Philo Gubb.

"Not Chones!" repeated the plumply benevolent-
looking German-American. "Dot vos stranche!
You vos sure he vos not Chones?"

"I'm quite almost positive upon that point of
knowledge," said Philo Gubb, "for I have under
my arm a golf cup I am returning back to Mr.
Medderbrook to receive five hundred dollars reward
from him for."

"So?" queried the stranger. "Fife hundredt dollars? Und it is his cup?"

"It is," said Philo Gubb. He raised the cup in
his hand that the stranger might read the inscription
stating that the cup was Jonas Medderbrook's.

The light of the window made the engraving easy
to read, but the old German-American first drew
from his pocket a pair of gold-rimmed spectacles and
adjusted them carefully on his nose. He then took
the cup and moved closer to the window and read
the inscription.

"Shess! Shess!" he agreed, nodding his head several times, and then he smiled at Mr. Gubb a broadly benevolent smile. "Oxcoose me!" he added, and with gentle deliberation he removed Mr. Gubb's hat. "Shoost a minute, please!" he continued, and with his free hand he felt gently of the top of Mr. Gubb's head. He turned Mr. Gubb's head gently to the right. "So!" he exclaimed: "Dot vos goot!" He raised the cup above his head and brought it down on top of Mr. Gubb's head in the exact spot he had selected. For two moments Mr. Gubb made motions with his hands resembling those of a swimmer, and then he collapsed in a heap. The kindly looking old German-American gentleman, seeing he was quite unconscious, tucked the golf cup under his own arm, and waddled slowly down the path to the club gates.

Ten minutes later a small automobile drove up and young Dr. Anson Briggs hopped out. Mr. Gubb was just getting to his feet, feeling the top of his head with his hand as he did so.

"Here!" said Dr. Briggs. "You must not do that!"

"Why can't I do it?" Mr. Gubb asked crossly. "It is my own personal head, and if I wish to desire to rub it, you are not concerned in the occasion whatever."

"Oh, rub your head if you want to!" exclaimed the doctor. "I say you must not stand up. A man that has just had a fit must not stand up."

THE EAGLE'S CLAWS

"Who had a fit?" asked Philo Gubb.

"You did," said Dr. Briggs. "I am told you had a very bad fit, and fell and knocked your head against the building. You're dazed. Lie down!"

"I prefer to wish to stand erect on my feet," said Mr. Gubb firmly. "Where's my cup?"

"What cup?"

"Who told you I was suffering from the symptom of a fit?" demanded Philo Gubb.

"Why, a short, plump little German did," said the doctor. "He sent me here. And he gave me this to give to you."

The doctor held an envelope toward Mr. Gubb, and the detective took it and tore it open. By the light of the window he read: —

Rec'd of J. Jones, golluf cup worth $500. P. H. SCHRECKENHEIM.

Philo Gubb turned to Dr. Briggs.

"I am much obliged for the hastiness with which you came to relieve one you considered to think in trouble, doctor," he said, "but fits are not in my line of sickness, which mainly is dyspeptic to date."

"Now, what is all this?" asked the doctor suspiciously. "What is that letter, anyway?"

"It is a clue," said Philo Gubb, "which, connected with the bump on the top of the cranium of my skull, will, no doubt, land somebody into jail. So good-evening, doctor."

He picked his hat from the lawn, and in his most

stately manner walked around the club-house and in at the door.

Inside the club-house, Mr. Gubb asked one of the waiters to call Mr. Medderbrook, and Mr. Medderbrook immediately appeared.

As he came from the dining-room rapidly, the napkin he had had tucked in his neck fell over his shoulder behind him, and Mr. Medderbrook, instead of turning around bent backward until he could pick up the napkin with his teeth, after which he resumed his normal upright position.

"Excuse me, Gubb," he said; "I did n't think what I was doing. Where is the cup?"

The detective explained. He handed Mr. Medderbrook the receipt that had been sent by Mr. Schreckenheim, and the moment Mr. Medderbrook's eyes fell upon it he turned red.

"That infernal Dutchman!" he cried, although Mr. Schreckenheim was not a Dutchman at all, but a German-American. "I'll jail him for this!"

He stopped short.

"Gubb," he said, "did that fellow tell you what his business was?"

"He did not," said Philo Gubb. "He failed to express any mention of it."

"That man," said Mr. Medderbrook bitterly, "is Schreckenheim, the greatest tattoo artist in the world. He is the king of them all. A connoisseur in tattooish art can tell a Schreckenheim as easily as a picture-dealer can tell a Corot. But no matter!

48

Mr. Gubb, you are a detective and I believe what is told detectives is held inviolable. Yes. You — and all Riverbank — see in me an ordinary citizen, wealthy, perhaps, but ordinary. As a matter of fact, I was once" — he looked cautiously around — "I was once a contortionist. I was once *the* contortionist. And now I am a wealthy man. My wife left me because she said I was stingy, and she took my child — my only daughter. I have never seen either of them since. I have searched high and low, but I cannot find them. Mr. Gubb, I would give the man that finds my daughter — if she is alive — a thousand dollars."

"You don't object to my attempting to try?" said Philo Gubb.

"No," said Mr. Jonas Medderbrook, "but that is not what I wish to explain. In my contortion act, Mr. Gubb, I was obliged to wear the most expensive silk tights. Wiggling on the floor destroys them rapidly. I had a happy thought. I was known as the Man-Serpent. Could I not save all expense of tights by having myself tattooed so that my skin would represent scales? Look."

Mr. Medderbrook pulled up his cuff and showed Mr. Gubb his arm. It was beautifully tattooed in red and blue, like the scales of a cobra.

"The cost," continued Mr. Medderbrook, "was great. Herr Schreckenheim worked continuously on me, and when he reached my manly chest I had a brilliant thought. I would have tattooed upon it

49

an American eagle. Imagine the enthusiasm of an audience when I stood straight, spread my arms and showed that noble emblem of our nation's strength and freedom! I told Herr Schreckenheim and he set to work. When — and the contract price, by the way, for doing that eagle was five hundred dollars — when the eagle was about completed, I said to Herr Schreckenheim, 'Of course you will do no more eagles?'

"'More eagles?' he said questioningly.

"'On other men,' I said. 'I want to be the only man with an eagle on my chest.'

"'I am doing an eagle on another man now,' he said.

"I was angry at once. I jumped from the table and threw on my clothes. 'Cheater!' I cried. 'Not another spot or dot shall you make on me! Go! I will never pay you a cent!'

"He was very angry. 'It is a contract!' he cried. 'Five hundred dollars you owe me!'

"'I owe it to you when the job is complete,' I declared. 'That was the contract. Is this job complete? Where are the eagle's claws? I'll never pay you a cent!'

"We had a lot of angry words. He demanded that I give him a chance to put the claws on the eagle. I refused. I said I would never pay. He said he would follow me to the end of the world and collect. He said he would do those eagle claws if he had to do them on my infant daughter. I dared him to touch the child. And now," said Mr. Medder-brook, "he has taken the golf cup I value at five hundred dollars. He has won."

At the mention of the threat regarding the child, Philo Gubb's eyes opened wide, but he kept silence.

"Gubb," said Mr. Medderbrook suddenly, "I'll give you a thousand dollars if you can recover my poor child."

"The deteckative profession is full of complicity of detail," said Mr. Gubb, "and the impossible is quite possible when put in the right hands. The cup —"

"Bother the cup!" said Mr. Medderbrook care-lessly. "I want my child — I'll give *ten* thousand dollars for my child, Gubb."

With difficulty could Philo Gubb restrain his eagerness to depart. He had a clue!

Ordinarily Mr. Gubb would have taken any dis-guise that seemed to him best suited for the work in hand; but now he was going to see and be seen by Syrilla!

Mr. Gubb ran down the list — Number Seven, Card Sharp; Number Nine, Minister of the Gospel; Number Twelve, Butcher; Number Sixteen, Negro Hack-Driver; Number Seventeen, Chinese Laun-dryman; Number Twenty, Cowboy. . . . Philo Gubb paused there. He would be a cowboy, for it was a jaunty disguise — "chaps," sombrero, spurs, buck-skin gloves, holsters and pistols, blue shirt, yellow hair, stubby mustache. He donned the complete

51

disguise, put his street garments in a suitcase and viewed himself in his small mirror. He highly approved of the disguise. He touched his cheeks with red to give himself a healthy, outdoor appearance.

Early the next morning, before the earliest merchants had opened their shops, Philo Gubb boarded the train for West Higgins, for it was there the World's Greatest Combined Shows were to appear. The few sleepy passengers did not open their eyes; the conductor, as he took Mr. Gubb's ticket, merely remarked, "Joining the show at West Higgins?" and passed on. Boys were already gathering on the West Higgins station platform when the train pulled in, and they cheered Mr. Gubb, thinking him part of the show. This greatly increased the difficulty of Mr. Gubb's detective work. He had hoped to steal unobserved to the circus grounds, but a dozen small boys immediately attached themselves to him, running before him and whooping with joy.

"Boys," said Mr. Gubb sternly, "I wish you to run away and play elsewhere than in front of me continuously and all the time," — and they cheered because he had spoken. Only the glad news that the circus trains had reached town finally dragged them reluctantly away. Detective Gubb hurried to the circus grounds. The cook tent was already up, and the grub tent was being put up. Presently the side-show tent was up and the "big top" rising. It was not until nine o'clock, however, that the side-show ladies and gentlemen began to appear, and when they arrived they went at once to the grub tent and seated themselves at the table. From a corner of the "big top's" side wall, Detective Gubb watched them.

"Look there, dearie," said Syrilla suddenly to Princess Zozo, "don't that cowboy look like Mr. Gubb that was at Bardville and got the golf cup?"

"It don't look like him," said Princess Zozo; "it *is* him. Why don't you ask him to come over and help at the eats? You seemed to like him yesterday."

"I thought he was a real gentlem'nly gentlemun, dearie, if that's what you mean," said Syrilla; and raising her voice she called to Mr. Gubb. For a moment he hesitated, and then he came forward. "We knowed you the minute we seen you, Mr. Gubb. Come and sit in beside me and have some breakfast if you ain't dined. I thought you went home last night. You ain't after no more crim'nals, are you?"

"There are variously many ends to the deteckative business," said Mr. Gubb, as he seated himself beside Syrilla. "I'm upon a most important case at the present time."

Syrilla reached for her fifth boiled potato, and as her arm passed Mr. Gubb's face he thrilled. He had not been mistaken. Upon that arm was a pair of eagle's claws, tattooed in red and blue! How little these had meant to him before, and how much they meant now!

"I presume you don't hardly ever long for a home in one place, Miss Syrilla," he began, with his eye fixed on her arm just above the elbow.

"Well, believe me, dearie," said Syrilla, "you don't want to think that just because I travel with a side-show I don't long for the refinements of a true home just like other folks. Some folks think I'm easy to see through and that I ain't nothin' but fat and appetite, but they've got me down wrong, Mr. Gubb. I was unfortunate in gettin' lost from my father and mother when a babe, but many is the time I've said to Zozo, 'I got a refined strain in my nature.' Have n't I, Zozo?"

"You say it every time we begin to rag you about fallin' in love with every new thin man you see," said Princess Zozo. "You said it last night when we was joshin' you about Mr. Gubb here."

Syrilla colored, but Mr. Gubb thrilled joyously.

"Just the same, dearie," Syrilla said to Princess Zozo, "I've got myself listed right when I say I got a refined nature. I've got all the instincts of a real society lady and sometimes it irks me awful not to be able to let myself loose and bant like —"

"Pant?" asked Mr. Gubb.

"*Bant* was the word I used, Mr. Gubb," Syrilla replied. "Maybe you would n't guess it, lookin' at me shovelin' in the eatables this way, but eatin' food is the croolest thing I have to do. It jars me somethin' terrible. Yes, dearie, what I long for day and night is a chance to take my place in the social stratums I was born for and bant off the fat like other social ladies is doin' right along. I don't eat food because I like it, Mr. Gubb, but because a lady in a profession like mine has got to keep fatted up. My outside may be fat, Mr. Gubb, but I got a soul inside of me as skinny as any fash'nable lady would care to have, and as soon as possible I'm goin' to quit the road and bant off six or seven hundred pounds. Would you believe it possible that I ain't dared to eat a pickle for over seven years, because it might start me on the thinward road?"

"I presume to suppose," said Mr. Gubb politely, "that if you was to be offered a home that was rich with wealth and I was to take you there and place you beside your parental father, you would n't refuse?"

Mr. Gubb awaited the reply with eagerness. He tried to remain calm, but in spite of himself he was nervous.

"Watch me!" said Syrilla. "If you could show me a nook like that, you could n't hold me in this show business with a tent-stake and bull tackle. But that's a rosy dream!"

"You ain't got a locket with the photo' of your mother's picture into it?" asked Mr. Gubb.

"No," said Syrilla. "My pa and ma was unknown to me. I dare say they got sick of hearin' me bawl and left me on a doorstep. The first I knew of things was that I was travelin' with a show, representin' a newborn babe in an incubator machine.

I was incubated up to the time I was five years old, and got too long to go in the glass case."

"But some one was your guardian in charge of you, no doubt?" asked Gubb.

"I had forty of them, dearie," said Syrilla. "Whenever money run low, they quit because they could n't get paid on Saturday night."

"Hah!" said Mr. Gubb. "And does the name Jones bring back the memory of any rememberance to you?"

"No, Mr. Gubb," said Syrilla regretfully, seeing how eager he was. "It don't."

"In that state of the case of things," said Mr. Gubb, "I 've got to go over to that wagon-pole and sit down and think awhile. I 've got a certain clue I 've got to think over and make sure it leads right, and if it does I 'll have something important to say to you."

The wagon-pole in question was attached to a canvas wagon near by, and Detective Gubb seated himself on it and thought. The side-show ladies and gentlemen, having finished, entered the side-show tent — with the exception of Syrilla, who remained to finish her meal. She ate a great deal at meals, before meals, and after meals. Mr. Gubb, from his seat on the wagon-pole, looked at Syrilla thoughtfully. He had not the least doubt that Syrilla was the lost daughter of Mr. Jones (or Medderbrook as he now called himself). The German-American tattoo artist had sworn to complete the eagle by putting its claws on Mr. Jones's daughter, if need be, and here were the claws on Syrilla's arm. But, just as it is desirable at times to have a handwriting expert identify a bit of writing, Mr. Gubb felt that if he could prove that the claws tattooed on Syrilla's arm were the work of Mr. Schreckenheim, his case would be complete. He longed for Mr. Schreckenheim's presence, but, lacking that, he had a happy idea. Mr. Enderbury, the tattooed man of the sideshow, should be a connoisseur and would perhaps be able to identify the eagle's claws. Leaving Syrilla still eating, Mr. Gubb entered the side-show tent.

Mr. Enderbury, seated on a blue property case, was engaged in biting the entire row of finger nails on his right hand, and a frown creased his brow. He was enwrapped by a long purple bathrobe which tied closely about his neck. As he caught sight of Mr. Gubb, he started slightly and doubled his hand into a fist, but he immediately calmed himself and assumed a nonchalant air. As a matter of fact, Mr. Enderbury led a dog's life. For years he had loved Syrilla devotedly, but he was so bashful he had never dared to confess his love to her, and year after year he saw her smile upon one thin man after another. Now it was Mr. Lonergan; again it was Mr. Winterberry — or it was Mr. Gubb, or Smith, or Jones, or Doe; but for Mr. Enderbury she seemed to have nothing but contempt. Mr. Enderbury had first seen her when she was posing in the infant incubator, and had loved her even then, for he was twenty when she was but five. The coming of a new rival always affected him as the coming of Mr. Gubb had, but for good reason he hated Mr. Gubb worse than any of the others.

"Excuse me for begging your pardon," said Mr. Gubb, "but in the deteckative business questions have to be asked. Have you ever chanced to happen to notice some tattoo work upon the arm of Miss Syrilla of this side-show?"

"I have," said Mr. Enderbury shortly.

"A pair of eagle's claws," said Mr. Gubb. "Can you tell me, from your knowledge and belief, if the work there done was the work of a Mr. Herr Schreckenheim?"

"I can tell you if I want to," said Mr. Enderbury. "What do you want to know for?"

"If those claws are the work of Mr. Herr Schreckenheim," said Mr. Gubb, "I am prepared to offer to Miss Syrilla her daughterly place in a home of wealth at Riverbank, Iowa. If those claws are Schreckenheim claws, Miss Syrilla is the daughter of Mr. Jonas Medderbrook of the said burg, beyond the question of a particle of doubt."

Mr. Enderbury looked at Mr. Gubb with surprise.

"That's non—" he began. "And if Schreckenheim did those claws, you'll take Syrilla away from this show? Forever?" he asked.

"I will," said Philo Gubb, "if she desires to wish to go."

"Then I have nothing whatever to say," said

Mr. Enderbury, and he shut his mouth firmly; nor would he say more.

"Do you desire to wish me to understand that they are not the work of Mr. Herr Schreckenheim?" persisted Mr. Gubb.

"I have nothing to say!" said Mr. Enderbury.

"I consider that conclusive circumstantial evidence that they are," said Detective Gubb, and he clanked out of the side-show.

Syrilla was still seated at the grub table, finishing her meal, and Mr. Gubb seated himself opposite her. As delicately as he could, he told of Jonas Medderbrook and his lost daughter, of the home of wealth that awaited that daughter, and finally, of his belief that Syrilla was that daughter. It was clear that Syrilla was quite willing to take up a life of refinement and dieting if she was given an opportunity such as Mr. Gubb was able to offer in the name of Jonas Medderbrook; and, this being so, he questioned her regarding the eagle's claws.

"Mr. Gubb," she said, "I wish to die on the spot if I know how I got them claws tattooed onto me. If you ask me, I'll say it is the mystery of my life. They've been on me since I was a little girl no bigger than — why, who is that?"

Mr. Gubb turned his head quickly, but he was not in time to see a plump, good-natured looking little German-American slip quickly out of sight behind the cook tent. Neither did he see the glitter of the sun on a large silver golf cup the plump

German-American carried under his arm; but the German-American had recognized Mr. Gubb, even through his disguise of a cowboy.

"No matter," said Syrilla. "But these claws have been on my arm since I was a wee little girl, Mr. Gubb. I always thought they was a trademark of a hospital."

"I was not knowingly aware that hospitals had trademarks," said Mr. Gubb.

"Maybe they don't," said Syrilla. "But when I was a small child I had an accident and had to be took to a hospital, and it was n't until after that that anybody saw the eagle's claws on me. I considered that maybe it was like the mark the laundry puts on a handkerchief it has laundered."

"I don't know much about the manners of the ways of hospitals," admitted Mr. Gubb, "and that may be so, but I have another idea. Did you ever hear of Mr. Herr Schreckenheim?"

"Only that Mr. Enderbury is always cross on the days of the month that he gets Mr. Schreckenheim's statements of money due. Mr. Schreckenheim is the man that tattooed Mr. Enderbury so beautiful, but poor Mr. Enderbury has never been able to pay him in full."

Philo Gubb arose.

"I am going to telegraph Mr. Medderbrook to come on to West Higgins immediately by the three P.M. afternoon train," he said, "and you will meet him as your paternal father and arrange to

make your home with him as soon as you desire
to wish it."

At five o'clock that afternoon, Mr. Medderbrook,
escorted by Mr. Gubb, entered the side-show tent.
The lady and gentlemen freaks were resting before
evening grub, and all were gathered around Syrilla's
platform, for the news that she was to leave the
show to enter a home of wealth and refinement had
spread quickly. Syrilla herself was in tears. Now
that the time had come she was loath to part from
her kind companions.

"I tell you, Mr. Gubb," Mr. Medderbrook said,
as they entered the side-show, "if you have indeed
found my daughter you have made me a happy man.
You cannot know how lonesome my life has been.
Now, which is she?"

"She is the female lady in the pink satin dress
on that platform," said Mr. Gubb.

Mr. Medderbrook looked toward Syrilla and
gasped.

"Why, that — that's the Fat Woman! That's
the Fat Woman of the side-show!" he exclaimed.
"I thought — I — why, my daughter would n't be
a Fat Woman in a side-show!"

"But she is," said Mr. Gubb.

"Great Scott!" exclaimed Mr. Medderbrook.

For years Mr. Medderbrook had retained a
memory of his daughter as he had seen her last,
a tender babe in long clothes. As he rode toward

West Higgins, however, he had thought about his daughter and he had revised his conception of her. She was older now, of course, and he had finally settled the matter by deciding that she would be a dainty slip of a girl — probably a tight-rope walker or one of the toe-dancers in the Grand Spectacle, or perhaps even engaged as the Ten-Thousand-Dollar Beauty. But a Fat Lady! Mr. Medderbrook walked toward Syrilla. Every eye in the tent was upon him. There was utter silence except for Syrilla's happy sobbing.

"Shess!" said a voice suddenly. "You bet I vos here! Und I vant my money! Years I haf been collecding dot bill, und still you owe me. Now I come, and you pay me all vot you owe or I make troubles!"

The voice came from outside the tent, and with surprising agility Detective Gubb dived under the platform and wriggled under the canvas wall.

"I don't owe you a cent!" exclaimed the voice of Mr. Enderbury. "I've paid you for every bit of tattoo I have on me."

"Seven hunderdt dollars vos der contract," cried the voice of Herr Schreckenheim. "Und ten dollars is due me yet. I vant it."

"Well, you'll keep on wanting it," said Mr. Enderbury's voice. "Look here! Look at my chest. There's the eagle you did on me — do you see any claws on it? No, you don't! Well, I'm not going to pay for claws that are not on me. No, sir!"

THE EAGLE'S CLAWS

"Claws? I do some claws on you, don't I, ven I do dot eagle?" asked the German-American.

"Yes, but they're not on me now, are they?" asked Mr. Enderbury. "You can go and collect from the person that has them. What do I care for her now? She's going to quit the circus business. I've paid for all the tattoo that's on me; you go and collect ten dollars for those claws from Syrilla."

"Und how does she get those claws on her?" asked Herr Schreckenheim shrewdly.

"I'll tell you how," said Mr. Enderbury. "You remember when Griggs' & Barton's Circus burned down years ago? Well, Syrilla was burned in that fire — burned on the arm — and they took her to a hospital and her arm would n't heal. So somebody had to furnish some skin for a skin-grafting job, and I did it. The piece they took had those claws on it. That's what happened. I gave those eagle's claws to cure her, and I've hung around her all these years like a faithful dog, and she don't care a hang for me, and now she's going away. Go and collect for those claws from her. I have n't got them. She's going to be rich; she can pay you!"

Simultaneously there was an exclamation from Mr. Medderbrook, a cry from Syrilla, and a short, sharp yell from outside the tent. Mr. Gubb entered, spurs first, creeping backward under the canvas. As he backed from under the platform it was observed that he held a shoe — about No. 8 size — in one hand, and that a foot was in the shoe, and the foot on a leg, and the leg on a short, plump, elderly German-American, who yelled as he was dragged into the tent on his back. In one hand of the German-American was a large silver golf cup with a deep dent on one side. As Mr. Gubb arose to his feet, still holding the German-American tattoo artist's foot in his hand, he said:—

"Mr. Medderbrook, the deteckative business is not always completely satisfactory in all kinds of respects, and it looks as if it appeared that the daughter I found for you is somebody else's, but if you will look at the other end of the assaulter and batterer I have in hand, you will see that I have recovered the silver golf cup trophy once again for the second time."

"And that," said Mr. Medderbrook as he took the cup from the German-American's hand, "is remarkable work. The ordinary detective is usually satisfied to recover stolen property once, but you have recovered this cup twice."

"The motto of my deteckative business," said Mr. Gubb modestly, "is 'Perfection, no matter how many times.'"

Mr. Gubb might have said more, but he was interrupted by Princess Zozo, the Snake Charmer, who had walked around Syrilla and unhooked two of the hooks at the top of Syrilla's low-necked gown.

"Look!" she exclaimed, and she pointed to a second pair of eagle's claws tattooed between Syrilla's shoulder blades. Without a word Mr. Medderbrook took five hundred dollars from his purse and handed them to Mr. Schreckenheim.

"That pays you for the cup," he said. And then, turning to Syrilla: "Come to my arms, my long-lost daughter!"

After Syrilla had hugged her father affectionately, Mr. Gubb and the freaks laid him on the ground and, by fanning him vigorously, were able to bring him back to life. Mr. Medderbrook's first act upon opening his eyes was to hold out his hand to Mr. Gubb.

"Thank you, Gubb," he panted. "It's a big price, but I'll keep my word. The ten thousand dollars shall be yours."

"Into ordinary circumstances," said Mr. Gubb gravely, "ten thousand dollars would be a largely big price to pay for recovering back a lost daughter, Mr. Medderbrook, but into the present case it don't amount to more than ten dollars per pound of daughter, which ain't a largely great rate per pound."

THE OUBLIETTE

THE discovery that Syrilla was the daughter of Jonas Medderbrook (born Jones) was a great triumph for Philo Gubb, but while the "Riverbank Eagle" made a great hurrah about it, Philo Gubb was not entirely happy over the matter. Having won a reward of ten thousand dollars for discovering Syrilla and five hundred dollars for recovering Mr. Medderbrook's golf cup, Mr. Gubb might have ventured to tell Syrilla of his love for her but for three reasons.

The first reason was that Mr. Gubb was so bashful that it was impossible for him to speak his love openly and immediatly. If Syrilla had returned to Riverbank with her father, Mr.Gubb would have courted her by degrees, or if Syrilla had weighed only two hundred pounds, Mr. Gubb might have had the bravery to propose to her instantly, but she weighed one thousand pounds, and it required five times the bravery to propose to a thousand pounds that was required to propose to two hundred pounds.

The second reason was that Mr. Dorgan, the manager of the side-show, would not release Syrilla from her contract.

"She's a beauty of a Fat Lady," said Mr. Dorgan, "and I've got a five-year contract with her and I'm going to hold her to it."

Mr. Medderbrook and Mr. Gubb would have been quite hopeless when Mr. Dorgan said this if Syrilla had not taken them to one side.

"Listen, dearies," she said, "he's a mean, old brute, but don't you fret! I got a hunch how to make him cancel my contract in a perfectly refined an' ladylike manner. Right now I start in bantin' and dietin' in the scientific-est manner an' the way I can lose three or four hundred pounds when I set out to do it is something grand. It won't be no time at all until I'm thin and wisp-like, an' Mr. Dorgan will be glad to get rid of me."

This information greatly cheered Mr. Gubb. While he admired Syrilla just as she was, a rapid mental calculation assured him that she would still be quite plump at seven hundred pounds and he knew he could love seven tenths of Syrilla more than he could love ten tenths of any other lady in the world.

The third reason had to do with the ten-thousand-dollar reward. When Mr. Gubb and Mr. Medderbrook were proceeding homeward on the train, Mr. Medderbrook brought up the subject of the reward again.

"I'm going to pay you that ten thousand dollars, Gubb," he said, "but I'm going to pay it so it will be worth a lot more than ten thousand dollars to you."

"You are very overly kind," said Mr. Gubb.

"It's because I know you are fond of Syrilla," said Mr. Medderbrook.

Mr. Gubb blushed.

"So I ain't going to give you ten thousand dollars in cash," said Mr. Medderbrook. "I'm going to do a lot better by you than that. I'm going to give you gold-mine stock. The only trouble —"

"Gold-mine stock sounds quite elegantly nice," said Mr. Gubb.

"The only trouble," said Mr. Medderbrook, "is that the gold-mine stock I want to give you is in a block of twenty-five thousand dollars. It's nice stock. It's as neatly engraved as any stock I ever saw, and it is genuine common stock in the Utterly Hopeless Gold-Mine Company."

"The name sounds sort of unhopeful," ventured Mr. Gubb timidly.

"That shows you don't know anything about gold mines," said Mr. Medderbrook cheerfully. "The reason I — the reason the miners gave it that name is because this mine lies right between two of the best gold-mines in Minnesota. One of them is the Utterly Good Gold-Mine, and the other is the Far-From-Hopeless. So when I — so when the miners named this mine they took part of the names of the two others and called this one the Utterly Hopeless. That's the way I — the way it is always done."

"It's very cleverly bright," said Mr. Gubb.

"It's an old trick — I should say an old and

approved method," said Mr. Medderbrook. "So what I'm going to do, Mr. Gubb, is to let you in on the ground floor on this mine. It's a chance I would n't offer to everybody. This mine has n't paid out all its money in dividends. I tell you as an actual fact, Mr. Gubb, that so far it has n't paid out a cent in dividends, not even to the preferred stock. No, sir! And it ain't one of these mines that has been mined until all the gold is mined out of it. No, sir! Not an ounce of gold has ever been taken out of the Utterly Hopeless Mine. Not an ounce."

"It is all there yet!" exclaimed Mr. Gubb.

"All there ever was," said Mr. Medderbrook. "Yes, sir! If you want me to I'll give you a written guarantee that the Utterly Hopeless Mine has never paid a cent in dividends and that not an ounce of gold has ever been taken out of the mine. That shows you I'm square about this. So what I'm going to do," he said impressively, "is to turn over to you a block of twenty-five thousand dollars' worth of Utterly Hopeless Gold-Mine stock and apply the ten thousand dollars I owe you as part of the purchase price. All you need to do then is to pay me the other fifteen thousand dollars as rapidly as you can."

"That's very kindly generous of you," said Mr. Gubb gratefully.

"And that is n't all," said Mr. Medderbrook. "I own every single share of the stock of that mine, Mr. Gubb, and as soon as you get the fifteen thousand dollars paid up I'll advance the price of that stock one hundred per cent! Yes, sir, I'll double the price of the stock, and what you own will be worth fifty thousand dollars!"

There were tears in Philo Gubb's eyes as he grasped Mr. Medderbrook's hand.

"And all I ask," said Mr. Medderbrook, "is that you hustle up and pay that fifteen thousand dollars as quick as you can. So that," he added, "you'll be worth fifty thousand dollars all the sooner."

Upon reaching Riverbank Mr. Medderbrook took Mr. Gubb to his home and turned over to him the stock in the Utterly Hopeless Mine.

"And here," said Mr. Medderbrook, "is a receipt for ten thousand five hundred dollars, and you can give me back that five hundred I paid you for recovering of my golf cup. That's to show you everything is fair and square when you deal with me. Now you owe me only fourteen thousand five hundred dollars."

While Mr. Gubb was handing the five hundred dollars back to Mr. Medderbrook the colored butler entered with a telegram. Mr. Medderbrook tore it open hastily.

"Good news already," he said and handed it to Mr. Gubb. It was from Syrilla and said: —

Be brave. Have lost four ounces already. Kind regards and best love to Mr. Gubb.

With only partial satisfaction Mr. Gubb left Mr. Medderbrook and proceeded downtown. He now had a double incentive for seeking the rewards that fall to detectives, for he had Syrilla to win and the Utterly Hopeless Gold-Mine stock to pay for. He started for the Pie-Wagon, for he was hungry, but on the way certain suspicious actions of Joe Henry (the liveryman who had twice beaten him up while he was working on the dynamiter case), stopped him, and it was much later when he entered the Pie-Wagon.

As Philo Gubb entered, Billy Getz sat on one of the stools and stirred his coffee. He held a dime novel with his other hand, reading; but Pie-Wagon Pete kept an eye on him. He knew Billy Getz and his practical jokes. If unwatched for a moment, the young whipper-snapper might empty the salt into the sugar-bowl, or play some other prank that came under his idea of fun.

Billy Getz was a good example of the spoiled only son. He went in for all the vice there was in town, and to occupy his spare time he planned practical jokes. He was thirty years old, rather bald, had a pale and leathery skin, and a preternaturally serious expression. In his pranks he was aided by the group of young poker-playing, cigarette-smoking fellows known as the "Kidders."

Billy Getz, as he read the last line of the thrilling tale of "The Pale Avengers," tucked the book in his pocket, and looked up and saw Philo Gubb. The hawk-eyes of Billy Getz sparkled.

"Hello, detective!" he cried. "Sit down and

have something! You're just the man I've been lookin' for. Was askin' Pete about you not a minute ago — was n't I, Pete?"

Pie-Wagon Pete nodded.

"Yes, sir," said Billy Getz eagerly, "I've got something right in your line — something big; mighty big — and — say, detective, have you ever read 'The Pale Avengers'?"

"I ain't had that pleasure, Mr. Getz," said Philo Gubb, straddling a stool.

"What's the matter? You're out of breath," said Pie-Wagon.

"I been runnin'," said Philo Gubb. "I had to run a little. Deteckatives have to run at times occasionally."

"You bet they do," said Billy Getz earnestly. "You ain't been after the dynamiters, have you?'

"I am from time to time working upon that case," said Philo Gubb with dignity.

"Well, you be careful. You be mighty careful! We can't afford to lose a man like you," said Billy Getz. "You can't be too careful. Got any of the ghouls yet?"

"Not yet," said Philo Gubb stiffly. "It's a difficult case for one that's just graduated out of a deteckative school. It's like Lesson Nine says — I got to proceed cautiously when workin' in the dark."

"Or they'll get you before you get them," said Billy Getz. "Like in 'The Pale Avengers.' Here, I want you to read this book. It'll teach you some things you don't know about crooks, maybe."

"Thank you," said Philo Gubb, taking the dime novel. "Anything that can help me in my deteckative career is real welcome. I'll read it, Mr. Getz, and — Look out!" he shouted, and in one leap was over the counter and crouching behind it.

Billy Getz turned toward the door, where a short, red-faced man was standing with a pine slab held in his hand. Intense anger glittered in his eyes, and he darted to the counter and, leaning over, brought the slab down on Philo Gubb's back with a resounding whack.

"Here! Here! None o' that stuff in here, Joe," cried Pie-Wagon Pete, grasping the intruder's arm.

"I'll kill him, that's what I'll do!" shouted the intruder. "Snoopin' around my place, and follerin' me up an' down all the time! I told him I was n't goin' to have him doggin' me an' pesterin' me. I've beat him up twice, an' now I'm goin' to give him the worst lickin' he ever had. Come out of there, you half-baked ostrich, you."

"Now, you stop that," said Pie-Wagon Pete sternly. "You're goin' to be sorry if you beat him up. He don't mean no harm. He's just foolish. He don't know no better. All you got to do is to explain it to him right."

"Explain?" said Joe Henry. "I'd look nice explainin' anything, would n't I? Hand him over here, Pete."

PHILO GUBB, THE DETECTIVE

"Now, listen," shouted Pie-Wagon Pete angrily.
"You ain't everything. I'm your pardner, ain't I?
Well, you let me fix this." He winked at Joe Henry.
"You let me explain to Mr. Gubb, an' if he ain't
satisfied, why — all right."

For a moment Joe Henry studied Pie-Wagon's
face, and then he put down the slab.

"All right, you explain," he said ungraciously, and
Philo Gubb raised his white face above the counter.

Upon the passage of the State prohibitory law
every saloon in Riverbank had been closed and there
had been growlings from the saloon element. Five
of the leading prohibitionists had received threatening letters and, a few nights later, the houses of four
of the five were blown up. Kegs of powder had been
placed in the cellar windows of each of the four
houses, wrecking them, and the fifth house was
saved only because the fuse there was damp. Luckily no one was killed, but that was not the fault of
the "dynamiters," as every one called them.

The town and State immediately offered a reward
of five thousand dollars for the arrest and conviction
of the dynamiters, and detectives flocked to Riverbank. Real detectives came to try for the noble
prize. Amateur detectives came in hordes. Citizens
who were not detectives at all tried their hands at
the work.

For the first few days rumors of the immediate
capture of the "ghouls" were flying everywhere,

but day followed day and week followed week, and no one was incarcerated. The citizen-detectives went back to their ordinary occupations, the amateur detectives went home, the real detectives were called off on other and more promising jobs, and soon the field was left clear for Philo Gubb.

Not that he made much progress. Each night he hid himself in the dark doorway of Willcox Hall waiting to pick up (Lesson Four, Rule Four) some suspicious-looking person, and having picked him up, he proceeded to trail and shadow him (Lesson Four, Rules Four to Seventeen). Six times — twice by Joe Henry — he was well beaten by those he followed. It became such a nuisance to be followed by Philo Gubb in false mustache or whiskers, that it was a public relief when Billy Getz and other young fellows took upon themselves the duty of being shadowed. With hats pulled over their eyes and coat-collars turned up, they would pass the dark doorway of Willcox Hall, let themselves be picked up, and then lead poor Detective Gubb across rubbish-encumbered vacant lots, over mud flats or among dark lumber piles, only to give him the slip with infinite ease when they tired of the game.

But Philo Gubb was back the next night, waiting in the shadow of the doorway of Willcox Hall. He did not progress very rapidly toward the goal of the reward, but he counted it all good practice.

But being beaten twice in succession by Joe Henry aroused his suspicion.

PHILO GUBB, THE DETECTIVE

Joe Henry ran a small carting business. He had three teams and three drays, and a small stable on Locust Street, on the alley corner. He was a great friend of Pie-Wagon Pete and he ate at the Pie-Wagon.

Philo Gubb, after leaving Mr. Medderbrook, had not intentionally picked up Joe Henry. On his way to the Pie-Wagon it had been necessary for him to pass the alley opposite Joe Henry's stable and his detective instinct told him to hide himself behind a manure bin in the alley and watch the stable. In the warm June dusk he had crouched there, watching and waiting.

Mr. Gubb could see into the stable, but there was not much to see. The stable boy sat at the door, his chair tipped back, until a few minutes after eleven, when one of Joe Henry's drays drove up with a load of baled hay.

Philo Gubb heard the voices of the men as they hoisted the hay to the hay-loft, and he saw Joe Henry helping with the hoisting-rope. The hay was water-soaked. Water dripped from it onto the floor of the stable.

But nothing exciting occurred, and Philo Gubb was about to consider this a dull evening's work, when Joe Henry appeared in the doorway, a pitch-fork in one hand and the slab of pine in the other. He looked up and down the street and then, with surprising agility, sprang across the street toward where Philo Gubb lay hid. With a wild cry, Philo

THE OUBLIETTE

Gubb fled. The pitchfork clattered at his feet, but missed him, and he had every advantage of long legs and speed. His heels clattered on the alley pave, and Joe Henry's clattered farther and farther behind at each leap of the Correspondence School detective.

"All right, you explain," said Joe Henry sullenly.

"Now you ain't to breathe a word of this, cross-your-heart, hope-to-die, Philo Gubb. Nor you neither, Billy," said Pie-Wagon Pete. "Listen! Me an' Joe Henry ain't what we let on to be. That's why we don't want to be follered. We're detectives. Reg'lar detectives. From Chicago. An' we're hired by the Law an' Order League to run down them gools. We're right clost onto 'em now, ain't we, Joe? An' that's why we don't want to have no one botherin' us. You would n't want no one shadowin' you when you was on a trail, would you, Gubby?"

"No, I don't feel like I would," admitted Philo Gubb.

"That's right," said Pie-Wagon Pete approvingly. "An' when these here dynamite gools is the kind of murderers they is, an' me and Joe is expectin' to be murdered by them any minute, it makes Joe nervous to be follered an' spied on, don't it, Joe?"

"You bet," said Joe. "I'm liable to turn an' maller up anybody I see sneakin' on me. I can't take chances."

"So you won't interfere with Joe in the pursoot

of his dooty no more, will you, Gubby?" said Pie-Wagon Pete.

"I don't aim to interfere with nobody, Peter," said Philo Gubb. "I just want to pursoo my own dooty, as I see it. I won't foller Mr. Henry no more, if he don't like it; but I got a dooty to do, as a full graduate of the Rising Sun Deteckative Agency's Correspondence School of Deteckating. I got to do my level best to catch them dynamiters myself."

Joe Henry frowned, and Pie-Wagon Pete shook his head.

"If you'll take my advice, Gubby," he said, "you'll drop that case right here an' now. You don't know what dangerous characters them gools are. If they start to get you —"

"You want to read that book — 'The Pale Avengers' — I just gave you," said Billy Getz, "and then you'll know more."

"Well, I won't interfere with you, Mr. Henry," said Philo Gubb. "But I'll do my dooty as I see it. Fear don't frighten me. The first words in Lesson One is these: 'The deteckative must be a man devoid of fear.' I can't go back on that. If them gools want to kill me, I can't object. Deteckating is a dangerous employment, and I know it."

He went out and closed the door.

"There," said Pie-Wagon Pete. "Ain't that better than beatin' him up?"

"Maybe," said Joe Henry grudgingly. "Chances are — he's such a dummy — he'll go right ahead follerin' me. He needs a good scare thrown into him."

Billy Getz slid from his stool and ran his hands deep into his pockets, jingling a few coins and a bunch of keys.

"Want me to scare him?" he asked pleasantly.

"Say! You can do it, too!" said Joe Henry eagerly. "You're the feller that can kid him to death. Go ahead. If you do, I'll give you a case of Six Star. Ain't that so, Pete?"

"Absolutely," said Pie-Wagon.

"That's a bet," said Billy Getz pleasantly. "Leave it to the Kidders."

Philo Gubb went straight to his room at the Widow Murphy's, and having taken off his shoes and coat, leaned back in his chair with his feet on the bed, and opened "The Pale Avengers." He had never before read a dime novel, and this opened a new world to him. He read breathlessly. The style of the story was somewhat like this: —

The picture on the wall swung aside and Detective Brown stared into the muzzles of two revolvers and the sharp eyes of the youngest of the Pale Avengers. A thrill of horror swept through the detective. He felt his doom was at hand. But he did not cringe.

"Your time has come!" said the Avenger.

"Be not too sure," said Detective Brown haughtily.

"Are you ready to die?"

"Ever ready!"

The detective extended his hand toward the table, on which his revolver lay. A cruel laugh greeted him. It was the last human voice he was to hear. As if by magic the floor under his feet gave way. Down, down, down, a thousand feet he was precipitated. He tried to grasp the well-like walls of masonry, but in vain. Nothing could stay him. As he plunged into the deep water of the oubliette a fiendish laugh echoed in his ears. The Pale Avengers had destroyed one more of their adversaries.

Until he read this thrilling tale, Philo Gubb had not guessed the fiendishness of malefactors when brought to bay, and yet here it was in black and white. The oubliette — a dark, dank dungeon hidden beneath the ground — was a favorite method of killing detectives, it seemed. Generally speaking, the oubliette seemed to be the prevailing fashion in vengeful murder. Sometimes the bed sank into the oubliette; sometimes the floor gave way and cast the victim into the oubliette; sometimes the whole room sank slowly into the oubliette; but death for the victim always lurked in the pit.

Before getting into bed Philo Gubb examined the walls, the floor, and the ceiling of his room. They seemed safe and secure, but twice during the night he awoke with a cry, imagining himself sinking through the floor.

Three nights later, as Philo Gubb stood in the dark doorway of the Willcox Building waiting to pick up any suspicious character, Billy Getz slipped in beside him and drew him hastily to the back of the entry.

"Hush! Not a word!" he whispered. "Did you

see a man in the window across the street? The third window on the top floor?"

"No," whispered Philo Gubb. "Was — was there one?"

"With a rifle!" whispered Billy Getz. "Ready to pick you off. Come! It is suicide for you to try to go out the front way now. Follow me; I have news for you. Step quietly!"

He led the paper-hanger through the back corridor to the open air and up the outside back stairs to the third floor and into the building. He tapped lightly on a door and it was opened the merest crack.

"Friends," whispered Billy Getz, and the door opened wide and admitted them.

The room was the club-room of the Kidders, where they gathered night after night to play cards and drink illicit whiskey. Green shades over which were hung heavy curtains protected the windows. A large, round table stood in the middle of the floor under the gas-lights; a couch was in one corner of the room; and these, with the chairs and a formless heap in a far corner, over which a couch-cover was thrown, constituted all the furniture, except for the iron cuspidors. Here the young fellows came for their sport, feeling safe from intrusion, for the possession of whiskey was against the law. There was a fine of five hundred dollars — one half to the informer — for the misdemeanor of having whiskey in one's possession, but the Kidders had no fear. They knew each other.

PHILO GUBB, THE DETECTIVE

For the moment the cards were put away and the couch-cover hid the four cases of Six Star that represented the club's stock of liquor. The five young men already in the room were sitting around the table.

"Sit down, Detective Gubb," said Billy Getz. "Here we are safe. Here we may talk freely. And we have something big to talk to-night."

Philo Gubb moved a chair to the table. He had to push one of the cuspidors aside to make room, and as he pushed it with his foot he saw an oblong of paper lying in it among the sand and cigar stubs. It was a Six Star whiskey label. He turned his head from it with his bird-like twist of the neck and let his eyes rest on Billy Getz.

"We know who dynamited those houses!" said Billy Getz suddenly. "Do you know Jack Harburger?"

"No," said Philo Gubb. "I don't know him."

"Well, we do," said Billy Getz. "He's the slickest ever. He was the boss of the gang. Read this!"

He slid a sheet of note-paper across to Philo Gubb, and the detective read it slowly: —

Billy: Send me five hundred dollars quick. I've got to get away from here.   J. H.

"And we made him our friend," said Billy Getz resentfully. "Why, he was here the night of the dynamiting — was n't he, boys?"

"He sure was," said the Kidders.

THE OUBLIETTE

"Now, he's nothing to us." said Billy Getz. "Now, what do you say, Detective Gubb? If we fix it so you can grab him, will you split the reward with us?"

"Half for you and half for me?" asked Philo Gubb, his eyes as big as poker chips.

"Three thousand for you and two for us, was what we figured was fair," said Billy Getz. "You ought to have the most. You put in your experience and your education in detective work."

"And that ought to be worth something," admitted Philo Gubb.

So it was agreed. They explained to Philo Gubb that Jack Harburger was the son of old Harburger of the Harburger House at Derlingport, and that they could count on the clerk of that hotel to help them. Billy Getz would go up and get things ready, and the next day Philo Gubb would appear at the hotel — in disguise, of course — and do his part. The clerk would give him a room next to Jack Harburger's room, and see that there was a hidden opening in the partition; and Billy Getz, pretending he was bringing the money, would wring a full confession from Jack Harburger. Then Philo Gubb need only step into the room and snap the handcuffs on Jack Harburger and collect the reward.

They shook hands all 'round, finally, and Billy Getz went to the window to see that no ghoul was lurking in the street, ready to murder Philo Gubb when he went out. As he turned away from the window the toe of his shoe caught in the fringe of the couch-cover and dragged it partially from the odd-shaped pile in the corner. With a quick sweep of his hand Billy Getz replaced the cover, but not before Philo Gubb had seen the necks of a full case of bottles and had caught the glint of the label on one of them, bearing the six silver stars, like that in the cuspidor. Billy Getz cast a quick glance at the Correspondence School detective's face, but Philo Gubb, his head well back on his stiff neck, was already gazing at the door.

Two days later Philo Gubb, with his telescope valise in his hand, boarded the morning train for Derlingport. The river was on one of its "rampages" and the water came close to the tracks. Here and there, on the way to Derlingport, the water was over the tracks, and in many places the wagon-road, which followed the railway, was completely swamped, and the passing vehicles sank in the muddy water to their hubs. The year is still known as the "year of the big flood." In Riverbank the water had flooded the Front Street cellars, and in Derlingport the sewers had backed up, flooding the entire lower part of the town.

When the train reached Derlingport Philo Gubb, with his telescope valise, which contained his twelve Correspondence School lessons, "The Pale Avengers," a pair of handcuffs, his revolver, and three extra disguises, walked toward the Harburger House. He was already thoroughly disguised, wear-

ing a coal-black beard and a red mustache and an
iron-gray wig with long hair. Luckily he passed no
one. With that disguise he would have drawn an
immense crowd. Nothing like it had ever been seen
on the streets of Derlingport — or elsewhere, for
that matter.

A full block away Philo Gubb saw the sign of the
hotel, and he immediately became cautious, as a
detective should. He crossed the street and observed
the exits. There was a main entrance on the corner,
a "Ladies' Entrance" at the side, and an entrance
to what had once been the bar-room. From the fire-
escape one could drop to the street without great
injury.

Philo Gubb noted all these, and then walked to
the alley. There were two doors opening on the
alley — one a cook's door, and the other evidently
leading to the cellar. At the latter a dray stood, and
as Philo Gubb paused there, two men came from
this door and laid a bale of hay on the dray, pushing
it forward carefully. They did not toss it carelessly
onto the dray but slid it onto the dray. And the
hay was wet. Moreover, the two men were two of
Joe Henry's men, and that was odd. It was odd that
Joe Henry should send a dray the full thirty miles
to Derlingport to get a load of wet hay, when he
could get all the dry hay he wanted in Riverbank.
But it did not impress Philo Gubb. He hurried to
the main entrance of the hotel, and entered.

The lobby of the Harburger House was large, and

gloomy in its old-fashioned black-walnut wood-work. Except for one man sitting at a desk by the window and writing industriously, and the clerk behind the counter, the lobby was untenanted. To the left a huge stairway led to the gloom above, for the hotel boasted no elevator except the huge "baggage lift," which had been put in in the palmy days of the house, when the great river packets were still a business factor.

Philo Gubb walked across the lobby to the clerk's desk. The industrious penman by the window glanced over his shoulder. He looked more like a hotel clerk than like a traveling salesman, but Philo Gubb gave this no thought. The clerk behind the desk put his fingers on his lips.

"Sh!" he whispered. "Are you Detective Gubb? Good! I've been expecting you. Have you a gun?"

"In my telescope case," whispered Philo Gubb.

"Take this one," said the clerk, handing the paper-hanger-detective a glittering revolver. "Be careful. Come — I'll show you the room."

He came from behind the desk and picked up Philo Gubb's telescope valise and led the way up the dingy stairway. Luckily for Billy Getz's great practical joke, Philo Gubb had never seen Jack Harburger, or he would have recognized him in the plump little man carrying his telescope valise. Up three flights of dark stairs, Jack Harburger led Philo Gubb, and at the landing of the fourth floor he stopped.

"THESE HERE IS FALSE WHISKERS AND HAIR"

"REBECCA, I PRAY YOU, WILL YOU TELL ME ALL YOUR HEART?"

THE OUBLIETTE

"You were taking a risk — a big risk — coming undisguised," he said.

"But I am disguised," said Philo Gubb. "These here is false whiskers and hair."

"What!" exclaimed Jack Harburger. "Wonderful work! A splendid make-up, detective! You fooled me with it, and I was on my guard. You'll do. Bend down like an old man. That's it! Now, listen: I have cut a hole through the wall from your room into Jack's. You can hear every word he speaks. Have you pencil and paper? Good! Jot down every word you hear. And don't make a sound. If you are discovered — well, they're a desperate gang. Come!"

He led the way through a long, dark corridor that turned and twisted. At the extreme end he stopped, put down the telescope valise, and drew a key from his pocket.

"That's Jack's room," he breathed softly, "and you go in here. Sorry it isn't a better room. We had to use it, and you won't be here long, anyway."

He opened the door. It was a large door that swung outward, and it occupied one half of one side of the room. The floor of the room was carpeted, and the walls were papered, as was the ceiling. There was no window, but an electric light burned in the center of the ceiling. Across the far side of the room stood a narrow iron bed, with a small bureau beside it. Jack Harburger pointed to a hole in the wall-paper.

"That's your ear-hole," he whispered, and Philo Gubb stepped into the room. Instantly the door slammed behind him, the key turned in the lock, and he heard a heavy iron bar clank as it fell into place outside. He was a prisoner, caught like a rat in a trap, and he knew it! He threw himself against the door, but it did not give. The electric light above his head went dark. He put out his hand, and the wall gave slightly. He drew the revolver and waited, dreading what might next occur. He heard soft footsteps outside the door, and, raising the revolver, pulled the trigger. The trigger snapped harmlessly. He had been tricked, tricked all around.

"Is the oubliette prepared?" whispered a voice outside.

"All ready for him. Twelve feet of water. He'll drown like a rat."

"Good. A slow death, like a rat in a trap — like we served the other two. Then get rid of his body the same way."

"A stone on it, and the river?"

"Yes. They never come up again."

The voices died away along the corridor, and Philo Gubb was left in utter silence. Oubliette! The fate of the detectives of "The Pale Avengers" was to be his! Suddenly the room began to quiver. The floor and the walls trembled and creaked, and Philo Gubb threw himself once more against the door. He shouted and beat upon it with his hands. Inch by inch, creaking and swaying, the room glided downward. The door seemed to glide upward beyond the ceiling, giving place to a solid wall. He turned and beat on the side of the room, and it gave forth a hollow sound. As he moved, the room swayed under his feet. He was doomed!

Alone in the darkness, his fear suddenly gave way to a feeling of pride. He was dangerous enough, then, to be thought worthy of death? His last drop of doubt oozed out of his mind. He was — he must be — a great detective, or such means would not have been taken to get rid of him. He felt a sort of calm joy in this. His murderers knew his prowess.

Locked in the room, going down to certain death, he exulted. And if he was as great as all that, it could not be that his position was hopeless. Time and again Carl Carroll, the Boy Detective, had been in equally precarious positions, but in the end he had brought the Pale Avengers low. And what a boy, untrained, could do, a graduate of the Rising Sun Correspondence School of Detecting ought to be able to do! He drew his knife from his pocket and cut into the wall-paper of the side wall.

Being a paper-hanger, the first touch of his hand against the side wall had told him the wall-paper was pasted on canvas and not on a solid wall, and now he ripped the canvas away. The wall was of rough boards, scarred and marred. The opposite wall was the same. He kneeled on the bed and tried the rear wall. He felt the plastered wall gliding

89

upward. He stood on the bed and ripped the canvas ceiling away.

As he ripped the ceiling away, light entered the cage from a dirty skylight far above. Just over his head a heavy iron grating covered the cage, barring him in, but high up he could see the great drum, from which the cable slowly unwound as the car descended. He was in an elevator, but this knowledge gave him small comfort. Cage, room, or elevator — call it what he chose — it was relentlessly descending into the flooded cellar. He watched the drum with fascinated eyes, as the wire cable unwound itself. He lay back on the bed, his feet hanging to the floor, and stared upward. He could not take his eyes from the revolving drum. It was like a clock, marking the moments he still had to live.

But suddenly he was galvanized into action. Over his feet something cold ran, making him jerk them from the floor. It was the water of the oubliette, and he gazed on it with horror as it rose, inch by inch, toward him. Slowly, as the car dropped, the water crept up. It reached the first drawer of the small bureau. It crept up to the side rails of the bed. It wet the mattress — and still it rose. He stood on the bed and grasped the iron grating above his head.

"Stop!" whispered a voice above his head, and the creaking cage stopped.

"Gubb! Detective Gubb!" whispered the voice, and Philo Gubb looked upward. "Listen, Detective

Gubb," said the voice. "One touch of my hand on the lever, and you will be dropped beneath the waters, never to appear again, except dead. One only chance remains for your life, and, blackened with crime though we are, we offer you that chance. If you will swear to leave the State, never to return, we will spare you. What say you, Philo Gubb?"

It was an offer no mortal could refuse. Life, after all, is sweet. Philo Gubb, the relentless Correspondence School detective, opened his mouth, but as he turned his head upward, he closed it again and licked his lips twice.

"No, durn ye!" he shouted angrily. "I won't never do no such thing!"

There was a hurried whispering of many voices above him.

"Think well," said the voice again. "We will give you until midnight to reconsider your rashness. Until midnight, Detective Gubb!"

"You can't scare *me!*" shouted Philo Gubb.

"Until midnight!" repeated the voice, and then there was silence.

Philo Gubb immediately drew his heavy pocket-knife from his pocket and began cutting out one of the panels of the door that shut him in on one side. He did not work hurriedly. He was not at all frightened. Looking up, he had seen the drum, and there was no more cable on the drum to be unwound. The car could descend no farther. His feet were as wet as they could get. Unless the river rose to unbelievable height, he could not be drowned in the makeshift oubliette, unless he voluntarily lay down in the shallow water and inhaled it. He worked on the panel slowly, but with the earnestness of a very angry victim of a hoax. The panel fell outward with a splash, and floated away. Philo Gubb bent sideways and squeezed out of the small opening into the cellar.

The huge cellar was dusky in the dim light that entered through the cobwebbed panes, high in the wall. It was an immense place, and now knee-deep in water, except for a gangway of boards laid on low trestles, which led from one side of the cellar to the cellar door. There were coal-bins and vegetable-bins, like watery bays leading from the general cellar sea, and — strange appliance to discover in a hotel cellar — a small hay-baling press stood on an extemporized platform against one wall, and alongside it, on a long table, such as are seen in factories, bales of hay, some complete and some torn open — and cases! The cases were labeled "Blue River Canned Tomatoes," but one, split across the end, gave evidence that their contents were not canned tomatoes at all. Through the crack in the case glittered the six silver stars of the Six Star whiskey. There were twenty-six of the cases.

Philo Gubb waded to the raised gangway and walked to the cellar door. It was double-barred on the inside, and he lifted the bars cautiously and stepped into the alley, closing the door carefully behind him. He pulled his false whiskers and wig from his face and stuffed them in his pockets and hurried down the alley.

When he returned, Billy Getz, Jack Harburger, and six of the Kidders were holding high revel in the closed barroom of the Harburger House, but they all fell silent when the door opened and the Sheriff of Derling County entered, with Philo Gubb and three deputies in company. It was evident that the Sheriff did not consider Philo Gubb a joke.

"Search-warrant, Jack," he said to Harburger. "Detective Gubb, of Riverbank, has been doing some sleuthing in your hotel, he says. We want to have a look at the cellar."

The next morning the "Riverbank Eagle" was full of Philo Gubb again. Through the superb acumen of that wonderful detective, three stores of whiskey had been discovered and confiscated — one in the cellar of the Harburger House at Derlingport; one in Joe Henry's stable at Riverbank; and a smaller one in the room in the Willcox Building frequented by the "Kidders."

"How I done it?" said Philo Gubb to one of his admirers. "I done it like a deteckative does it — a deteckative that wants to detect — picks up some feller that looks suspicious-like, like it says in Lesson Four, Rule Four. And then he shadows and trails him, like it says in Lesson Four, Rules Four to Seventeen. And then somethin's bound to happen."

PHILO GUBB, THE DETECTIVE

"But how can you tell what's goin' to happen?" asked his admirer.

"Well, sir," said Philo Gubb, "that's the beauty of the deteckative business. You don't ever know what's goin' to happen until it happens."

THE UN-BURGLARS

ALTHOUGH Detective Gubb's experience with the oubliette-elevator did not lead to the detection of the dynamiters for whom a reward of five thousand dollars was offered, it resulted in the payment to him of one half of three fines of five hundred dollars for each of the three stores of whiskey he had unearthed. With this money, amounting to seven hundred and fifty dollars, Mr. Gubb went to the home of Jonas Medderbrook and paid that gentleman the entire amount.

"That there payment," Mr. Gubb said, "deducted from what I owe onto them shares of Perfectly Worthless Gold-Mine Stock — "

"The name of the mine, if you please, is Utterly Hopeless and not Perfectly Worthless," said Mr. Medderbrook severely.

"Just so," said Mr. Gubb apologetically. "You must excuse me, Mr. Medderbrook. I ain't no expert onto gold-mines' names and, offhand, them two names seem about the same to me. But my remark was to be that the indebtedness of the liability I now owe you is only thirteen thousand seven hundred and fifty dollars."

"And the sooner you get it paid up the better it will suit me," said Mr. Medderbrook.

"Yes, sir," said Mr. Gubb, and hesitated. Then,

assuming an air of little concern, he asked: "It ain't likely to suppose we 've had any word from Miss Syrilla, is it, Mr. Medderbrook?"

For answer Mr. Medderbrook went to his desk and brought Mr. Gubb a telegram. It was from Syrilla. It said: —

Eating no potatoes, drinking no water. Have lost eight pounds. Kind love to Mr. Gubb.

"She 's wore herself down to nine hundred and ninety-two pounds, according to that," said Mr. Gubb. "She has only got to wear off two hundred and ninety-two pounds more before Mr. Dorgan will discharge her away from the side-show."

"And at the rate she is wearing herself away," said Mr. Medderbrook, "that will be in about ten years! What interests me more is that the telegram came collect and cost me forty cents. If you want to do the square thing, Mr. Gubb, you 'll pay me twenty cents for your share of that telegram."

Mr. Gubb immediately gave Mr. Medderbrook twenty cents and Mr. Medderbrook kindly allowed him to keep the telegram. Mr. Gubb placed it in the pocket nearest his heart and proceeded to a house on Tenth Street where he had a job of paper-hanging.

At about this same time Smith Wittaker, the Riverbank Marshal — or Chief of Police, as he would have been called in a larger city — knocked the ashes from his pipe against the edge of his much-whittled desk in the dingy Marshal's room on the ground floor of the City Hall, and grinned at Mr. Griscom, one of Riverbank's citizens.

"Well, I don't know," he said with a grin. "I don't know but what I'd be glad to be un-burgled like that. I guess it was just somebody playing a joke on you."

"If it was," said Mr. Griscom, "I am ready to do a little joking myself. I'm just enough of a joker to want to see whoever it was in jail. My house is my house — it is my castle, as the saying is — and I don't want strangers wandering in and out of it, whether they come to take away my property, or leave property that is not mine. Is there, or is there not, a law against such things as happened at my house?"

"Oh, there's a law all right," said Marshal Wittaker. "It's burglary, whether the burglar breaks into your house or breaks out of it. How do you know he broke out?"

"Well, my wife and I went to the Riverbank Theater last night," said Mr. Griscom, "and when I got home and went to put the key in the keyhole, there was another key in it. Here are the two keys."

Marshal Wittaker took the two keys and examined them. One was an old doorkey, much worn, and the other a new key, evidently the work of an amateur key-maker.

"All right," said Marshal Wittaker, when he had examined the keys. "This new one was made out of an old spoon. Go ahead."

"We never had a key like that in the house," said Mr. Griscom. "But when we reached home last night, this nickel-silver key was sticking in the lock of the front door, on the outside, and the door was unlocked and standing ajar."

"Just as if some one had gone in at the front door and left it unlocked," said Mr. Wittaker.

"Exactly!" said Mr. Griscom. "So the first thing we thought was 'Burglars!' and the first place my wife looked was the sideboard, in the dining-room, and there —"

"Yes," said Mr. Wittaker. "There, on the sideboard, were a dozen solid silver spoons you had never seen before."

"And marked with my wife's initials — understand!" said Mr. Griscom. "And the cellar window — the one on the east side of the house — had been broken out of."

"Why not broken into?" asked the Marshal.

"Well, I 'm not quite a fool," said Mr. Griscom with some heat. "I know because of the marks his jimmy made on the sill."

"Some one has been playing a joke on you," said Mr. Wittaker. "You wait, and you 'll see. You won't be offended if I ask you a question?"

"My wife knows no more about it than I do," said Mr. Griscom hotly.

"Now, now," said Mr. Wittaker soothingly. "I did n't mean that. What are your own spoons, solid or plated?"

THE UN-BURGLARS

"Plated," said Mr. Griscom.

"Well," said Mr. Wittaker, "there's where to look for the joke. Try to think who would consider it a joke to send you solid silver spoons."

"Billy Getz!" exclaimed Mr. Griscom, mentioning the town joker.

"That's the man I had in mind," said Mr. Wittaker. "Now, I guess you can handle this alone, Mr. Griscom."

"I guess I can," agreed Mr. Griscom. And he went out.

The Marshal chuckled.

"Un-burgled!" he said to himself. "That's a new one for sure! That's the sort of burglary to set Philo Gubb, the un-detective, on."

He was still grinning as he went out, but he tried to hide the grin when he met Billy Getz on Main Street. Billy uttered a hasty "Can't stop now, Wittaker!" but the head of the Riverbank police grasped his arm.

"What's your rush? I've got some fun for you," said Wittaker.

"Some other time," said Billy. "I just borrowed this from Doc Mortimer and promised to take it back quick."

"What is it?" asked the Marshal, gazing at the curious affair Billy had in his hands. It looked very much like a coffeepot, and on the lid was a wheel, like a small tin windmill. Just below the lid, and above the spout, was a hole as large as a dime.

"Lung-tester," said Billy, trying to pull away. "Let me go, will you, Wittaker? I'm in a hurry. Just borrowed it to settle a bet with Sam Simmons. I show two pounds more lung pressure than he does. Twenty-six pounds."

"You?" scoffed Wittaker. "I bet I can show twenty-eight, if you can show twenty-six."

"Oh, well! I suppose I can't get away until baby tries the new toy. But hurry up, will you?"

The Marshal put his lips to the spout and blew. Instantly, from the hole under the lid, a great cloud of flour shot out, covering his face and head, and deluging his garments. From up and down the street came shouts of joy, and the Marshal, brushing at his face, grinned.

"One on me, Billy," he said, good-naturedly, patting the flour out of his hair, "and just when I was coming to put you onto some fun, too. What do you know about the Griscom un-burglary?"

"Not a thing!" Billy said. "Tell me."

"I did n't expect you would know anything about it," said the Marshal with a wink. "But how about putting Correspondence School Detective Gubb onto the job?"

"Fine!" said Billy. "Tell me what the unburgled Griscom thing is, and I'll do the rest."

Billy found Philo Gubb at work in the house on Tenth Street, hanging paper on the second floor, and the lank detective looked at Billy solemnly as the story of the Griscom affair was explained to him.

THE UN-BURGLARS

"When I started in takin' lessons from the Rising Sun Deteckative Agency's Correspondence School of Deteckating," said Mr. Gubb solemnly, "I aimed to do a strictly retail business in deteckating, and let the wholesale alone."

"Seeing that you learned by mail," said Billy Getz, "I should think you'd be better fitted to do a mail-order business."

"Them terms of retail and wholesale is my own," said Mr. Gubb.

"You don't believe anybody would un-burgle a house, I guess," said Billy.

"Yes, I do," Philo Gubb said. "A fellow can tie a knot, or he can un-tie it, can't he? He can hitch a horse, or he can un-hitch it. And if a man can burgle, he can un-burgle. A mercenary burglar would naturally burgle things out of a house after he had burgled himself in, but a generous-hearted burglar would just as naturally un-burgle things into a house and then un-burgle himself out. That stands to reason."

"Of course it does," said Billy Getz. "And I knew you would see it that way."

"I see things reasonable," said Philo Gubb. "But I guess I won't take up the case; un-burgling ain't no common crime. It ain't mentioned in the twelve lessons I got from the Rising Sun Correspondence School. I would n't hardly know how to go about catching an un-burglar —"

"Just do the opposite from what it says to do to

catch a burglar," said Billy Getz. "Common sense would tell you that, would n't it? But, listen, Mr. Gubb: I 'd let Wittaker catch his own burglars. The reason I ask you to take this case is because I know you have a good heart."

"It 's good, but it 's hard," said Philo Gubb. "A deteckative has to have a hard heart."

"All right! Here is this man, un-burgling houses. For all we know he is honest and upright," said Billy Getz. "He continues un-burgling houses. The habit grows. Each house he un-burgles tempts him to un-burgle two. Each set of spoons he leaves in a house tempts him to leave two sets in the next house, or four sets, or a solid silver punch-bowl. In a short time he wipes out his little fortune. He borrows. He begs. At last he steals! In order to un-burgle one house he burgles another. He leads a dual life, a sort of Jekyll-Hyde life — "

"But what if I caught him?" said Mr. Gubb.

"Oh, you won't catch — I mean, we will leave that to you. Frighten him out of the un-burgling habit. I 'll tell Marshal Wittaker you will get on the trail?"

"Yes," said Philo Gubb. "I feel sorry for the feller. Maybe he 's lettin' his wife and children suffer for food whilst he un-burgles away his substance."

"Then," said Billy Getz, taking up his lung-tester, "suppose you stop in at the Marshal's office to-night at eight-thirty. Wittaker will tell you all about it."

THE UN-BURGLARS

Philo Gubb waited until Billy was well out of the house, and then he said: "He done it, and I know he done it, and he done it to make a fool out of me, but I guess I owe Billy Getz a scare, and if I can prove that un-burglary onto him, he 'll get the scare all right!"

Detective Gubb, when it was time to go to the Marshal's office, pinned his large nickel-plated star on his vest, put three false beards in his pocket, and went.

The Marshal received him cordially. Billy Getz was there.

"You understand," said Wittaker, "I have nothing to do with putting you on this case. But I want to ask you to report to me every evening."

"I could write out a docket," said Philo Gubb. "That's what them French deteckatives did always."

"Good idea!" said Wittaker. "Write out a docket, and bring it in every night. Now, I'll go over this Griscom case, so you 'll understand how to go at it. Here, for instance, is the house —"

The clock on the Marshal's desk marked ten before they were aware. Billy had arisen from his chair, for he had a poker game waiting for him at the Kidders' Club, when the telephone bell rang. The Marshal drew the 'phone toward him.

"Yes!" he said, into the telephone. "Yes, this is Marshal Wittaker. Mr. Millbrook? Yes, I know — 765 Locust Avenue. Broken into? What? Oh, broken out of! While you were out at dinner. Yes.

Opened the front door with a key. Yes. What kind of a key, Mr. Millbrook? Thin, nickel-silver key. Nothing taken? What s that? Left a dozen solid silver spoons engraved with your wife's initials? I see. And broke out through a cellar window. Yes, I understand. No, it does n't seem possible, but such things have happened. I'll send —"

He looked around, but Philo Gubb, who had heard the name and address, was already gone.

"I 'll attend to it at once," he concluded, and hung up the receiver. He turned to Billy Getz. "Billy," he said severely, "is this another of your jokes?"

"Wittaker," said Billy, "I give you my word I had nothing to do with this."

"Well, I 'll believe you," said Wittaker rather reluctantly. "I thought it was you. Who do you suppose is trying to take the honor of town cut-up from you?"

"I can't imagine," said Billy. "Are you going to leave the thing in Gubb's hands?"

"That mail-order detective? Not much! It is getting serious. I 'll send Purcell up to look the ground over. A man can't make nickel-silver keys, and break out of houses and leave engraved spoons and forks around without leaving plenty of traces. We 'll have the man to-morrow, and give him a good scare."

Detective Gubb in the meanwhile had gone directly to Mr. Millbrook's un-burgled house at 765 Locust Avenue. Mr. Millbrook, a short, stout man with a husky voice that gurgled when he was excited, opened the door.

"I 'm Deteckative Gubb, of the Rising Sun Deteckative Agency's Correspondence School of Deteckating, come to see about your un-burglary," said Philo Gubb, opening his coat to show his badge. "This is a most peculiar case."

"I never heard anything like it in my life!" gurgled Mr. Millbrook. "Did n't take a thing. Left a dozen spoons. Came in at the front door and broke out through the cellar window."

"How long have you been married?" asked Mr. Gubb, seating himself on the edge of a chair and drawing out a notebook and pencil.

"Married? Married? What 's that got to do with it?" asked Mr. Millbrook. "Twenty years next June, if you want to know."

"That makes it a difficult case," said Philo Gubb. "If you was a bride and a groom it would be easier, but I guess maybe you can tell me the names of some of the folks you 've had to dinner."

"Dinner?" gurgled Mr. Millbrook. "Dinner? When? "

"Since you were married," said Mr. Gubb.

"My dear man," exclaimed Mr. Millbrook, "we 've had thousands to dinner! Dining out and giving dinners is our favorite amusement. I can't see what you mean. I can't understand you."

"Well, you got plated spoons and forks, ain't you?" asked Philo Gubb.

"What if we have?" gurgled Mr. Millbrook. "That's our affair, ain't it?"

"It's my affair too," said Detective Gubb. "Mr. Griscom's house was unburgled last night, and he had plated spoons. The un-burglar left solid ones on him, like he did on you. Now, I reason induc-i-tively, like Sherlock Holmes. You both got plated spoons. An un-burglar leaves you solid ones. So he must have known you had plated ones and needed solid ones. So it must be some one who has had dinner with you."

"My dear man," gurgled Mr. Millbrook, "we never have had a plated spoon in this house! Who sent you here, anyway?"

"Nobody," said Philo Gubb. "I come of my-self."

"Well, you can go of yourself!" gurgled Mr. Mill-brook angrily. "There's the door. Get out!"

On his way out Mr. Gubb met Patrolman Purcell coming in.

Detective Gubb, outside the house, examined the cellar window as well as he could. There was not a mark to be seen from the outside, but a pansy-bed bore the marks of the un-burglar's exit. To get out of the cellar, the un-burglar had had to wiggle him-self out of the small window, and had crushed the pansies flat. Detective Gubb felt carefully among the crushed pansies, and his hand found something hard and round. It was the drumstick bone of a chicken's leg. Detective Gubb threw it away. Even

"WHO SENT YOU HERE, ANYWAY?"

an un-burglar would not have chosen a chicken's leg bone as a weapon. Evidently Billy Getz had not left any clue in the pansy-bed.

Philo Gubb had no doubt that Billy was putting up a joke on him. The detective decided that his best method would be to shadow Billy Getz from sundown each day, until he caught him un-burgling another house, or found something to connect him with the un-burglaries. So he went home. It was eleven when he began to undress.

It was then he first realized that the knees of his light trousers were damp from kneeling in the pansy-bed, and he looked at them ruefully. The knees were stained like Joseph's coat of many colors, and they were his best trousers. He hung them carefully over the back of his chair, and went to bed.

The next morning he rolled the trousers in a bundle and took them with him on his way to his paper-hanging job. On Main Street he stopped at Frank the Tailor's — "Pants Cleaned and Pressed, 35 Cents." He unrolled the trousers and laid them across the counter.

"Can you remove those stains?" he asked.

"Oh, sure I couldt!" said Frank. "I make me no droubles by dot, Mister Gupp. Shust dis morning alretty I didt it der same ding. You fall ofer der vire too, yes?"

"Certainly. I expect it was the same wire. Into a flower-bed."

"Chess," said Frank. "Like Misder Vestcote,

yes? Cudding across der corner, yes, und did n't
see der vire?"

"That so?" said Detective Gubb. "You don't
mean old Mr. Westcote, do you?"

"Sure, yes!" said Frank. "He falls by der flower-
bed in, und stains his knees alretty, shust like dot.
Vell, I have me dese pants retty by you dis efenings.
You vant dem pressed too?"

"Press 'em, an' clean 'em, an' make 'em nice,"
said Philo Gubb, and went out.

Old John Westcote, and pansy stains on his
trouser knees, was it? The thing seemed impossible,
but so did un-burglary, for that matter. Old John
Westcote was one of the richest men in Riverbank.
He was a retired merchant and as mean as sin. He
was the last man in Riverbank any one would suspect of leaving spoons and forks in other people's
houses. But how did it come that he had pansy
stains on the knees of his trousers? Philo Gubb
thought of old John Westcote all day, and toward
night he hit on a solution. Wedding presents! From
what he had heard, old John was — or had been —
the sort of man to accept a wedding invitation, go to
the reception and eat his fill, and never send the
bride so much as a black wire hairpin. And now,
grown old, his conscience might be hurting him. He
might be in that semi-senile state when restitution
becomes a craze, and the ungiven wedding presents
might press upon his conscience. It was not at all
unlikely that he had chosen the un-burglary method

UNDER HIS ARM HE CARRIED A SMALL BUNDLE

of giving the presents at this late date. The form of the un-burgled goods — forks and spoons — and the initials engraved upon them, made this more likely.

That night Detective Gubb did not report in person or by docket to Marshal Wittaker. At seven o'clock he was hiding in the hazel brush opposite old John Westcote's lonely house on Pottex Lane. At seven-fifteen the old man tottered from his gate and tottered down the lane toward the more thickly settled part of the town. Under his arm he carried a small bundle — a bundle wrapped in newspaper!

Detective Gubb waited until the old man was well in advance, and then slipped from the hazel brush and followed him, observing all the rules for Shadowing and Trailing as taught by the Rising Sun Detective Agency's Correspondence School of Detecting. For three hours the old man wandered the streets. Now he walked along Main Street, peering anxiously into the faces of the pedestrians, with purblind eyes, and now walking the residence streets. Detective Gubb kept close behind.

As ten o'clock struck from the clock in the High School tower, old John Westcote quickened his steps a little and walked toward the opposite end of the town, where the lumber-yards are. Down the hill into the lumber district he walked, and Detective Gubb dodged from tree to tree. Halfway down the hill the old man hesitated. He glanced around. At his side was a mass of lilac bushes, seeming strangely out of place among the huge piles of lumber. Without stopping, the old man let the bundle slide from under his arm and fall on the walk. For a moment it lay like a white spot on the walk, and then it moved rapidly out of sight into the bushes.

Bundles do not move thus, unless assisted, but Philo Gubb was too far away to see the hand he knew must have reached out for the bundle. He ran rapidly, keeping in the sawdust that formed the unfruitful soil of the lumber-yard, until he dared come no nearer, and then he climbed to the top of the tallest lumber-pile and lay flat. He commanded every side of the hillside lumber-yard, and he did not have long to wait. From the lower side of the yard he saw a black figure emerge, cross the street and disappear over the bank into the railway switch-yard below. Mr. Gubb scrambled down and followed.

At the bank above the switch-yard he paused, keeping in a shadow, and looked here and there. Flat cars and box cars stood on the tracks in great numbers, most of them closed and sealed — some partly open. He heard a car door grate as it was closed. He slipped down the bank and crept on his hands and knees. He was halfway down the line of cars when he heard a voice. It came from car 7887, C. B. & Q.

"Run all the breath out of me," said the voice in a wheeze.

"Well, did you get it?" whispered another voice.

"Sure I got it! Got something, anyway. Strike a match, Bill, and let's see if he put up a job on us. If he did, we'll blow him up to-morrow night, hey?"

"That's right. We got a can o' powder left under the pile by the laylocks. How much is it?"

"We tol' him one thousand, didn't we? Same as he give the Law and Order to help grab us. Now, listen! You take half of this and go one way, an' I'll take half an' go the other. We can get away with five hundred apiece."

"And we got the five hundred apiece we got for doin' the dynamite job, too. Say, I never thought to have a thousand dollars at once in me life. What's that?"

It was Philo Gubb, slipping the car door latch over the staple and hammering home the hasp with a rock. It was the engine, backing against the long row of cars to make a coupling, and then moving slowly forward toward Derlingport as the heavy train got under way. The two rascals hammered on the side of the car with their fists. They swore. They kicked against the doors. Philo Gubb drew himself into the next open car as the train moved away.

About the same time, Officer Purcell entered the Marshal's office, where Wittaker and Billy Getz sat awaiting the coming of Philo Gubb. Purcell led John Gutman, the town half-wit.

"I got him," he said proudly. "Caught him comin' out of Sam Wentz's cellar window. Says he did n't mean no harm. Had a dream he was to leave spoons on all the society folks an' he 'd be invited to all their parties."

"Did he fight you?" asked Wittaker. "Your pants is all stained up."

"Fight? No, he would n't fight a sheep. I tripped over a wire fence cuttin' a corner an' fell into a flower-bed. Got Hail Columbia from the lady, too. She said old man Westcote fell into the flowers yesterday, and she did n't mean to have her flower-bed used as no landin' place. Heard from Detective Gubb yet?"

Wittaker grinned. "We ought to hear from him soon. And I reckon he 'll be worth waiting to hear from."

And he was. Word came from him about an hour later. It was a telegram from the Sheriff of Derling County: —

Detective Gubb captured two of the dynamiters tonight. Have their confession. Arrest Pie-Wagon Pete, Long Sam Underbury, and Shorty Billings. All implicated.

"An' the rewards tot up to five thousand dollars," said Officer Purcell. "Let 's hustle out an' nab the other three, an' maybe we can split it with Gubb."

"And us sitting here thinking we had a joke on him!" exclaimed Marshal Wittaker with disgust. "It makes me sick!"

"Well, I feel a little bilious myself," said Billy Getz.

THE TWO-CENT STAMP

THE house in Tenth Street where Philo Gubb was doing a job of paper-hanging when he made the happy error of capturing the dynamiters while seeking the un-burglars was the home of Aunt Martha Turner, a member of the Ladies' Temperance League of Riverbank.

The members of the Ladies' Temperance League — and Aunt Martha Turner particularly — had recently begun a movement to have City Attorney Mullen impeached and thrown out of office, for they claimed that while he had been elected by the Prohibition-Republican Party, and had pledged himself to close every saloon, he had not closed one single saloon. Aunt Martha Turner and her associates believed this was because Attorney Mullen was himself a drinker of beer, and it was to get proof of this that the hot-headed ladies had engaged a youth named Slippery Williams to make a raid on his home.

Detective Gubb was, however, quite unconscious of all this when he proceeded to the home of Aunt Martha to complete his work there. He was in an unhappy frame of mind, for he had in his pocket nothing but one two-cent stamp and he had immediate need for one hundred dollars.

Mr. Gubb had, early that morning, visited the

home of Mr. Medderbrook, from whom he hoped to have news of Syrilla, but the colored butler informed him that Mr. Medderbrook had been called to Chicago.

"He done lef' word, howsomedever," said the butler, "dat ef you come an' was willin' to pay thutty cents you could have dis telegraf whut come from Mis' Syrilla. An' he lef' dis note fo' you, whut you can have whever you pay or not."

Mr. Gubb quite willingly gave the negro thirty cents, the very last money he possessed, and read the telegram. It said: —

Hope on, hope ever. Have given up wheat bread, corn bread, rye bread, home-made bread, bakers' bread, biscuit and rolls. Have lost six pounds more. Love to Gubby.

This would have sent Mr. Gubb to his work in a happy frame of mind, had it not been for the note Mr. Medderbrook had left. This note said: —

Called to Chicago suddenly. I must have one hundred dollars payment on account of the gold stock immediately. Cannot let my daughter marry a man who puts off paying for gold stock forever. Unless I hear from you with money to-morrow, all is over between us.

Such a letter would have made any lover sad. Mr. Gubb had no idea where he could raise one hundred dollars during the day and he saw his promising romance cut short just when Syrilla was beginning to lose weight handsomely. The greeting he received when he reached Aunt Martha Turner's was not of a sort to cheer him. Mrs. Turner met him with a sour face.

"No, you can't go ahead with puttin' the wall-paper on this kitchen ceilin' to-day, Mr. Gubb," she said.

"I'd like to, if I could," said Philo Gubb wistfully. "My financial condition ain't such as to allow me to waste a day. I'm very low in a monetary shape, right now."

Aunt Martha Turner seemed worried.

"Well," she said reluctantly, "I guess if that's the case you might as well go ahead. I expect I'll have to be out of the house 'most all day. If you get done before I get back, lock the kitchen door and put the key behind a shutter."

She departed, and Philo Gubb set up his trestle, unrolled and trimmed a strip of ceiling-paper, pasted it, and climbed his ladder. At the top he seated himself a moment and shook his head.

He sighed and picked up the paste-covered strip of ceiling-paper, but before he could get to his feet the kitchen door opened and "Snooks" Turner put his head in cautiously.

"Say, Gubb, where's Aunt Martha?" he asked in a whisper.

"She's gone out," said Philo Gubb. "She won't be back for quite some time, I guess, Snocksy."

"Good!" said Snooks, and he entered the kitchen. Some weeks before he had met Nan Kilfillan. He was deeply in love with Nan, and Nan was a good girl, although Aunt Martha Turner did not approve of her, because she was "hired girl" to City Attorney Mullen. Before she had met Snooks Nan had done her best to "make something" of "Slippery" Williams, who was courting her then, but that task was beyond even Nan's powers.

Snooks held a job on the "Eagle" as city reporter, with the dignified title of City Editor, and he was making good. He got the news. He seemed able to smell news. When there was big news in the air he would become uneasy and feel nervous.

"I got the twitches again," he would say to the editor of the "Eagle." "There's some big item around. I've got to get it." And he would get it.

"She's gone out, has she?" said Snooks, when he had entered his aunt's kitchen and asked Philo Gubb about Aunt Martha. "That's good. I wanted to see you on a matter of business — detective business."

He put his hand in his pocket and drew out a small roll of bills. He was not the usually neat Snooks. One eye was blackened and one side of his face was scratched. His clothes were badly torn and soiled. He looked as if some one had tried to murder him.

"There!" he said, holding the bills up to Philo Gubb after counting them. "There's twenty-five dollars. You take that and find out what I have done, and what's the matter with me, and all about it."

"What do you want me to find out?" asked Mr. Gubb, fondling the bills.

"If I knew, I would n't ask you," said Snooks peevishly. "I don't know what it is. I 'd go and find out myself, but I 'm in jail."

"Where did you say you was?" asked Philo Gubb.

"In jail," said Snooks. "I 'm in jail, and I 'm in bad. When the marshal put me in last night I gave him my word I 'd stay in all day to-day, and it ain't right for me to be here now.

"'Dog-gone you, Snooks!' he says, 'you ain't got no consideration for me at all. Here I figgered that there would n't be no wave of crime strike town for some days, and I went and took the jail door down to the blacksmith to have a panel put in where the one rusted out, and my wife made me promise to drive out to the farm with her to-morrow, and now you come and spoil everything. I got to stay in town and watch you.'

"'Go on,' I says, 'and take your drive. I 'll stay in jail. I got a strong imagination. I 'll imagine there 's a door.'

"'Honor bright?' he says.

"'Yes, honor bright,' I says.

"So he went," said Snooks, "and he 's trusting me, and here I am. You can see it would n't do for me to be running all over town when, by rights, I 'm locked and barred and bolted in jail. I 'm locked and barred and bolted in jail, and well started on my way to the penitentiary as a burglar."

"As a burglar!" exclaimed Gubb.

"That's it!" said Snooks. "I can't see head or tail of it. You got to help me out, Gubb. See if you can make any sense of this: —

"Last night I went out for a walk with Nan. She's my girl, you know, and she's going to marry me. Maybe she won't now, but she was going to. She works for Mullen. We got back to Mullen's house about eleven o'clock, and Mrs. Mullen always locks the door at half-past ten, whether Nan is in or not. So, being late, we had to ring the doorbell, and Mr. Mullen came to the door to let Nan in, and when he saw I was with her he shook hands with me and asked me to come in and have a cigar, and sit awhile, but I told him I had to hustle up some news for to-day's paper, and he let me go. That's how pleasant he was. So I went downtown, and the first fellow I met was Sammy Wilmerton."

"Widow Wilmerton's boy?" asked Philo Gubb.

"Exactly!" said Snooks, feeling his eye with his finger. "And he says, 'Snooks, did you hear what the Ladies' Temperance League did last night?' I had n't heard. 'I heard ma say,' says Sammy, 'but don't say I told you. They got up a petition to have City Attorney Mullen impeached by the City Council.'

"Well, that was news! I went into the 'Eagle' office and called up Mullen.

"'Hello! Is that Attorney Mullen?' I says.

"'Yes,' he says.

"'Well, something happened last night,' I says, 'and I'd like to see you about it.'

"'How do you know what happened?' he says.

"'No matter,' I says; 'can I come up?'

"After a half a minute he says, 'Oh, yes! Come up. Come right away. I'll be waiting for you.'

"So I went."

"Nothing strange about that," said Philo Gubb, shifting himself on the ladder.

"So I went," continued Snooks. "I rang the doorbell and, the moment it rang, the door flew open and — *bliff!* — down came a bed-blanket over me and somebody grabbed me in his arms and lugged me into the house. I guess it was Attorney Mullen — you know how big and husky he is. But I could n't see him. I could n't see anything. Only, every two seconds, bump! he hit at my head through the blanket. That's how I got this eye. And, all the time, he was talking to me, mad as a hatter, and I could n't hear a word he said. But I could hear his wife screaming at the top of the stairs, and I could hear Nan screaming, and I heard a window go up.

"'Stop that yelling!' says Mullen, in a voice I *could* hear, and then he picked me up again and carried me to the back door, and opened it and threw me all the way down the eight steps. I chucked off the blanket, and I was going up the steps again, to show him he could n't treat me that way, when — *bing!* — somebody next door took a shot at me with a revolver. Thought I was a burglar, I guess. I started to run for the back gate, when — *bing!* — somebody shot at me from the other house. What do you think of that? For a few minutes it sounded like the battle of San Juan, and I can't understand yet why I did n't suffer an awful loss of life."

"But you did n't?" asked Philo Gubb.

"No, siree! I made a dive for the cellar door, just as they got the range. I stayed in the cellarway, with the bullets pattering on it like hail, until the cop came. Tim Fogarty was the cop. He ordered 'Cease firing!' and the shower stopped, and I let him capture me. He took me to the calaboose, and this morning, early, he had me before the judge, and I'm held for the grand jury, and the charge is burglary and petit larceny. Now what is the answer?"

"Being pulled into a house and thrown out the other door is n't burglary," said Philo Gubb. "Burglary is breaking in or breaking out. Maybe Attorney Mullen mistook you for some one else."

"Mistook nothing!" said Snooks. "He was in the court-room this morning. He handled the case against me. Who is that?"

Some one was climbing the back steps, and Snooks made one dive for the cellar door, and slipped inside. He knew how to get out through the cellar, for he was familiar with it. He did not wait now, but opened the outside cellar door, and after looking to see that the way was clear, hurried back to the jail.

THE TWO-CENT STAMP

Philo Gubb did not have time to descend from his ladder before the kitchen door opened. The visitor was Policeman Fogarty.

"Mawrnin'!" he said, removing his hat and wiping the sweat-band with his red handkerchief. "Don't ye get down, Misther Gubb, sor. I want but a wurrd with ye. I seen Snooksy Tur-rner here but a sicond ago, me lookin' in at the windy, an' you an' him conversin'. Mayhap he was speakin' t' ye iv his arrist?"

"He was conversing with me of that occurrence," said Philo Gubb. "He was consulting me in my professional capacity."

"An' a fine young lad he is!" said Policeman Fogarty, reaching into his pocket. "I got th' divvil for arristin' him. 'T was that dark, ye see, Misther Gubb, I cud not see who I was arristin'. Maybe he was consultin' ye about gettin' clear iv th' charge ag'inst him?"

"He retained my deteckative services," said Philo Gubb.

"Poor young man!" said Fogarty. "I'll warrant he has none too much money. Me hear-rt bleeds for him. Ye'll have no ind iv trailin' an' shadowin' an' other detective wurrk to do awn th' case, no doubt. 'T is ixpinsive wurrk, that! I was thinkin' maybe ye'd permit me t' contribute a five-dollar bill t' th' wurrk, for I'm that sad t' have had a hand in arristin' him."

Fogarty held up the bill and Philo Gubb took it.

PHILO GUBB, THE DETECTIVE

"Contingent expenses are always numerously present in deteckative operations," he said.

"Right ye ar-re!" said Fogarty. "An' ye 'll remimber, if anny wan asks ye, that I ixprissed me contrition for arristin' Snooksy. Whist!" he said, putting his hand alongside his mouth and whispering: "Some wan wanted me t' search th' house here t' see did Snooksy have sivin bottles iv beer an' a silver beer-opener in his room."

Philo Gubb sat on the ladder and contemplated the five-dollar bill until he heard Fogarty returning.

"Hist!" Fogarty said. "I did not see him, mind ye!"

Fogarty slipped out of the back door and was gone, and Philo Gubb, after a thoughtful moment, decided that the five-dollar bill was rightfully his, and slipped it into his pocket. To earn it, however, he must get to work on the case. He raised the pasted strip of paper, but before he could place the loose end on the ceiling, some one tapped at the kitchen door.

"Come in!" he called, and the door opened.

"Slippery" Williams glided into the room. His crafty eyes sought Philo Gubb.

"'Lo, Gubby! Watcha doin' up there? Where's Miss Turner?" he asked.

"Miss Turner is out on business, I presume," said the Correspondence School detective coldly, "and I am pursuing my professional duties in the deteckating line."

"Yar, hey?" said Slippery. "Who you detectin' for now?"

"Snooks Turner," said Philo Gubb. "I'm solving a case for him."

Instantly Slippery's manner changed. From rough he became smooth. From bold he became cringing.

"Why, I'm Snooksy's friend," he said. "You know me and Snooksy was always chums, don't you, Gubby? Yes, sir, I think a lot of Snooksy. He says, 'Slippery, you go up to my room and get me a bundle of clean clothes — these are all torn and dirty, and —' Well, I guess I'll get 'em, and get back. Snooks is waitin' for me."

He turned to the hall, but Philo Gubb called him back.

"You can't go up there," said Philo Gubb, from his ladder-top. "There's been enough folks up there already."

"Who was up?" asked Slippery hastily.

"Policeman Fogarty was," said Philo Gubb.

"What'd he find up there?" asked Slippery anxiously.

"Nothin'," said Philo Gubb. "He told me he couldn't find seven bottles of beer and a beer-opener."

"Look here!" said Slippery sweetly. "If I gave you five dollars to hire you to hunt for them, could you find them seven bottles of beer and that beer-opener for me? Straight detective work? Could you?"

"I could try to find them," said Philo Gubb.

"Well, that's all I want," said Slippery. "I don't want to do nothin' with them. All I want to know is — where are they? Here's five dollars."

Philo Gubb took the money.

"All right," said Slippery, "now, you find them. They're upstairs in Mrs. Turner's bed, between the quilt and the mattress. Go find them."

"Not until Miss Turner comes home," said Philo firmly. "It's her house."

"Why, you long-legged stork you!" said Slippery, "she knows I'm here for that beer. She sent me."

"I thought you said Snooks sent you for his clothes," said Philo.

"Never you mind who sent me for what!" said Slippery, angrily. "You're a dandy detective, ain't you? Sittin' on top of a ladder, and not lettin' a friend of Snooks help him out. Say, listen, Gubby! Everybody's goin' to get into worse trouble if I don't get away with that beer. Understand? Come on! Let me take it away!"

"When Miss Turner comes back!" said Philo Gubb.

A new knock on the door interrupted them, and Slippery glided to the cellar door, through which Snooks had so recently fled. The kitchen door opened to admit Attorney Smith. He was a thin man, but intelligent-looking, as thin men quite frequently are.

"Don't get down, Mr. Gubb, don't get down!"

he said. "I came in the back way, hoping to find Miss Turner. She is not here?"

"She's out," said Philo.

"Too bad!" said Attorney Smith. "I wanted to see her about her nephew. You have heard he is in jail?"

"Why, yes," said Philo, crossing one leg over the other. "He hired me to do some deteckating. I'm sort of in charge of that case. I'm just going to start in looking it up."

Attorney Smith took a turn to the end of the room and back. He was known in Riverbank as the unsuccessful competitor against Attorney Mullen for the City Attorneyship, and was supposed to be the counselor of the liquor interests.

"You have done nothing yet?" he asked suddenly, stopping below Philo Gubb's elevated seat.

"No, I'm just about beginning to commence," said Philo.

"Then you know nothing regarding the — the articles young Turner is charged with stealing?"

"Well, maybe I do know something about that," said Philo. "If you mean seven bottles of beer and a beer-opener, I do."

"Where are they?" asked Attorney Smith in the sharp tone he used in addressing a witness for the other side when he was trying a case.

"I guess I've told about all I'm going to tell about them," said Philo thoughtfully. "I don't want to be disobliging, Mister Smith, but I look on them bottles of beer as a clue, and that beer-opener as a clue, and they're about the only clue I've got. I got to save up my clues."

"Are they in this house?" asked Mr. Smith sharply.

"If they ain't, they're somewheres else," said Philo.

"Mr. Gubb," said Mr. Smith impressively "there are large interests at stake in this case. Larger interests than you imagine. We are all interested at this moment in clearing your client of the suspicion — which I hope is an unjust suspicion — now resting over and upon him. I need not say what the interests are, but they are very powerful. I feel confident that those interests could succeed in clearing Snooks Turner."

"Well, I guess, if I was left alone long enough to get down from this ladder, I could clear him myself. I didn't study in the Rising Sun Deteckative Agency's Correspondence School of Deteckating for nothing," said Philo Gubb. "Snooks hired me —"

"And he did well!" said Attorney Smith heartily. "I praise his acumen. I wonder if I might be permitted, on behalf of the powerful interests I represent, to contribute to the expense of the work you will do?"

"I guess you might," said Philo Gubb. "Deteckating runs into money."

"The interests I represent," said Mr. Smith, taking out his wallet, "will contribute ten dollars."

And they did. They put a crisp ten-dollar bill in Philo Gubb's hands.

"And now, having shown our unity of interest with young Mr. Turner, there can be no harm in telling us where that beer is, can there?"

He turned toward the kitchen door — for Nan Kilfillan stood there. Her eyes were red and swollen. Attorney Smith hastily excused himself and went away, and Nan came into the kitchen.

"Oh, Mr. Gubb!" she exclaimed. "You *will* get Snooks out of jail, won't you? It would break my heart if he was sent to the penitentiary, and I *know* he has done nothing wrong! He is depending on you, Mr. Gubb. I brought you ten dollars — it is all I have left of last month's wages, but it will help a little, won't it?"

"Thank you," said Philo Gubb, taking the money. "I cannot estimate in advance what the cost of his clearance will be. It may be more, and it may be less. It is a complicated case. I am just about going to get down from this ladder and start working on it vigorously. If you —"

He stopped.

"If you wish to help us in this case, Miss Kilfillan," he said, "will you go to the jail and ask Snooks where is the beer and the beer-opener?"

"Where is —" Her face went white. "What beer and what beer-opener?" she asked tensely.

"Seven bottles and a beer-opener," said Philo Gubb.

"Oh!" she moaned. "And he said he did n't do it! He swore he did n't do it! Oh, Snooks, how could you — how could you!"

"Now, don't you weep like that," said Philo Gubb soothingly. "You go and ask him. I'll have my things ready for my immediate departure onto the case by the time you get back."

Nan hurried away, and Philo Gubb waited only to count the money he had so far received. It amounted to fifty-five dollars. He slipped it into his pocket and stood up on the stepladder. He had even proceeded so far as to put one foot on a lower step, when Mrs. Wilmerton entered the kitchen.

She was a stout woman, and she was almost out of breath. She had to stand a minute before she could speak, but as she stood she made gestures with her hands, as if *that* much of her delivery could be given, at any rate, and the words might catch up with their appropriate gestures if they could.

"Mister Gubb! Mister Gubb!" she gasped. "Oh, this is terrible! Terrible! Miss Turner should never have dared it! Oh, my breath! Do you — do you know where the beer is?"

"I would n't advise you to take beer for shortness of the breath," said Philo Gubb. "Just rest a minute."

"But," gasped poor Mrs. Wilmerton, "I *told* Miss Turner it was folly! She's so stubborn! Ah—h! I thought I'd never get a full breath again as long as I lived. How can we get rid of the beer?"

SHE MADE GESTURES WITH HER HANDS

THE TWO-CENT STAMP

"There's plenty want to take it," said Mr. Gubb. "Attorney Smith —"

"Oh, I knew it! I knew it!" moaned Mrs. Wilmerton. "He threatened it!"

"Threatened what?" asked Philo Gubb.

"That he would find the beer in this house!" cried Mrs. Wilmerton. "He threatened Aunt Martha that if she did not give it to him freely, he would have it found here, and make a scandal! Beer hidden between the quilt and the mattress of Aunt Martha's bed, and she Secretary of the Ladies' Temperance League! It's awful! Martha is so headstrong! She's getting herself in an awful fix! She never should have had a thing to do with that Slippery fellow!"

"With who? With Slippery Williams?" asked Philo Gubb, intensely surprised. "Aunt Martha Turner? What did she have to do with Slippery Williams?"

"Well, she had plenty, and enough, and more than that to do with him," said Mrs. Wilmerton angrily. "Getting bottles of beer in her bed, and robbing houses at her time of life, and wanting the Ladies' Temperance League to have a special meeting this morning to approve of burglary and larceny! At her age!"

"Now, Miss Wilmerton," said Philo Gubb, from the top of the ladder, "I'd ought to warn you, before you go any farther, that Snooks Turner has engaged me and my services to detect for him in this burglar case. If Aunt Martha Turner burgled the burglary that Snooks is in jail for, maybe you ought not say anything about it to me. I got to do what I can to free Snooksy, no matter who it gets into trouble."

"Mr. Gubb!" exclaimed Mrs. Wilmerton suddenly — "Mr. Gubb, I'm not authorized so to do, but I'll warrant I'll get the other ladies to authorize, or I'll know why. If I was to give you twenty dollars on behalf of the Ladies' Temperance League to help get Snooksy out of jail, — and land only knows why he is in jail, — would you be so kind as to beg and plead with Snooksy to leave Attorney Mullen alone, in the 'Eagle,' after this?"

She held four five-dollar bills up to Philo Gubb, and he took them.

"From what I saw of his eye," said Mr. Gubb, "I guess Snooks will be willing to leave Attorney Mullen alone in every shape and form from now on. Now, maybe you can tell me how Snooks got into this business."

"I have n't the slightest idea in the world!" said Mrs. Wilmerton. "All I know about it is —"

Both Mrs. Wilmerton and Philo Gubb turned their heads toward the door. The greater duskiness of the kitchen was caused by the large form of City Attorney Mullen. He bowed ceremoniously to Mrs. Wilmerton, who turned bright red with embarrassment, probably because of her part in the efforts of the League to have Mr. Mullen impeached by the

City Council. Attorney Mullen was not, however, embarrassed.

"I am glad you are here, Mrs. Wilmerton," he said, "for I wish a witness. I do not wish to have any stigma of bribery rest on me. I came here," he continued, taking a leather purse from the inner pocket of his coat, "to give these twenty-five dollars to Mr. Gubb. Mr. Gubb, I have just visited Snooks — so called — Turner at the jail. I went there with the intention of bailing him out, pending the simple process of his ultimate and speedy release from the charges against him. I am convinced that I was wrong when I made the charge of burglary against him. I am convinced that no burglary was ever committed on my premises —"

"Oh!" exclaimed Mrs. Wilmerton. "Not even seven bottles of beer and a beer-opener, I suppose!"

Attorney Mullen turned on her like a flash.

"What do you know about beer and beer-openers?" he snapped.

"I may not know as much as Detective Gubb, but I know what I know!" she answered, and Mr. Mullen restrained himself sufficiently to hide the glare of hatred in his eyes by turning to Philo Gubb.

"Exactly!" he said with forced calmness. "And perhaps I know more about them than Mr. Gubb knows. In fact, I do know more about them. I know they are upstairs between a blanket and a mattress. I know, Mrs. Wilmerton," he almost

shouted, turning on her with an accusing forefinger, "that they were stolen from a house in this
town by some one representing the Ladies' Temperance League. I know that burglary was committed by, or at the behest of, some one representing the Ladies' Temperance League! I know that,
if this matter is carried to the end, a respectable old
lady — a leader in the Ladies' Temperance League
— will go behind the bars, sentenced as a burglar!
That's what I know!"

"Oh, my!" gasped Mrs. Wilmerton, and sank
into a chair.

"Now, then!" said Attorney Mullen, turning to
Philo Gubb again, and handing him the twenty-five
dollars, "I give you this money as my share of the
fund that is to pay you for the work you do for
Snooks Turner. I make no request, because of
the money. It is yours. But if you love justice, for
Heaven's sake, send word to him to come out of
jail!"

"Won't he come out?" asked Philo Gubb,
puzzled.

"No, he won't!" said Attorney Mullen. "I
begged him to, but he said, 'No! Not until Philo
Gubb gets to the bottom of this case. But should
we, as citizens, and as members of the Prohibition
Party, permit you, Mr. Gubb, to land Aunt Martha
Turner in the calaboose?"

"Well, if what I find out, when I get down from
this ladder and start to work, sends her there, I

don't see that I can help it," said Philo Gubb. "Deteckative work is a science, as operated by them that has studied in the Rising Sun Deteckative Agency's Correspondence School of Deteckating — "

"Snooks says he don't know anything about any beer," said Nan Kilfillan, entering hastily, and then pausing, as she saw Mr. Mullen.

"Did you tell him it was upstairs, in bed?" asked Philo Gubb.

"In his room? In his bed?" said Attorney Mullen eagerly. "Why, that puts an entirely different aspect on the matter! That gives me, as City Attorney, all the proof I shall need to convict the respectable Miss Martha Turner and her honorable nephew of the 'Eagle.' And, by the gods! I *will* convict them!"

He glared at Mrs. Wilmerton. Nan broke into sobs.

"Unless," he added gently, "this whole matter is dropped."

Philo Gubb took out all the money he had received and counted it, sitting cross-legged on the ladder.

"I guess," he said thoughtfully, "you had better run up to the jail and tell Snooksy I want to see him right away, Miss Kilfillan. Maybe he can stretch the jail that much again. Tell him I'm just going to get down from this ladder and start to work, and I want to ask his advice."

"What do you want to ask him?" inquired Attorney Mullen, as Nan hurried away.

"I want to ask him about those seven bottles of beer and that beer-opener," said Philo Gubb.

"Mr. Gubb," said the City Attorney, "I can tell you about those bottles of beer. If those bottles of beer came from my house Aunt Martha Turner goes to the penitentiary. If she does not go to the penitentiary, there are no bottles of beer and there is no beer-opener. And never were!"

"I told her she had done a foolish, foolish thing!" exclaimed Mrs. Wilmerton.

"Just so! And it *was* foolish," said Attorney Mullen. "*If* it was done. And, if it was done, and Snooks Turner telephoned, and I thought he meant the burglary, I would, naturally, assault him."

"You hurt him bad," said Philo Gubb.

"And I meant to!" said Attorney Mullen.

All turned toward the door, where Policeman Fogarty entered with Snooksy and Nan.

"I've done ivrything I cud t' quiet th' matter up," said Fogarty to Mullen, thus explaining his interest in the affair.

"I like jail," said Snooks cheerfully. "I'm going to stay in jail."

Aunt Martha Turner interrupted him. She came into the kitchen like a gust of wind, scattering the others like leaves, and threw her arms around her nephew Snooksy.

"Oh, my Snooksy! My Snooksy!" she moaned.

THE TWO-CENT STAMP

"Don't you love your old auntie any more? Won't you be a good boy for your poor old auntie? Don't you love her at all any more?"

"Sure," said Snooks happily. "A fellow can love you in jail, can't he?"

"But won't you come out?" she pleaded. "Everybody wants you to come out, dear, dear boy. See — they all want you to come out. Every last one of them. Please come out."

"Oh, I like it in jail," said Snooks. "It gives me time for meditation. Well, good-bye, folks, I'll be going back."

His aunt grasped him firmly by the arm and wailed. So did Nan.

"But, Snooksy," begged Mrs. Turner, "don't you know they'll send me to the penitentiary if you go back to that old jail?"

"Yes, but don't you care, auntie. They say the penitentiary is nicer than the jail. Better doors. Nobody can break in and steal things from you."

"Snooks Turner!" said his aunt. "You know as well as I do that Mr. Mullen will forgive and forget, if you will. Would you rather see me go to prison — suffer?"

"No, of course not, auntie," said Snooks, laughing. "But you see, I've hired Detective Gubb to work on this case, and if there's no case, it will not be fair to him. He's all worked up about it. He's so eager to be at it that he has almost come down from the top of that ladder. In another day or two

135

he would come all the way down, and then there's no telling what would happen. No, I'm a newspaper man. I want Philo Gubb to discover something we don't know anything about."

"I might start in trailing and shadowing somebody that has n't anything to do with this case," suggested Philo Gubb. "That would n't discommode none of you folks, and I'd sort of feel as if I was giving you your money's worth. Somebody has been writin' on the front of the Methodist Church with black chalk. I might try to detect who done that."

"But that would be a very difficult job," said Snooks.

"It would be some hard," admitted Philo Gubb.

"Then you ought to have more money," said Snooks. "Aunt Martha ought to contribute to the fund. If Aunt Martha contributes to the fund, I'll be good. I'll come out of jail."

Aunt Martha opened her shopping bag, and fumbled in it with her old fingers. Philo Gubb took from his pocket the bills he had been given during the morning. He counted them. He had exactly one hundred dollars, just enough to send to Mr. Medderbrook.

"How much should I give you, Mr. Gubb?" asked Aunt Martha tremulously, and Philo Gubb stared thoughtfully at the ceiling for a few minutes. When he spoke, his words were cryptic to all those in the room.

THE TWO-CENT STAMP

"Well, ma'am," he said, "I guess ten cents will be about enough. I've got a two-cent postage stamp myself."

"Ain't detectives wonderful?" whispered Nan, clinging to Snooks's arm. "You can't ever tell what they really mean."

Nobody seemed to care what Philo Gubb meant, but a week later Snooks stopped him on the street and asked him why he had asked for ten cents.

"For to register a letter," said Philo Gubb. "A letter I had to send off."

THE CHICKEN

PHILO GUBB, with three rolls of wall-paper under his arm and a pail of mixed paste in one hand, walked along Cherry Street near the brick-yard.

On this occasion Mr. Gubb was in a reasonably contented frame of mind, for he had just received his share of the reward for capturing the dynamiters and had this very morning paid the full amount to Mr. Medderbrook, leaving but eleven thousand six hundred and fifty dollars still to be paid that gentleman for the Utterly Hopeless Gold-Mine Stock, and upon the further payment of seventy-five cents — half its cost — Mr. Medderbrook gave him a telegram he had received from Syrilla. The telegram was as follows: —

Rapidly shrinking. Have given up all soups, including tomato soup, chicken soup, mulligatawny, mock turtle, green pea, vegetable, gumbo, lentil, consommé, bouillon and clam broth. Now weigh only nine hundred and fifty pounds. Wire at once whether clam chowder is a soup or a food. Fond remembrances to Gubby.

Mr. Gubb was thinking of this telegram as he walked toward his work. Just ahead of him a short lane led, between Mrs. Smith's house and the Cherry Street Methodist Chapel, to the brick-yard. Mrs. Smith's chicken coop stood on the fence line between her property and the brick-yard!

"DETECKATING IS MY AIM AND MY PROFESSION"

THE CHICKEN

Philo Gubb had passed Mrs. Smith's front gate when Mrs. Smith waddled to her fence and hailed him.

"Oh, Mr. Gubb!" she panted. "You got to excuse me for speakin' to you when I don't know you. Mrs. Miffin says you're a detective."

"Deteckating is my aim and my profession," said Mr. Gubb.

"Well," said Mrs. Smith, "I want to ask a word of you about crime. I've had a chicken stole."

"Chicken-stealing is a crime if ever there was one," said Philo Gubb seriously. "What was the chicken worth?"

"Forty cents," said Mrs. Smith.

"Well," said Philo Gubb, "it wouldn't hardly pay me."

"It ain't much," admitted Mrs. Smith.

"No. You're right, it ain't," said Philo Gubb. "Was this a rooster or a hen?"

"It was a hen," said Mrs. Smith.

"Well," said Mr. Gubb, "if you was to offer a reward of a hundred dollars for the capture of the thief —"

"Oh, my land!" exclaimed Mrs. Smith. "It would be cheaper for me to pay somebody five dollars to come and steal the rest of the chickens. It seems to me, that you ought to make the thief pay. I ain't the one that did the crime, am I? It's only right that a thief should pay for the time and trouble he puts you to, ain't it?"

139

"I never before looked at it that way," said Mr. Gubb thoughtfully, "but it stands to reason."

"Of course it does!" said Mrs. Smith. "You catch that thief and you can offer yourself a million dollars reward if you want to. That's none of my business."

"Well," said Philo Gubb, picking up his paste-pail, "I guess if there ain't any important murders or things turn up by seven to-night, I'll start in to work for that reward. I guess I can't ask more than five dollars reward."

At seven the evening was still light, and Philo Gubb, to cover his intentions and avert suspicion in case his interview with Mrs. Smith had been observed by the thief, put a false beard in his pocket and a revolver beside it and left his office in the Opera House Block cautiously. He slipped into the alley and glided down it, keeping close to the stables. A detective must be cautious.

The abandoned brick-kilns offered admirable seclusion. A brick-kiln is built entirely, or almost so, of the brick that are to be burned, and the kilns are torn down and carted away as the brick are sold. The over-structure of the kilns was a mere roof of half-inch planks laid on timbers that were upheld by poles.

A ladder leaning against one of the poles gave access to the roof. In the darkness it was impossible for Philo Gubb to find a finger-print of the culprit on the kilns, although he looked for one. He did not even find the usual and highly helpful button, torn from its place in the criminal's eagerness to depart. He found only an old horseshoe and a broken tobacco pipe. As there were evidences that the pipe had been abandoned on that spot several years earlier, neither of these was a very valuable clue.

Mr. Gubb next gave his attention to the chicken coop. It was preëminently a hand-made chicken coop of the rough-and-ready variety.

Philo Gubb entered the chicken-house and looked around, lighting his dark lantern and throwing its rays here and there that he might see better. The house was so low of roof that he had to stoop to avoid the roosts, and the tails of the chickens brushed his hat. It needed brushing, so this did no harm. The hens and the two roosters complained gently of this interruption of their beauty sleep, and moved along the roosts, and Mr. Gubb went outside again. It was quite evident that the thief had had no great hardships to undergo in robbing that roost. All he had to do was to enter the chicken-house, choose a chicken, and walk away with it.

Why had he not taken ten chickens? Mr. Gubb, as he put the keg hoop over the end board of the gate, studied this.

The theory that Mr. Gubb adopted was that the thief, coming for a raid on the coop, had been surprised to find it so poorly guarded. It had been so easy to enter the coop and steal the chicken that he had decided it would be folly to take eight or ten chickens and thus arouse instant suspicion and reprisal. Instead of this he had taken but one, trusting that the loss of one would be unnoticed or laid to rats or cats or weasels. Thus he would be able to return again and again as fowl meat was needed or desired, and the chickens would be like money in the bank — a fund on which to draw. This theory was so sound that Mr. Gubb believed it would require nothing more than patience to capture the criminal. The thief would come back for more chickens!

Philo Gubb looked around for an advantageous position in which to await the coming of the thief, and be unseen himself, and the loose board roof of the brick-kiln met his eye. No position could be better. He climbed the ladder inside the kiln, pushed one of the boards aside enough to permit him to squeeze through onto the roof, and creeping carefully over the loose boards, reached the edge of the roof. Here he stretched himself out flat on the boards, and waited.

Nothing — absolutely nothing — happened! The mosquitoes, numerous indeed because of the nearness of the pond, buzzed around his head and stung him on the neck and hands, but he did not dare slap at them lest he betray his hiding-place. Hour followed hour and no chicken thief appeared. And when the first rays of the sun lighted the east he climbed down and stalked stiffly away to a short hour of sleep.

The next night the Correspondence School detective wasted no time in preliminary observations of the lay of the land. He kept out of sight until the sun had set and dusk covered the land with shade, and then he went at once to the roof of the brick-kiln. This time he was disguised in a red mustache, a pair of flowing white side-whiskers, and a woolen cap. And he wore two revolvers — large ones — in a belt about his waist.

It was still too early for brisk business in chicken-stealing when Philo Gubb climbed to the roof of the kiln and spread himself out there, and he felt that he had time for a few minutes' sleep.

He was tremendously sleepy. Sleep fairly pushed his eyelids down over his eyes, and he put his crooked arm under his head and, after thinking fondly of Syrilla for a few minutes, went to sleep so suddenly that it was like falling off a cliff into dream-land. He dreamed, uneasily, of having been captured by an array of forty chicken thieves, of having been led in triumph before the Supreme Court of the United States, and of having been condemned as a Detective Trust on the charge of acting in restraint of trade — as injuring the Chicken Stealers' Association's business — and required to dissolve himself.

The dream was agonizing as he tried one dissolvent after another without success. Turpentine merely dissolved his skin; alcohol had no effect whatever. He imagined himself in a long room in which stood vast rows of vats bearing different

143

labels, and in and out of these he climbed, trying to obey the order of the court, but nothing seemed capable of dissolving him, and he suddenly discovered that he was made of rubber. He seemed to remember that rubber was soluble in benzine, and he started on a tour of the vats, trying to find a benzine vat.

He walked many miles. Sometimes he arose in the air, with ease and grace, and flew a few miles. Finally he found the vat of benzine, immersed himself in it, and began to dissolve calmly and with a blessed sense of having done his duty.

It was then that Philo Gubb entered the dreamless sleep of the utterly weary, and, about the same time, two men slunk under the roof of the brick-kiln and after looking carefully around took seats on the fallen bricks, resting their backs against the partly demolished kiln. They arranged the bricks as comfortably as possible before seating themselves, and when they were seated, one of them drew a whiskey bottle from his pocket and, after taking a good swig, offered it to his partner.

"Nope!" said he. "I'm going to steer clear of that stuff until I know where I'm at, and you're a fool for not doing the same, Wixy. First thing you know you'll be soused, and if you are, and anything turns up, what'll I do? I got all I can do to take care of you sober."

"Ah, turn up! What's goin' to turn up 'way out here?" asked Wixy. "They ain't nobody follerin' us anyway. That's just a notion you got. Your nerves has gone back on you, Sandlot."

"My nerve is all right, and don't you worry about that," said Sandlot. "I've got plenty of nerve so I don't have to brace it up with booze, and you ain't. That's what's the matter with you. You saw that feller as well as I did. Did n't you see him at Bureau?"

"That feller with the white whiskers?"

"Yes, him. And did n't you see him again at Derlingport? Well, what was he follerin' us that way for when he told us at Joliet he was goin' East?"

"A tramp has as good a right to change his mind as what we have," said Wixy. "Did n't we tell him we was goin' East ourselves? Maybe he ain't lookin' for steady company any more than we be. Maybe he come this way to get away from us, like we did to get away from — say! — Sandlot," he said almost pleadingly, "you don't really think old White-Whiskers was a-trailin' us, do you? You ain't got a notion he's a detective?"

"How do I know what he is?" asked Sandlot. "All I know is that when I see a feller like that once, and then again, and he looks like he was tryin' to keep hid from us, I want to shake him off. I know that. And I know I'm goin' to shake him off. And I know that if you get all boozed up, and full of liquor, and can't walk, and that feller shows up, I'm a-goin' to quit you and look out for myself. When a feller steals something, or does any little harmless thing like that, it's different. He can afford to stick to a pal, even if he gets nabbed. But when it's a case of —"

"Now, don't use that word!" said Wixy angrily. "It was n't no more murder than nothing. Was we going to let Chicago Chicken bash our heads in just because we stood up for our rights? Him wantin' a full half just because he put us onto the job! He'd ought to been killed for askin' such a thing."

"Well, he was, was n't he?" asked Sandlot. "You killed him all right. It was you swung on him with the rock, Wixy, remember that!"

"Tryin' to put it off on me, ain't you!" said Wixy angrily. "Well, you can't do it. If I hang, you hang. Maybe I did take a rock to him, but you had him strangled to death before I ever hit him."

"What's the use gabbin' about it?" said Sandlot. "He's dead, and we made our get-away, and all we got to do is to keep got away. There ain't anybody ever goin' to find him, not where we sunk him in that deep water."

"Ain't I been sayin' that right along?" asked Wixy. "Ain't I been tellin' you you was a fool to be scared of an old feller like White-Whiskers? Cuttin' across country this way when we might as well be forty miles more down the Rock Island, travelin' along as nice as you please in a box car."

"Now, look here!" said Sandlot menacingly. "I ain't goin' to take no abuse from you, drunk or sober. If you don't like my way, you go back to the railroad and leave me go my own way. I'm goin' on across country until I come to another railroad, I am. And if I come to a river, and I run across a boat, I'm goin' to take that boat and float a ways. When I says nobody is goin' to know anything about what we did to the Chicken, over there in Chicago, I mean it. Nobody is. But did n't Sal know all three of us was goin' out on that job that night? And when the Chicken don't come back, ain't she goin' to guess something happened to the Chicken?"

"She's goin' to think he made a rich haul, like he did, and that he up and quit her," said Wixy. "That's what she'll think."

"And what if she does?" said Sandlot. "She and him has been boardin' with Mother Smith, ain't they? Ain't Mother Smith been handin' the Chicken money when he needed it, because he said he was workin' up this job with us? I bet the Chicken owed Mother Smith a hundred dollars, and when he don't come back, then what? Sal will say she ain't got no money because the Chicken quit her, and Mother Smith will —"

"Well, what?" asked Wixy.

"She'll send word to every crook in the country to spot the Chicken, and you know it. And when word comes back that there ain't no trace of him —"

"You've lost your nerve, that's what ails you," said Wixy scornfully.

"No, I ain't," Sandlot insisted. "I've heard plenty of fellers tell how Mother Smith keeps tabs on anybody that tries to do her out of ten cents even. Why, maybe the Chicken promised to come back that night and pay up. I bet he did! And I bet he *was* sour on Sal. And I bet Mother Smith knew it all the time, and that when he did n't come back that night she sent out word to spot him or us. I bet you!"

"You 've lost your nerve!" said Wixy drunkenly. "You never did have no nerve. You're so scared you're seein' ghosts."

"All right!" said Sandlot, rising. "I'll see ghosts, then. But I'll see them by myself. You can go —"

"Goo'-bye!" said Wixy carelessly, and finished the last drop in his bottle. "Goo'-bye, ol' Sandlot! Goo'-bye!"

Sandlot hesitated a moment and then arose and, after a parting glance at Wixy, struck out across the drying floor of the brick-yard, and was lost in the darkness. Wixy blinked and balanced the empty bottle in his hand.

"He's afraid!" he boasted to himself. "He's coward. 'Fraid of dark. 'Fraid of ghosts. Los' his nerve. I ain' 'fraid."

He arose to his feet unsteadily.

"Sandlot's coward!" he said, and threw down the empty bottle with a motion of disgust at the cowardice of Sandlot. The bottle burst with a jangling of glass.

THE CHICKEN

On the loose board roof Philo Gubb raised his head suddenly. For an instant he imagined he was a disembodied spirit, his body having been dissolved in benzine, but as he became wider awake he was conscious of a noise beneath him. Wixy was shifting twenty or thirty bricks that had fallen from the kiln upon a truss of straw, used the last winter to cover new-moulded bricks to protect them from the frost against their drying. He was preparing a bed. He muttered to himself as he worked, and Philo Gubb, placing his eye to a crack between the boards of the roof, tried to observe him. The darkness was so absolute he could see nothing whatever.

He heard Wixy stretch out on the straw, and in a minute more he heard the heavy breathing of a sleeper. Wixy was not letting any cowardice disturb his repose, at all events, and Philo Gubb considered how he could best get himself off the roof.

The sleeping man was immediately beneath him; the ladder was a full ten yards away; every motion made the loose boards complain. Looking down, Mr. Gubb saw that the top of the kiln reached within a few feet of where he lay, and that the partially removed sides had left a series of giant steps.

Mr. Gubb loosened his pistols in his belt. Now that he had the chicken thief so near, he meant to capture him. With the utmost care he slid one of the boards of the roof aside and put his long legs into the opening thus made, feeling for the kiln until he touched it, and when he had a firm footing on it he lowered the upper part of his body through the roof.

Five feet away a cross-timber reached from one pillar of the roof to another, and just below that was one of the steps of the kiln. Philo Gubb lighted his dark lantern, and casting its ray, saw this cross-piece. If he could jump and reach it he could drop to the lower step and avoid the danger of bringing the side of the kiln down with him. He slipped the lantern into his pocket, reached out his hands, and jumped into the dark.

For an instant his fingers grappled with the cross-piece; he struggled to gain a firmer hold; and then he dropped straight upon the sleeping Wixy. He alighted fair and square on the murderer's stomach, and the air went out of Wixy in a sudden *whoof!*

Philo Gubb, in the unreasoning excitement of the moment, grappled with Wixy, but the unresistance of the man told that he was unconscious, and the Correspondence School detective released him and stood up. He uncovered the lens of his dark lantern and turned the ray on Wixy.

The murderer lay flat on his back, his eyes closed and his mouth open. Mr. Gubb put his hand on Wixy's heart. It still beat! The man was not dead!

With the dark lantern in one hand and a rusty tin can in the other, Mr. Gubb hurried to the pond and returned with the can full of water, but even in this crisis he did not act thoughtlessly. He set the dark lantern on a shelf of the kiln, so that its rays

WITH ANOTHER GROAN WIXY RAISED HIS HANDS

might illuminate Wixy and himself alike, drew one of his pistols and pointed it full at Wixy's head, and holding it so, he dashed the can of water in the face of the unconscious man. Wixy moved uneasily. He emitted a long sigh and opened his eyes.

"I got you!" said Philo Gubb sternly. "There ain't no use to make a move, because I'm a deteckative, and if you do I'll shoot this pistol at you. If you're able so to do, just put up your hands."

Wixy blinked in the strong light of the lantern. He groaned and placed one of his hands on his stomach.

"Put 'em up!" said Philo Gubb, and with another groan Wixy raised his hands. He was still flat on his back. He looked as if he were doing some sort of health exercise. In a minute the hands fell to the ground.

"I guess you'd better set up," said Philo Gubb. "You ain't goin' to be able to hold up your hands if you lay down that way."

As he helped Wixy to a sitting position, he kept his pistol against the fellow's head.

"Now, then," said Philo Gubb, when he had arranged his captive to suit his taste, "what you got to say?"

"I got to say I never done what you think I done, whatever it is," said Wixy. "I don't know what it is, but I never done it. Some other feller done it."

"That don't bother me none," said Philo Gubb. "If you didn't do it, I don't know who did. Just about the best thing you can do is to account for the chicken and pay my expenses of getting you, and the quicker you do it the better off you'll be."

Pale as Wixy was, he turned still paler when Philo Gubb mentioned the chicken.

"I never killed the Chicken!" he almost shouted. "I never did it!"

"I don't care whether you killed the chicken or not," said Philo Gubb calmly. "The chicken is gone, and I reckon that's the end of the chicken. But Mrs. Smith has got to be paid."

"Did she send you?" asked Wixy, trembling. "Did Mother Smith put you onto me?"

"She did so," said the Correspondence School detective. "And you can pay up or go to jail. How'd you like that?"

Wixy studied the tall detective.

"Look here," he said. "S'pose I give you fifty and we call it square." He meant fifty dollars.

"Maybe that would satisfy Mrs. Smith," said Philo Gubb, thinking of fifty cents, "but it don't satisfy me. My time's valuable and it's got to be paid for. Ten times fifty ain't a bit too much, and if it had took longer to catch you I'd have asked more. If you want to give that much, all right. And if you don't, all right too."

Wixy studied the face of Philo Gubb carefully. There was no sign of mercy in the bird-like face of the paper-hanger detective. Indeed, his face was severe. It was relentless in its sternness. Five dollars was little enough to ask for two nights of first-class Correspondence School detective work. Rather than take less he would lead the chicken thief to jail. And Wixy, with his third, and half of the Chicken's third, of the proceeds of the criminal job that had led to the death of the Chicken, knowing the relentlessness of Mother Smith, that female Fagin of Chicago, considered that he would be doing well to purchase his freedom for five hundred dollars.

"All right, pal," he said suddenly. "You're on. It's a bet. Here you are."

He slipped his hand into his pocket and drew out a great roll of money. With the muzzle of Philo Gubb's pistol hovering just out of reach before him, he counted out five crisp one hundred dollar bills. He held them out with a sickly grin. Philo Gubb took them and looked at them, puzzled.

"What's this for?" he asked, and Wixy suddenly blazed forth in anger.

"Now, don't come any of that!" he cried. "A bargain is a bargain. Don't you come a-pretendin' you did n't say you'd take five hundred, and try to get more out of me! I won't give you no more — I won't! You can jug me, if you want to. You can't prove nothin' on me, and you know it. Have you found the body of the Chicken? Well, you got to have the corpus what-you-call-it, ain't you? Huh? Ain't five hundred enough? I bet the Chicken never cost Mother Smith more than a hundred and fifty —"

"I was only thinkin' —" began Philo Gubb.

153

"Don't think, then," said Wixy.

"Five hundred dollars seemed too —" Philo began again.

"It's all you'll get, if I hang for it," said Wixy firmly. "You can give Mother Smith what you want, and keep what you want. That's all you'll get."

Philo Gubb could not understand it. He tried to, but he could not understand it at all. And then suddenly a great light dawned in his brain. There was something this chicken thief knew that he and Mrs. Smith did not know. The stolen chicken must have been of some rare and much-sought strain. So it was all right. The thief was paying what the chicken was worth, and not what Mrs. Smith thought it was worth in her ignorance. He slipped the money into his pocket.

"All right," he said. "I'm satisfied if you are. The chicken was a fancy bird, ain't it so?"

"The Chicken was a tough old rooster, that's what he was," said Wixy, staggering to his feet.

"I thought he was a hen," said Philo Gubb. "Mrs. Smith said he was a hen."

Wixy laughed a sickly laugh.

"That ain't much of a joke. That's why everybody called him Chicken, because his first name was Hen."

Philo Gubb's mouth fell open. He was convinced now that he had to do with an insane man. Wixy moved toward the open drying-floor.

"Well, so 'long, pard," he said to Philo Gubb.

THE CHICKEN

"Give my regards to Mother Smith. And say," he added, "if you see Sal, don't let her know what happened to the Chicken. Don't say anybody made away with the Chicken, see? Tell Sal the Chicken flew the coop himself, see?"

"Who is Sal?" asked Philo Gubb.

"You ask Mother Smith," said Wixy. "She'll tell you." And he went out into the dark. Philo Gubb heard him shuffle across the drying-floor, and when the sound had died away in the distance he put up his revolver.

"Five hundred dollars!" he said, and he routed Mrs. Smith out of bed. He did not tell her the amount of reward he had made the chicken thief pay. He asked her what the most expensive chicken in the world might be worth, and she reluctantly accepted ten dollars as being far too much. Then he asked her who Sal was.

"Sal?" queried Mrs. Smith.

"The chicken thief declared the statement that you would know," said Mr. Gubb. "He said to tell her —"

"Well, Mr. Gubb," said Mrs. Smith tartly, "I don't know any Sal, and if I did I would n't carry messages to her for a chicken thief, and it is past midnight, and the draught on my bare feet is giving me my death of cold, and if you think this is a pink tea for me to stand around and hold fool conversation at, I don't!"

And she slammed the door.

THE DRAGON'S EYE

It was with great pleasure that Mr. Gubb carried four hundred and ninety dollars to Mr. Medderbrook, and his intended father-in-law received him quite graciously.

"This is more like it, Gubb," he said. "Keep the money coming right along and you'll find I'm a good friend and a faithful one."

"I aim so to do to the best of my ability," said Mr. Gubb, delighted to find Mr. Medderbrook in a good humor. "I hope to get the eleven thousand two hundred and sixty dollars I owe you paid up —"

"Where do you get that?" asked Mr. Medderbrook. "You owe me twelve thousand dollars, Gubb."

"It was eleven thousand seven hundred and fifty," said Mr. Gubb, "and this here payment of four hundred and ninety —"

"Ah!" said Mr. Medderbrook, "but the Utterly Hopeless Gold-Mine has declared a dividend —"

"But," ventured Mr. Gubb timidly, "I thought dividends was money that came to the owner of the stock."

"Often so," said Mr. Medderbrook. "I may say, not infrequently so. But in this case it was a compound ten per cent reversible dividend, cumulative and retroactive, payable to prior owners of the stock, on account of the second mortgage debenture lien. In such a case," he explained, "unless the priority is waived by the party of the first part, you have to pay it to me."

"Oh!" said Mr. Gubb.

"Luckily," said Mr. Medderbrook, "I was able to prevail upon the registrar of the company to make the dividend only ten cumulative per cents instead of eleven retroactive geometrical per cents, or you would now owe me thirteen thousand dollars."

"Well, I'm sure I'm much obliged to you," said Mr. Gubb with sincere gratitude. "I appreciate your kindness of good-will most greatly."

He stood for a minute or two uneasily, while Mr. Medderbrook frowned like a great financier burdened with cares.

"I don't suppose," said Mr. Gubb, when he had screwed up his courage, "you have had no telegraphic communications from Miss Syrilla?"

"Why, yes, I have," said Mr. Medderbrook, taking a telegram from his pocket, "and it will only cost you one dollar to read it. I paid two dollars."

Mr. Gubb was very glad to pay the small sum and he eagerly devoured the telegram, which read:—

Oh be joyful! Have given up all meat diet. Have given up beef, pork, lamb, mutton, veal, chicken, pigs' feet, bacon, hash, corned beef, venison, bear steak, frogs' legs, opossum, and fried snails. Weigh only nine hundred and forty pounds. Affectionate thoughts to little Gubby.

PHILO GUBB, THE DETECTIVE

"I wish," said Mr. Gubb wistfully, when he had read the message, "that Miss Syrilla could be here present this week in Riverbank whilst the Carnival is going on."

"She would draw a big crowd at twenty-five cents admission," said Mr. Medderbrook.

"I was thinking how pleasantly nice it would be for her to enjoy the festivities of the occasion," said Mr. Gubb, but this was not quite true. What he wished was that she could be present to see him in the handsome disguise he had obtained for his work as Official Detective of the Carnival, and which he was now about to don.

This, the second day of the Third Riverbank Carnival, opened with a sun hot enough to frizzle bacon, and the ladies in charge of the lemonade, ice-cream and ice-cream cone booths were pleased, while the committee from Riverbank Lodge P. & G. M., No. 788, selling broiled frankfurters (known as "hot dogs"), groaned. It was no day for hot food. But it was grand Carnival weather.

The grounds opened at one-thirty and the amateur circus began at two-thirty, but Philo Gubb, the detective, was on the grounds in full regalia by ten o'clock in the morning. Through some awful error on the part of the Chicago costumer, Philo Gubb's regalia had not arrived in time for the first day of the Carnival, so he had absented himself rather than let the crooks and thieves who were supposed to swarm the grounds have an opportunity to

158

become acquainted with his appearance and thus be put on their guard against the famous Correspondence School detective.

When the Committee on Organization of the Third Carnival and Circus for the benefit of the Riverbank Free Hospital held its first public mass meeting in Willcox Hall, Philo Gubb had been there. Like all the rest of Riverbank, he was willing to assist the good cause in any way he could, and he had meant to donate his services as official paperhanger, but a grander opportunity offered. Mr. Beech, the Chairman of the Committee on Peanuts and Police Protection, offered Mr. Gubb the position of Official Detective. Mr. Gubb accepted eagerly.

During the weeks of preparation for the Carnival, a thousand plans for getting the better of pickpockets and other crooks passed through Philo Gubb's mind. He finally decided to disguise himself as Ali Baba. He had a slight recollection that Ali Baba had something to do with forty thieves. It seemed an appropriate *alias*.

His disguise he ordered from the Supply Department of the Rising Sun Detective Agency, where he bought all his disguises. It consisted of a tall conical cap spangled with stars, a sort of red Mother-Hubbard gown bespattered with black crescents, a small metal tube, and a wand. With the metal tube came several hundred sheets of apparently blank paper, but, when these were rolled into cylinders and inserted in the metal tube for half a minute, characters appeared on the sheets. A child could work the magic tube, and so could Philo Gubb.

It was not until the second day that Mr. Beech thought of Mr. Gubb at all. Then Mrs. Phillipetti, daughter-in-law of General Phillipetti, who was Ambassador to Siberia in 1867, asked for Mr. Gubb. Mrs. Phillipetti was in charge of the Hot Waffles Booth, No. 13, aided by seventeen ladies of the highest society Riverbank could boast, and they served hot waffles with their own fair hands to all who chose to buy. The cooking of the waffles, being a warm task in late June, had been turned over to three colored women, hired for the occasion, and to complete the "ongsomble" and make things perfectly "apropos" — two of Mrs. Phillipetti's favorite words — the three colored women had been dressed as Turkish slaves, while Mrs. Phillipetti and her aides dressed as Beauties of the Harem.

To judge by Mrs. Phillipetti's costume, the Beauties of the Harem were expensive to clothe. She had more silk, gold lace, and tinsel strung upon her ample form than would set a theatrical costumer up in business, but the star feature of her costume was her turban. It was a gorgeous creation, and would have been a comfortable piece of headgear in midwinter, although slightly heating for a hot June day, but it came near being the talk of the Carnival, for in the center of the front, just above her forehead, Mrs. Phillipetti had pinned the celebrated brooch containing the Dragon's Eye — the priceless ruby given to old General Phillipetti by the Dugosh of Zind after the old diplomat had saved the worthless life of the old reprobate by appealing to the Vice-Regent of Siberia in his behalf.

The Dragon's Eye was about the size of a lemon and weighed nearly as much as a pound of creamery butter, so it required considerable turban to make it "apropos" and complete its "ongsomble." Pinned on her shelf-like chest, Mrs. Phillipetti wore a small mirror somewhat smaller than a tea saucer. By tipping the outer edge of the mirror upward and glancing down into it, Mrs. Phillipetti had a good view of the entire façade of her turban, reflected in the mirror, and she was thus able to keep an eye on the Dragon's Eye.

"Oh, Mr. Beech!" cried Mrs. Phillipetti, stopping him as he was bustling past her booth, "*do* you know where Mr. Gubb is?"

"Gubb? Gubb?" said Mr. Beech. "Oh! that paper-hanger-detective fellow? No, I don't know where he is. Why?"

"It's gone! The Dragon's Eye is gone!" moaned Mrs. Phillipetti.

Mr. Beech, although greatly concerned, tried to maintain his composure. Mrs. Phillipetti explained that she had removed her turban and placed it under a chair at the back of the booth. A little later she had noticed that the turban, with the priceless Dragon's Eye, was gone.

"Now, this — now — was not wholly unexpected," Beech said. "It's a — now — unfortunate thing, but it's the sort of thing that happens. Now, Mrs. Phillipetti, just let me beg you not to say anything about it to anybody, and I'll have Detective Gubb get right on the case. The matter is in my hands. Rest easy! We will attend to it."

"I — I hate to lose the Dragon's Eye," said Mrs. Phillipetti, wiping her eyes, "but the worst is to have my turban stolen. Mr. Beech, I will give one hundred dollars to whoever returns the Dragon's Eye to me. The 'ongsomble' of my costume is ruined. I haven't anything else 'apropos' to wear on my head."

"You look fine just as you are," said Mr. Beech. "But if you want something to wear, you can get a Turkish hat at the Paper Hat Booth for twenty-five cents."

"Thank you!" said Mrs. Phillipetti scornfully. "I don't wear twenty-five-cent hats!"

Within twenty minutes the Boy Scouts, who were acting as Aides to the Executive Committee, had tacked in ten prominent places ten hastily daubed placards that read: —

Philo Gubb, please report at Executive Booth.
                    Beech, Chmn. Police Committee.

And the members of the Board of Managers had, singly and by roundabout routes, approached the scene of the theft and had studied it.

"THE 'ONGSOMBLE' OF MY COSTUME IS RUINED"

To the left of Mrs. Phillipetti's booth was the Ethiopian Dip. Here, some thirty feet back from a counter and shielded by a net, a negro sat on an elevated perch just over a canvas tub full of water. In front of the net was a small target, and if a patron of the game hit the target with a baseball, the negro suddenly and unexpectedly dropped into the tub of water. The price was three throws for five cents.

As Riverbank had some remarkably clever baseball throwers, the Ethiopian was dipped quite frequently. As the water was cold and such a bath an unusual luxury for the Riverbank Ethiopians, no one Ethiopian cared to be dipped very often in succession. Therefore the Committee of Seven of the Exempt Firemen's Association, which had the Dip in charge, had arranged for a quick change of Ethiopians, and while one sat on the perch to be dipped, three others lolled in bathing costumes just back of Mrs. Phillipetti's booth.

Mr. Beech questioned the colored men quietly.

"Turbine?" said one of them. "We ain't seen no turbine. We ain't seen nuffin'. We ain't done nuffin' but sit here an' play craps."

"But you were here?" said Mr. Beech.

"Yes, we was heah," said the blackest negro. "We was right heah all de time. Dey ain't been no turbine took from nowhar whilst we was heah, neither. Ain't been nobody back heah but us, an' we's been heah all de time."

"Well, perhaps you can tell how this board got

pried loose, if you were here all the time," said Mr. Beech.

"It wa'n't pried loose," said the yellow negro. "Hit got kicked loose f'om de hinside. I know dat much, annerways. I seen dat oc-cur. I seen dat board bulge out an' bulge out an' bulge out twell hit bust out. An' dey hain't no turbine come out, nuther. No, sah!"

Mr. Beech went away. The detective business was not his business. He specialized in coal and not in crime. But in going he passed by Mrs. Phillipetti's booth and spoke to her.

"It will be all right," he said reassuringly. "We are on the track."

"Oh, thank you!" said Mrs. Phillipetti, who had completed the "apropriety" of her "ongsomble" by wrapping a green silk handkerchief about her head.

"I hope to return the turban and the jewel sometime to-morrow," said Mr. Beech, bluffing bravely.

But Philo Gubb did not heed the notices posted to call him to the Executive Booth. The evening passed and he did not appear, and Mr. Beech, on his way home, stopped at the police station. It was after midnight, but Chief of Police Wittaker was still on duty. He never slept during the Carnival.

Mr. Beech explained the loss of the turban and the Dragon's Eye, and early the next morning the Chief himself took up the hunt. By three o'clock in the afternoon he had discovered several things.

He discovered that the yellow man who had claimed to see the board pushed out from the inside was the husband of one of the waffle cooks in Mrs. Phillipetti's booth. He learned that the yellow man had been in jail. He learned that for a few minutes the yellow negro had been alone behind the waffle booth. The Chief thereupon arrested the yellow negro.

As he led the negro from the grounds by the back way, in order to cause as little commotion as possible, he brushed by a strange creature dressed as a wizard, who was standing by the rear entrance, droning: "Tell your fortune, ten cents! Tell your fortune, ten cents!" The wizard was tall and thin and wore a long white beard, a sort of Mother-Hubbard gown, and a pointed cap. As the Chief passed with his prisoner the wizard turned his eyes on the two, and then droned on. It was Philo Gubb, the paperhanger detective, on the job!

Philo Gubb, having received his costume, had come to the Carnival grounds the back way. He had wandered about the grounds, peeking and peering, seeking malefactors unsuccessfully. He felt the whole weight of the Carnival on his shoulders. When he suspected a youth he followed him at a safe distance, stopping when he stopped, going on when he went on. He was so intent on trailing and shadowing that he did not even notice the placards calling him to the Executive Booth. Every few minutes he had to stop and tell a fortune with the magic tube. So far he had collected two dollars and sixty cents.

The Chief, with his prisoner walking quietly by his side, — to avoid unpleasant commotion in an otherwise orderly crowd, — had just passed the wizard when he heard voices that made him look back.

"There he is!" said one voice. "Kick him off the grounds!"

"Here, you!" said another voice. "You've got to get out of here. And you've got to give up the money you've taken. Quick now. We don't allow any professionals on these grounds."

The voices were those of Henry P. Cross, Officer of the Day for this day of the Carnival, and Sam Green, Jr., Vice-Chairman of Police, and they were speaking to the wizard.

"Sh!" said the wizard, in a mysterious voice. "It's all right! Don't make a fuss. It's all right!"

"Let me kick him off the grounds!" said Mr. Cross. "All I want is a chance to kick him off the grounds. The cheap professional fakir, sneaking in to get money that ought to go to the Hospital! Let me kick —"

"Now, wait!" said Mr. Green irritably. "We want to make him disgorge first, don't we? Just keep your head on, Cross. Let me handle this."

"It's all right! Don't make a fuss," whispered the wizard. "I belong here."

"You belong nowhere!" shouted Mr. Cross.

"You belong here, indeed! Why, you could n't tell that to a baby! I guess not! Telling fortunes and putting the cash in your pocket. Don't the Ladies' Aid of the Second Baptist Church have the exclusive fortune-telling privilege? Did n't they put us onto you?"

The Chief turned back.

"What's up?" he asked.

"Professional," said Mr. Green. "Some Chicago grafter trying to make money out of our show."

"I'm all right, I tell you," said Philo Gubb earnestly. "I'm no crook. You see Beech. Ask Beech. Have Beech come here."

Mr. Cross looked at Mr. Green.

"You mean you fixed it with Beech so you could tell fortunes here?" asked Mr. Cross.

"Yes, that's what I mean," said Philo Gubb. "You get Beech."

"Get Beech," said Mr. Green. "Beech will throw him out."

"I'll watch him," said the Chief. "If he tries to move I'll club him."

Mr. Cross and Mr. Green hurried away, and the Chief dangled his club meaningly. The yellow man, who had been standing awaiting the end of the controversy, seated himself on the grass and leaned his back against a tree. Philo Gubb, as evidence that he did not mean to run, also seated himself, and leaned back against the same tree. The Chief stood a short distance away, his eyes keenly on them.

"How about it, Chicago man?" asked the yellow man in a low tone, bending down to pick a blade of grass. "Kin you he'p a feller out?"

"How?" asked Philo Gubb.

"I got in trouble," said the yellow man. "I'm gwine git hit in de neck ef some one don't he'p me mighty quick. Ef I hand you somethin' is you gwine take it?"

"Sure," said Philo Gubb.

"Grab it!" whispered the yellow man, and his hand slid the Dragon's Eye into the hand of Philo Gubb.

The Chief moved nearer.

"I guess dey let me go whin dey git me to de calaboose," said the yellow man in a louder voice. "Kaze I ain' done nuffin' nohow."

"They'll let you go when we get that ruby," said the Chief meaningly; "and if we can prove it on you, you go to the pen'."

Mr. Cross and Mr. Green returned with Mr. Beech.

"There he is," said Mr. Cross, pointing to the wizard Gubb.

"Never saw him in my life!" said Mr. Beech. "Now, then, what is this now? What's this story you —"

The paper-hanger detective arose and leaned close to Mr. Beech's ear. He whispered three words and Mr. Beech's attitude changed entirely.

"Oh!" he said. "I wondered where — now — all

right! It's all right! It's all right, Cross. All right, Green. All right, Chief!" Then he turned to Gubb. "We've been wanting you, detective. Put up placards for you. Now, listen! Mrs. Phillipetti had a turban stolen from her booth, and that infernal ton and a half or so of ruby was in it. The Dragon's Eye, she calls it. Well, that turban was stolen —"

"I am quite well acquainted with that fact," said Philo Gubb.

"Well, why don't you hunt for it, then?" asked Mr. Beech crossly. "I thought you were going to be of some use. Fooling around here with your silly ten-cent fortune-telling, having the time of your life while all of us are worrying about that Dragon's Eye. Why don't you hunt for it?"

"It ain't hardly necessary to engage in deteckative exertions at the present moment on account of that ruby," said Philo Gubb slowly, "because when I want it, all I got to do is to consult the magic deteckative tube."

"You're crazy!" said Mr. Beech. "You're crazy as a loon!"

"The usual price for consulting the oracle is ten cents," said Philo Gubb, "but I'll make a special exception out of this time."

He put the end of the magic tube to his ear and listened.

"The genyi of the tube says I've got the Dragon's Eye into my pocket, and if you ask this yellow negro black-man he'll tell you where the turban is at."

"Honest!" exclaimed Mr. Beech. "Gubb, you're a wonder!"

The negro, thus trapped, told where he had hidden the turban, and in a few minutes Mr. Beech, Mr. Cross, and Mr. Green returned with Mrs. Phillipetti, on whose head again towered the turban with the Dragon's Eye gleaming in it, making her "ongsomble" thoroughly "apropos."

"Gubb," said Mr. Beech, "I want Mrs. Phillipetti to meet you. You certainly are a wizard."

"Yes, indeed!" said Mrs. Phillipetti. "The wizardry of your whole ongsomble is completely apropos to your detective ability."

THE PROGRESSIVE MURDER

WHEN Philo Gubb paid Mr. Medderbrook the one hundred dollars he had received for retrieving the Dragon's Eye, Mr. Medderbrook was not extremely gracious.

"I'll take it on account," he said grudgingly, "but it ought to be more. It only brings what you owe me for that Utterly Hopeless Gold-Mine stock down to eleven thousand nine hundred dollars and, at this rate, you'll never get me paid up. I can't tell when there'll come along another dividend of ten cumulative per cents on that stock, that I will have to charge up against you. Unless you can do better I have half a mind not to let you see the telegram I got from my daughter Syrilla this morning."

"Was the news into it good?" asked Mr. Gubb eagerly.

"As good as gold," said Mr. Medderbrook. "As good as Utterly Hopeless Gold-Mine stock."

"What did Miss Syrilla convey the remark of?" asked the lovelorn paper-hanger detective.

"Well, now," said Mr. Medderbrook, "I went and paid two dollars and fifty cents for that telegram. For one dollar and twenty-five cents I'll give you the telegram, and you can read it from start to finish."

Mr. Gubb, his heart palpitating as only a lover's heart can palpitate, paid Mr. Medderbrook the sum

he asked and eagerly read the telegram from Syrilla.
It said: —

Grand news! Have given up all fish diet. Have given
up codfish, weak fish, sole, flounder, shark's fins, bass,
trout, herring (dried, kippered, smoked, and fresh),
finnan haddie, perch, pike, pickerel, lobster, halibut,
and stewed eels. Gross weight now only nine hundred
and thirty pounds averdupois. Sweet thoughts to
Gubby-lubby.

"You are touched," said Mr. Medderbrook as
Mr. Gubb put the dear missive to his lips, "but
unless I am mistaken you will be still more deeply
touched when you pay for — when you read
Syrilla's next telegram."

"I so hope and trust," said Mr. Gubb, and he
returned to his office in the Opera House Block with
a light heart.

With the increase of fame that came to him as a
detective Mr. Gubb's paper-hanging business had
grown, and he had left Mrs. Murphy's house and
taken a room on the second floor of Opera House
Block, near the offices of ex-Judge Gilroy, attorney-
at-law, and C. M. Dillman, loans and real estate.
The door now bore the sign

> **PHILO GUBB**
> **DETECKATIVE**
> **Also Paper-hanging**

THE PROGRESSIVE MURDER

On this morning Detective Gubb had hardly reached his office when Uncle Gabriel Hostetter, a shrewd smile on his face, opened Mr. Gubb's door.

Uncle Gabriel Hostetter was a round-shouldered old man with a long white beard that came to a thin point. He wore old-fashioned gold-rimmed spectacles, the rims forming irregular octagons, and on his head he wore one of the grandest old silk hats that ever saw the light of day in 1865. His principal garment was a frock coat, once black, but now grayish green. He was the wealthiest man in town, and it was said that when he once got his hands on a silver dollar he squeezed it so hard that the bird of freedom on it uttered a squawk.

He opened Philo Gubb's door hesitatingly. He expected to see an array of mahogany desks and filing cabinets for which he would have to pay every time the detective turned around. When he peered into the room he saw a tall, thin man in white overalls with a bib, sitting on an up-ended bundle of wall-paper, stirring a pail of paste with one hand while he ate a ham sandwich by means of the other.

"I guess I got in the wrong place," said Uncle Gabe. "Thought this was a detective office. All right! All right!"

"I'm him," said Philo Gubb, swallowing a hunk of sandwich with a gulp and wiping his hand on his overalls.

"You're who?" asked Uncle Gabe.

"I'm the deteckative," said Philo Gubb.

"You are, hey?" said Uncle Gabe. "All disguised up, I reckon."

"Disguised up?" said Philo questioningly. "Oh, this here paper-hanging and decorating stuff? No, this ain't no disguise. Even a deteckative has got to earn a living while his practice is building up."

"Humph!" said old Gabe. "Detecting ain't very good right now?"

"It ain't, for a fact," said Philo.

"Well, if that's so," said old Gabe, "maybe you and me could do business. If you want to do a little detective work to sort of keep your hand in, maybe we can do business."

"I ought to git paid something," said Philo doubtfully.

"Pay!" exclaimed old Gabe. "Pay for bein' allowed to sharpen up and keep bright? Why, you'd ought to pay me for lettin' you have the practice. It ain't goin' to do me no good, is it?"

"I don't know what you want me to detect yet," said Philo. "I might pay some if it was a case that would do me good to practice on. I might pay a little."

"I knew it," said old Gabe. "Now, this case of mine — What sort of a case *would* you pay to work on?"

"Well," said Philo thoughtfully, "if I was to have a chance at a real tough murder case, for instance."

THE PROGRESSIVE MURDER

"Humph!" said old Gabe. "How much might you pay to be let work on a case like that?"

"Well, I dunno!" said Philo Gubb thoughtfully. "If it looked like a mighty hard case I might pay a dollar a day — if it was a murder case."

"This case of mine," said old Gabe, coming farther into the room, "is just that sort of a case. And I'll let you work on it for a dollar and a quatter a day."

"Well, if it's that kind of a case," said Philo slowly, "I'll give you a dollar a day, and I'll work on it hard and faithful."

"A dollar and a quatter a day," insisted old Gabe.

"No, sir, a dollar is all I can afford to pay," said Philo.

"All right, I won't be mean," said old Gabe. "Make it a dollar an' fifteen cents and we'll call it a go."

"One dollar a day," said Philo.

"A dollar, ten cents," urged old Gabe.

"One dollar," said Philo.

"Tell you what let's do," said old Gabe. "We ain't but ten cents apart. You add on a nickel and I'll knock off a nickel, and we'll make it a dollar five. What say? That's fair enough. You ain't come up any. I come all the way down."

"All right, then," said Philo. "It's a go. Now, who was murdered, and when was he murdered, and why was he murdered? Them's the things I've got to know first."

PHILO GUBB, THE DETECTIVE

"You pay me a dollar five for the first day's work, and I'll tell you," said old Gabe.

Philo dug into his pocket and drew out some money. "There," he said. "There's two dollars and ten cents. That pays for two days. Now, go ahead."

He drew out his notebook and wet the end of a pencil and waited.

"The reason this is such a hard case," said old Gabe slowly, and choosing his words with care, "is because the murder ain't completed yet. It's being did."

"Right now?" exclaimed Philo excitedly. "Why, we ought n't to be sitting here like this. We ought —"

"Now, don't be in such a hurry," said old Gabe. "If you mean we ought to be where the victim of the murder is, we are. He's right here now. I'm him. I'm the one that's being murdered. I'm being murdered by slow murder. I'm liable to drop down dead any minute. But I don't want to be murdered and not have the feller that murders me hang like he ought. I can't be expected to. It ain't human nature."

"No, it ain't," agreed Philo. "A man can't help feeling revengeful against the man that murders him. If anybody murdered me I'd feel the same way. How's he killing you? Slow poison?"

"Gun-shot," said old Gabe. "Shootin' me to death with a gun."

THE PROGRESSIVE MURDER

The correspondence school detective looked at old Gabe with amazement.

"Shootin' you to death with a gun!" he exclaimed. "Ain't you told the police?"

"I come to you, did n't I?" asked old Gabe. "If I was to set the police on the feller he might rouse up and shoot me to death all at once."

"How is he shootin' you to death?" asked Philo.

"By inches, b'gee," said old Gabe. "Yes, sir, by inches. Every once in a while he takes a shot at me. Sometimes through the window of my house, and sometimes when I 'm walkin' on the street."

"And he ain't ever hit you yet?" asked Philo Gubb.

"Hit me?" exclaimed old Gabe. "Why, he don't ever miss me. He hits me every time. There ain't a day he don't shoot and hit me, and some days he hits me two or three times. I dare say I 'm almost dead now, if I knowed it."

Philo Gubb fondled his notebook uncertainly.

"What — what does he shoot you with?" he asked.

"Well, I dunno exactly," said old Gabe. "With a pea-shooter."

Philo Gubb closed his notebook, and slipped it into his pocket.

"If all you was after was to get that two dollars and ten cents, you might have got it without wastin' so much of my time," he said reproachfully.

But old Gabe did not move.

"What's the matter?" he asked.

"Maybe I'm a fool," Gubb said bitterly, "but I ain't no such fool as to think anybody is murdering nobody with a pea-shooter."

"Was you ever shot with a cannon?" asked old Gabe calmly.

"No, nor nobody ever tried to murder me with a pea-shooter," said Philo Gubb.

"If you ever *was* shot by a thirteen-inch cannon ball," said old Gabe, "you'd know it. When a thirteen-inch cannon ball hits you, there ain't nothin' left of you at all. But when a one-inch cannon ball hits you, you've got a chance to live a minute or two, maybe. That's the difference between a thirteen-inch cannon ball shootin' you, and a one-inch cannon ball shootin' you. And a rifle ball is different, too."

"I got a job of paper-hangin' as soon as I can get away from here," said Philo Gubb meaningly.

"You got a job of detectin' on hand now," said old Gabe. "And, as I was sayin', a rifle ball acts different. Maybe it kills you the first shot, and maybe you can hold three or four rifle bullets before you die, but if they keep on shootin' at you, you get killed sooner or later. Probably five shots is all any man could stand. I guess that's about it.

"And then you come down to one of them little twenty-two caliber revolvers. If he don't hit you in the heart, a murderer could easy enough shoot at you twenty-five times with one of them little

"THERE AIN'T A DAY HE DON'T SHOOT AND HIT ME"

twenty-two's before he killed you dead. But you'd be dead sooner or later. It's just a matter of what a man shoots you with that makes the difference in time.

"Of course," he continued agreeably, "you don't expect no pea-shooter to kill me as quick as a thirteen-inch gun would. If you expect that you're unreasonable. But the principle is just the same. Shootin' is shootin'. You know how that pome goes—

> 'The constant drip of water
> Wears away the hardest stone—'

and that's just as true of murderin' a man with a pea-shooter.

"And the beauty of it is that nobody knows you're committin' a murder. If anybody catches you and asks you what you're doin' you just say, 'Oh, nothin'. Just shootin' peas.'"

"Maybe that's so," agreed Philo Gubb. "It sounds reasonable. But the thing for me to do is to wait until you're dead and then catch the feller. It ain't a murder until you're dead."

"It ain't, ain't it?" sneered old Gabe. "You'd wait until I am dead, I suppose, and then start out to catch the feller. And you'd lose all the help I can give you. It ain't often a detective can get the corpse to help him like this."

"No, it ain't," agreed Philo Gubb.

"I got a suspicion who the feller is," said Gabe.

"Who?" asked Philo Gubb.

"You'll go ahead with the case? On the terms we settled on?" asked old Gabe.

Philo Gubb considered this carefully.

"Why, yes," he said at length, "I will. Who is the feller you think is doin' it?"

"Farrin'ton Pierce, the cashier of the Farmers' and Citizens' Bank," said old Gabe, his eyes shining with malice and shrewdness, as he leaned forward and whispered the words. "My own son-in-law, he is. An' I'll tell you why he's tryin' it. For my money. So his wife'll get it, an' he can be president of the bank in my place."

"You've seen him have a pea-shooter?" asked Philo Gubb.

"No, sir!" said old Gabe. "And I never seen one of the peas. All I ever felt was the sting of it when it hit me."

"Maybe," said Philo Gubb eagerly, "maybe it ain't a pea-shooter. Maybe it's a twenty-two short pistol with a silencer onto it. Maybe it's only because he's been afraid to come nigh enough to you that he ain't killed you yet. It don't seem to me that any man would try to murder any one with a pea-shooter."

"Humph!" said old Gabe. "Maybe you are right, at that. That's something I never thought of. It sounds likely, too."

"A deteckative has to think of all them things," said Philo simply. "If I was you I'd be more careful."

THE PROGRESSIVE MURDER

"I will!" said old Gabe. "See here, if he's shootin' at me like that, it ain't no joke, is it? Tell you what I'll do. I'll let you off from payin' me that dollar five a day. Just you hustle onto this case and keep at it, and I'll leave you work on it for nothin'. All I want is that you should send me word reg'lar of what you find out."

"It is the custom of all the graduates of the Rising Sun Correspondence School deteckatives to make reg'lar reports in writing," said Philo Gubb. "I'll start right in shadowing and trailing Mister Farrington Pierce, according to Lessons Three and Four, and I'll report reg'lar every day."

"Everything you find out," said old Gabe. "Don't leave out a thing. And particularly at night. That's when he shoots me the most."

"I won't leave him a minute," said Philo Gubb. "I've got a man I hire to help me on my paperhangin', and I'll get him to finish up this job. I'll start trailin' and shadowin' Farry Pierce right away."

Old Gabe shook hands with Philo and went out. When the door was closed behind him he chuckled, and all the way home his face was creased in a grin. He felt that he had done a good bit of business and saved himself a good sum of money. Philo Gubb, in the meantime, having put a false beard and a wig in his pocket, went out.

Across the street from the bank was Grammill's Cigar Store, where the idler men of the town loafed when they had nothing better on hand, and Philo Gubb entered and bought a cigar and took an easy loafing position near the front window. He commanded a view of the only entrance to the bank, and here he waited. At fifteen minutes after three Farry Pierce came out of the bank.

"There's a man with an easy job," said one of the loafers. "That Farry Pierce. Nothing to do till to-morrow."

"Too much time on his hands, I guess," said another, who — by the way — had more spare time than Farry Pierce. "From what I hear he'd be better off if he had to work all day *and* all night."

"The widow?" asked the first speaker.

"That's what they say," said the second. "They tell me he's blowing all his salary and more on that widow. Must make old Gabe crazy to see any of his kin spend money that way. Or any way. He's a close one, old Gabe is."

"What you hear about Farry and the widow?" asked the first.

"Makes old Gabe crazy, they tell me. He wants his girl to get a divorce."

"Who told you that?"

"My girl. My girl is workin' for his girl. Fr'm what she tells me old Gabe is pretty well worked up about it. Said he'd get a spotter to foller Farry and get some evidence on him if it did n't cost so blame much. I bet the' won't be any divorces in that family if old Gabe has to pay out any money."

"I bet they won't. And the' ain't no detectives workin' for nothin' so far as I hear. Not this year."

"No, nor next year, neither," said the other; and as this was in the nature of a joke they both laughed.

But Philo Gubb did not join their laughter. He felt his face grow red. His lean hands folded and unfolded as he watched Farry Pierce disappear around the corner of the bank building. If any one felt like murdering old Gabe with a pea-shooter at that moment, Philo Gubb did. Shadow and trail Farry Pierce! The old skin-flint, coming with a fairy tale and getting the only fully graduated de-teckative in Riverbank to shadow and trail a son-in-law and report daily! Divorce case evidence, hey? Talking murderer and working a deteckative into doing scandal sleuthing free of charge! Philo Gubb's face reddened again with new anger as he put his hand in his pocket and touched the beard and wig he had placed there. But for this chance conversation he would have been following Farry Pierce now, and making a fool of himself. But for this chance conversation he would not have lost sight of Farry Pierce by day or by night. He went back to his office, put on his overalls, and went to his work on a paper-hanging job.

At six he started for home. A block down the street he met one of the loafers he had heard speaking in Grammill's Cigar Store.

"What do you think about it?" he asked Philo Gubb.

"About what?" asked Philo in return.

"Ain't you heerd?" asked the man. "Why, it's all over town by now. Farry Pierce murdered old Gabe Hostetter not more'n twenty minutes after we seen him comin' out of the bank. Shot him. Killed him first shot. Yes, sir! Killed him instantly with a little mite of a pistol with about as much carry as a pea-shooter. Must have hit him in just the right spot."

"Did you see the pistol?" asked Philo Gubb nervously.

"No, I did n't," said his informant, "but that's what the feller told me. 'Killed him instantly with one of these here little pea-shooters,' was what he said. What you lookin' so funny about?"

"If you insist to wish to know," said Philo Gubb, "Mr. Gabe Hostetter was n't murdered instantly at all. He was progressively murdered by inches over a long considerable period of time, like little drops of water."

For a minute the loafer stared at Mr. Gubb. Then he laughed.

"Crazy!" he scoffed. "Crazy as a loon!" and he walked away and left Mr. Gubb struggling for a suitably crushing retort.

THE MISSING MR. MASTER

THAT evening Mr. Gubb received a short note from Mr. Medderbrook that was in the form of a bill or statement. It read: "Due from P. Gubb to J. Medderbrook, $11,900. Please remit," — so he put on his hat and walked to Mr. Medderbrook's elegant home.

"I want you to hurry up with what you owe me," said Mr. Medderbrook, when Mr. Gubb explained that he could pay nothing on the Utterly Hopeless Gold-Mine stock at the moment, "because I know you are soft on Syrilla, and from a telegram I got from her to-day it looks as if it would be no time at all before she reduced her weight down to seven hundred pounds and Mr. Dorgan of the side-show broke his contract with her. And if you want to read the telegram you can do so by paying half what it cost me, which was three dollars."

Mr. Gubb paid Mr. Medderbrook one dollar and a half, as any lover would, and read the telegram from Syrilla. It said: —

Love is triumphing. Have given up all cereal diet. Have given up oatmeal, rice, farina, puffed wheat, corn flakes, hominy, shredded wheat, force, cream of wheat, grapenuts, boiled barley, popcorn, flour paste, and rice powder. Weigh now only nine hundred and twenty-five pounds. Soft thoughts to dearest Gubby.

Mr. Gubb hesitated a moment and then said: —

"Far be it from me to say aught or anything, Mr. Medderbrook, but I would wish the cost of telegrams would reduce themselves down a little. This one is marked onto its upper corner 'PAID'—"

"Yes, the telegraph boy said that was a mistake," said Mr. Medderbrook hastily.

"And very likely so," said Mr. Gubb, "but for a reduction of five pounds one dollar fifty is a highish price to pay. Thirty cents a pound is too much."

"Well," said Mr. Medderbrook, "I don't want to have any quarrel with you, so I'll do this for you: I will make you a flat price of twenty-five cents per pound."

"Which is a fair and reasonable price for glad tidings to a fond heart," said Mr. Gubb, and this matter having been amicably settled, he returned to his office.

That evening he sat on the edge of his cot bed minus his coat, vest, and trousers, with his bare feet comfortably extended. At his back a pillow made a back-rest, and a bundle of wall-paper served as a rather lofty footstool. He was deeply immersed in Lesson Eleven, his bird-like face screwed into tensity. From time to time he wiggled one toe or another as a fly alighted on it. Sometimes, when more than one fly alighted on his toes at once, he wiggled all ten toes simultaneously.

A trunk, a varnished oak washstand and a cot showed that the room was not only a decorator's shop, but a living-place; and that this was the office of Philo Gubb, detective, was shown by a row of hooks from which hung various disguises used by the celebrated detective, by a portrait of William J. Burns, cut from a magazine and pasted on the wall, and by a placard which read, "P. Gubb, Graduate and Diploma-ist of the Rising Sun Detective Agency's Correspondence School of Detecting. Detecting done by the Day or Job. Terms on Application."

On the cot at Philo Gubb's side lay a copy of that day's morning Chicago paper, with a two-column spread headline reading, "Wife Offers $5000 Reward," and it was this that had driven Philo Gubb, the paper-hanger detective, to renewed study of Lesson Eleven — "Procedure in Abduction and Missing Men Cases."

Mr. Custer Master, of Chicago, had mysteriously disappeared. One paragraph in the article had caught Mr. Gubb's particular attention: —

Mrs. Master feels that her husband is still alive, and insists that Mr. Master will be found in one of the Iowa towns on the Mississippi River. The police of these towns have been notified, and detectives have gone to investigate. The Masters stand high in South-Side society. Mr. Master, it is understood, recently inherited $450,000 from a maternal uncle. At the time the will was probated considerable interest was aroused by the fact that the legacy was to go to Mr. Master only on condition that he carried out certain provisions contained in a sealed envelope, to be read only by the executors and Mr. Master.

And so on. The paper pointed out that Mr. Master had been a sufferer from dyspepsia for many years, but this had not had a permanently depressing effect on his mind. His home relations were most satisfactory. His own business — he was a dealer in laundry supplies and laundry machinery — was doing well, and no trace of outside troubles could be discovered.

On the morning of his disappearance, Mr. Master had shown some signs of mental eccentricity. A neighbor, happening to be at her window, saw Mr. Master come hurriedly from the door of his house. An hour later a friend passed him as he was standing on a corner six blocks from home. Mr. Master seemed greatly distressed.

"I can't do it! It kills me; I can't do it!" he was muttering to himself. "I never could do it. I said so."

The next news of Mr. Master was gained from the keeper of a bath-house and swimming-pool known as the Imperial Natatorium. About ten o'clock, Mr. Master entered the Natatorium hurriedly, asked the price of baths, and chose to pay for a plunge in the big swimming-pool. He paid in advance, removed his garments in one of the small dressing-rooms, put on a swimming-suit and went to the edge of the big pool. Here he grasped the rail and extended one foot until his toes touched the cold water, when he uttered a cry, rushed to the dressing-room, and, as soon as he had thrown on his clothes, dashed from the building. That was the last seen of Mr. Master.

Philo Gubb, having finished reading Lesson Eleven for the third time, had picked up the Chicago paper when the silence of the Opera House Building was disturbed by the sound of feet ascending the brass-clad stairs.

The nocturnal visitors seemed unacquainted with the building, for, after two or three steps had been taken, one lighted a match. It was evident to the detective that these visitors were reading the names on the doors as they progressed along the corridor, and he was about to extinguish his lamp and prepare for the worst, when the two men stopped again, struck a match, and, after an instant's hesitation, rapped sharply upon his door.

"Come in!" called Philo Gubb, at the same time drawing his bed-sheet over his scantily clad legs. He knotted the sheet behind, like an apron, and arose to greet the comers. They were two. One of them Mr. Gubb recognized at once; he was Billy Gribble, proprietor of the Gold Star Hand Laundry, just across the way on Main Street. The other man was a stranger.

Under his arm, Billy Gribble carried a long, cylindrical parcel enclosed in heavy wrapping paper. The parcel was about six feet long and nearly as large around as Billy himself. Under his other arm, Billy carried a second parcel. This was about three feet square. The trained eye of Detective Gubb noted all this at a glance. Billy Gribble dropped the two parcels on the floor.

"Gubby, old sport!" he said in his noisy way, "this is —"

"Now, now!" said the stranger irritably. "Now, wait! I said I would talk to him, did n't I? What do you mean by — if you'll please let — you are Detective Gubb, are you not?" he asked.

Philo Gubb gazed at the man. The man was tall and thin, taller and thinner than Mr. Gubb himself. He was clean-shaven and his face showed deep lines about the mouth and nose. His hair was closely clipped, making his head seem pea-like in its smallness.

But Mr. Gubb was not gazing at these things. His bird-like eyes were fastened on the end of the suitcase the stranger still held in his hand. On the end of the case were painted in black the letters "C. M." and the word "Chicago." The stranger glanced down at the suitcase and put it on the floor with a suddenness that brought forth a thumping sound.

"Clue!" he said, and he kicked the suitcase.

"I presume the honor of this call at this late hour of time," said Philo Gubb, shifting his sheet a little, "is on a matter of business. If it is of a social, society sort, I'll have to ask to be kindly excused whilst I assume my pants."

"Business call, business call entirely, Mr. Gubb," said the tall stranger. "Don't put anything on. If

— if you feel embarrassed I'll take some off. My name is — is —"

"Phineas Burke," said Billy Gribble, in a loud whisper.

"Can't you keep still?" asked the stranger crossly. "Don't you think I know my own name? Phineas — that's my name, and I know it as well as you do. Phineas Burns."

"Burke, not Burns," whispered Billy Gribble.

The stranger turned red with exasperation.

"Look here! Don't I know my own name?" he asked angrily. "My name is Phineas Burns."

"All right! All right!" said Billy Gribble. "Have it your own way. You ought to know. Only — you said Burke over at my place."

Mr. Burke-Burns glared at Billy Gribble.

"Now! There, now!" he cried. "Just for that I'll tell you you don't know anything about it. My name is n't Burke, and it is n't Burns. It's — it's Charles Augustus Witzel. Mr. Gubb, my name is Charles Augustus Witzel."

"Glad to know your acquaintance, sir," said Philo Gubb. "Won't you be seated upon one of them bundles of wall-paper?"

"I'm a detective," said Mr. Charles Augustus Witzel. "Tell him about me, Gribble."

"Well, he — whatever his name is, but Burke was what he told me — is a Chicago detective," said Billy Gribble. "Yes, sir, Mr. Gubb, Mr. — ah, what is it?"

"Witzel," said Mr. Witzel.

"Mr. Witzel is one of the celebratedest Chicago detectives," said Mr. Gribble, "and he's come over here to hunt up this man Master that's disappeared. See? So when he strikes town he comes straight to me. That's how it is, ain't it?"

"Ex-act-ly!" said Mr. Witzel.

"Yes, sir," said Billy Gribble. "So he comes to my laundry, and I'm in the washroom —"

"You ain't!" said Mr. Witzel. "You're out, and you know you're out!"

"And I'm out," said Billy Gribble. "Maybe I was in the washroom and went out the back way. Anyway, I'm out. Say," he said, as Mr. Witzel squirmed, "if you don't like the way I'm telling this, tell it yourself."

"I entered Mr. Gribble's laundry," said Mr. Witzel. "You'll understand, being a detective, Mr. Gubb. I entered the laundry. Here is the counter. I walked up to the counter. I leaned over and spoke to the girl there. 'My dear young lady,' I said, 'is Mr. Gribble in?' 'Out,' she says. Naturally, I looked down. A detective observes everything. My toe has hit a suitcase. On the end of the suitcase are the initials 'C. M.' and 'Chicago.' In other words, 'Custer Master, Chicago,' — the man I'm looking for."

"And did you get him?" asked Philo Gubb tensely.

"Gone! Gone like a bird!" said Mr. Witzel.

"I waited for Gribble. I questioned Gribble. I asked him if Mr. Master had been there —"

"Hold on!" said Mr. Gribble, and then, "Oh, all right!"

"And he said, 'No,'" said Mr. Witzel, frowning. "'Very well,' I said to Gribble, 'he'll be back. He'll come back after the suitcase.' So Gribble hid me in his private office. I waited."

"And he came back?" asked Detective Gubb eagerly.

"He did not," said Mr. Witzel.

Philo Gubb sighed with relief. "Then I've got a chance at an opportunity to get that five thousand dollars," he said.

"Mr. Gubb," said Mr. Witzel, "you have a chance to get twenty-five hundred. It was to offer you the chance to get twenty-five hundred that I came here. What did I say to you, Gribble?"

"You go ahead and tell it, if you want it told," said Gribble. "You don't like the way I tell things. Tell 'em yourself."

"I said to Gribble," said Mr. Witzel slowly, "'Gribble, is this the town where a detective by the name of Grubb lives?'"

"Gubb is the name," said Mr. Gubb.

"Gubb. That's what I said," said Mr. Witzel. "That made me think a bit. 'Gribble,' I says, 'by to-morrow there will be forty Chicago detectives in this town, all looking for Master. And I don't care a whoop for any of them,' I says. 'I'm the leader of them all, as anybody who has read the exploits of — of George Augustus Wechsler —.'"

"Charles Augustus Witzel," said Gribble, correctingly.

"I have so many *aliases* I forget them," said Mr. Witzel to Mr. Gubb. "You'll understand that perfectly. You are a detective, and I'm a detective, Witzel or Wotzel or Wutzel — who cares? We understand each other. Don't we?"

"I presume to suppose we will do so in the course of time," said Philo Gubb politely.

"Pre-cise-ly!" said Mr. Witzel. "So I said to Gribble, 'I'm afraid of Gubb! He's the man who will find Master, if I don't. But I've got an advantage. I've got the clue.'"

He pointed to the suitcase.

"So Gribble says to me," said Mr. Witzel, "'Why don't you and Gubb combine?' 'Great idea!' I says, and — here I am. How about it, Mr. Gobb?"

"Gubb is the name I adhere to when not deteckating," said Mr. Gubb kindly. "And as to how about it, I wouldn't want to enter into a combination shutting me out from using the ability taught to me in Chapters One to Twelve inclusive, of the Correspondence course. For the twenty-five hundred which would fall to my share, I should expect to detect to some considerable extent."

"Quite right! *Quite* right!" said Mr. Witzel promptly. "That meets my plans entirely. I make my headquarters here. I give you a free hand. I am a — an inductive detective."

"Yes, sir. A Sherlock Holmes deteckative," said Philo Gubb.

"Ex-act-ly!" said Mr. Witzel. "I think things out. But you go out. You shadow and snoop and trail. I remain here. For you see," he added, "I'm so well known that if Master saw me he would disappear instantly. Instantly!"

"I'm willing to transact it as a business bargain onto them terms," said Philo Gubb, and it was agreed.

Mr. Gribble immediately cut the cords that bound the two bundles, and released a canvas cot and a bundle of bedding. Then he said good-night and withdrew, closing the door behind him.

Mr. Gubb waited until he heard Mr. Gribble's footsteps on the brass-clad stairs.

"That Gribble man ain't what I'd term by name of a — of a —" He hesitated. "He's not known as a strictly reliable citizen in any respect," he ended. "I wouldn't trust him any more than need be necessary."

"Thank you," said Mr. Witzel, who was already removing his garments. "I don't mean to. And now, if you don't mind, I'll retire. Let's see if Mr. Master has a night-shirt in his suitcase. I think it helps the inductive mind to sleep in the night-shirt of the man it is hunting."

He opened the suitcase, using — oddly enough — a key from his own bunch of keys. He found a night-shirt and put it on. To his surprise it fitted him exactly, which was odd, for Mr. Witzel was an unusually tall and thin man. Without wasting time, he climbed into the cot and closed his eyes. Mr. Gubb also retired.

Philo Gubb, from his cot, watched Mr. Witzel until he was sure he was thoroughly asleep. Then the Correspondence School detective slipped out of bed and knelt over the suitcase.

The suitcase contained linen all plainly marked. The name "C. Master" was written in indelible ink on each piece. An extra suit of outer garments was marked with Mr. Master's name. There were silver-backed toilet articles, engraved with Mr. Master's name, and these Mr. Gubb examined closely, but what caught and held his interest most was a folded document, covered in light-blue paper and endorsed, "Last Will and Testament of Orlando J. Higgins. Copy."

The will began with the usual preamble, but the clause that caught Philo Gubb's bird-like eye, and held it, was the next.

"To my nephew, Custer Master," this clause said, "I give and bequeath $450,000; but, be it understood, my said nephew, Custer Master, shall benefit by this clause only in case he faithfully carries out the instructions contained in the sealed envelope attached hereto, the contents of said envelope to be read by my hereinafter named Executors, and the said Custer Master, and not by any other persons whatsoever; the said Executors are to be the sole judges of whether the said Custer Master has carried out the instructions therein contained."

This document was worn at the corners of the folds, and slightly soiled, as if Mr. Master had carried it in his pocket some time before dropping it in his suitcase.

With the same caution, and following closely Lesson Three and its directions for "Searching Occupied Apartments, Etc.," Mr. Gubb examined the articles of dress the Chicago detective had cast aside. All were marked "C. Master" or "C. M." or with a monogram composed of the letters "C. M." interwoven.

As cautiously as he could, Philo Gubb crossed to his trunk and took from the left-hand compartment of the tray his trusty pistol. It was a large and deadly looking pistol, about a foot and a half long, with a small ramrod beneath the barrel. It was a muzzle-loader of the crop of 1854, and carried a bullet the size of a well-matured cherry. It was as heavy as a vitrified paving-brick. Its efficiency as a firearm was unknown, as Mr. Gubb had never discharged it, but it looked dangerous. A man, facing Philo Gubb's trusty weapon, felt that if the gun went off he would be utterly and disastrously blown to flinders. Mr. Gubb pointed it at the sleeping Mr. Witzel, using both hands, and sighting along the barrel.

"Wake up!" he exclaimed sternly.

Mr. Witzel sat straight up on the cot. For an instant he was still dazed with sleep and did not seem to know where he was; then a look of joy spread over his face and he jumped from the cot and, with both hands extended, moved toward Detective Gubb.

"Superb!" he exclaimed. "A perfect specimen! Wonderfully preserved!"

"Go back!" said Philo Gubb sternly. "This article is a loaded pistol gun, prepared for momentary explosion at any time at all. Go back!"

"Remarkable!" cried Mr. Witzel joyously. "A superb specimen. Let me see it. Let me look at it."

He walked up to the gun and peered into its muzzle with one eye. He bent his head to read the engraving on the top of the barrel.

"A real Briggs & Bolton $53\frac{1}{2}$ caliber, muzzleloading, 1854!" he exclaimed rapturously.

Mr. Gubb pushed him away with one hand.

"Go back there into range," he said sternly. "In shooting I aim to kill, but not to blow into particles of pieces."

"But, my dear sir!" exclaimed Mr. Witzel. "Do you know what you have there?"

"It's a pistol gun," said Philo Gubb. "If you don't stand back, I'll shoot you anyway."

"It's a Briggs & Bolton," said Mr. Witzel. "That's what it is. It is the only well-preserved specimen of Briggs & Bolton I ever saw."

Mr. Gubb shook off the hand that clasped his arm.

"I don't care what it is," said Mr. Gubb. "It's a pistol gun, and it's bung full of powder and bullet, and when I point it at you I mean that if you make a move I'm a-going to shoot."

"And I don't care what you mean," said Mr. Witzel. "It's a Briggs & Bolton, and I warn you that you have that gun so full of powder that if you pull that trigger you'll blow it to bits and ruin the only perfect specimen of that gun I ever saw!"

"And I tell *you*," said Philo Gubb sternly, "that I can't shoot you whilst you're rubbing your nose right into this gun. Go back there where I can shoot you."

"I won't!" said Mr. Witzel angrily.

Philo Gubb was slow to anger, but he was sorely pressed now, and his temper failed him.

"Look here," he said to Mr. Witzel. "If you don't go back where I can get a shot at you, I'll — I'll smack you on the face."

"If you shoot off that gun, and bust it," said Mr. Witzel, with equal anger, "I'll — I'll hit you on the head."

"Go back!" cried Philo Gubb menacingly. "One!"

"I'll give you fifty dollars for that gun, just as she is," said Mr. Witzel.

"Two!" said Mr. Gubb.

"Sixty dollars!" said Mr. Witzel.

"Th—" said the paper-hanger detective, step-

ping backward to get room to sight along the long
barrel. Unfortunately the trunk was just behind
him and as he stepped back he tripped over it and
fell backward, doubling up like a jack-knife. But he
kept his presence of mind. The long barrel of the
Briggs & Bolton protruded from between the soles
of Philo Gubb's feet in Mr. Witzel's direction.

"Hands up!" he said.

Instantly Mr. Witzel raised his hands in the air.

"I'll give you seventy dollars," he said.

"Make it seventy-five," said Mr. Gubb, "and
as soon as I'm done with it, you can have it."

"It's a bargain!" said Mr. Witzel happily. "It's
my pistol. Now, what's all this nonsense about
shooting me?"

"*Nonsense* is an insufficient word to use in rela-
tion to this here case," said Philo Gubb grimly.
"It won't be nonsense for you when you get through
with it. What did you do with the corpse?"

"With the — with the *what?*" cried Mr. Witzel.

"The remains," said Mr. Gubb. "What did you
do with them?"

"The remains of what?" asked Mr. Witzel.

"Of Mister Custer Master," said Philo Gubb,
easing himself a little by shifting one waving foot.
"There is no need to pretend to play innocent.
Where is the body?"

"My dear Mr. Detective Gubb!" exclaimed Mr.
Witzel. "I know nothing about any body. I am
George Augustus Wetzler —"

THE MISSING MR. MASTER

"Maybe you are," said Philo Gubb. "Maybe so. But your clothes ain't. Your clothes are the clothes of Mister Custer Master. The question is, 'Did you murder him alone, or did you and William Gribble murder him together?'"

Mr. Witzel-Wetzel-Wetzler's mouth fell open.

"Murder him!" he exclaimed aghast. "But — but —"

"In the name of the law," said Philo Gubb, "I take you into custody for the murder and disappearing bodyliness of Mister Custer Master. Turn your back and keep your hands up until I get from behind this trunk, and I'll put handcuffs on you in proper shape and manner. Turn!"

Mr. Witzel turned — all but his head. He kept his face toward the priceless (or, more properly) seventy-five-dollar Briggs & Bolton.

"Mr. Gubb," he said, "you are making a serious mistake. I am a detective."

"You ain't!" said Philo Gubb. "I searched all your things and you ain't got a silver badge nor a false mustache nowhere. I'm going to turn you right over to the police to-morrow morning."

"To the police!" exclaimed Mr. Witzel. "Don't do that! Whatever you do, don't do that!" And suddenly, like a nervous dyspeptic suddenly overwrought, Mr. Witzel broke down and, falling on the cot, began to sob. Philo Gubb looked at him a moment with amazement. Then he dug a pair of handcuffs out of his trunk and, walking to where Mr.

Witzel lay, prodded him in the back with the muzzle of the pistol. Mr. Witzel turned quickly, rolling over like an eel.

"Stop it! You're tickling me. I can't stand tickling!" he cried. "I — I can't stand lots of things. I'm — I'm the most sensitive man in the world. I — I can't stand cold water at all."

"Well, nobody is cold-watering you," said Philo Gubb. "Handcuffs ain't cold water."

"But cold water is," said Mr. Witzel. "Cold water kills me! It makes me shiver, and turn blue, and goose-fleshy, and gives me cramps in the palms of my hands and the soles of my feet. I — listen: my doctor says cold baths will kill me. The shock of 'em. Bad heart, you understand."

Philo Gubb's eyes blinked.

"I'll tell *you*," said Mr. Witzel, grasping Mr. Gubb's hand. "I can't *stand* cold baths. They'd kill me, you understand. It would be suicide! So — so I knew Billy Gribble. Did n't I set him up in business here, to get rid of him? Don't he owe me a good turn?"

"Does he?" asked Philo Gubb.

"Has n't he two bathrooms in connection with his laundry. 'Hot and Cold Baths, All hours. Ladies Tuesdays and Wednesdays Only?'" asked Mr. Witzel. "Mr. Gubb, I will be frank. I am Custer Master!"

"The reward for who — for who the reward," said Philo Gubb, seeking a grammatical form that

THE MISSING MR. MASTER

would sound right, "for information as to which five thousand dollars reward is offered!"

"Exactly!" said Mr. Master. "And I will make it six thousand if you do not give information. I admit I am Master. I am Custer Master. Here, read this!"

He reached for his vest and from the pocket took a slip of paper. It was typewritten and headed "Secret Stipulation Regarding Custer Master Clause of Orlando J. Higgins Will. Copy": —

Being a firm believer in the efficacy of cold baths for the cure of dyspepsia and having been laughed at for same by my nephew, Custer Master, and feeling that a course of ice-cold baths would cure him, I make it a part of my will and testament that the sum or sums bequeathed to him shall be given to him only after he has faithfully, and upon the sworn testimony of an eye-witness, bathed for twelve minutes, every morning for one month of thirty days, in ice-cold water.

"Cleanliness may be next to godliness," said Mr. Master, "but ice-water baths are my shortest road to a future state, and I'm not ready for that yet. Still, I did not like to give up $450,000. To Billy Gribble," he added, with a meaning smile, "all baths are cold baths. I hold a mortgage on his laundry machinery."

"And so you came up here to my office to hide whilst bathing in so-called ice-water at Mister Gribble's?" said Philo Gubb.

"Exactly!" said Mr. Master.

"If you ain't got six thousand and seventy-five

dollars by you," said Philo Gubb simply, "you can give me a check for the whole amount in the morning, but if you go to take the bullet out of this pistol you'll have to get an auger. I made the bullet myself and it was too big, and I had to pound it into the gun with a hammer and screw-driver. It's in good and safe."

"And you would have dared to pull the trigger?" asked Mr. Master.

"I would have dared so to do," said Mr. Gubb.

"It would have blown the pistol to atoms!" exclaimed Mr. Master.

"It would so have done," said Mr. Gubb, "except for the time I loaded it being the first beginning time I ever loaded a pistol. In loading a Briggs & Bolton, I have since subsequently learned, the powder ought to go into it first, and the bullet second. I put the bullet in first."

"Well, bless my stars!" exclaimed Mr. Master. "Bless my stars! If that is the case — if that is the case, I'm going to bed again. I have to get up before daylight to take a bath."

WAFFLES AND MUSTARD

It would not be true to say that Mr. Gubb had become suspicious of Mr. Medderbrook's honesty. The fact that the cashier of the Riverbank National Bank told him the Utterly Hopeless Gold-Mine stock was not worth the paper it was printed on did pain him, however.

It pained Mr. Gubb to think his father-in-law-to-be might be guilty of even unconscious duplicity, and when Mr. Master paid him the six thousand and seventy-five dollars Mr. Gubb decided that only three thousand dollars of it should pass immediately into Mr. Medderbrook's hands. Mr. Gubb put two thousand dollars in the bank and invested the balance in furniture for his office and in articles and instruments that were needed for his detective career. The three thousand dollars he took to Mr. Medderbrook and paid it to him, leaving only eight thousand nine hundred dollars unpaid.

Mr. Medderbrook was greatly pleased with this and told Mr. Gubb so.

"This is a bully payment on account," he said, "and if you keep on this way you'll soon be all paid up, but you don't want to let that worry you, for I'm having a brand-new lot of stock in a brand-new mine printed, and I'll sell you a whole lot of it

205

as soon as we are square. I'm going to call it the Little Syrilla Gold-Mine —"

"I don't think I'll buy any more gold-mine stock after the present lot is paid up completely full," said Mr. Gubb.

"That's all right," said Mr. Medderbrook. "I have n't given the printer final orders yet and if you prefer something else I'll make it Oil-Well stock. It is all the same to me. The property will produce just as much oil as it will gold. Every bit!"

"Have you heard from Miss Syrilla recently of late?" asked Mr. Gubb.

"Yes, I have," said Mr. Medderbrook. "I have heard two dollars and a half's worth."

The telegram, which Mr. Medderbrook permitted Mr. Gubb to read after he had paid the cash in hand, said: —

Heaven smiles on us. Have given up all vegetable diet. Have given up potatoes, beets, artichokes, fried parsnips, Swiss chard, turnips, squash, kohl-rabi, boiled radishes, sugar beets, corn on the cob, cow pumpkin, mushrooms, string beans, asparagus, spinach, and canned and fresh tomatoes. Have lost ten pounds more. Weight now only nine hundred and fifteen pounds. Dorgan worried. I dream of Gubby and love.

Mr. Gubb sighed happily. "I suppose," he said blissfully, "that by the present moment of time Miss Syrilla has only got left a remainder of six double chins out of seven, dear little one!" And he went back to his office feeling that it would not be long now before the apple of his eye was released from her side-show contract.

The next day Mr. Gubb had begun his labors on a new and interesting case when the door opened.

"Gubb, come across the hall here!"

Gubb looked up from the labor in which he was engaged and blinked at Lawyer Higgins.

"At the present time I am momently engaged upon a case," said Mr. Gubb. "As soon as I am disengaged away from what I am at, I expect to be engaged at the next thing I have to do. I should n't wish to assume to be rude, Mr. Higgins, but when a deteckative is working up a case, and has a sign on his door 'Out — Back at Midnight,' he generally means he ain't receiving callers on no account."

"That's all right," said Higgins briskly, "but this is business. I've got a real job for you."

"I am engaged upon a real job now," said Philo Gubb.

"This is a detective job," said Mr. Higgins. "We want you to find a man, and if you find him, there's two hundred dollars in it for you. What sort of a job is it you have on hand?"

"I am searching out the whereabouts of a lost party," said Gubb earnestly. "I'm investigating clues at the present time and moment."

Higgins stepped inside the door. He walked to where Philo Gubb sat at an elaborate mahogany desk, and looked at the apparatus Mr. Gubb was using.

"What the dickens?" he asked.

On the slide of the desk were grouped a number of small articles, and a large and powerful microscope. Through the lens of the microscope Mr. Gubb was inspecting something that looked like frayed yellow-brown wool yarn.

"You don't expect to find your missing party in that wad of wool, do you, Gubb?" asked Mr. Higgins jestingly.

"Maybe I do, and maybe the operations of the deteckative mind are none of your particular affair when conducted in the private seclusion of my laboratory," said Gubb.

"Now, don't get mad," said Higgins. "It just struck me as funny. Looks as if you were hunting for fleas in a wisp of dog hair."

Philo Gubb looked up quickly. As a matter of fact, he had but a moment before found a flea in the wool he was examining, and the wool was indeed a wisp of dog hair. The party Mr. Gubb had been engaged to find was a dog, and Mr. Gubb was — by the inductive method of detecting — trying to reason out the location of the dog. By the aid of the microscope, Mr. Gubb was searching for the slight indications that mean so much to detectives. Unfortunately, however, Mr. Gubb had not yet found anything from which he could deduce anything whatever, unless the flea in the wool might lead to the conclusion that the dog now, or once, had fleas.

WAFFLES AND MUSTARD

"Tell you what I want," said Mr. Higgins: "I want you to find Mustard."

Detective Gubb swung suddenly in his chair and faced Mr. Higgins.

"I don't want nothing more to do with that will!" he said.

"I'm with you there!" said Higgins, laughing. "When O'Hara made his will so that my client could n't get her rights at once he did a mean trick, and I dare say Mrs. Doblin will think so when she gets my bill. But, just the same, Gubb, you're in the detective business more or less, and it strikes me you ought to take a job when it's offered to you. You signed the will as a witness, and this man Bilton, commonly known as Mustard on account of his yellow complexion and hair, was the other witness, was n't he? Now, if you can't give us the information we want, and Mustard can, it looks to me as if it was your duty, as a fellow witness, to hunt him up. But we don't ask that. We're willing to pay you if you find him."

"Are you prepared to contract to say you'll pay me just for hunting for him?" asked Mr. Gubb.

"We'll give you two hundred dollars if you can produce Mustard here in Riverbank," said Higgins.

"The job I've took on to hunt up another missing party will occupy me for quite a while, I guess," said Gubb, "but maybe I might put in what extra time I can spare looking for your party."

"Do it!" said Higgins. "I don't say you're the

best detective in the world, Gubb, but you do have luck. You must have a magic talisman."

"The operation of the deteckative mind is always like magic to the common folks," said Gubb gravely.

"All right, then," said Higgins. "Two hundred if you find him. And now, will you just come across the hall for one minute?"

Gubb left his microscope reluctantly. He was sick and tired of the O'Hara will, but he followed Mr. Higgins.

The second floor of the Opera House Block was laid out in small offices arranged on two sides of a corridor. One of these offices had been for many years the office of Haddon O'Hara, who specialized in commercial law, collections, and jokes, and he had accumulated a snug little fortune. It was said he could draw a contract no one could break except himself.

On the streets and in his home and at his office — except when at work on some especially difficult case — his face always wore a quizzical smile. O'Hara seemed to enjoy himself every moment. Walking along the street he would suddenly stop some citizen, enunciate a dozen or twenty cryptic words, laugh, and proceed on his way, leaving the citizen to puzzle over the affair, lose interest in it and forget it. A week, a month, or a year later O'Hara would stop the same citizen and utter ten more words, the key to the cryptic joke. Then, chuckling, he would hurry away. He had a lot of fun. His keen

brain felt equal to making fun of the whole town and
not letting the town know it. Money came to him
easily; he had no wife; his pleasure was in his books
— and he was probably a happy man. But he died.
He died and left a will.

For some years O'Hara lived with his niece, an
orphan. She was eighteen, and there might have
been some gossip, but O'Hara forestalled it by hir-
ing old Mrs. Mullarky.

O'Hara bought his niece a pup and had a dog-
house built and put in the yard. He christened the
pup himself, naming it Waffles, because, he said,
the minute he saw the pup it reminded him of Dolly.
The pup was just the color of the waffles Dolly
baked — "baked" is O'Hara's word. So he bought
Waffles and brought him home to Dolly, and the girl
loved the dog from the first minute. Then, just as
the dog had outgrown puppyhood, O'Hara died.

His will was found in the safe in his office. Old
Judge Mackinnon, who shared the office with
O'Hara, found the will the day after O'Hara died.
It was in a white legal envelope endorsed, "My Will,
Haddon O'Hara." The Judge opened the envelope
— it was not sealed — and took out the will. The
will was not filled in on a printed form — it was a
holograph will, written in O'Hara's own hand. It
began in the usual formal manner and there were
two bequests. The first read: "To my niece,
Dorothy O'Hara, since she is so extremely fond
of her dog Waffles, I give and bequeath the dog-

house now on my property at 342 Locust Street, Riverbank, Iowa." The second read: "Secondly, to my cousin Ardelia Doblin I bequeath the entire remainder and residue of my estate," etc.

Judge Mackinnon frowned as he read these two bequests. He knew Ardelia Doblin as a spiteful, scandal-mongering woman. To cut off Dolly O'Hara with a dog-house and give his entire estate to Ardelia Doblin might be O'Hara's idea of a joke, but the Judge did not like it. He read the final clause, appointing him sole executor without bond. O'Hara's signature was correctly appended. The will was dated July 1, 1913. It was witnessed by Philo Gubb and Max Bilton. The Judge knew both witnesses. Gubb was the eccentric paperhanger who thought he was a detective because he had taken a correspondence course, and Bilton was a jaundiced loafer, commonly called Mustard. The good old man sighed and was about to put the will back in the envelope when he noticed three letters at the bottom of the sheet. They were "P.T.O." Now "P.T.O." is an English abbreviation that means "Please Turn Over." The Judge turned the paper over.

Suddenly he smiled. Then he looked grave again. And then he grinned. After which he shook his head.

The reverse of the sheet contained a will exactly like that on the obverse. Word for word it was the same. Line for line, punctuation mark for punctuation mark, the two wills on the opposite sides of the sheet were identical except for two words. In the will the Judge was now reading, the name Sarah P. Kinsey was substituted for the name Ardelia Doblin. The date was the same. The witnesses were the same. There were two wills, one written on one side of the sheet and the other written on the other side of the sheet, of the same date, with the same signature, and with the same witnesses. O'Hara had joked to the last.

"This is a dickens of a joke!" exclaimed Judge Mackinnon. "O'Hara should not have done this!"

He saw the property of Haddon O'Hara being dissipated in lawsuits over this remarkable will. He knew Sarah P. Kinsey as well as he knew Ardelia Doblin, and she was just such another mean cantankerous individual.

"A joke's a joke, but you should n't have done this, O'Hara!" said the Judge.

There was nothing to do but notify the parties concerned. He went to see Dolly O'Hara first and told her, as gently as he could, about the will. She cried a little, softly, at first, and then she smiled bravely.

"You must n't worry about it, Judge Mackinnon," she said. "I — of course I never thought what Uncle Haddon would do with his money. And — and we used to joke about the dog-house. He always said he would leave it to me in his will. Uncle Haddon loved to joke, Judge Mackinnon."

PHILO GUBB, THE DETECTIVE

"He was a joking jackanapes!" said Judge Mackinnon angrily.

Ardelia Doblin and Sarah P. Kinsey took the matter in quite a different spirit. Mrs. Doblin could hardly wait until Judge Mackinnon was out of the house before she hurried down to see Lawyer Higgins, and Mrs. Kinsey did not wait until the Judge was ready to go, but put on her hat in his presence, so eager was she to hurry down to see Lawyer Burch.

Ten hours later the O'Hara will was the one matter talked about in Riverbank. Evidently there must be some clue leading to the solution of the mystery — some well-hidden, cleverly planned key such as Haddon O'Hara would undoubtedly have left in perpetrating such a joke. Common sense was sufficient to tell any one that O'Hara could not have written both wills simultaneously, that he had written one will on one side of the paper, after which he had turned the paper over and had written the other will on the other side of the paper. The difficulty was to tell which side he had written last.

Lawyer Higgins, Lawyer Burch, and Judge Mackinnon went over both sides of the paper with a microscope. The same ink had been used on both sides. O'Hara's writing was the same on both sides. Often, in writing as many words as occupied both sides of the paper in question, a man's hand grows involuntarily weary. There was nothing of this sort. There seemed to be absolutely nothing on which the

214

greatest penmanship expert could base a plea that either side was, in fact, the *last* will of Haddon O'Hara. Either might be the last.

Nothing was left untested by Higgins and Burch. The two sides of the paper on which the wills were written were subjected to the minutest scrutiny.

Each will was witnessed by the same pair of witnesses, and these were Philo Gubb and Max Bilton. It was no trouble to get Philo Gubb to tell about signing the will. Judge Mackinnon crossed the hall and brought Philo Gubb to the office.

"Yes, sir," said Mr. Gubb. "I signed my signature onto that document two times as requested so to do by the late deceased. He come over to my official deteckative headquarters and asked me to step across and do him the pleasure of a small favor and I done so. Yes, sir, that's my signed signature. And that's my signed signature also likewise."

"Did he say anything, Mr. Gubb?" asked the Judge.

"He says, 'Gubb, this is my last will and testament, and I wish you to sign your signature onto it as a witness.' So he put the paper in front of me. 'Where'll I sign it?' I says. 'Sign it right here under Mr. Bilton's name,' he says. So I signed my signature like he told me."

"Yes," said the Judge, "and Mr. O'Hara blotted it with a piece of blotting-paper, did he not?"

"He so done," said Mr. Gubb.

"And then what?"

"Then he turned the paper over," said Mr. Gubb, "and he says, 'Now, please sign this one.' So I signed it."

"Under Mr. Bilton's name again?" said the Judge.

"Why, no," said the paper-hanger detective. "Not under it, because it was n't located nowhere to have an under to it. Mr. Bilton had n't signed on that side yet."

There was an instant sensation.

"Bilton had n't signed that side?" said Mr. Higgins. "Which side had n't he signed?"

"The other side from the side he had signed," said Mr. Gubb.

"Did you notice which side he had not signed?" insisted Mr. Higgins. "Was it this side that mentions Mrs. Doblin, or this side that mentions Mrs. Kinsey? Which was it?"

Mr. Gubb took the paper and examined it carefully. He turned it over and over.

"Could n't say," he said briefly.

"In other words," said Mr. Burch, "you signed one side before Mr. Bilton signed and one side after he signed, but you don't know which?"

"Yes, sir, I don't," said Mr. Gubb.

"So," said Judge Mackinnon, with a smile, "you can swear you signed both these wills as witness, but you have no idea which you signed last, Mr. Gubb."

"E-zactly so!" said Mr. Gubb with emphasis.

"Now, just a minute," said Mr. Burch. "One of these Bilton signatures is 'M. Bilton' and the other is 'Max Bilton.' You don't recall which was on the paper when you signed, do you?"

"Mr. Burch," said Mr. Gubb, "I was n't taking no extra time to find out if a no-account feller like Mustard Bilton signed his name M. or Max or Methuselah. No, sir."

"Do you know where Mustard Bilton is now?" asked Judge Mackinnon.

"Don't know," said Mr. Gubb.

The three lawyers consulted for a minute or two. Then the Judge turned to Gubb again.

"And did Mr. O'Hara say anything more on the occasion when you signed the will?" asked the Judge.

"He said, 'Thank you,'" said Mr. Gubb. "He said, 'Thank you, Sherlock Holmes.'"

Higgins and Burch laughed, and even the Judge smiled, and they told Mr. Gubb he could go.

An hour or three quarters of an hour after he had been called to identify his signature to the wills, a gentle tap at Mr. Gubb's door caused him to look up from the pamphlet — Lesson Four, Rising Sun Detective Agency's Correspondence School of Detecting — he was reading.

"Come on right in," he called, and in answer the door opened and a young woman entered. She was a sweet-faced, modest-appearing girl, and when she pushed back her veil, Mr. Gubb saw she had been

217

weeping, for her eyes were red. Mr. Gubb hastily pulled out his desk chair.

"Take a seat and set down, ma'am," he said politely. "Is there anything in my lines I can be doing for you to-day?"

"Are you Mr. Philo Gubb?" she asked, seating herself.

"Yes'm, paper-hanging and deteckating done," he said.

"It's about a dog, my dog," said the young woman. "He's lost, or stolen, and —"

Emotion choked her words.

"I know it sounds foolish to ask a detective to look for a dog," she said with a poor attempt at a smile, "but —"

"In the deteckative line nothing sounds foolish," said Mr. Gubb with politeness.

"But Uncle Haddon told me once that if ever I needed a — a detective I should come to you," the young woman continued. "You knew Uncle Haddon, Mr. Gubb?"

"I had the pleasure of being known to and knowing of him," said Mr. Gubb.

"My name is Dolly O'Hara! I am his niece."

"Glad to make your acquaintance, ma'am," said Philo Gubb, and he shook hands gravely.

"He gave me my dog," said Miss O'Hara. "He gave him to me when the dog was just a puppy, and he called him Waffles. He used to joke about my loving the dog more than I loved him. He used to say —"

WAFFLES AND MUSTARD

Miss O'Hara wiped her eyes. For a moment she could not speak.

"He used to say," she continued in a moment, "that I'd never break my heart over a lost uncle, but that if I lost Waffles I'd die of grief. It was n't so, of course. But I'm heart-broken to have Waffles gone. He is all I'll have to remember Uncle Haddon by. And then — to have him — go!"

"I should take it a pleasure to be employed upon a case to fetch him back," said Mr. Gubb.

"Oh, would you?" cried Miss O'Hara. "I'm so glad! I was afraid a — a real detective might not want to bother with a dog. Of course I'll pay —"

"The remuneration will be minimum on account of the smallness of the crime under the statutes made and provided," said Mr. Gubb.

"But you must let me pay!" urged Miss O'Hara. "One of the things Uncle Haddon said was, 'If you ever lose that dog, Dolly, hire Detective Gubb. Understand? He's a wonderful detective. He'll leave no stone unturned. He'll find your dog. He'll pry the roof off the dog-house to find a flea, and when he's found the flea he'll hunt up a blond dog to match it. Remember,' he said, 'if you lose the dog, get Gubb.'"

"I consider the compliment the highest form of flattery," said Mr. Gubb.

"So I want you to try to find Waffles, please, if it is n't beneath you to hunt a dog," said Miss

O'Hara. "How much will you charge to find Waffles, Mr. Gubb?"

"I'd ought to have five dollars — " Mr. Gubb began doubtfully.

"Of course!" exclaimed Miss O'Hara. "Why, I expected to pay far more."

"Well and good," said Mr. Gubb. "And now, how aged was the dog when he was purloined away from you?"

Philo Gubb secured a complete history of the dog. Miss O'Hara had brought, also, two photographs of Waffles in pleasing poses, and when she left, Mr. Gubb accompanied her to the late home of Waffles. It was there he gathered the clues over which he was poring with his microscope when Mr. Higgins came to ask him to step across the hall and to offer him two hundred dollars if he could produce Mustard Bilton. Mr. Gubb went across the hall.

"Gubb," said Judge Mackinnon, when he had introduced the detective to Mrs. Kinsey and Mrs. Doblin, "was Mustard Bilton in this office when you signed your name to these wills?"

"No, sir, he was not present in person," said Mr. Gubb. "He was elsewhere."

"Well, ladies," said the Judge, "it seems to me that until we can find Mustard we cannot proceed. Mr. O'Hara's last will — whichever it is — must be probated. If I took this will to the courthouse, whichever side happened to be uppermost would be probated first and the other side would naturally appear on the record as the latest will. It is a responsibility I do not care to undertake. If you will not agree to compromise and divide the estate —"

"Never!" said both ladies.

"We must find Mustard!" said the Judge.

Mr. Gubb went into the hall, but Lawyer Burch followed him.

"Gubb," he said, "just a word! Find Mustard for me. Now, don't talk — find him. Bring Mustard to Judge Mackinnon's office and I'll put two hundred dollars in your hand! That's all!"

Detective Gubb returned to his office and resumed his work on his lost dog clues. One by one he submitted the clues to inspection under the microscope. He tried the five processes of the Sherlock Holmes inductive method on them. By some strange quirk, quite out of keeping with the usual detective-story logic, he could make nothing of them. Even the flea in the bit of dog hair did not point direct to the location of the dog. They were blind clues. Mr. Gubb swept them into an empty envelope, sealed the envelope, put on his hat and went out.

On the stair he met Judge Mackinnon.

"Well, if O'Hara meant to have a little joke — and he did — he's had it," said the Judge with a chuckle. "You should have been in that room just now. Cat fights? Those two women all but jumped on each other with claws and teeth. I don't know why O'Hara wanted to worry them, but he has paid them back well for whatever they ever did to him."

"And the dog has disappeared away, too," said Mr. Gubb. "I am proceeding on my way at the present time to help discover where the dog is."

"Hope you find the poor child's pet," said the Judge as he turned off in the opposite direction.

Mr. Gubb proceeded to the late home of Haddon O'Hara. He followed the brick walk to the back of the house. He was already familiar with the premises.

The dog-house — the only recently painted structure in the neighborhood — stood opposite the kitchen door. It was perhaps three feet in height and four feet long, with a pointed roof. As a door it had an open arch, and at one side of this was a staple to which a chain could be attached. The grass in front of the dog-house was worn away, leaving the soil packed hard. The detective, arriving at the dog-house, walked around it, gazing at it closely.

The inductive method had failed — as it always failed for Mr. Gubb — and he meant now to try following a clue in person, if he could find a clue to follow. Mr. Gubb dropped to his hands and knees and crept around the dog-house, seeking a clue hidden in the grass. When he reached the front of the dog-house he paused.

"Ye look that like a dog I was thinkin' ye'd howl for a bone," said Mrs. Mullarky suddenly from the kitchen door.

222

WAFFLES AND MUSTARD

Mr. Gubb turned and eyed her with disapproval.
"The operations of deteckating are strange to the
lay mind," he said haughtily. "Those not under-
standing them should be seen and not heard."

"An' hear the man!" cried Mrs. Mullarky. "Does
a dog-house drive all of ye crazy? T' see a human
bein' crawlin' around on his four legs an' callin' it
detectin' where a dog is that ain't there! Go awn,
if ye wish! Crawl inside of ut!"

"I'm going to do so," said Mr. Gubb, and he
did.

Inside, or as far inside as he could get, Mr. Gubb
struck a match and examined the floor of the house.
There was straw on it, but nothing even remotely
suggesting a clue. No dog thief had left a glove
there. Mr. Gubb began to back out, and as he
backed his head touched something softer than a
pine board. He craned his long neck and looked upward. Tacked to the inside of the roof of the house
was a long envelope. Mr. Gubb put up his hand
and pulled it loose. Then he backed into the daylight. He sat on the bare spot before the dog-house
and examined the envelope.

The envelope was sealed, but on the face of it was
written: —

To be delivered to Judge Mackinnon, after Waffles has
been returned to his house and home. Waffles will be
found in the old cattle-shed on the Illinois side of the
river, north from the turnpike at the far end of the
bridge.   H. O'H.

PHILO GUBB, THE DETECTIVE

It was a clue! Without stopping to silence the scornful laughter of Mrs. Mullarky, Philo Gubb jumped to his feet and made for the Illinois side of the long bridge as rapidly as his long legs could carry him. He reached the old cattle-shed and there he found Mustard Bilton seated at the door, smoking a cob pipe in lazy comfort.

"Come for the dog?" asked Mustard carelessly. "Sort of thought you'd come for him about now. Been expectin' you the last couple o' days."

"Expecting me?" said Philo Gubb. "I've been doing deteckative work on this case —"

"Yes, Had' O'Hara reckoned you'd detect around awhile before you got track of me," said Mustard without emotion. "He says, when I'd signed that there will for him, 'Day or so after I kick the bucket, Mustard, you go up and steal Waffles,' he says, 'and fetch him over to the cattle-shed on the Illinoy side,' he says, 'and keep him there until Gubb comes for him. Take a day or so, maybe,' he says, 'for Dolly to remember I told her to get Gubb, and take Gubb a day or two to scrooge round before he hits on the clue I've fixed up to point him to you, but he'll come. He's a wonder, Gubb is,' says O'Hara, 'and no mistake. If a feller was to steal the sardines out of a can,' he says, 'bet you Gubb would want to see what was inside the empty can before he'd start out to find the feller. You just sit quiet an' wait till Gubb snoops round enough,' he says, 'and he'll come.'"

WAFFLES AND MUSTARD

"You have possession of the Waffles dog at the present time?" asked Detective Gubb.

"In yonder," said Mustard, pointing over his shoulder. "Say, what's the joke O'Hara was cookin' up, anyway?"

"You accompany yourself with me to the office of Judge Mackinnon," said Mr. Gubb, "and you'll discover it out for yourself and I'll remunerate you to twenty dollars also. Fetch the dog."

Mr. Gubb, quite properly, left Mustard and Waffles in his own office while he visited Mr. Higgins and Mr. Burch, collecting two hundred dollars from each. Then he turned Mr. Mustard Bilton over to them.

"You signed those wills of O'Hara's," said Mr. Burch when all had gathered in Judge Mackinnon's office. "Do you know which you signed last?"

"Sure, I do," said Mustard.

Mr. Burch handed him the double will.

"Which did you sign last?" asked Mr. Burch energetically.

Mustard took the document and looked at it. The Kinsey side was toward him.

"It wasn't this one," he said positively.

"Ah, ha!" cried Lawyer Higgins, turning the paper over. "Then it was this one you signed last!"

"No," said Mustard, glancing at the Doblin side of the paper. "I signed this'n the same time as I signed the other side of it. I signed both these the

225

first day of the month. The one I signed last I signed on the second of the month."

"Ah, yes!" said Judge Mackinnon, looking at a document he had taken from the envelope Philo Gubb had handed him. "You mean this one: —

Last will and testament — and all else with which I may die possessed — to my niece Dorothy O'Hara — and hope she can take a joke — Haddon O'Hara.

You mean this one, Mr. Bilton?"

"Yep," said Mustard, looking at the document that gave to Dolly O'Hara every jot and tittle of Haddon O'Hara's property. "That's the one. That's the one I signed last. Me and old Sam Fliggis signed her — same day O'Hara hired me to steal the dog. Well, I guess I'll be takin' the dog back home. So 'long, gents. Old Had' was bound to have his joke, wasn't he?"

"Mr. Gubb," said Judge Mackinnon suddenly, "would you be betraying a professional secret if you told us how you found this document?"

"In the pursuit of following my deteckative profession," said Detective Gubb, "according to Lesson Six, Page Thirty-two."

THE ANONYMOUS WIGGLE

ANY one reading a history of the detective work of Philo Gubb, the paper-hanger detective, might imagine that crime stalked abroad endlessly in Riverbank and that criminals crowded the streets, but this would be mere imagination. For weeks before he took on the case of the Anonymous Wiggle, he had been obliged to revert to his side-line of paper-hanging and decorating.

Four hundred of the dollars he had earned by solving the mystery of the missing Mustard and Waffles he had paid to Mr. Medderbrook, together with five dollars for a telegram Mr. Medderbrook had received from Syrilla. This telegram was a great satisfaction to Mr. Gubb. It brought the day when she might be his nearer, and showed that the fair creature was fighting nobly to reduce. It had read: —

None but the brave deserve the thin. Have given up all liquids. Have given up water, milk, coca-cola, beer, chocolate, champagne, buttermilk, cider, soda-water, root beer, tea, koumyss, coffee, ginger ale, bevo, Bronx cocktails, grape juice, and absinthe frappé. Weigh eight hundred ninety-five net. Love to Gubby from little Syrilla.

Crime is not rampant in Riverbank. P. Gubb therefore welcomed gladly Miss Petunia Scroggs

227

when she came to his office in the Opera House Block and said: "Mr. Gubb? Mr. Philo Gubb, the detective? Well, my name is Miss Petunia Scroggs, and I want to talk to you about detecting something for me."

"I'm pleased to," said Mr. Gubb, placing a chair for the lady. "Anything in the deteckative line which I can do for you will be so done gladly and in good shape. At the present moment of time, I'm engaged upon a job of kitchen paper for Mrs. Horton up on Eleventh Street, but the same will not occupy long, as she wants it hung over what is already on the wall, to minimize the cost of the expense."

"Different people, different ways," said Miss Scroggs, smiling sweetly. "Scrape it off and be clean, is my idea."

"Yes, ma'am," said Philo Gubb.

"Well, I didn't come here to talk about Mrs. Horton's notion of how a kitchen ought to be papered," said Miss Scroggs. "How do you detect, by the day or by the job?"

"My terms in such matters is various and sundry, to suit the taste," said Mr. Gubb.

"Then I'll hire you by the job," said Miss Scroggs, "if your rates ain't too high. Now, first off, I ain't ever been married; I'm a maiden lady."

"Yes, ma'am," said Philo Gubb, jotting this down on a sheet of paper.

"Not but what I could have been a wedded wife many's the time," said Miss Scroggs hastily, "but

228

I says to myself, 'Peace of mind, Petunia, peace of mind!'"

"Yes'm," said Philo Gubb. "I'm a unmarried bachelor man myself."

"Well, I'm surprised to hear you say it in a boasting tone," said Miss Petunia gently. "You ought to be ashamed of it."

"Yes, ma'am," said Philo Gubb, "but you was conversationally speaking of some deteckative work—"

"And I'm leading right up to it all the time," said Miss Scroggs. "Peace of mind is why I have remained single up to now, and peace of mind I have had, but I won't have it much longer if this Anonymous Wiggle keeps on writing me letters."

"Somebody named with that cognomen is writing letters to you like a Black Hand would?" asked Mr. Gubb eagerly.

"Cognomen or not," said Miss Scroggs, "that's what I call him or her or whoever it is. Snake would be a better name," she added, "but I must say the thing looks more like a fish-worm. Now, here," she said, opening her black hand-bag, "is letter Number One. Read it."

Mr. Gubb took the envelope and looked at the address. It was written in a hand evidently disguised by slanting the letters backward, and had been mailed at the Riverbank post-office.

"Hum!" said Mr. Gubb. "Lesson Nine of the Rising Sun Deteckative Agency's Correspondence

School of Deteckating gives the full rules and regulations for to elucidate the mystery of threatening letters, scurrilous letters, et cetery. Now, is this a threatening letter or a scurrilous letter?"

"Well, it may be threatening, and it may not be threatening," said Miss Scroggs. "If it is a threat, I must say I never heard of a threat just like it. And if it is scurrilous, I must say I never heard of anything that scurriled in the words used. Read it."

Philo Gubb pulled the letter from the envelope and read it. It ran thus: —

PETUNIA: —

Open any book at page fourteen and read the first complete sentence at the top of the page. Go thou and do likewise.

For signature there was nothing but a waved line, drawn with a pen. In some respects it did resemble an angle-worm.

Philo Gubb frowned. "The advice of the inditer that wrote this letter seemingly appears to be sort of unexact," he said. "'Most every book is apt to have a different lot of words at the top of page fourteen."

"Just so!" said Miss Scroggs. "You may well say that. And say it to myself I did until I started to open a book. I went to the book-case and I took down my Bible and I turned to page fourteen."

"As the writer beyond no doubt thought you would," said P. Gubb.

"I don't know what he thought," said Miss

Scroggs, "but when I opened my Bible and turned to page fourteen there was n't any page fourteen in it. Page fourteen is part of the 'Brief Foreword from the Translators to the Reader,' so I thought maybe it had got lost and never been missed. So I took up another book. I took up Emerson's Essays. Volume Two."

"And what did you read?" asked Philo Gubb.

"Nothing," said Miss Scroggs, "because I could n't. Page fourteen was tore out of the book. So I went through all my books, and every page fourteen was tore out of every book. There was only one book in the house that had a page fourteen left in it."

"And what did that say?" asked Mr. Gubb.

"It said," said Miss Petunia, "'To one quart of flour add a cup of water, beat well, and add the beaten whites of two eggs.'"

"Did you do all that?" inquired Mr. Gubb.

"Well," said Miss Petunia, "I did n't see any harm in trying it, just to see what happened, so I did it."

"And what happened?" asked Mr. Gubb.

"Nothing," said Miss Petunia. "In a couple of days the water dried up and the dough got pasty and moulded, and I threw it out."

"Just so!" said Philo Gubb. "You'd sort of expect it to get mouldy, but you would n't call it threatening at the first look."

"No," said Miss Petunia. "And then I got this letter Number Two."

231

She handed the second letter to Mr. Gubb. It ran thus: —

P. SCROGGS: —

A complete study of the history and antiquities of Diocese of Ossory fails to reveal the presence of a single individual bearing the name of Scroggs from the year 1085 to date.

Like the first letter this was signed with a waved line. Mr. Gubb studied it carefully.

"I don't see no sign of a threat in that," he said.

"Not unless you should say it was belittling me to tell me to my face that no Scroggs ever lived wherever that says they didn't live," said Miss Petunia. "Now, here's the next letter."

Mr. Gubb read it. It ran thus: —

MISS PETUNIA: —

For to-morrow: Rising temperature accompanied by falling barometer, followed by heavy showers. Lower temperature will follow in the North Central States and Northern Missouri.

"I shouldn't call that exactly scurrilous, neither," said Mr. Gubb.

"It ain't," said Miss Petunia, "and unless you can call a mention of threatening weather a threat, I wouldn't call it a threatening letter. And then I got this letter."

She handed Mr. Gubb the fourth letter, and he read it. It ran: —

PETUNIA SCROGGS: —

Trout are rising freely in the Maine waters. The Parmacheene Belle is one of the best flies to use.

THE ANONYMOUS WIGGLE

Mr. Gubb, having read this letter, shook his head and placed the letter on top of those he had previously read. It was signed with the wiggle like the others.

"Speaking as a deteckative," he said, "I don't see anything into these letters yet that would fetch the writer into the grasp of the law. Are they all like this?"

"If you mean do they say they are going to murder me, or do they call me names," said Miss Scroggs, "they don't. Here, take them!"

Mr. Gubb took the remaining letters and read them. There were about a dozen of them. While peculiar epistles to write to a maiden lady of forty-five years, they were not what one might call violent. They were, in part, as follows:—

PETUNIA:—
Although a cat with a fit is a lively object, it has seldom been known to attack human beings. Cause of fits — too rich food. Cure of fits — less rich food.

MISS SCROGGS:—
If soil is inclined to be sour, a liberal sprinkling of lime, well ploughed in, has a good effect. Marble dust, where easily obtainable, serves as well.

MISS PETUNIA:—
Swedish iron is largely used in the manufacture of upholstery tacks because of its peculiar ductile qualities.

"I don't see nothing much into them," said Mr. Gubb, when he had read them all. "I don't see much of a deteckative case into them. If I was to

233

get letters like these I would n't worry much about them. I'd let them come."

"You may say that," said Miss Petunia, "because you are a man, and big and strong and brave-like. But when a person is a woman, and lives alone, and has some money laid by that some folks would be glad enough to get, letters coming right along from she don't know who, scare her. Every time I get another of those Anonymous Wiggle letters I get more and more nervous. If they said, 'Give me five thousand dollars or I will kill you,' I would know what to do, but when a letter comes that says, like that one does, 'Swedish iron is largely used in the manufacture of upholstery tacks,' I don't know what to think or what to do."

"I can see to understand that it might worry you some," said Mr. Gubb sympathetically. "What do you want I should do?"

"I want you should find out who wrote the letters," said Miss Scroggs.

Mr. Gubb looked at the pile of letters.

"It's going to be a hard job," he said. "I've got to try to guess out a cryptogram in these letters. I ought to have a hundred dollars."

"It's a good deal, but I'll pay it," said Miss Petunia. "I ain't rich, but I've got quite a little money in the bank, and I own the house I live in and a farm I rent. Pa left me money and property worth about ten thousand dollars, and I have n't wasted it. So go ahead."

"YOU ARE A MAN, AND BIG AND STRONG AND BRAVE-LIKE"

"I'll so do," said Philo Gubb; "and first off I'll ask you who your neighbors are."

"My neighbors!" exclaimed Miss Petunia.

"On both sides," said Mr. Gubb, "and who comes to your house most?"

"Well, I declare!" said Miss Petunia. "I don't know what you are getting at, but on one side I have no neighbors at all, and on the other side is Mrs. Canterby. I guess she comes to my house oftener than anybody else."

"I am acquainted with Mrs. Canterby," said Mr. Gubb. "I did a job of paper-hanging there only last week."

"Did you, indeed?" said Miss Scroggs politely. "She's a real nice lady."

"I don't give opinions on deteckative matters until I'm sure," said Mr. Gubb. "She seems nice enough to the naked eye. I don't want to get you to suspicion her or nobody, Miss Scroggs, but about the only clue I can grab hold of is that first letter you got. It said to look on page fourteen, and all the pages by that number was torn out of your books —"

"Except my cook-book," said Miss Petunia.

"And a person naturally would n't go to think of a cook-book as a real book," said Mr. Gubb. "If you stop to think, you'll see that whoever wrote that letter must have beforehand tore out all the page fourteens from the books into your house, for some reason."

235

"Why, yes!" exclaimed Miss Scroggs, clapping her hands together. "How wise you are!"

"Deteckative work fetches deteckative wisdom," said Mr. Gubb modestly. "I don't want to throw suspicion at Mrs. Canterby, but Letter Number One points at her first of all."

"O—h, yes! O—h my! And I never even thought of that!" cried Miss Petunia admiringly.

"Us deteckatives have to think of things," said Philo Gubb. "And so we will say, just for cod, like, that Mrs. Canterby got at your books and ripped out the pages. She'd think: 'What will Miss Petunia do when she finds she has n't any page fourteens to look at? She'll rush out to borrow a book to look at.' Now, where would you rush out to borrow a book if you wanted to borrow one in a hurry?"

"To Mrs. Canterby's house!" exclaimed Miss Petunia.

"Just so!" said Mr. Gubb. "You'd rush over and you'd say, 'Mrs. Canterby, lend me a book!' And she would hand you a book, and when you looked at page fourteen, and read the first full sentence on the page, what would you read?"

"What would I read?" asked Miss Scroggs breathlessly.

"You would read what she meant you to read," said Mr. Gubb triumphantly. "So, then what? If I was in her place and I had written a letter to you, meaning to give you a threat in a roundabout way, and it went dead, I'd write some foolish letters to you to make you think the whole thing was just foolishness. I'd write you letters about weather and tacks and cats and lime and trout, and such things, to throw you off the scent. Maybe," said Mr. Gubb, with a smile, "I'd just copy bits out of a newspaper."

"How wonderfully wonderful!" exclaimed Miss Petunia.

"That is what us deteckatives spend the midnight oil learning the Rising Sun Deteckative Agency's Correspondence School lessons for," said Mr. Gubb. "So, if my theory is right, what you want to do when you get back home is to rush over to Mrs. Canterby's and ask to borrow a book, and look on page fourteen."

"And then come back and tell you what it says?" asked Miss Petunia.

"Just so!" said Philo Gubb.

Miss Petunia arose with a simper, and Mr. Gubb arose to open the door for her. He felt particularly gracious. Never in his career had he been able to apply the inductive system before, and he was well pleased with himself. His somewhat melancholy eyes almost beamed on Miss Petunia, and he felt a warm glow in his heart for the poor little thing who had come to him in her trouble. As he stood waiting for Miss Scroggs to gather up her feather boa and her parasol and her black hand-bag, he felt the dangerous pity of the strong for the weak.

Miss Petunia held out her hand with a pretty

gesture. She was fully forty-five, but she was kittenish for her age. There was something almost girlish in her manner, and the long, dancing brown curls that hung below her very youthful hat added to the effect. When she had shaken Mr. Gubb's hand she half-skipped, half-minced out of his office.

"An admirable creature," said Mr. Gubb to himself, and he turned to his microscope and began to study the ink of the letters under that instrument. His next work must be to find the identical ink and the identical writing-paper. He had no doubt he would find them in Mrs. Canterby's home. The ink was a pale blue in places, deepening to a strong blue in other places, with grainy blue specks. He decided, rightly, that this "ink" had been made of laundry blue. The paper was plain note-paper, glossy of surface and with blue lines, and, in the upper left corner, the maker's impress. This was composed of three feathers with the word "Excellent" beneath. The envelopes were of the proper size to receive the letters. They bore an unmistakable odor of toilet soap and chewing-gum.

"Dusenberry!" said Mr. Gubb, and smiled.

Hod Dusenberry kept a small store near the home of Mrs. Canterby. There seemed no doubt that the coils of the investigation were tightening around Mrs. Canterby, and Mr. Gubb put on his hat and went out. He went to Hod Dusenberry's store. Mr. Dusenberry sat behind the counter.

"I came in," said Mr. Gubb, "to purchase a bottle of ink off of you."

"There, now!" said Mr. Dusenberry self-accusingly. "That's the third call for ink I've had in less'n two months. I been meanin' to lay in more ink right along and it allus slips my mind. I told Miss Scroggs when she asked for ink —"

"And what did you tell Mrs. Canterby when she asked for ink?" asked Mr. Gubb.

"Mrs. Canterby?" said Hod Dusenberry. "Maybe I ought to see the joke, but I'm feelin' stupid today, I reckon. What's the laugh part?"

"It wasn't my intentional aim to furnish laughable amusement," said Detective Gubb seriously. "What did Mrs. Canterby say when she asked for ink and you didn't have none?"

"She didn't say nothin'," said Mr. Dusenberry, "because she never asked me for no ink, never! She don't trade here. That's all about Mrs. Canterby."

The Correspondence School detective had been leaning on the show-case, and with the shrewdness of his kind had let his eyes search its contents. In the show-case was writing-paper of the very sort the Anonymous Wiggle letters had been written on — also envelopes strangely similar to those that had held the letters.

Mr. Gubb smiled pleasantly at Mr. Dusenberry.

"I'd make a guess that Mrs. Canterby don't buy her writing-paper off you neither?" he hazarded.

"You guess mighty right she don't," said Mr. Dusenberry.

"And maybe you don't recall who ever bought writing-paper like this into the case here?" said Mr. Gubb.

"I guess maybe I do, just the same," said Mr. Dusenberry promptly. "And it ain't hard to recall, either, because nobody buys it but Miss 'Tunie Scroggs. 'Tunie is the all-firedest female I ever did see. Crazy after a husband, 'Tunie is." He chuckled. "If I was n't married already I dare say 'Tunie would have worried me into matrimony before now. 'Tunie's trouble is that everybody knows her too well — men all keep out of her way. But she's a dandy, 'Tunie is. They tell me that when Hinterman, the plumber, hired a new man up to Derlingport and 'Tunie found out he was a single feller, she went to work and had new plumbing put in her house, just so's the feller would have to come within her reach. But he got away."

"He did?" said Mr. Gubb nervously.

"Oh, yes," said Mr. Dusenberry. "He stood 'Tunie as long as he could, and then he threw up his job and went back to Derlingport. They tell me she don't do nothin' much now but set around the house and think up new ways to git acquainted with men that ain't heard enough of her to stay shy of her. Sorry I ain't got no ink, Mr. Gubb."

"It's a matter of no consequential importance, thank you," said Mr. Gubb, and he went out. He was distinctly troubled. He recalled now that Miss Scroggs had smiled in a winning way when she spoke to him, and that she had quite warmly pressed his hand when she departed. With a timid bachelor's extreme fear of designing women, Mr. Gubb dreaded another meeting with Miss Scroggs. Only his faithfulness to his Correspondence School diploma had power to keep him at work on the Anonymous Wiggle case, and he walked thoughtfully toward the home of Mrs. Canterby. He went to the back door and knocked gently. Mrs. Canterby came to the door.

"Good-afternoon," said Mr. Gubb. "I been a little nervous about that paper I hung onto your walls. If I could take a look at it —"

"Well, now, Mr. Gubb, that's real kind of you," said Mrs. Canterby. "You can look and welcome. If you just wait until I excuse myself to Miss Scroggs —"

"Is she here?" asked Mr. Gubb with a hasty glance toward his avenues of escape.

"She just run in to borrow a book to read," said Mrs. Canterby, "and she's having some trouble finding one to suit her taste. She's in my lib'ry sort of glancing through some books."

"Does — does she glance through to about near to page fourteen?" asked Mr. Gubb nervously.

"Now that you call it to mind," said Mrs. Canterby, "that's about how far she is glancing through them. She's glanced through about sixteen, and she's still glancing. She thinks maybe she'll take 'Myra's Lover, or The Hidden Secret,' but she ain't sure. She come over to borrow 'Weldon Shirmer,' but I had lent that to a friend. She was real disappointed I did n't have it."

Mr. Gubb wiped the perspiration from his face. He too would have liked at that moment to have seen a copy of "Weldon Shirmer," and to have read what stood at the top of page fourteen.

"If it ain't too much trouble, Mrs. Canterby," he said, "I wish you would sort of fetch that Myra book out here without Miss Scroggs's knowing you done so. I got a special reason for it, in my deteckative capacity. And I wish you would n't mention to Miss Scroggs about my being here."

"Land sakes!" said Mrs. Canterby. "What's up now? Miss Scroggs she's right interested in you, too. She made inquiries of me about you when you was working here. She says she thinks you are a real handsome gentleman."

Mrs. Canterby laughed coyly and went out, and Mr. Gubb dropped into a chair and wiped his face again nervously. His eye, falling on the kitchen table, noted a sheet of writing-paper. It was the same style of paper as that on which the Anonymous Wiggle letters had been written. He bent forward and glanced at it. In blue ink evidently made of indigo dissolved in water, was written on the sheet a recipe. The writing, although undisguised and slanting properly, was beyond doubt the same as that of the Wiggle letters. When Mrs. Canterby returned to the kitchen with "Myra's Lover" hidden in the folds of her skirt, the perplexed Mr. Gubb held the recipe in his hand.

"By any chance of doubt," he said, "do you happen to be aware of whom wrote this?"

"Petunia wrote it," said Mrs. Canterby promptly, "and whatever are you being so mysterious for? There's no mystery about that, for it's her mincemeat recipe."

"There is often mystery hidden into mince-meat recipes when least expected," said Mr. Gubb. "I see you got the book."

He took it and turned to page fourteen. At the top of the page were the words, completing a sentence, "— without turning a hair of his head." Then followed the first complete sentence. It ran: "'A woman like you,' said Lord Cyril, 'should be loved, cherished, and obeyed.'"

"Goodness!" exclaimed Mr. Gubb, and handed the book back to Mrs. Canterby.

"Why did you say that?" asked Mrs. Canterby.

"I was just judging by the book that Miss Scroggs is fond of love and affection in fiction tales," he said.

"Fond of!" exclaimed Mrs. Canterby. "Far be it from me to say anything about a neighbor lady, but if Petunia Scroggs ain't crazy over love and marriage I don't know what. She'd do anything in the world to get a husband. I recall about Tim

243

Wentworth — Furnaces Put In and Repaired — and how hungry Petunia used to look after him when he went by in his wagon, but she could n't get after him because she has n't a furnace in her house, but the minute he hung up the sign 'Chimneys Cleaned,' she was down to his shop and had him up to the place, and I know it for a fact, for I took some of the soot out of her eye myself, that she courted him so hard when he got to her house that even when he went to the roof to clean the chimney she stuck her head in the fireplace and talked up the flue at him."

"Goodness!" said Mr. Gubb again. "I guess I 'll go on my way and look at your wall-paper some other day."

Mrs. Canterby laughed.

"Just as you wish," she said, "but if Petunia has set out after you, you won't get away from her that easy."

But Mr. Gubb was already moving to the door. He heard Miss Petunia's voice calling Mrs. Canterby, and coming nearer and nearer, and he fled.

At Higgins's book-store he stopped and asked to see a copy of "Weldon Shirmer," and turned to page fourteen. "'Fate,'" ran the first full sentence, "'has decreed that you wed a solver of mysteries.'" Mr. Gubb shivered. This was the mysterious passage Miss Scroggs had meant to bring to his eyes in an impressive manner. He was sure of one thing: whatever Fate had decreed in the case of the heroine of "Weldon Shirmer," Philo Gubb had no intention of allowing Fate to decree that one particular Correspondence School solver of mysteries should marry Miss Petunia Scroggs. He hurried to his office.

At the office door he paused to take his key from his pocket, but when he tried it in the lock he found the door had been left unlocked and he opened the door hastily and hurried inside. Miss Petunia Scroggs was sitting in his desk-chair, a winning smile on her lips and "Myra's Lover, or The Hidden Secret," in her lap.

"Dear, wonderful Mr. Gubb!" she said sweetly. "It was just as you said it would be. Here is the book Mrs. Canterby loaned me."

For a moment Mr. Gubb stood like a flamingo fascinated by a serpent.

"You detectives are such wonderful men!" cooed Miss Petunia. "You live such thrilling lives! Ah, me!" she sighed. "When I think of how noble and how strong and how protective such as you are —"

Mr. Gubb kept his bird-like eyes fixed on Miss Petunia's face, but he pawed behind himself for the door. He felt his hand touch the knob.

"And when I think of how helpless and alone I am," said Miss Petunia, rising from her chair, "although I have ample money in the bank —"

Bang! slammed the door behind Mr. Gubb. *Click!* went the lock as he turned the key. His feet hurried to the stairs and down to the nearest street almost falling over Silas Washington, seated on the lowest step. The little negro looked up in surprise.

245

"Do you want to earn half a dollar?" asked Mr. Gubb hastily.

"'Co'se Ah do," said Silas Washington. "What you want Ah shu'd do fo' it?"

"Wait a portion of time where you are," said Mr. Gubb, "and when you hear a sound of noise upstairs, go up and unlock Mister Philo Gubb, Deteckative, his door, and let out the lady."

"Yassah!" said Silas.

"And when you let her exit out of the room," said Mr. Gubb, "say to her: 'Mister Gubb gives up the case.' Understand?"

"Yassah!"

"Yes," said Mr. Gubb, and he glanced up and down the street. "And say '— because it don't make no particle bit of difference who the lady is, Mister Gubb would n't marry nobody at no time of his life.'"

"Yassah!" said the little negro.

THE HALF OF A THOUSAND

PHILO GUBB sat in his office in the Opera House Block with a large green volume open on his knees, reading a paragraph of some ten lines. He had read this paragraph twenty times before, but he never tired of reading it. It began —

Gubb, Philo. Detective and decorator. *b.* Higginsville, Ia., June 26, 1868. Educated Higginsville, Ia., primary schools. Entered decorating profession, 1888. Graduated with honors, Rising Sun Detective Agency's Correspondence School of Detecting, 1910.

He hoped that some day this short record of his life might be lengthened by at least one line, which would say that he had "*m.* Syrilla Medderbrook," and since his escape from Petunia Scroggs and her wiles, and the latest telegram from Syrilla, he had reason for the hope. As Mr. Gubb had not tried to collect the one hundred dollars due him from Miss Scroggs, he had nothing with which to pay Mr. Medderbrook more on account of the Utterly Hopeless mining stock, but under his agreement with Mr. Medderbrook he had paid that gentleman thirty-seven dollars and fifty cents for the last telegram from Syrilla. This had read: —

Joy and rapture! Have given up all forms of food. Have given up spaghetti, fried rabbit, truffles, brown betty, prunes, goulash, welsh rabbit, hoecake, sauerkraut,

PHILO GUBB, THE DETECTIVE

Philadelphia scrapple, haggis, chop suey, and mush. Have lost one hundred and fifty pounds more. Weigh seven hundred forty-five. Going down every hour. Kiss Gubby for me.

Mr. Gubb, therefore, mused pleasantly as he read the book that contained the short but interesting reference to himself.

The book with the green cover was "Iowa's Prominent Citizens," sixth edition, and was a sort of local, or state, "Who's Who." In its pages, for the first time, Philo Gubb appeared, and he took great delight in reading there how great he was. We all do. We are never so sure we are great as when we read it in print.

It is always comforting to a great man to be reassured that he was "*b*. Dobbinsville, Ia., 1869," that he "*m*. Jane, dau. of Oscar and Siluria Botts, 1897," and that he is not yet "*d*." There are some of us who are never sure we are not "*d*." except when we see our names in the current volume of "Who's Who," "Who's It," or "Iowa's Prominent Citizens."

Outside Philo Gubb's door a man was standing, studying that part of "Iowa's Prominent Citizens" devoted to the town of Riverbank. The man was not as young as he appeared to be. His garments were of a youthful cut and cloth, being of the sort generally known as "College Youth Style," but they were themselves no longer youthful. In fact, the man looked seedy.

Notwithstanding this he had an air — a something — that attracted and held the attention. A cane gave some of it. The extreme good style of his Panama hat gave some of it. His carriage and the gold-rimmed eyeglasses with the black silk neck-ribbon gave still more. When, however, he removed his hat, one saw that he was partly bald and that his reddish hair was combed carefully to cover the bald spot.

The book in his hand was a small memorandum book, and in this he had pasted the various notices cut from "Iowa's Prominent Citizens" and one — only — cut from "Who's Who," relating to citizens of Riverbank. He had done this for convenience as well as for safety, for thus he had all the Riverbank prominents in compact form, and avoided the necessity of carrying "Iowa's Prominent Citizens" and "Who's Who" about with him. That would have been more or less dangerous. Particularly so, since he had been exposed by the New York "Sun" as The Bald Impostor.

The Bald Impostor, to explain him briefly, was a professional relative. He was the greatest son-cousin-nephew in the United States, and always he was the son, cousin, or nephew of one of the great, of one of the great mentioned in "Who's Who." He was as variable as a chameleon. Sometimes he was a son, cousin, or nephew of some one beginning with *A*, and sometimes of some one beginning with *Z*, but usually of some one with about twelve to fourteen lines in "Who's Who."

The great theory he had established and which was the basis of all his operations was this: "Every Who's Who is proud of every other Who's Who," and "No Who's Who can refuse the son, cousin, or nephew of any other Who's Who five dollars when asked for one dollar and eighty cents."

The Bald Impostor's operation was simple in the extreme. He went to Riverbank. He found, let us say, the name of Judge Orley Morvis in "Who's Who." Then he looked up Chief Justice Bassio Bates in the latest "Who's Who," gathered a few facts regarding him from that useful volume, and called on Judge Orley Morvis. Having a judge to impose upon he began by introducing himself as the favorite nephew of Chief Justice Bassio Bates.

"Being in town," he would say, when the Judge was mellowed by the thought that a nephew of Bassio Bates was before him, "I remembered that you were located here. My uncle has often spoken to me of your admirable decision in the Higgins-Hoopmeyer calf case."

The Higgins-Hoopmeyer case is mentioned in "Who's Who." The Judge can't help being pleased to learn that Chief Justice Bassio Bates approved of his decision in the Higgins-Hoopmeyer case.

"My uncle has often regretted that you have never met," says the Bald Impostor. "If he had known I was to be in Riverbank he would have sent his copy of your work, 'Liens and Torts,' to be autographed."

THE HALF OF A THOUSAND

"Liens and Torts" is the one volume written by Judge Orley Morvis mentioned in "Who's Who." The Judge becomes mellower than ever.

"Ah, yes!" says the Judge, tickled, "and how is your uncle, may I ask?"

"In excellent health considering his age. You know he is ninety-seven," says the Bald Impostor, having got the "*b.* June 23, 1817" from "Who's Who." "But his toe still bothers him. A man of his age, you know. Such things heal slowly."

"No! I did n't hear of that," says the Judge, intensely interested. He is going to get some intimate details.

"Oh, it was quite dreadful!" says the Bald Impostor. "He dropped a volume of Coke on Littleton on it last March — no, it was April, because it was April he spent at my mother's."

All this is pure invention, and that is where the Bald Impostor leads all others. Even as he invents details of the sore toe, you see, he introduces his mother.

"She was taken sick early in April," he says, and presently he has Dr. Somebody-Big out of "Who's Who" attending to the Chief Justice's sore toe and advising the mother to try the Denver climate. And the next thing the Judge knows the Bald Impostor is telling that he is now on his way back from Denver to Chicago.

So then it comes out. The Bald Imposter sits on the edge of his chair and becomes nervous and perspires. Perspiring is a sure sign a man is unaccustomed to asking a loan, and the Bald Impostor is entitled to start the first School of Free Perspiring in America. He can perspire in December, when the furnace is out and the windows are open. All his head pores have self-sprinklers or something of the sort. He is as free with beads of perspiration as the early Indian traders were with beads of glass. He mops them with a white silk handkerchief.

So he perspires, and out comes the cruel admission. He needs just one dollar and eighty cents! As a matter of fact, he has stopped at Riverbank because his uncle had so often spoken of Judge Orley Morvis — and really, one dollar and eighty cents would see him through nicely.

"But, my dear boy!" says the Judge kindly. "The fare is six dollars. And your meals?"

"A dollar-eighty is enough," insists the Bald Impostor. "I have enough to make up the fare, with one-eighty added. And I could n't ask you to pay for my meals. I 'll — I have a few cents and can buy a sandwich."

"My dear boy!" says Judge Orley Morvis, of Riverbank (and it is what he did say), "I could n't think of the nephew of a Chief Justice of the United States existing for that length of time on a sandwich. Here! Here are twenty dollars! Take them — I insist! I must insist!"

Some give him more than that. We usually give him five dollars.

HE PERSPIRES, AND OUT COMES THE CRUEL ADMISSION

THE HALF OF A THOUSAND

I admit that when the Bald Impostor visited me and asked for one dollar and eighty cents I gave him five dollars and an autographed copy of one of my books. He was to send the five back by money-order the next day. Unfortunately he seems to have no idea of the flight of time. For him to-morrow never seems to arrive. For me it is the five that does not arrive. The great body of us consider those who give him more than five to be purse-proud plutocrats. But then we sometimes give him autographed copies of our books or other touching souvenirs. And write in them, "*In memory of a pleasant visit.*" I *do* wonder what he did with my book!

Judge Orley Morvis was the only Who's Whoer in Riverbank, but the town was well represented in "Iowa's Prominent Citizens," and after collecting twenty dollars from the Judge the Bald Impostor proceeded to Mr. Gubb's office.

"Detective and decorator," he said to himself. "I wonder if William J. Burns has a son? Better not! A crank detective might know all about Burns. I'm his cousin. Let me see — I'm Jared Burns. Of Chicago. And mother has been to Denver for the air." He took out the memorandum book again. "The Waffles-Mustard case. The Waffles-Mustard case. Waffles! Mustard! I must remember that." He knocked on the door.

"Mr. Gubb?" he asked, as Philo Gubb opened the door. "Mr. Philo Gubb?"

PHILO GUBB, THE DETECTIVE

"I am him, yes, sir," said the paper-hanger detective. "Will you step inside into the room?"

"Thank you, yes," said the Bald Impostor, as he entered.

Philo Gubb drew a chair to his desk, and the Bald Impostor took it. He leaned forward, ready to begin with the words, "Mr. Gubb, my name is Jared Burns. Mr. William J. Burns is my cousin —" when there came another rap at the door. Mr. Gubb's visitor moved uneasily in his chair, and Mr. Gubb went to the door, dropping an open letter carelessly on the desk-slide before the Bald Impostor. The new visitor was an Italian selling oranges, and as Mr. Gubb had fairly to push the Italian out of the door, the Bald Impostor had time to read the letter and, quite a little ahead of time, began wiping perspiration from his forehead.

The letter was from the Headquarters of the Rising Sun Detective Agency, and was brutally frank in denouncing the Bald Impostor as an impostor, and painfully plain in describing him as bald. It described in the simplest terms his mode of getting money and it warned Mr. Gubb to be on the outlook for him "as he is supposed to be working in your district at present." The Bald Impostor gasped. "A number of victims have organized," continued the letter, "what they call the Easy Marks' Association of America and have posted a reward of fifty dollars for the arrest of the fraud."

The Bald Impostor glanced toward Philo Gubb

and hastily turned the letter upside down. When Mr. Gubb returned, the Bald Impostor was rubbing the palms of his hands together and smiling.

"My name, Mr. Gubb," he said, "is Allwood Burns. I am a detective. I have heard of your wonderful work in the so-called Muffins-Mustard case."

"Waffles-Mustard," said Mr. Gubb.

"I should say Waffles," said the Bald Impostor hastily. "I consider it one of the most remarkable cases of detective acumen on record. We in the Rising Sun Detective Agency were delighted. It was a proof that the methods of our Correspondence School of Detecting were not short of the best."

Philo Gubb stared at his visitor with unconcealed admiration.

"Are you out from the Rising Sun Deteckative Agency yourself?" he asked.

The Bald Impostor smiled.

"I wrote you a letter yesterday," he said. "If you have not received it yet you will soon, but I can give you the contents here and now. A certain impostor is going about the country —"

Philo Gubb picked up the letter and glanced at the signature. It was indeed signed "Allwood Burns." Mr. Gubb extended his hand again and once more shook the hand of his visitor — this time far more heartily.

"Most glad, indeed, to meet your acquaintance,

255

Mr. Burns," said Philo Gubb heartily. "It is a pleasure to meet anybody from the offices of the Rising Sun Deteckative Agency. And if you ever see the man that wrote the 'Complete Correspondence Course of Deteckating,' I wish —"

The false Mr. Burns smiled.

"I wrote it," he said modestly.

"I am *most* very glad to meet you, sir!" exclaimed Philo Gubb, and again he shook his visitor's hand. "Because —"

"Ah, yes, because —" queried the Bald Impostor pleasantly.

"Because," said Philo Gubb, "there's a question I want to ask. I refer to Lesson Seven, 'Petty Thievery, Detecting Same, Charges Therefor.' I have had some trouble with 'Charges Therefor.'"

"Indeed? Let me see the lesson, please," said the Bald Impostor.

"'The charges for such services,'" Philo Gubb read, pointing to the paragraph with his long forefinger, "'should be not less than ten dollars per diem.' That's what it says, ain't it?"

"It does," said the Bald Impostor.

"Well, Mr. Burns," said Philo Gubb, "I took on a job of chicken-thief detecting, and I had to detect for two diems to do it, and that would be twenty dollars, would n't it?"

"It would," said the Bald Impostor.

"Which is fair and proper," said Philo Gubb, "but the old gent would n't pay it. So I ask you if you'd be kindly willing to go to him along with me in company and tell him I charged right and according to rates as low as possible?"

"Of course I will go," said the Bald Impostor.

"All right!" said Philo Gubb, rising. "And the old gent is a man you'll be glad to meet. He's a prominent citizen gentleman of the town. His name is Judge Orley Morvis."

The Bald Impostor gasped. Every free-acting pore on his head worked immediately.

"And, so he won't suspicion that I'm running in some outsider on him," said Philo Gubb, "I'll fetch along this letter you wrote me, to certify your identical identity."

He picked up the warning letter from the Rising Sun Agency, and stood waiting for the Bald Impostor to arise. But the Bald Impostor did not arise. For once at least he was flabbergasted. He opened and shut his mouth, like a fish out of water. His head seemed to exude millions of moist beads. He saw a smile of triumph on Philo Gubb's face. Mr. Gubb was smiling triumphantly because he was able now to show Judge Orley Morvis a thing or two, but the Bald Impostor was sure Philo Gubb knew he was the Bald Impostor. He was caught and he knew it. So he surrendered.

"All right!" he said nervously. "You've got me. I won't give you any trouble."

"It's me that's being a troubling nuisance to you, Mr. Burns," said Philo Gubb.

PHILO GUBB, THE DETECTIVE

The paper-hanger detective stopped short. A look of shame passed across his face.

"I hope you will humbly pardon me, Mr. Burns," he said contritely. "I am ashamed of myself. To think of me starting to get you to attend to my business when prob'ly you have business much more important that fetched you to Riverbank."

A sudden light seemed to break upon Philo Gubb.

"Of a certain course!" he exclaimed. "What you come about was this — this" — he looked at the letter in his hand — "this Bald Impostor, was n't it?"

Philo Gubb's visitor, who had begun to breathe normally again, gasped like a fish once more. He saw Philo Gubb finish reading the description of the Bald Impostor, and then Philo Gubb looked up and looked the Bald Impostor full in the face. He looked the Bald Impostor over, from bald spot to shoes, and looked back again at the description. Item by item he compared the description in the letter with the appearance of the man before him, while the Impostor continued to wipe the palms of his hands with the balled handkerchief. At last Philo Gubb nodded his head.

"Exactly similar to the most nominal respects," he said. "Quite identical in every shape and manner.'"

"Oh, I admit it! I admit it!" said the Bald Impostor hopelessly.

"Yes, sir!" said Philo Gubb. "And I admit it

the whilst I admire it. It is the most perfect disguise of an imitation I ever looked at."

"What?" asked the Bald Impostor.

"The disguise you've got onto yourself," said Philo Gubb. "It is most marvelously similar in likeness to the description in the letter. If you will take the complimentary flattery of a student, Mr. Burns, I will say I never seen no better disguise got up in the world. You are a real deteckative artist."

The Bald Impostor could not speak. He could only gasp.

"If I didn't know who you were of your own self," said Philo Gubb in the most complimentary tones, "I'd have thought you were this here descriptioned Bald Impostor himself."

His visitor moistened his lips to speak, but Mr. Gubb did not give him an opportunity.

"I presume," said Mr. Gubb, "you have so done because you are working upon this Bald Impostor yourself."

"Yes. Oh, yes!" said the Bald Impostor hoarsely. "Exactly."

"In that case," said Mr. Gubb, "I consider it a high compliment for you to call upon me. Us deteckatives don't usually visit around in disguises."

The visitor moistened his lips again.

"I wanted to see," he said, but the words were so hoarse they could hardly be heard, — "I wanted to see —"

"Well, now," said Philo Gubb contritely, "you

must n't feel bad that I did n't take you for that fraud feller right away off. I had n't read the letter through down to the description quite. If I had I would have mistook you for him at once. The resemblance is most remarkably unique."

"Thank you!" said the Bald Impostor, regaining more of his usual confidence. "And it was a hard disguise for me to assume. I'm not naturally reddish like this. My hair is long. And black. And — and my taste in clothes is quiet — mostly blacks or dark blues. Now the reason I am in this disguise — "

He was interrupted by a loud and strenuous knock on the door.

Mr. Gubb went to the door, but before he reached it his visitor had made one leap and was hidden behind the office desk, for a voice had called, impatiently, "Gubb!" and it was the voice of Judge Orley Morvis. When Detective Gubb had greeted his new visitor he turned to introduce the Judge — and a look of blank surprise swept his features. Detective Burns was gone!

For a moment only, Detective Gubb was puzzled. There was but one place in the room capable of concealing a full-grown human being, and that was the space behind the desk. He placed a chair for the Judge exactly in front of the desk and himself stood in a negligent attitude with one elbow on the top of the desk. In this position he was able to turn his head and, by craning his neck a little, look down upon the false Mr. Burns. Mr. Burns made violent gestures, urging secrecy. Mr. Gubb allayed his fears.

"I'm glad you come just now, Judge," he said, "because we can say a few or more words together, there being nobody here but you and me. I presume you come to talk about the per diem charge I charged to you, did n't you?"

"Yes, I did," said the Judge.

"Well, I'll be able to prove quite presently or sooner that the price is correctly O.K.," said Mr. Gubb, "because the leading head of the Rising Sun Deteckative Agency is right in town to-day, and as soon as he gets done with a job he has on hand he's going up to see you. Maybe you've heard of Allwood Burns. He wrote the 'Twelve Correspondence Lessons in Deteckating' by which I graduated out of the Deteckative Correspondence School."

"Never heard of him in my life," said the Judge.

"This here," said Mr. Gubb, not without pride, "is a personal letter I got from him this A.M. just now," and he handed the Judge the letter.

Judge Orley Morvis took the letter with an air of disdain and began to read it with a certain irritating superciliousness. Almost immediately he began to turn red behind the ears. Then his ears turned red. Then his whole face turned red. He breathed hard. His hand shook with rage.

"Well, of all the infernal—" he began and stopped.

"Has the aforesaid impostor been to see *you?*" asked Philo Gubb eagerly.

"Me? Nonsense!" exclaimed the Judge violently. "Do you think I would be taken in by a child's trick like this? Nonsense, Mr. Gubb, nonsense!"

"I did n't hardly think it was possible," said Detective Gubb.

"Possible?" cried the Judge with anger. "Do you think a common faker like that could hood-wink *me?* Me give an impostor twenty dollars! Nonsense, sir!"

He arose. He was in a great rage about it. He stamped to the door.

"And don't let me hear you retailing any such lie about me around this town, sir!" he exclaimed.

He slammed the door, and then the Bald Impostor slowly raised his head above the desk.

"What did you hide for?" asked Philo Gubb.

The Bald Impostor wiped his bedewed brow.

"Hide?" he said questioningly. "Oh, yes, I did hide, did n't I? Yes. Yes, I hid. You see — you see the Judge came in."

"If you had n't hid," said Philo Gubb, "I could have got that business of the per diem charge per day fixed up right here. I was going to introduce him to you."

"Yes — going to introduce him to me," said the Bald Impostor. "That was it. That was why I hid. You were going to introduce him to me, don't you see?"

"I don't quite comprehend the meaning of the reason," said Philo Gubb.

"Why, you see," said the Bald Impostor glibly, — "you see — if you introduced me to him — why — why, he'd know me."

"He'd know you?" said Philo Gubb.

"He'd know me," repeated the false Mr. Burns. "I'll tell you why. The Bald Impostor *did* call on him."

"Honest?"

"I was there," said the Bald Impostor. "The Judge gave him twenty dollars and a copy of some book or other he had written, and he wrote his autograph in the book. Remember that. The Judge wrote his autograph in a book — and gave it to the fellow. I'm telling you this so you can tell the Judge. Tell him I told you. Tell him the fellow's mother is much better now. Tell him Judge Bassic Bates's toe is quite well. And then ask him for the twenty dollars he owes you. You'll get it."

"And you was there?" asked Philo Gubb, amazed.

"Out of sight, but there," said the false Mr. Burns glibly. "Just ready to put my hand on the fellow — but I could n't. I had n't the heart to do it. I thought of the ridicule it would bring down on the poor old Judge. You know he's an uncle of mine. I'm his nephew."

"He said," said Philo Gubb hesitatingly, "he'd never heard of you."

"He never did," said the Bald Impostor promptly. "I was his third sister's adopted child — I am an adopted nephew. And of course you know he would never have anything to do with his sister after she married—ah—General Winston Wells. Not a thing! It was what killed my poor foster mother. Grief!"

He wiped his eyes with his silk handkerchief.

"Grief. Yes, grief. And I had n't the heart to bring shame to the old man by arresting the Impostor in his house — by showing that the good old man was such a silly old fellow as to be done by a simple trick. And what did it matter? I can pick up the Bald Impostor in Derlingport."

"In Derlingport?" queried Philo Gubb.

"In Derlingport," said the Bald Impostor nervously, "for that is where he went. I'll get him there. But half of the thousand dollars is rightfully yours, and you shall have it."

"Thousand dollars?" queried Philo Gubb in amazement.

"The reward has been increased," said the false Mr. Burns. "The — the publishers of 'Who's Who' increased it to a thousand because the Bald Impostor works on the names in their book. They thought they ought to. But you shall have your half of the thousand. I can pick him up in Derlingport this afternoon if — if I can get there in time. And of course I *should* have arrested him here in Riverbank where you are our correspondent and thus entitled to half the reward earned by any one in the head office. You knew that, did n't you?"

"No!" said Philo Gubb. "Am I?"

THE HALF OF A THOUSAND

"Did n't you get circular No. 786?" asked the Bald Impostor.

"I did n't ever get the receipt of it at all," said Mr. Gubb.

"An oversight," said the Bald Impostor. "I 'll send you one the minute I get back to Chicago. I 'll pick up the Bald Impostor at Derlingport this afternoon — if — Mr. Gubb, I am ashamed to make an admission to you. I —"

The Bald Impostor sat on the edge of his chair and pearls of perspiration came upon his brow. He took out his silk handkerchief and wiped his forehead.

"Go right on ahead and say whatever you 've got upon your mind to say," said Mr. Gubb.

"Well, the fact is," said the false Mr. Burns nervously, "I 'm short of cash. I need just one dollar and eighty cents to get to Derlingport!"

"Why, of course!" said Philo Gubb heartily. "All of us get into similar or like predicaments at various often times, Mr. Burns. It is a pleasure to be able to help out a feller deteckative in such a time and manner. Only —"

"Yes?" said the Bald Impostor nervously.

"Only I could n't think of giving you only the bare mere sum to get to Derlingport," said the graduate of the Rising Sun Detective Agency's Correspondence School of Detecting, generously. "I could n't think of letting you start off away with anything less than a ten-dollar bill."

DIETZ'S 7462 BESSIE JOHN

PHILO GUBB sat on an upturned bundle of rolls of wall-paper in the dining-room of Mrs. Pilker's famous Pilker mansion, in Riverbank, biting into a thick ham sandwich. It was noon.

Mr. Gubb ate methodically, taking a large bite of sandwich, chewing the bite long and well, and then swallowing it with a wonderful up and down gliding of his knobby Adam's apple. From time to time he turned his head and looked at the walls of the dining-room. The time was Saturday noon, and but one wall was covered with the new wall-paper, a natural forest tapestry paper, with lifelike representations of leafy trees. He had promised to have the Pilker dining-room completed by Saturday night. It seemed quite impossible to Philo Gubb that he could finish the Pilker dining-room before dark, and it worried him.

Other matters, even closer to his heart, worried Mr. Gubb. He had had a great quarrel with Mr. Medderbrook, the father of the fair Fat Lady of the World's Greatest Combined Shows. Judge Orley Morvis had paid Mr. Gubb twenty dollars for certain detective work, but Mr. Gubb had not turned all this over to Mr. Medderbrook, and Mr. Medderbrook had resented this. He told Mr. Gubb he was a cheap, tank-town sport.

DIETZ'S 7462 BESSIE JOHN

"I worked hard," said Mr. Medderbrook, "to sell you that Utterly Hopeless Gold-Mine stock and now you hold out on me. That's not the way I expect a jay-town easy-mark —"

"I beg your pardon, but what was that term of phrase you called me?" asked Mr. Gubb.

"I called you," said Mr. Medderbrook, changing his tone to one of politeness, "an easy-mark. In high financial circles the term is short for 'easy-market-investor,' meaning one who never buys stocks unless he is sure they are of the highest class and at the lowest price."

"Well, I should hereafter prefer not to be so called," said Mr. Gubb.

Almost as soon as he had said the cruel words he regretted them, but the next day Mr. Medderbrook's colored butler came to Mr. Gubb's office with a telegram for which he demanded thirty-six dollars and fifty cents.

Mr. Gubb trembled with emotion as he paid, for it meant that Syrilla was still losing flesh and that Mr. Dorgan must surely cancel his contract with her soon. The telegram read: —

Happy days! Still shrinking. Have lost one hundred and forty-five pounds since last wire. Contract sure to be canceled as soon as Dorgan gets back from hurried trip to Siam. Weather very hot. Can feel myself shrink. Fond thoughts to my Gubby.

The very next day the colored butler brought Mr. Gubb another telegram.

"Fifty dollars, please, sah," he said.

"What!" cried Mr. Gubb.

"Yes, sah," said the negro. "That's the amount Mistah Meddahbrook done say."

Mr. Gubb could hardly believe it, but he wrote his check for the fifty dollars and then read the telegram. It ran: —

Excelsior! Have lost two hundred pounds since last wire. Now weigh only four hundred pounds. Every one guys me when I am ballyhooed as Fat Lady. Affection to Gubby.

Mr. Gubb was greatly pleased by this, but when, the next day, the colored butler again appeared and asked for fifty dollars Mr. Gubb was worried. The telegram this time read: —

Frightened. Have lost two hundred pounds since last wire, now weigh only two hundred. If lose two hundred more will weigh nothing. Have resumed potatoes and water. Love to Gubby.

That same afternoon the negro brought Mr. Gubb another telegram, on which he collected seven dollars and fifty cents. This telegram contained these words: —

Am indeed frightened. Have resumed bread diet, soup, fish, meat, and cereals, but have lost fifty pounds more. Weigh only one hundred and fifty. Taking tonic. Hope for the best. Tell Gubby I think of him as much as when I weighed half a ton.

Mr. Gubb was much distressed. He had no doubt that his Syrilla would rapidly recover a part of her

A MAN WHO LOOKED LIKE NAPOLEON BONAPARTE GONE TO SEED

lost weight, but he felt as if at the moment he had
lost Syrilla. He could not picture her as a sylph of
one hundred and fifty pounds. He was worried,
indeed, as he sat eating his lunch in Mrs. Pilker's
mansion. It was then he heard a voice: —

"Say, are you the feller they call Bugg?"

Mr. Gubb looked up. In the dining-room door
stood a man who looked like Napoleon Bonaparte
gone to seed.

"If the party you are looking for to seek," said
Mr. Gubb with somewhat offended pride, "is Mister
P. Gubb, him and me are one and the same party.
My name is P. Gubb, deteckative and paper-
hanger."

"Well, youse is the party I'm looking for," said
the stranger. "I got a hunch from Horton, the wall-
paper-store feller, that youse was up here and that
youse wanted a helper. Does youse?"

"If you know paper-hanging as a trade and profession and can go to work immediately at once, I
could use you," said Mr. Gubb. "I've got more jobs
than I can handle alone by myself."

"Say, me a paper-hanger?" said the stranger
scornfully. "Why, sport, I've hung more wall-
paper than youse ever saw, see? Honest, when I
butted in here and saw that there Dietz's 7462
Bessie John on the wall —"

"That what?" asked Philo Gubb.

"That there Dietz's 7462 Bessie John, on the
wall there," explained the stranger. "Don't youse

even know the right name of that wall-paper there, that's been a Six Best Seller for the last three years?"

"It is a forest tapestry," said Mr. Gubb.

"Sure, Mike!" said the stranger. "And one of the finest youse ever seen. Looks like youse could walk right into it and pick hickory nuts off them oak trees, don't it? It's one of me old friends."

Philo Gubb took another bite of sandwich and masticated it slowly.

"Let me teach youse something," said the stranger, and he took a roll of the tapestry paper in his hand and unrolled a few feet. He pointed to the margin of the printed side of the paper with his oily forefinger. "Do youse see them printings?" he asked. "Says 7462 B J, don't it?"

"It does," mumbled Philo Gubb.

"Well, say! This here wall-paper feller Dietz — he makes this here paper, don't he? And that there 7462 is the number of this here forest tap. pattern, see? And B J — that's Bessie John — that tells youse what the coloring is, see? Bessie John is the regular nature coloring, see? They got one with pink trees and yeller sky, for bood-u-wars and bedrooms. That's M S — Mary Sam."

"It is a very ingenious way to proceed to do," said Philo Gubb, "and if regular union wages is all right you can take that straight-edge and trim all them Bessie John letters off this bundle of 7462 Bessie John I'm sitting onto."

This was satisfactory to the stranger. He removed his greasy coat, threw his greasy cap into a corner, wiped his greasy hands on a wad of trimmings and set to work. When Mr. Gubb had completed his modest luncheon he asked his name.

"Youse might as well call me Greasy," said the new employee. "I'm greasier than anything. Got it off 'n my motor-boat."

During the afternoon Philo Gubb learned something of his assistant's immediate past. "Greasy" had saved some money, working at St. Paul, and had bought a motor-boat — "Some boat!" he said; "Streak o' Lightnin'" was what I named her, and she was" — and he had come down the Mississippi. "She can beat anything on the Dad," he said.

The "Dad" was his disrespectful paraphrase of "The Father of Waters," the title of the giant Mississippi. He told of his adventures until he mentioned the Silver Sides. Then he swore in a manner that suited his piratical countenance exactly.

He had been floating peacefully down the river with the current, his power shut off and himself asleep in the bottom of the boat, doing no harm to any one, when along came the Silver Sides, and without giving him a warning signal, ran him down.

"Done it a-purpose, too," he said angrily.

He had managed to keep the boat afloat until he reached Riverbank, but to fix her up would take more money than he had. So he had hunted a job in his own line, and found Philo Gubb.

The Silver Sides, Captain Brooks, owner, was a

271

small packet plying between Derlingport and Bardenton, stopping at Riverbank, which was midway between the two. No one knowing Captain Brooks would have suspected him of running down anything whatever. He was a kind, stout, gray-haired old gentleman. He had a nice, motherly old wife and eight children, mainly girls, and they made their home on the Silver Sides. Mrs. Brooks and the girls cooked for the crew and kept the boat as neat as a new pin. Captain Brooks occupied the pilot-house; Tom Brooks served as first mate, and Bill Brooks acted as purser. Altogether they were a delightfully good-natured and well-meaning family. It was hard to believe they would run down a helpless motor-boat in mid-river, but Greasy swore to it, and about it.

During the next few weeks Greasy and the detective worked side by side. Greasy had every night and all Sunday for his own purposes. Once Mr. Gubb met Greasy carrying a large bundle of canvas, and Mr. Gubb imagined Greasy was fitting a mast and sail to the motor-boat.

On July 15 the Independent Horde of Kalmucks gave a moonlight excursion on the Mississippi, chartering the Silver Sides for the purpose. The Kalmucks were the leading lodge of the town, and leaders also in social affairs. They gave frequent dramatic entertainments — in their hall in winter, and outdoors in the big yard back of Kalmuck Temple in the summer. In the entire history of the lodge there had never been so much as an untoward incident, but at eleven o'clock on the night of July 15 something frightful did occur. It spread it across the top of the first page of the "Daily Eagle" in the one shocking word — PIRATES!

The Silver Star had started on the return trip and had reached a point about two miles below Towhead Island when a rifle or revolver bullet crashed through the glass window on the western side of the pilot-house. Uncle Jerry — as most people called Captain Brooks — turned his head, stared out at the moonlit waters of the river, and saw bearing down upon him from the northwest a long, low craft. Four men stood in the forward part of the boat, and a fifth sat beside the motor. In the bright moonlight, Captain Brooks could see that all the men wore black masks. He also saw that all were armed, and that from the staff at the stern of the boat floated a jet-black flag on which was painted in white the skull and cross-bones that have always been the insignia of pirates. Even as he looked one of the men in the motor-boat raised his arm: Uncle Jerry saw a flash of fire, and another pane of glass at his side jingled to the floor.

The low black craft swept rapidly across the bows of the Silver Sides; the sputtering of its motor ceased; and the next moment the pirates were aboard the barge, lining up the dancers at the points of their pistols, and preparing to take away their ice-cream money.

And they did take it. They began at the bow of

the barge and walked to the stern, making one after another of the excursionists deliver his valuables, and then slipped quietly over the stern of the barge; the pirate craft began to spit and sputter furiously; and the next moment it was tearing through the water like a streak of lightning.

To chase a speed-boat in an elderly river packet would have been nonsense. Uncle Jerry signaled full speed ahead and kept to the channel, where his boat belonged. Presently Mrs. Brooks, panting, climbed to the pilot-house.

"Well, Pa," she said, "pirates has been and robbed us."

"Don't I know it?" said Uncle Jerry testily. "No need of comin' to tell me."

"They got all the ice-cream money," said Mrs. Brooks.

"Well, 't wa'n't ourn, was it?" snapped Uncle Jerry.

"Why, Pa, what a way to talk!" exclaimed Mrs. Brooks. "It's like you thought it wa'n't nothin', to be pirated right here in the forepart of the twentieth century in the middle of the Mississippi River in broad daylight —"

"'T ain't daylight," said Uncle Jerry shortly. "It's midnight, and it's goin' to be long past midnight before we git ashore. A man can't get even part of a night's rest no more. Everybody pirootin' round, stoppin' boats an' stealin' ice-cream money! Makes me 'tarnel mad, it do."

"Pa," said Mrs. Brooks.

"Well, what is it now?" asked Uncle Jerry testily.

"Philo Gubb, the detective-man, is on board," said his wife. "I come up because I thought maybe you'd want to hire him right off to find out who was them pirates, and if —"

"Me? Hire a fool detective?" snapped Mr. Brooks. "Why 'n't you come up and ask me to throw my money into the river?"

Philo Gubb, although not a dancer, had been on the barge when it was attacked, because he was a lover of ice-cream. He too had been lined up and robbed. He had been robbed not only of forty perfectly good cents, but his pirate had seen his opal scarf-pin and had rudely taken it from Mr. Gubb's tie. The pirate was, Mr. Gubb noticed, a short, heavy man with greasy hands. As the motor-boat dashed away, Mr. Gubb pressed to the rear of the barge and looked after it.

As the boat regained her speed, Philomela Brooks approached him.

"Oh, Mr. Gubb!" she exclaimed, "I'm so tremulous."

"If you will kindly not interrupt me at the present moment of time," said Mr. Gubb, "I will be much obliged. I am making an endeavor to try to do some deteckative work onto this case."

"Oh, Mr. Gubb!" Miss Philomela cried. "And *do* you think you'll do any good?"

"In the deteckative business," said Mr. Gubb

sternly, "we try to do all the good we can do, whether we can do it or not." And he turned away and sought a more secluded spot.

The affair of the pirate craft caused a tremendous sensation in Riverbank. Before eight o'clock the next morning every one in Riverbank seemed to have heard of the affair, and when, at eight o'clock, Philo Gubb entered the vacant Himmeldinger house, which he was decorating, he started with surprise to see Greasy already there. He had not expected to see him at all. But there he was, trimming the edge of a roll of Dietz's 7462 Bessie John, and as he turned to greet Mr. Gubb, the detective saw in Greasy's greasy tie what seemed to be his own opal scarf-pin.

"That there," said Mr. Gubb sternly, "is a nice scarf-pin you've got into your tie."

"Ain't it?" said Greasy proudly. "Me new lady-friend give it to me last night."

To Greasy, Detective Gubb said nothing. He was not yet ready to act. But to himself he muttered:—

"Scarf-pin — scarf-pin. That there is a clue I had ought to look into."

In the town excitement was high all day. There was some time wasted while the Chief of Police and the County Sheriff tried to discover which was compelled by law to fight pirates, but the Chief of Police finally put the job on the Sheriff's hands, and the old Fourth of July cannon was loaded with powder and nails and put on the bow of the good ferry-boat Haddon P. Rogers, a posse of about three hundred men with shotguns and army muskets was crowded aboard, and the pirate-catcher got under way.

This was, of course, Monday, and Monday the Silver Sides made her usual down-river trip to Bardenton, leaving in the morning and returning late at night. It was usually two o'clock at night when she tied up at the Riverbank levee, but this time two o'clock came without the Silver Sides. There was a good reason. As the packet neared Hog Island, about two miles below the Towhead, on her return trip, Uncle Jerry heard the sputter of a gas engine and saw dart out from below Hog Island the same low black craft that had carried the pirates before. Even before the craft was within range, the revolvers began to spit at the Silver Sides.

"Well, dang them pirates to the dickens!" exclaimed Uncle Jerry. "If they be goin' to keep up this nonsense I'm goin' to get down-right mad at 'em." But he signaled the engine-room to slow down, as if it was getting to be a habit with him. One of the upper panes, just above his line of vision, clattered down as he pulled the bell-rope.

At the first volley, Ma Brooks and her daughters dashed into the galley and slammed the door. The remainder of the male Brookses made two jumps to the coal bins and began burrowing into the coal, and the three non-Brooks members of the crew dived into openings between the small piles of cargo stuff and tried to become invisible. When the pirates clambered aboard the Silver Star they seemed to be boarding a deserted vessel. They worked quickly and thoroughly. Piece by piece they threw the cargo of the Silver Sides into the motor-boat until they uncovered the three members of the crew, who leaped from their hiding-place like startled rabbits and loped wildly to places of greater safety. Half a dozen revolver shots followed them. The pirates then leisurely reëmbarked, fired a parting salute, and glided away.

The next morning Greasy appeared at work with his pocket full of Sultana raisins, and offered some to Mr. Gubb.

"Thank you," said Mr. Gubb; "raisins are one of my foremost fondnesses. Nice ones like these are hard to find obtainable."

"You're right they are," said Greasy. "Me lady-friend give me these last night. She's the girl that knows good raisins, ain't she?"

Evidently she was, but Philo Gubb had taken occasion to discover, before he went to work that morning, whether the Silver Sides had been pirated again, and he had learned that a half-dozen boxes of Sultana raisins had formed part of the cargo of the Silver Sides. He looked at Greasy severely.

"Your lady-friend is considerably generous in giving things, ain't she?" he said, trying to hide the guile of his questions in an indifferent tone. "You ain't cared to mention her name to me as yet to this time."

"Ain't I?" said Greasy carelessly. "Well, I ain't ashamed of her. Her name is Maggie Tiffkins. She's some girl!"

"You spend most of your evenings with or about her, I presume to suppose?" asked Mr. Gubb carelessly.

"You bet!" said Greasy. "Me and her is going to get married before long, we are. Yep. And I'll be right glad to have a home to sleep in, instead of a barn."

"A barn?" queried Philo Gubb.

"I been sleepin' in a barn," said Greasy. "I thought youse knowed it. I been doin' a piece or two of scene paintin' for them Kalmucks, and I sort of hired a barn to do it in, and so long as I had to have the barn I just slept in it. Keeps me up late," he said, yawning, "seein' my lady-friend till midnight and then paintin' scenery till I don't know when."

"I presume you ain't spent much time on your motor-boat of late times," said Mr. Gubb.

"Ain't had no time," said Greasy briefly.

Detective Gubb, as he pasted paper on the walls of the Himmeldinger house, turned various matters over and over in his mind. His clues pointed as clearly to Greasy as the Great Dipper points to the North Star. He had decided to join the posse on the Haddon P. Rogers when she set out on her next voyage of vengeance, but now he changed his mind.

A barn, large and vacant, would be an excellent place in which to hide the proceeds of a pirate raid. Lest — possibly — the barn should recognize him and hide itself, Mr. Gubb first went to his office in the Opera House Building, disguised himself as a hostler, with cowhide boots, a cob pipe, a battered straw hat, and blue jean trousers. Lest his face be recognized by the barn he wore a set of red under-chin whiskers, which would have been more natural had they been a paler shade of scarlet. Thus disguised, he crept softly down the Opera House Building stairs and ran full into Billy Getz, Riverbank's best example of the spoiled only-son species, and the town's inveterate jester. Mr. Getz put a hand on Mr. Gubb's arm.

"Sh-h!" he said mysteriously. "Not a word. Only by chance did I recognize you, Mr. Gubb. Now, about this pirate business — it has to stop."

"I am proceeding to the deteckative work preliminary to so doing," said Mr. Gubb.

"Good!" said Billy Getz. "Because I can't have such things happening on my Mississippi River. I hate to see the dear old river get a bad name, Mr. Gubb. I'm just organizing the Dear Old River Anti-Pirate League — to suppress pirates, you know. And we want you as our official detective. In the meantime — Greasy! That's all I say — just Greasy! Tough-looking character. Lives in a barn."

HE WORE A SET OF RED UNDER-CHIN
WHISKERS

"I am just proceeding to locate the whereabouts of the barn," said Mr. Gubb.

"That's easy," said Billy Getz. "Hampton's barn — Eighth Street alley. I know, because I've been there. He's doing our scenery for the Kalmuck summer show. You go straight up this street — or no, *you'd* go in the opposite direction, and three miles into the country, and back across the cemetery, as advised in Lesson Thirteen, would n't you?"

"There are only twelve lessons," said Mr. Gubb haughtily and stalked away. He went, however, to Hampton's barn, climbed in through the alley window, and searched the place.

The barn contained nothing of interest. A cot stood at one end of the hay-loft; and stretched across the wall at the other end was a canvas on which was a partly completed scene of a ruined castle, with mountains in the distance. On the floor were pails and brushes, bundles of dry colors, glue, and the various articles needed by a scene-painter. Mr. Gubb looked behind the canvas. No loot was concealed there. He returned to his office, discarded his disguise, and went back to the Himmeldinger house. Seated on the front steps, quite neglecting his work, was Greasy, and beside him sat a girl.

"This," said Greasy, "is Maggie Tiffkins. Youse ought to know her. Mag, consider this a proper knockdown to P. Gubb, my boss."

That night the Silver Sides was attacked by the pirates on her return from Derlingport. The next morning Mr. Gubb awaited Greasy's coming impatiently, hoping for a new clue, but Greasy had none. He was glum. He had had a quarrel with Maggie, and he was cross.

"Last job of work I'll ever do for Billy Getz and them Kalmucks of his'n," he said crossly. "He's gettin' worse and worse. Them first two scenes I painted he kicked enough about: said the forest scene looked like a roast-beef sandwich, and asked me if the parlor scene was a bar-room or a cow-pasture, but when I do a first-class old bum castle and he wants to know if it's a lib'ry interior, I get hot. And so would youse."

For three nights the Silver Sides, now protected by the presence of part of the armed posse, was not disturbed, but on the fourth night the low, black pirate craft boldly attacked the steamer, carrying on a running fight. The pirates did not venture to board her, but the piratical business was getting to be an unbearable nuisance to Uncle Jerry Brooks. A dozen small craft were armed and patrolled the river. On the fourteenth night, when the Silver Sides was up-river on her Derlingport trip, the Jane P., the opposition steamer making the same ports, was boldly attacked by the pirates and lost the most precious part of her cargo. It was then determined to exterminate the pirates at any cost.

Once only had a steamer been attacked above the town, and this seemed to indicate that the pirates had their nest below Riverbank, and this was the more likely as the river below town gave far greater opportunities for hiding the pirate boat during the day. There were several sloughs or bayous and many indentations of the shore-line, while above the town there was none. Above the town the shores sloped back from the river's edge, and even a skiff on the shore could be seen from across the river. The search for the pirate vessel was therefore, conducted below the town, but most unsuccessfully.

Mr. Gubb, in the three weeks during which the search went on, exhausted all his disguises and every page of the twelve lessons of the Rising Sun Detective Agency's Correspondence School of Detecting. He was in a condition bordering on despair. Each day he donned a disguise and visited the barn, and saw nothing but scenery and more scenery. He had reached a point where detective skill seemed to fail, and where he feared he might have to go openly to Greasy and ask him whether he was the pirate, or at least go to Maggie and ask her where she had obtained the scarf-pin and the raisins. And that would not have been detecting. Nothing like it was mentioned in the twelve lessons.

A reward of One Hundred Dollars (rewards are always in capital letters) had been offered by the Business Men's Association for the capture of the pirate craft, but no one seemed likely to earn the reward.

PHILO GUBB, THE DETECTIVE

"Say, honest!" said Greasy, "if my boat was workin' I'd go out alone in her and cop off them hundred dollars. Youse is a detective, Gubb; why don't youse get to work and grab them dollars?"

"Your boat is not into a workable condition?" asked Philo Gubb.

"She's all but that," said Greasy. "She's hauled up on the levee, rottin' like a tomato. I tried to sell her to Muller, the grocery feller where Mag gets them raisins you liked, and I tried to trade her for a ring to Calloway, the jewelry man what Mag got my opal scarf-pin of, but I can't get rid of her no-how. If I had her workin' I'd find them pirates or I'd know why."

"I have remembered the thought of something; I've got to go downtown," said Mr. Gubb, and he left Greasy and went to question Mr. Muller and Mr. Calloway. The one admitted selling Mag the raisins, and the other the pin, and thus two perfectly good clues went bad. Mr. Gubb turned toward Fifth Street, when Billy Getz caught him by the arm.

"Come on and hunt pirates," he said. "The good cruiser Haddon P. Rogers is going to hit a new trail — up-river this time. Come on along."

Billy Getz escorted him aboard the Haddon P. Rogers and led him straight to the Sheriff on the upper deck.

"Sheriff," he said, "we've got 'em now! This time we've got 'em sure. Here's Gubb, the famous

P. Gubb, detective, and after many solicitations he has consented to accompany us. We will have the pirate craft ere we return. P. Gubb never fails."

The Sheriff smiled good-naturedly.

"Always kidding, ain't you, Billy," he said.

The boat started. She steamed slowly up the river, the members of the posse on the upper deck on either side, scanning the shores carefully. Occasionally the ferry-boat backed and ran closer to shore to permit a nearer inspection of some skiff or to view some log left on the shore by the last flood. Billy Getz, standing beside the Sheriff and P. Gubb, called their attention to every shadow and lump on the shore. The boat proceeded on her slow course and reached the channel between an island and the Illinois shore. The wooded bank of the island rose directly from the water, some of the water-elms dipping their roots into the river. There was no place where a boat could be hidden, and the ferry steamed slowly along. Billy Getz poked solemn-faced fun at Mr. Gubb in the most serious manner, and Mr. Gubb was sternly haughty, knowing he was being made sport of. His eyes rested with bird-like intensity on the wooded shore of the island.

"Now, this combination of paper-hanging and detecting has its advantages," said Billy Getz, with a wink at the Sheriff. "When a man —"

Philo Gubb was not hearing him.

"The remarkableness of the similarity of nature to art is quite often remarkable to observe," he said

285

to the Sheriff, "and is seeming to grow more so now and then from time to time. That piece of section of woods right there is so naturally grown you might say it was torn right off a roll of Dietz's 7462 Bessie John."

He stopped short.

"What's the matter?" asked Billy Getz nervously.

"Run the boat in there," said Philo Gubb excitedly. "Those verdures ain't *like* 7462 Bessie John; they *are* 7462 Bessie John."

The Sheriff stared keenly at the spot indicated by Detective Gubb's extended hand and, turning suddenly, said a word to the pilot in the house at his side. The ferry veered and ran in toward the island. Not until the boat was nearer the shore than a front row of the orchestra seats to the back drop of a theater did the others on the boat understand. Then the trick was seen and understood. The trees of the shore were not all trees. One group was a painted canvas, copied carefully by Greasy from Dietz's 7462 Bessie John at the behest of Billy Getz. Stretched across a small indentation of the shore it made a safe screen, unrecognizable a few rods from the shore, and behind this bit of painted forest they found the long, low, black pirate craft — Billy Getz's motor-boat.

When the Sheriff had torn down the canvas and his men had hoisted and heaved the pirate craft to the broad deck of the ferry, Billy Getz was gone. Riverbank never saw him again, and a half-dozen of his roistering companions also disappeared completely.

"Sometimes occasionally," said Philo Gubb, as the ferry turned toward town, "the combination of paper-hanging and deteckative work is detrimental to one or both, as the case may be, but at other occasional times they are worth one hundred dollars."

"That's right!" said the Sheriff suddenly. "You get that reward, don't you?"

"Most certainly sure," said Philo Gubb.

HENRY

Philo Gubb entered his office and placed on his cutting-table the express package he had found leaning against his door. With his trimming-knife he cut the cord that bound the package. It contained, he knew, the new disguise for which he had sent twenty-five dollars to the Rising Sun Detective Agency's Supply Bureau, and he was eager to examine his purchase, which, in the catalogue, was known as "No. 34. French Count, with beard and wig complete. List, $40.00. Special price to our graduates, $25.00, express paid."

Mr. Gubb wore a face more solemn than usual, for he had just had bad news. He had hidden his distrust of Mr. Medderbrook, the father of his beloved Syrilla, and had carried that gentleman the one hundred dollars he had earned by aiding in the capture of the river pirates, but he had found Mr. Medderbrook close to tears.

"Read this, Gubb," Mr. Medderbrook said; and that he was deeply affected was shown by the fact that he did not ask Mr. Gubb to pay any part of the cost of the telegram from Syrilla which had, this time, come "Collect." The telegram read: —

Scared crazy. Resumed vegetables and all kinds of food, eating steadily all day and night, but have lost twenty-five pounds more. Now weigh only one hundred and twenty-five and going down rapidly. If worse goes to worst, love to Gubby.

It is not surprising that Mr. Gubb sighed as he lifted the exaggeratedly thin-waisted frock coat from the package, but there came a tap on the door and he hastily covered the coat with the wrapping paper and turned to the door.

"Enter in," he said. And the door opened cautiously and a short, ruddy-faced man entered, peering into the room first and then closing the door behind him as cautiously as he had opened it.

"Are you this here detective feller?" he asked bluntly.

"I am Mister P. Gubb, deteckating and paperhanging done, to command at your service," admitted Mr. Gubb. "Won't you take a seat onto a chair?"

"Depends," said Mr. Gubb's visitor, keeping his hand on the doorknob. "I'll put it to you like this: Say some guy stole something from me, and I was willing to pay you for finding out who stole it and for getting it back — you'd take a job like that and say nothing about it to anybody, would n't you?"

"Most certainly sure," agreed Mr. Gubb.

"That's the idee! You'd keep it dark. It would n't be nobody's business but yours and mine, would it? It would be a quiet little deal between you and me, and nobody would know anything about it. Hey?"

"Exactly sure," said Philo Gubb. "The deteckative business is conducted onto an absolutely quiet Q.T. basis."

"Correct!" said his visitor. "I see you and me can do business. Now, my name is Gus P. Smith, and I've had one of the rawest deals handed me a man ever had handed him. I was coming along down one of these alleys between streets this morning and —"

He stopped short and turned to the door. Some one had tapped on the panels. Mr. Smith opened the door the merest crack and peered out. He closed it again instantly.

"Somebody to see you," he whispered. "What I've got to say I want kept private. I'll be back."

He opened the door and slipped out, and as he went a second visitor entered. The newcomer was somewhat tall and thin, and his hair was long, so long it fell upon his shoulders in greasy curls. He wore a rather ancient frock coat and a black slouch hat, and a touch of style was added by his gray kid gloves, although the weather was average summer weather. His face was thin and adorned by a silky brown beard, divided at the chin and falling in two carefully arranged points. He closed the door carefully, first looking into the hall to see that Mr. Gus P. Smith had disappeared.

"Mr. P. Gubb, the detective?" he asked.

"Most absolutely sure," said Mr. P. Gubb.

"My name," said Mr. Gubb's visitor, "is one you are doubtless familiar with. I am Alibaba Singh."

HENRY

"Pleased to meet your acquaintance," said Mr. Gubb. "What can I aim to do for you?"

Mr. Alibaba Singh brought a chair close to Mr. Gubb's desk and seated himself. He leaned close to Mr. Gubb — so close that Mr. Gubb scented the rank odor of cheap hair-oil — and whispered.

"Everything is to be strictly confidential — most strictly confidential. That's understood?"

"Most absolutely sure."

"Of course! Now, you must have heard of me — I've made quite a stir here in Riverbank since I came. Theosophical lectures — first lessons in Nirvana — Buddhistic philosophy — mysteries of Vedaism — et cetery."

"I read your advertisement notices into the newspapers," admitted Mr. Gubb.

"Just so. I have done well here. Many sought the mysteries. I have been unusually successful in Riverbank." He stopped short and looked at Philo Gubb suspiciously. "You don't believe in transmigration, do you?" he asked.

"Not without I do without knowing it," said Mr. Gubb. "What is it?"

"Transmigration," repeated Alibaba Singh. "It — Hindoos believe in it. At death the souls of the good enter higher forms of life; the souls of the bad enter lower forms of life. If you were a bad man and died you would become a — a dog, or a horse, or — or something. You don't believe that, do you?"

"Most certainly not at all!" said Mr. Gubb.

"I — I teach it," said Alibaba Singh uneasily. "It is part of my teaching."

"You don't aim to believe nothing of that sort, do you?" asked Mr. Gubb as if he could not imagine any man so foolish.

"Now, that's it!" said Alibaba Singh. "That's why I came to you. All this is strictly confidential, of course? Thanks. I can speak right out, Mr. Gubb? I have in the past taught some things I did not absolutely believe."

"Quite likely true," admitted Philo Gubb.

"We — we occulists get carried on by our eloquence," said Alibaba Singh. "We — we go too far sometimes. Far too far! I admit it. I admit that frankly. When our clients reach out to us for more and more, we — we sometimes go too far. I won't say we string them along. I would n't say that. But we — we lead them farther than we have gone ourselves, perhaps. You understand?"

"Almost absolutely," said Mr. Gubb.

"Just so! Mr. Gubb, one of my clients was greatly interested in transmigration of souls — greatly interested. She was interested in all things mystical — in reincarnation; in the return of the spirits of the dead; in everything like that. I — really, Mr. Gubb, it was hard for me to keep up with her."

"And you proceeded to go ahead and teach her about this transmigration of souls that you don't believe into yourself," said Mr. Gubb helpfully.

"And when she found out you was a faker she set out to sue you for her money back."

"No. Not that!" said Alibaba Singh energetically. "That's not it. She doesn't want her money back. She — she's *almost* satisfied. She's willing to accept what had happened philosophically. She's almost content. Mr. Gubb, the reason I came to you was that I did not want her to land in —"

Alibaba Singh looked carefully around.

"I don't want her to land in jail," he whispered. "It would make trouble for me. The lady, Mr. Gubb, is Mrs. Henry K. Lippett."

"Well?" queried Mr. Gubb.

"What I don't know," said Alibaba Singh, wiping his brow nervously, "is whether I *did* reincarnate her late husband or whether she's liable to be arrested for stealing a —"

Alibaba Singh stopped short and arose hastily. Some one had knocked on Mr. Gubb's door. Alibaba Singh moved toward the door.

"I don't want to talk about this with anybody around," he said nervously. "I'll come back later. Not a word about it!"

He brushed past Mr. Gubb's new visitor as he went out, and Mr. Gubb arose to greet the newcomer.

This third visitor was a large, red-faced man with an extremely loud vest. He wore a high hat of gray beaver, and a large but questionable diamond sparkled on his finger. He walked directly up to Mr. Gubb and shook hands.

PHILO GUBB, THE DETECTIVE

"Sit down," he commanded. "Now, you're Gubb, the detective, ain't you? Good enough! My name is Stephen Watts, but they mostly call me Steve for short — Three-Finger Steve," he added, holding up his right hand to show that one finger was missing. "I'm in the show business. Ever hear of John, the Educated Horse? Ever hear of Hogo, the Human Trilobite? Ever hear of Henry, the Educated Pig? Well, them are me! That's my show. Did you ever hear of a sheriff?"

"Frequently often," said Mr. Gubb with a smile.

"Well, up to Derlingport this here Human Trilobite of mine got loose from my side-show tent, and when they found him he had eat about half of the marble cornerstone out from under the Dawkins Building. He's crazy after white marble. It's like candy to him. So Dawkins attaches my show and sends the Sheriff with an execution to grab the whole business unless I pay for a new cornerstone. Said it would cost two hundred and fifty dollars. I did n't have the money."

"So he took the show," said Philo Gubb.

"*Ex*-act-ly!" said Mr. Three-Finger Steve. "He grabbed the whole caboodle. *Ex*-cept Henry, the Educated Pig. That's why I'm here. That Sheriff's attachment is out against that pig; it was a felony to remove that pig from Derling County while that attachment was out against it. *And* the pig was removed."

HENRY

"You removed it away from there?" asked Philo Gubb.

"Listen," said Three-Finger Steve. "I did n't remove that pig from Derling County. It was stole from me. Greasy Gus stole it. Augustus P. Smith, my bally-hoo man, stole Henry, the Educated Pig, and made a get-away with him. See? See what I want?"

"Not positively exact," said Philo Gubb.

"Well, it's a little bit delicate," said Three-Finger Steve, "and that's why I come to you instead of to the police. I want that pig. But if I go to the police and they find the pig they'll send it back to the Sheriff in Derling County. See?"

"Do you want I should arrest Greasy Augustus P. Smith?" asked Philo Gubb.

"Not on your life!" said Three-Finger vigorously. "No arrests! You just get the pig."

"How big is the size of the pig?" asked Philo Gubb.

"It's a big pig," said Mr. Watts. "Henry has been getting almost too fat, and that's a fact. I've been thinking right along I'd have to diet Henry, but I never got to it. He's one of these big, double-chinned pinkish-white pigs — looks like a prize pig in a county fair. And, listen! He's in this town!"

"Really, indeed?" said Mr. Gubb.

"I know it!" said Three-Finger Steve. "I seen Greasy Gus load that pig into a farm wagon at Derlingport, and I thought Gus was trying to salvage the pig for me, like one feller will help out another in time of trouble. So I come down to Riverbank on the train, expecting Gus would show up at the hotel and tell me where the pig was hid. All right! Gus shows up. 'Gus,' I says, 'where's Henry?' Gus lets on to be worried. 'Stolen!' he says. 'Some guy lifted him when I was n't looking.' Of course I knew that was a lie, and I told him so. 'Now,' he says, ' you 'll never get Henry back. I meant to give him back to you, but after you have talked to me like that I 'll never give him back. I 'll keep him,' he says, 'if I can find him.' So there you are, Mr. Gubb. Henry is in Riverbank, and I want Henry. This story about Henry being stolen is a lie. Henry is hid, and Gus Smith knows where."

Mr. Gubb looked at Mr. Watts thoughtfully.

"Now, if you're one of these fellers with a conscience," said Three-Finger, "you can send Henry back to the Sheriff. But I won't have Greasy Gus putting a trick like this over on me! No, sir!"

He shook hands with Mr. Gubb again and went out. It was fully fifteen minutes before Mr. Gus P. Smith, who must have been waiting across the street, came in. He closed the door and locked it.

"I saw old Three-Finger come out of this building," he said. "What did he want?"

"He came upon confidential business which can't be mentioned," said Mr. Gubb.

"Just so!" said Mr. Smith. "He wanted you to find Henry, the Educated Pig. Now, listen to me.

HENRY

I skipped out with that pig to do Three-Finger a
favor and save part of his show for him, and that's
the truth, but he don't believe it — not him! He
called me a thief and worse, he did. He had the
nerve to say I wanted that pig myself, to start in
business with, and that's a lie. No man can insult
me like that, Mr. Gubb. Look at this —"

He took from his pocket a couple of feet of whipcord and handed it to Philo Gubb.

"What is this?" asked Mr. Gubb.

"That's all that's left of Henry," said Greasy
Gus. "That's his total remains up to date. That's
the rope I led Henry with after I quit the wagon of
a farmer that rode us out of Derlingport. That cord
was tied to Henry's left hind foot. Look at the end
without the knot — was that cut or wasn't it?"

"I most generally reserve my opinion until later
than right at first," said Philo Gubb.

"All right, reserve it!" said Greasy Gus. "Looks
to me like it was cut. No matter. The main thing
I want is for you to find Henry. How's that?"

"Under them certain specifications," said Philo
Gubb, "I can take up the case and get right to
work onto it."

"All right, then," said Greasy Gus. "Now, here's
what I know about it. I got out of Derlingport with
Henry, and when the farmer dumped us from his
wagon I hitched this whipcord to Henry's leg and
drove him along the road. After while I hit this town
of Riverbank. I thought maybe the police would

297

be looking for Henry. So I took to an alley instead of a regular street, and along we came. We came down the alley, and of a sudden I began to wonder what I'd do with Henry now I'd got him into town. It would look kind of suspicious for me and Henry to go to a hotel. 'I know what I'll do,' I says to myself: 'What I want to do is to go alone and rent a barn and say I'm thinking of buying a pig if I can get a place to keep him.' So that's what I did."

"You left the pig alone in the alley by itself?" asked Philo Gubb.

"Yes, sir!" said Mr. Smith. "I found an alley fence that had a staple in it, and I tied one end of the whipcord to the staple and went down the alley to find a barn I could put Henry in. About the fifth barn I tried I found a place for Henry and then I went back to get him, and he was gone!"

"And no clue?" asked Mr. Gubb.

"This tag end of the rope," said Greasy Gus. "And that's all I know about where Henry went, but my idee is somebody come along and seen him there and just thought he'd have a pig cheap."

"It's a pretty hard case to work onto," said Mr. Gubb doubtfully. "Somebody might have come along with a wagon and loaded him in."

"Sure!" said Mr. Smith. "No telling at all. That's why I come to you. If he was where I could fall over him, I wouldn't need a detective, would I? And if you find Henry I'll just give you these four five-dollar bills. I'm no millionaire, but I'll blow that much for the satisfaction of getting back at Three-Finger Watts. Is it a go?"

"Under them certain specifications," said Mr. Gubb, using the exact words he had used before, "I can take up the case and get right to work onto it."

Mr. Smith shook hands to bind the bargain and departed.

He had hardly disappeared before Mr. Alibaba Singh opened the door cautiously, put his head inside and then entered.

"I thought that man would stay forever," he said with annoyance. "He isn't in any way interested in my affairs or in the affairs of Mrs. Henry K. Lippett, is he?"

"Nobody has been here that is interested into anything you are interested into in the slightest form or manner," Mr. Gubb assured him, and Alibaba Singh sighed with relief.

"You never knew Henry K. Lippett, did you?" he asked.

"Never at all," said Mr. Gubb.

"He broke his neck," said Alibaba Singh, "and it killed him."

He hesitated and seemed lost in thought. He drew himself together sharply.

"It isn't *possible!*" he exclaimed with irritation and with no connection with what he had just said. "I *don't* believe it! I — I —"

299

His distress was great. He wrung one hand inside the other. He almost wept.

"Mr. Gubb," he said, "since I was here I have been up to Mrs. Lippett's house again, and it is worse than ever. It can't be possible! I have n't the power. I know I have n't the power."

"You'd ought to try to explain yourself more plain to your deteckative," said Mr. Gubb.

"I'll tell you everything!" said Alibaba Singh in a sudden burst of confidence. "Mr. Gubb, I am an impostor. I am a fraud. I am not a Hindoo. My name is Guffins, James Guffins. I did sleight-of-hand stuff in a Bowery show. I took up this mystic, yogi, Hindoo stuff because I thought it would pay and it was easy to fool the dames. They fell for it fast enough, and I made good money. But I'm no yogi. I'm no miracle man. I could n't bring a man back to life in his own form or any other form, could I?"

"Undoubtedly hardly so," said Mr. Gubb.

"Glad to hear you say it," said Mr. Guffins with relief. "A man gets so interested in his work — and there is a lot you can learn in books about this Hindoo mumbo-jumbo business — but of course I could n't bring Mr. Lippett back. I'm no spiritualistic medium. I could n't materialize the spirit of a pig."

As he said the word, Mr. Guffins shuddered. It had come out unintentionally, but it seemed to jar him to the depth of his being. He had evidently not meant to say *pig*.

"Mr. Gubb, I will be frank with you. I need your help," he continued. "Mrs. Lippett attended my lecture, and she became interested. She formed a class to study yogi philosophy. We went deep into it. I had to read up one week what I taught them the next. The lights turned low and my Hindoo costume helped, of course. Air of mystery, strange perfumes, and all that. You said you never knew Henry K. Lippett?"

"Never at all," said Mr. Gubb.

"Fat man," said Mr. Guffins. "He must have been a very fat man. And a hearty eater. Rather — rather an over-hearty eater. He must have lived to eat."

Mr. Guffins sighed again.

"Of course there was remuneration," Mr. Guffins went on. "For me, I mean. To pay for my time. Mrs. Lippett was most generous. I *told* her," he said angrily, "I could n't guarantee to materialize her dead husband. I said to her: 'Mrs. Lippett, we had better not try it. My power may be too weak. And think of the risk. He *may* be pure spirit, floating in Nirvana, and come to us as a pure spirit, but what if his life was not all it should have been on earth? What if his spirit has passed into a lower form as a punishment for misdeeds? You will pardon me for speaking so of him, but men are weak,' I said, 'and he may now be a — a bird of the air. It would be a shock,' I said, 'to see him changed into a bird of the air.'"

Mr. Guffins paused and groaned.

"But she would have it," he went on. "She would have me make the attempt. So —"

Mr. Guffins looked at Mr. Gubb appealingly.

"You *don't* believe I could do it, do you?" he pleaded.

"Not in any manner of means," said Mr. Gubb.

"That's what I want you to prove to her," said Mr. Guffins. "That's why I came to you. Everybody knows you are a detective. I want you to — to get on my trail."

"You want me to arrest you!" cried Mr. Gubb with surprise.

"I want you to be looking for me as if you wanted to arrest me," said poor Mr. Guffins; "as if you had received word that I was a fraud, and that you had traced me to Mrs. Lippett's. You can go there and say: 'Gone! I am too late! He has escaped.' And then you can tell her it could n't be."

"That what could n't be?" asked Mr. Gubb.

"The room was darkish," said Mr. Guffins. "The lights were dim. I stood in the light of the red globe, and it gave me a weird look. I held the crystal globe in one hand and the jade talisman in the other. The incense arose from the incense-burner. As if out of the empty air, a sweet-toned bell rang three times. I bowed low three times as the bell rang and muttered the magic words. I made them up as I said them, but they sounded mystic. Mrs. Lippett was sitting on the edge of her chair, breathless with emotion. The curtains were drawn across the door at the back of the room. You could have heard a pin drop. We were alone, just we two. I felt creepy myself. I turned toward the curtains. I said, 'Henry, appear!'"

"Yes?" queried Philo Gubb.

Mr. Guffins threw out both hands with a gesture of utter despair.

"A pig came under the curtains," he groaned. "A pig — a great, fat, double-chinned, pinky-white pig, the kind you see at county fairs — came under the curtains and grunted twice. It stood there and raised its head and grunted twice."

Mr. Guffins wrung his hands nervously.

"It — it surprised me," he said, — "but only for a minute. I said, 'Get out, you beast!' and was going to kick it, but Mrs. Lippett rose slowly from her chair. She half-tottered for an instant, and then she covered her face with her hands. She began to weep. 'I knew it!' she sobbed; 'I knew it! Oh, Henry, I knew you ate too much. I told you and *told* you again and again you were making a pig of yourself. Oh, Henry, if you had only been less of a pig when you were alive before!' And what do you think that pig did?"

"What did it do?" asked Philo Gubb.

"It sat up on its hind legs and begged," said Mr. Guffins, "begged for food. It was awful! Mrs. Lippett could n't stand it. She wept. 'He was always so hungry in his other life,' she said. 'I

303

can't begin to be stern with him now. To-morrow, but not when he has just come back to me. Come, Henry!'

"She went into the dining-room," continued Mr. Guffins, "and Henry — or the pig, for it *could n't* have been Henry — followed her. And what do you think it did?"

"What?" asked Mr. Gubb.

"It went right to the dining-room table and climbed into a chair. Pigs don't do that, do they? But you don't believe it could have been Henry, do you? It got up in the chair and *sat* in it, and put its front feet on the table and grunted. And Mrs. Lippett hurried about saying, 'Oh, Henry! Oh, poor, dear Henry!' and brought a plate of fried hominy and sliced apple and set it before him. And he would n't touch it! He would n't eat. So Mrs. Lippett wept harder and got a napkin and tied it around the pig's neck. Then the pig ate. He almost climbed into the plate, and gobbled the food down. And then he grunted for more. And Mrs. Lippett wept and said: 'It's Henry! He always did tie a napkin around his neck — he spilled his soup so. It's Henry! It acts just like Henry. He never did anything at the table but eat and grunt.' And so," said Mr. Guffins sadly, "she thinks it's Henry. She's fixed up the guest bedroom for him."

"The idea of such a notion!" said Mr. Gubb.

"Well, that's it," said Mr. Guffins sadly. "I ain't sure but it *is* Henry. Do you know, that pig

'SHE THINKS IT'S HENRY. SHE'S FIXED UP THE GUEST
BEDROOM FOR HIM''

walks on its hind feet like a man? She says it walks like Henry. . . . Oh!"

"What is it?" asked Mr. Gubb.

"I told you Henry —"

"Yes?"

"I told you Henry broke his neck. He fell down and broke his neck, in his store. He was coming down the back stairs in the dark, and his foot caught in a piece of rope and he fell. And — this pig came into the parlor with a piece of string on its leg! Here's the string."

Mr. Gubb took it. From his desk he took the string Mr. Greasy Gus had left. The two ends joined perfectly.

"I'll get you out of this fix, and fix it so Mrs. Lippett won't have that pig onto her hands," he said. "I'll go tell her what a fraud of a faker you are, and it won't cost you but twenty-five dollars."

"Willingly paid," said Mr. Guffins, reaching into his pocket.

"And don't you worry about that pig being Henry K. Lippett," said Mr. Gubb. "That pig was a stranger into Riverbank. And," he went on, as if reading the words from the end of the whipcord, "it was tied to the alley fence. Tied to an iron staple," he said, "by a short, stoutish man with a ruddish face." He took up the other piece of cord and looked at it closely. "And the pig jerked the cord in two and went into the yard and in at the open door and into the room. And what is moreover also, the pig is an educated show-pig, and its name is Henry, and —"

"And what?" asked Mr. Guffins eagerly.

"If you want to get rid of the pig out of Mrs. Lippett's house, all you have to do is to write to the Sheriff of Derling County, Derlingport, Iowa, and you need n't trouble yourself into it no further."

"Great Scott!" cried Mr. Guffins. "And you can tell all that from that piece of cord!"

Mr. Gubb assumed a look of wisdom.

"Us gents that is into the deteckative business," he said carelessly, "has to learn twelve correspondence lessons before we get our diplomas. The deteckative mind is educated up to such things."

BURIED BONES

WHEN Mr. Gubb went to the house of Mr. Jonas Medderbrook to pay him the money he had received for solving the mystery of Henry, the Educated Pig, he found the house closed, locked and deserted, and on the door was pinned a card that said simply, and in a neat handwriting: —

Gone to Patagonia. Will be back in one hundred years. Please wait.

This was signed "Jonas Medderbrook," but not until the next day did Mr. Gubb learn from the "Riverbank Eagle" that Mr. Medderbrook had decamped after selling his friends and neighbors an immense amount of stock in the Utterly Hopeless Gold-Mine, of which Mr. Gubb had a very large and entirely worthless quantity.

The departure of Mr. Medderbrook was a great shock to Mr. Gubb, as it seemed to indicate that serious complications in his wooing of Syrilla might result from it, especially as he had only heard from Syrilla through Mr. Medderbrook, but, disturbed as he was by this fear, he was even more upset by a telegram that came to him direct that afternoon. It was from Syrilla herself —

Alas! [it read], the worst has happened. Weighed myself this morning and weighed only one hundred

307

pounds. Later discovered scales were one hundred and five pounds out of balance, registering one hundred and five pounds too much. I cannot marry you, now or ever, Gubby dear, as cannot permit your faithful heart to wed one who weighs five pounds less than nothing. Good-bye forever.   SYRILLA.

The blow was a severe one to Mr. Gubb, as it would have been to any lover who loved a half-ton of beauty only to have her shrink to five pounds less than nothing. For several days he remained locked in his office, hardly touching food, and then, with a sad heart he resumed his customary occupations. He would never have learned the truth about Syrilla had it not been for a tramp called Chi Foxy.

Chi Foxy made the long walk from Derlingport, and night found him on the outskirts of Riverbank. He begged a hand-out from one of the small houses and hunted a place to spend the night. He found it underneath a tool-house alongside the railway tracks, and that it had been used as sleeping-quarters by other tramps was shown by the heap of crushed straw, the bread-crusts, and the remnants of a small fire.

Chi Foxy crawled in and stretched himself out for a comfortable night. He lighted his pipe, loosened the laces of his shoes, and settled back for a comfortable smoke.

Just outside the rear of his sleeping quarters ran the wire right-of-way fence, which was also the back fence of a small piece of property on which stood a rickety old house. The house was devoid of paint, but it was a cheerful sight from where Chi Foxy reclined. He had a clear view of the kitchen window, from which the light came in a yellow glow. and he could see a woman cooking something in a frying-pan on a kitchen stove. A man sat beside the stove, his elbows on his knees, waiting for supper.

Chi Foxy almost decided to climb the fence and knock at the door of the kitchen at the moment the woman took the frying-pan off the stove, but he was feeling well filled and comfortable, and he decided to wait and to use the house as his breakfasting-place. This required no little strength of character, for the perfume of fried veal chops was wafted to his nostrils, but he held himself in hand, and when he had burned his pipeful of tobacco he curled down and went to sleep.

He was awakened by the sound of voices near at hand, and peered out between the ties. The night was not dark. The voices had come from a man and a woman, and as Chi Foxy watched them the man began digging in the sandy soil with a spade. He made quite a hole in the soil and turned to the woman.

"Hand me the bag," he said.

The woman dragged a heavy gunny-sack to the edge of the hole. The man untwisted the neck of the bag and up-ended it over the hole. There followed the rattle of bones, one striking against the other, and the man handed the bag back to the woman. Chi Foxy peered eagerly at the hole. He saw bones.

He looked up at the stars and saw it must be well after midnight. He saw the man hastily spade the soft soil over the bones, saw him scatter loose dry top-sand over the completed job, and saw the man and woman hurry back to the dark house.

The next morning Chi Foxy left his resting-place and climbed over the wire fence. He looked curiously at the spot where the weird burial had taken place, and went on toward the house. He knocked on the door, and it was opened by the man — a tall, lanky, coarse-bearded specimen.

"Say, friend, how about givin' a feller some breakfast?" asked Chi Foxy.

"How 'bout it, ma?" asked the man, turning his head. "Got some breakfast for this feller?"

The woman looked toward the tramp. She evidently decided in his favor.

"Let him set on the step and I kin hand him out some coffee and some meat, if that'll do him," she said, and Chi Foxy seated himself. The breakfast she brought him on a chipped plate was all he could have desired. There was a half of a veal cutlet, browned to a nicety, a portion of fried potatoes, a thick slice of bread without butter, and a cup of coffee. Chi Foxy ate and drank.

"Thanks, folks," he said. "I won't forget you." And he continued on his way toward Riverbank.

"So you're here," said the first policeman he met. "Right on time with the first frosty breeze, ain't you?. Well, my friend, you can blow out of town on the breeze, just like you blew in. No more free board and gentle stone-pile massage in this town. Drift along, bo!"

He turned up the first cross-street. He went from house to house begging a hand-out, but the residents were colder than the weather. At the twelfth house he knocked on the back door, but he was beginning to feel hopeless. A thin streamer of smoke was issuing from the kitchen chimney, and where there is smoke there is food; but here, instead of a hard-faced woman coming to the door, a man put his face to the kitchen window and looked out. It was the face of a tall, thin man with a long neck and prominent Adam's-apple, and as the man peered out of the window he looked something like a flamingo. He opened the door.

"Come right into the inside," said Philo Gubb pleasantly, "and heat yourself up warm. The temperature is full of cold weather to-day."

Chi Foxy entered. He looked around the kitchen. There was a brisk fire in the stove, but no sign of food.

"Say, pard," he said, "how about giving me a bite? I have n't had a bite this morning. I ain't too late, am I?"

His host looked at him.

"You are not too late," he answered, "because it may be some days of time before there is any eats here, for what's burning into that stove is the un-valueless trimmings off of wall-paper. I'm not the regular resider at this house by no means."

Chi Foxy looked at his host again.

"You're a paper-hanger, ain't you?" he said.

"Paper-hanger and deteckative," said his host proudly. "My name is Mister P. Gubb, graduate of the Rising Sun Deteckative Agency's Correspondence School of Deteckating in twelve lessons. And paper-hanging done in a neat manner."

Chi Foxy held out his hand eagerly.

"Shake, pard!" he asked. "That's my line, too."

"Paper-hanging?" asked Philo Gubb.

"Detecting," said Chi Foxy promptly. "I'm one of the most famousest gum-shoe fellers in the world. Me and this here great detective feller — what's his name, now? — used to work team-work together."

"Burns?" suggested Philo Gubb.

"Holmes," said Chi Foxy, "Shermlock Holmes. Me and him pulled off all them big jobs you maybe have read about in the papers."

He pronounced the name of the celebrated detective of fiction "Shermlock Hol-lums."

"Oh, yes," said the tramp, "me and Shermlock is great chums. And me and the kid!"

"To what kid do you refer to?" asked Philo Gubb.

"Why, my old side partner's little son, Shermlock Hollums the Twoth," said Chi Foxy without a blink. "And a cunnin' little feller he was — took after his father like a cat after fish, he did. Me and old Shermlock we used to hide things — candy and — and oranges — and let little Shermlock go and detect where they was. He was a great little codger, he was."

He noticed that Mr. Gubb was looking at him sharply. He looked down at his ragged garments.

"Disguise," he said briefly. "Nobody'd know a swell dresser like I am in this rig, would he? Say, pard, how about giving me a half-dollar to get breakfast? Us detectives ought to have es-*spirit dee corpse*, hey? We ought to stick by each other, hey?"

The celebrated paper-hanger detective considered Chi Foxy. It was evident that P. Gubb doubted the authenticity of the tramp-detective.

"In times of necessary need," he said slowly, "I often assume onto me the disguise of a tramp, but I don't assume it onto me so complete that I go asking for money to buy breakfast."

"You don't, hey?" said Chi Foxy scornfully. "Well, you must be a swell detective, you must. When I get into a tramp disguise I'm a tramp all through."

"Most certainly," said P. Gubb. "And so am I. But there's a difference into the way you are doing it now. You ain't deteckating now. You are coming at me as one deteckative unto another."

Chi Foxy laughed.

"Say," he said, "I'd like to see this here Correspondence School you graduated out of, I would. I'd like to see the lessons they learn you, I would.

313

Why, the first thing my old pard Shermlock Hollums told me was *never* to be anything but what I was disguised to be as long as I was disguised to be it. That's right. Maybe I'd be disguised as a tramp and I'd meet our old friend and college chum, the Dook of Sluff. He'd want to take me into some swell place and blow me off to a swell dinner. Would I let on? No, sir! I'd sort of whine at him and say, 'Mister, won't you give a poor feller a penny for to hire a bed?' That's how me and Shermlock stuck to a disguise. And Shermlock! Me and him was like twins, we was, and yet when I was in this tramp disguise and went up to his room to report, I'd knock at the door and say, 'Mister, give a poor cove a hand-out, won't you?' and Shermlock would turn and say, 'Watson, throw this tramp downstairs.' And Watson would do it. Yes, sir! I've been so sore and bruised from being thrown downstairs when I went to report to Shermlock that sometimes I'd have to go to the hospital to get plastered up. That's detecting!"

Chi Foxy looked at P. Gubb, but P. Gubb did not seem to have melted.

"That's livin' up to your disguise," continued Chi Foxy. "Me and Shermlock, when we had on tramp disguises we *were* tramps. Why, I used to go home and my valet would throw me downstairs. I was so thoroughly disguised, and I kept actin' so trampish while I had the disguise on, that he used to come at me with a golluf stick and whack me on the head. And when I got into my own room I kept right on being a tramp. Took off my clothes — still a tramp. Took off my false whiskers — still a tramp. I'd be there stark naked and I'd still be a tramp. Yes, sir. That's the kind of detective disguising I did. And then I'd take a bath. Then I was myself again. Yes, sir. When I'd scrubbed myself in the bathtub I figured I'd got rid of the tramp disguise right down into the skin, and I'd be myself again — and not until then."

He looked at P. Gubb out of the corner of his eye.

"Why, I remember one time," he said briskly, "I was asked to the Dook's palace to a swell party. Me and Shermlock was both asked, because they knew one of us would n't go unless the other did. Well, sir, I had been out detecting in a tramp disguise that day — findin' stolen jools and murderers and that sort of business — and I went and took my bath and rigged all up in swell clothes, and called my limmy-seen automobile, and when the feller I hired to drive the limmy-seen come to open the door of the car at the Dook's palace I dodged. Yes, sir, I dodged like I thought he was going to hit me because I had n't no business in my own limmy-seen automobile. That was funny, was n't it? So I went up the steps into the Dook's palace, and the gentleman he had to open the door opened the door, and he called out my name and up come the Dookess — Mrs. Dook of Sluff, as they call her, but I always called her Maggie, like she called me Mike. So she says to me, 'Mike, I'm mighty glad to see you here. We're going to have a swell party.' And I started to say back something pleasant, but what I said was, 'Please, missus, won't you give a poor cove a hand-out?'"

"What seemed to be the reason you said that?" asked Philo Gubb with interest.

"That's what worried me," said Chi Foxy. "I did n't mean to say it. I just said it against my will, as you might say. But I guess she thought I was tryin' to be smart, for she just says, 'Naughty, naughty, Mike,' and whistled to the Dook to come and blow me off to the feeds. So the Dook come and led me into the dining-room, and stacked me up against the table for a stand-up feed. Swell feed, bo! Samwiches till you could n't rest — ham sam-wiches and chicken samwiches and tongue sam-wiches and club samwiches and — and all kinds of samwiches. And what did I do? I grabbed half a dozen of them samwiches and rammed them into my pants pocket, just like a tramp would do it. The Dook looked surprised, but he begun to haw-haw, and he slapped me on the back and said, 'Good joke, ol' chap, good joke!' So that passed off all right. Then I went into the jool room, because the Dook had told me his son, the Dookette, or what you might call the little Dookerino, was in there. So in I went, and the first thing I knew I was hiding one of the Dook's gold crowns inside my vest. In a minute in come the Dook to pick out a crown to wear at dinner —"

"I thought you said they had a stand-up dinner at the table," said Philo Gubb.

"Pshaw, that was nothing but the appetizer," said Chi Foxy. "Well, in he come and began lookin' through his crowns for the one he wanted, and all at once he saw how my vest bulged out, and he knew by the rough edges of the bulge it was n't samwiches because them dookal samwiches is all boneless. So he puts his hand on my shoulder and he says, 'Mike, ain't you carryin' the joke a bit too far?' That's what he says, and I wish you could have heard how sad his voice was. He says, 'You know me, Mike, and you know that anything I've got is yours — *except* that crown you've got inside your vest.'

"For a minute I did n't know what to do. I was n't in tramp disguise and I thought he would think I was a thief in real life, so I says, 'Dook, search me!' 'I don't have to search you,' he says, 'for I can see my favorite crown bulging out your vest.' 'I don't mean that, Dook, old chap,' I says; 'I mean take me up to your bood-u-war or the bathroom and give me the twice-over. Something's wrong with me, and I don't know what, but some of my tramp disguise must be sticking to me somewhere.' So we went up to the bathroom and he went over me with this one-eyed monocule he always wore, and then he went over me with a reading-glass, and then he went over me with a microscope, but he could n't see a speck of tramp disguise on me. Not a speck. 'Keep lookin'!' I says. 'It must be there somewhere, Dook,' I says, 'or I would n't act so pernicious.' So he begun again, and all at once I hear him chuckle. He was lookin' in my ear with the microscope."

"What was it?" asked Philo Gubb eagerly.

"A hair," said Chi Foxy. "Just one hair. It was a hair out of my tramp whiskers that had got in my ear, and the minute he pulled it out I was all right again and no more tramp than he was. So you see that's the way I keep acting tramp as long as I have even one hair of tramp disguise about me. Come on, be a good feller and let me have half a dollar to get some feeds with."

P. Gubb put his hand in his pocket and withdrew it again. "I much admire to like the way you act right up to the disguise," he said, "and it does you proud, but of course when you ask for fifty cents it's nothing but part of the disguise, ain't it?"

"Now, see here, bo!" said Chi Foxy earnestly. "Don't you go and misunderstand me. I did n't mean to be mistook that way. I *do* want fifty cents. I'm hungry, I am."

P. Gubb smiled approvingly. "Most excellent trampish disguise work," he said. "Nobody could n't do it better. A real tramp could n't do it better."

Chi Foxy frowned. "Say," he said, "cut that out, won't you, cully? Your head ain't solid ivory, is it?

I'm starvin'. Gimme fifty cents, mister. Gimme a quarter if you won't give me fifty. Come on, now, be a good feller."

"A deteckative like you are ought n't to need twenty-five cents so bad as that," said P. Gubb. "A deteckative acquainted with the knowing of a Dook and of Sherlock Holmes don't have to beg."

Chi Foxy actually gritted his teeth. He was angry with himself. He had talked too well. He had proved so thoroughly that he was a detective that P. Gubb would not believe he was hungry.

"See here, bo," he said suddenly, "is this straight about you being a detective, or is that a bluff, too?"

Philo Gubb showed Chi Foxy the badge he had received upon completion of his correspondence course of twelve lessons.

"I'm the most celebrated and only deteckative in the town of Riverbank, Iowa," he said seriously, "and you can ask the Sheriff or the Chief of Police if you don't believe me. I'm working right now onto a case of quite some importance, into which a calf was stolen, but up to now the clues ain't what they should be. If you don't think I'm a deteckative you can ask Farmer Hopper. He hired me for to get the capture of the guilty calf-stealer aforesaid."

Chi Foxy studied P. Gubb's simple face.

"And you can arrest a feller and lodge him in jail?" he asked.

"I've arrested many and lodged them into jail," P. Gubb assured him.

"Well, bo," said Chi Foxy frankly, "I'm the man you're looking for. Arrest me."

The tramp knew enough about arrests to know that even a suspect, when lodged in jail, would be fed, and he was hungry and getting hungrier every moment. P. Gubb looked at him with surprise.

"I thought you said you was a deteckative," he said.

"I am," said Chi Foxy. "Or I would n't know I was a criminal. I detected it myself, because nobody else could. Even my old friend Shermlock Hollums could n't detect it, but I did. I'm a — a murderer, I am. There's a thousand-dollar reward offered for me."

"Then why don't you arrest yourself and get the reward?" asked P. Gubb.

"Say," said Chi Foxy with disgust. "It can't be done. I know, for I've tried. I'm a fugitive, that's what I am, and right behind me, no matter where I flee to, comes myself ready to grab me and arrest me. I've chased myself all over Europe, Asia and Africa, and I can't get away from myself, and I can't grab myself. It's — it's just awful."

Chi Foxy wiped an imaginary tear from his eye.

"And I can't keep away from the scene of my crime," he said. "I come back here time after time — "

"Did you do the murder here?" asked P. Gubb with increased interest.

"That's what I did," said Chi Foxy. "I did it

"A DETECKATIVE LIKE YOU ARE OUGHT N'T TO NEED
TWENTY-FIVE CENTS SO BAD AS THAT"

here. Take me down to the lock-up. Me and you can hold me all right."

"It's somewhat out of the ordinary common run for a feller to be a deteckative and the criminal murderer he's chasing both at once," said P. Gubb doubtfully.

"That's so, ain't it?" agreed Chi Foxy. "It looks that way. But facts are facts, ain't they?"

"Quite occasionally they are such," agreed P. Gubb.

"That's right," said Chi Foxy. "And all you've got to do is to explain them. You see, bo, I was a young feller when I murdered this old miser —"

"What did you say his name was?" asked P. Gubb.

"Smith," said Chi Foxy promptly. "John J. Smith, and he lived right here in this town. And I murdered the old feller and got away. Nobody cared much whether the old feller was murdered or not, and nothin' much might have been said of it except that the old feller had a nephew. His name was Smith — Peter P. Smith."

"What did he do?" asked P. Gubb.

"He offered a reward of a thousand dollars," said Chi Foxy. "It was one of them unsolved mystery cases — one of them cases that never get solved because no detective is smart enough to solve it. Nobody knew who killed old John J. Smith but me, and I was 't going around telling it."

"I should think not," said P. Gubb.

"No, sir!" said Chi Foxy. "So I was as safe as a babe unborn. I skipped up the river to Minneapolis, and nobody thought of lookin' for me, because I was n't suspected. And then I did a fool thing."

"Murderers 'most always does," said P. Gubb.

"Sure!" said Chi Foxy. "I thought I'd go to New Orleans. It was all right — nice trip — until we got to Dubuque, and then what happened? The old steamboat blew up. I went sailin' up in the air like one of these here skyrockets, I did, and when I come down I lit head first."

"It is a remarkable wonder it did n't kill you to death," said P. Gubb.

"Ain't it?" said Chi Foxy. "But it did worse than kill me. It knocked my senses out of me. When I come to I did n't know what had happened. I did n't remember a thing out of my past — not a thing. I was like a newborn babe. I did n't have an idea or a memory left in me. When they picked me up and I opened my eyes I could just say 'Ahgoo' and 'Da-da' and things like that, and I did n't know who I was or where I'd been or anything. So some kind folks took me and sent me to kindergarden, and I started in to learn my A-B-C's and things like that. I learned fast, and pretty soon I was in the high school, and pretty soon I graduated, and the name I graduated under was Mike Higgs, Higgs being the name of the family that adopted me."

BURIED BONES

"Mike Higgs?" repeated P. Gubb, trying to remember a celebrated detective of that name.

"Yes," said Chi Foxy, "they named me Mike after the old gran'pa of the family. He was a butcher, and they wanted me to be a butcher, but I wanted to be a detective. So Gran'pa Higgs he lent me enough money to go to London and take lessons in detecting from Shermlock Hollums, and I did. He says to me, when I'd finished the course, 'Mike, I hate to say it, but I can't call you a rival. You're so far ahead of me in detective knowledge that I'm like a half-witted child beside you.' That's what my old friend and teacher, Shermlock Hollums, says to me."

"That was exceedingly high praising from one so great," said P. Gubb.

"You bet it was!" said Chi Foxy, "So cne day Shermlock says to me, 'Mike you're so good at this detecting work, why don't you try to solve The Great Mystery?'

"'What's that?' I says.

"'Why, the greatest unsolved mystery of the world,' he says. 'The mystery of the Riverbank, Iowa, miser.'

"So he told me what he knew about it," continued Chi Foxy, "and I set to work. I come here to Riverbank to hunt up a clue, and I found just one clue."

"What was it?" asked Philo Gubb.

"It was a speck of red pepper no bigger than the

point of a pin," said Chi Foxy, "crushed into the carpet by the old miser's bed, where he had been killed. I picked up the speck of red pepper and microscoped it, and I saw that along one edge it was sort of brown, where it had been burned a little."

"Have you got it now?" asked P. Gubb.

"Got it?" said Chi Foxy. "I should say not. While I was lookin' at it a breeze come and blowed it away, and I never saw it again, but that was enough for me. 'Red pepper,' I says, 'partly burned,' and I began to tremble. 'Cause why? 'Cause I never was able to get smoking tobacco strong enough to suit me, and to make it taste snappy I always put a little red pepper in my pipe. I turned as white as a sheet. 'Red pepper partly burned!' I says to myself. 'Nobody in the world but me puts red pepper in his tobacco.'

"Well, sir, I started tracing myself back and I found out I was the murderer. And I was the detective after the murderer. I was everybody concerned. In a moment I was overcome by criminal fear and I fled. I fled all over Europe, Asia, and Africa, and wherever I went I was right after myself, ready to arrest me."

Chi Foxy paused and glanced at P. Gubb questioningly. With a solemn face the great Correspondence School detective blinked his bird-like eyes at Chi Foxy.

"So now arrest me," said Chi Foxy.

Philo Gubb rubbed his chin. "I'd like to favor

you by so doing, Mr. Jones," he said, "for I can easy see, Mr. Higgs, that you can't arrest yourself, but it is against the instructions in Lesson Six of the Rising Sun Correspondence School of Deteckating for a graduate to arrest a man without a good clue, and the only clue you had was blowed away."

For a moment this seemed to annoy Chi Foxy, but his face suddenly brightened.

"Clue?" he said. "Say, friend, I would n't ask you to arrest me on any such clue as a speck of red pepper. No, sir! But I've got a clue that'll mean something. I can tell you right where I buried that old miser's bones, I can. You go up the river road until you come to a tool-house on the railway, and just back of the tool-house is a dwellin'-house — old and unpainted. All right! Right in that yard, close to the railway fence, the bones is buried. Now, you turn me over to the law, and you go up there —"

"We'd best go up there immediately first before anything else," said Philo Gubb, starting to remove his paper-hanger's apron. "Putting off clues until sometime else is against Paragraph Four, Lesson One. If you come up there with me —"

"Look here," said Chi Foxy, "will you buy me a feed on the way up if I go with you?"

"Quite certainly sure," said P. Gubb, and so it was agreed.

The paper-hanger detective and the criminal-detective stopped at Hank's restaurant and Chi

Foxy ate a heavy meal, and then led the way to the tool-house, and pointed over the wire fence to the spot where the bones of the murdered miser were supposed to repose.

"Right there!" he said, but when P. Gubb had climbed the fence and had turned to look for Chi Foxy, the late detective-criminal was gone. Mr. Gubb's face turned red, but as he hung his head in shame he noticed that the ground at his feet had lately been spaded. He stooped to look at it, and then walked to the weather-beaten house and knocked. A lanky, loose-jointed man came to the door, and a woman peered at Mr. Gubb from behind the man.

"I hope you'll pardon," said Mr. Gubb politely, "but my name is P. Gubb, deteckative and paper-hanger, and I'm looking up a case. Might I trouble you for the loan of a spade or shovel?"

"What you want with it?" asked the man gruffly.

"To dig," said Mr. Gubb.

The man reluctantly handed Mr. Gubb a spade on which there were still traces of soft, sandy soil. Mr. Gubb walked to the rear of the yard and jabbed the spade into the soft soil. It struck something hard. In a moment or two Mr. Gubb had the evidences of crime completely uncovered. There were bones buried there — many bones. Mr. Gubb looked up and wiped his brow. Then he looked down at the bones. One was a skull. Mr. Gubb stared at it. It was indeed a skull, but it was the skull of a calf. All the bones were calf bones — not bones of the human calf, but bones of the veal calf. Mr. Gubb turned his head and saw the long lanky man approaching.

"All right," said the long, lanky man, "I give up. You've got me. I surrender. When a detective gets that close, a man has n't any chance. I own up. I did it."

"You did what?"

"Now, quit!" said the long, lanky man. "No use rubbin' it in after I've owned up. You know as well as I do — I'm the man that stole Farmer Hopper's calf. I give up. I surrender."

"I'm much obliged to you," said Philo Gubb.

"Well, I ain't obliged to *you*," said the lanky man, "but I wish you'd tell me how you found out I was the calf thief."

Mr. Gubb smiled an inscrutable smile.

"A deteckative acquires dexterity in the way of capturing up the criminal classes," he said with oracular yet modest simplicity.

The next day, when Mr. Gubb returned to his paper-hanging job he found Chi Foxy waiting for him.

"Boss," he said with a laugh, "I showed you where that murdered man's bones was buried, won't you stake me to a meal?"

"Are you hungry again?" asked Mr. Gubb.

"Hungry?" said Chi Foxy. "I'm so hungry that I feel like a living skeleton. I'm so hungry that a square meal would make me feel like Syrilla, that Fat Lady I seen at Derlingport a couple of days ago."

"What's that you remarked about?" asked Mr. Gubb, pinning Chi Foxy with his eye. "Did I understand the meaning of what you said was that you saw a Fat Lady named Syrilla?"

"At Derlingport," said Chi Foxy. "A swell guy named Medderbrook give me a meal and a ticket to the big show. It was a performance *de luxe*, so to say. Special attraction, bo. You'd have laughed your head off. This here Syrilla Fat Lady got married to the Living Skeleton in the middle ring, and she had the Snake Charmer for a bridesmaid. Say! you'd have laughed —"

But Mr. Gubb did not laugh. He never laughed again.

PHILO GUBB'S GREATEST CASE

Philo Gubb, wrapped in his bathrobe, went to the door of the room that was the headquarters of his business of paper-hanging and decorating as well as the office of his detective business, and opened the door a crack. It was still early in the morning, but Mr. Gubb was a modest man, and, lest any one should see him in his scanty attire, he peered through the crack of the door before he stepped hastily into the hall and captured his copy of the "Riverbank Daily Eagle." When he had secured the still damp newspaper, he returned to his cot bed and spread himself out to read comfortably.

It was a hot Iowa morning. Business was so slack that if Mr. Gubb had not taken out his set of eight varieties of false whiskers daily and brushed them carefully, the moths would have been able to devour them at leisure.

P. Gubb opened the "Eagle." The first words that met his eye caused him to sit upright on his cot. At the top of the first column of the first page were the headlines.

MYSTERIOUS DEATH OF HENRY SMITZ

Body Found In Mississippi River By Boatman Early This A.M.

Foul Play Suspected

329

PHILO GUBB, THE DETECTIVE

Mr. Gubb unfolded the paper and read the item under the headlines with the most intense interest. Foul play meant the possibility of an opportunity to put to 'use once more the precepts of the Course of Twelve Lessons, and with them fresh in his mind Detective Gubb was eager to undertake the solution of any mystery that Riverbank could furnish. This was the article: —

Just as we go to press we receive word through Policeman Michael O'Toole that the well-known mussel-dredger and boatman, Samuel Fliggis (Long Sam), while dredging for mussels last night just below the bridge, recovered the body of Henry Smitz, late of this place.

Mr. Smitz had been missing for three days and his wife had been greatly worried. Mr. Brownson, of the Brownson Packing Company, by whom he was employed, admitted that Mr. Smitz had been missing for several days.

The body was found sewed in a sack. Foul play is suspected.

"I should think foul play would be suspected," exclaimed Philo Gubb, "if a man was sewed into a bag and deposited into the Mississippi River until dead."

He propped the paper against the foot of the cot bed and was still reading when some one knocked on his door. He wrapped his bathrobe carefully about him and opened the door. A young woman with tear-dimmed eyes stood in the doorway.

"Mr. P. Gubb?" she asked. "I'm sorry to disturb you so early in the morning, Mr. Gubb, but I could n't sleep all night. I came on a matter of

330

business, as you might say. There's a couple of things I want you to do."

"Paper-hanging or deteckating?" asked P. Gubb.

"Both," said the young woman. "My name is Smitz — Emily Smitz. My husband —"

"I'm aware of the knowledge of your loss, ma'am," said the paper-hanger detective gently.

"Lots of people know of it," said Mrs. Smitz. "I guess everybody knows of it — I told the police to try to find Henry, so it is no secret. And I want you to come up as soon as you get dressed, and paper my bedroom."

Mr. Gubb looked at the young woman as if he thought she had gone insane under the burden of her woe.

"And then I want you to find Henry," she said, "because I've heard you can do so well in the detecting line."

Mr. Gubb suddenly realized that the poor creature did not yet know the full extent of her loss. He gazed down upon her with pity in his bird-like eyes.

"I know you'll think it strange," the young woman went on, "that I should ask you to paper a bedroom first, when my husband is lost; but if he is gone it is because I was a mean, stubborn thing. We never quarreled in our lives, Mr. Gubb, until I picked out the wall-paper for our bedroom, and Henry said parrots and birds-of-paradise and tropical flowers that were as big as umbrellas would look awful on our bedroom wall. So I said he had n't

331

anything but Low Dutch taste, and he got mad.
'All right, have it your own way,' he said, and I
went and had Mr. Skaggs put the paper on the wall,
and the next day Henry did n't come home at all.

"If I'd thought Henry would take it that way,
I'd rather had the wall bare, Mr. Gubb. I've cried
and cried, and last night I made up my mind it was
all my fault and that when Henry came home he'd
find a decent paper on the wall. I don't mind telling
you, Mr. Gubb, that when the paper was on the wall
it looked worse than it looked in the roll. It looked
crazy."

"Yes'm," said Mr. Gubb, "it often does. But,
however, there's something you'd ought to know
right away about Henry."

The young woman stared wide-eyed at Mr. Gubb
for a moment; she turned as white as her shirt-
waist.

"Henry is dead!" she cried, and collapsed into
Mr. Gubb's long, thin arms.

Mr. Gubb, the inert form of the young woman in
his arms, glanced around with a startled gaze.
He stood miserably, not knowing what to do, when
suddenly he saw Policeman O'Toole coming toward
him down the hall. Policeman O'Toole was leading by the arm a man whose wrists bore clanking
handcuffs.

"What's this now?" asked the policeman none
too gently, as he saw the bathrobed Mr. Gubb holding the fainting woman in his arms.

"I am exceedingly glad you have come," said Mr. Gubb. "The only meaning into it, is that this is Mrs. H. Smitz, widow-lady, fainted onto me against my will and wishes."

"I was only askin'," said Policeman O'Toole politely enough.

"You should n't ask such things until you're asked to ask," said Mr. Gubb.

After looking into Mr. Gubb's room to see that there was no easy means of escape, O'Toole pushed his prisoner into the room and took the limp form of Mrs. Smitz from Mr. Gubb, who entered the room and closed the door.

"I may as well say what I want to say right now," said the handcuffed man as soon as he was alone with Mr. Gubb. "I've heard of Detective Gubb, off and on, many a time, and as soon as I got into this trouble I said, 'Gubb's the man that can get me out if any one can.' My name is Herman Wiggins."

"Glad to meet you," said Mr. Gubb, slipping his long legs into his trousers.

"And I give you my word for what it is worth," continued Mr. Wiggins, "that I'm as innocent of this crime as the babe unborn."

"What crime?" asked Mr. Gubb.

"Why, killing Hen Smitz — what crime did you think?" said Mr. Wiggins. "Do I look like a man that would go and murder a man just because —"

He hesitated and Mr. Gubb, who was slipping his

suspenders over his bony shoulders, looked at Mr. Wiggins with keen eyes.

"Well, just because him and me had words in fun," said Mr. Wiggins, "I leave it to you, can't a man say words in fun once in a while?"

"Certainly sure," said Mr. Gubb.

"I guess so," said Mr. Wiggins. "Anybody'd know a man don't mean all he says. When I went and told Hen Smitz I'd murder him as sure as green apples grow on a tree, I was just fooling. But this fool policeman —"

"Mr. O'Toole?"

"Yes. They gave him this Hen Smitz case to look into, and the first thing he did was to arrest me for murder. Nervy, I call it."

Policeman O'Toole opened the door a crack and peeked in. Seeing Mr. Gubb well along in his dressing operations, he opened the door wider and assisted Mrs. Smitz to a chair. She was still limp, but she was a brave little woman and was trying to control her sobs.

"Through?" O'Toole asked Wiggins. "If you are, come along back to jail."

"Now, don't talk to me in that tone of voice," said Mr. Wiggins angrily. "No, I'm not through. You don't know how to treat a gentleman like a gentleman, and never did."

He turned to Mr. Gubb.

"The long and short of it is this: I'm arrested for the murder of Hen Smitz, and I did n't murder him and I want you to take my case and get me out of jail."

"Ah, stuff!" exclaimed O'Toole. "You murdered him and you know you did. What's the use talkin'?"

Mrs. Smitz leaned forward in her chair.

"Murdered Henry?" she cried. "He never murdered Henry. I murdered him."

"Now, ma'am," said O'Toole politely, "I hate to contradict a lady, but you never murdered him at all. This man here murdered him, and I've got the proof on him."

"I murdered him!" cried Mrs. Smitz again. "I drove him out of his right mind and made him kill himself."

"Nothing of the sort," declared O'Toole. "This man Wiggins murdered him."

"I did not!" exclaimed Mr. Wiggins indignantly. "Some other man did it."

It seemed a deadlock, for each was quite positive. Mr. Gubb looked from one to the other doubtfully.

"All right, take me back to jail," said Mr. Wiggins. "You look up the case, Mr. Gubb; that's all I came here for. Will you do it? Dig into it, hey?"

"I most certainly shall be glad to so do," said Mr. Gubb, "at the regular terms."

O'Toole led his prisoner away.

For a few minutes Mrs. Smitz sat silent, her hands clasped, staring at the floor. Then she looked up into Mr. Gubb's eyes.

"You will work on this case, Mr. Gubb, won't you?" she begged. "I have a little money — I'll give it all to have you do your best. It is cruel — cruel to have that poor man suffer under the charge of murder when I know so well Henry killed himself because I was cross with him. You can prove he killed himself — that it was my fault. You will?"

"The way the deteckative profession operates onto a case," said Mr. Gubb, "is n't to go to work to prove anything particularly especial. It finds a clue or clues and follows them to where they lead to. That I shall be willing to do."

"That is all I could ask," said Mrs. Smitz gratefully.

Arising from her seat with difficulty, she walked tremblingly to the door. Mr. Gubb assisted her down the stairs, and it was not until she was gone that he remembered that she did not know the body of her husband had been found — sewed in a sack and at the bottom of the river. Young husbands have been known to quarrel with their wives over matters as trivial as bedroom wall-paper; they have even been known to leave home for several days at a time when angry; in extreme cases they have even been known to seek death at their own hands; but it is not at all usual for a young husband to leave home for several days and then in cold blood sew himself in a sack and jump into the river. In the first place there are easier ways of terminating one's life; in the second place a man can jump into the river with perfect ease without going to the trouble of sewing himself in a sack; and in the third place it is exceedingly difficult for a man to sew himself into a sack. It is almost impossible.

To sew himself into a sack a man must have no little skill, and he must have a large, roomy sack. He takes, let us say, a sack-needle, threaded with a good length of twine; he steps into the sack and pulls it up over his head; he then reaches above his head, holding the mouth of the sack together with one hand while he sews with the other hand. In hot anger this would be quite impossible.

Philo Gubb thought of all this as he looked through his disguises, selecting one suitable for the work he had in hand. He had just decided that the most appropriate disguise would be "Number 13, Undertaker," and had picked up the close black wig, and long, drooping mustache, when he had another thought. Given a bag sufficiently loose to permit free motion of the hands and arms, and a man, even in hot anger, might sew himself in. A man, intent on suicidally bagging himself, would sew the mouth of the bag shut and would then cut a slit in the front of the bag large enough to crawl into. He would then crawl into the bag and sew up the slit, which would be immediately in front of his hands. It could be done! Philo Gubb chose from his wardrobe a black frock coat and a silk hat with a wide band of crape. He carefully locked his door and went down to the street.

On a day as hot as this day promised to be, a frock

coat and a silk hat could be nothing but distressingly uncomfortable. Between his door and the corner, eight various citizens spoke to Philo Gubb, calling him by name. In fact, Riverbank was as accustomed to seeing P. Gubb in disguise as out of disguise, and while a few children might be interested by the sight of Detective Gubb in disguise, the older citizens thought no more of it, as a rule, than of seeing Banker Jennings appear in a pink shirt one day and a blue striped one the next. No one ever accused Banker Jennings of trying to hide his identity by a change of shirts, and no one imagined that P. Gubb was trying to disguise himself when he put on a disguise. They considered it a mere business custom, just as a butcher tied on a white apron before he went behind his counter.

This was why, instead of wondering who the tall, dark-garbed stranger might be, Banker Jennings greeted Philo Gubb cheerfully.

"Ah, Gubb!" he said. "So you are going to work on this Smitz case, are you? Glad of it, and wish you luck. Hope you place the crime on the right man and get him the full penalty. Let me tell you there's nothing in this rumor of Smitz being short of money. We did lend him money, but we never pressed him for it. We never even asked him for interest. I told him a dozen times he could have as much more from us as he wanted, within reason, whenever he wanted it, and that he could pay me when his invention was on the market."

"No report of news of any such rumor has as yet come to my hearing," said P. Gubb, "but since you mention it, I'll take it for less than it is worth."

"And that's less than nothing," said the banker. "Have you any clue?"

"I'm on my way to find one at the present moment of time," said Mr. Gubb.

"Well, let me give you a pointer," said the banker. "Get a line on Herman Wiggins or some of his crew, understand? Don't say I said a word, — I don't want to be brought into this, — but Smitz was afraid of Wiggins and his crew. He told me so. He said Wiggins had threatened to murder him."

"Mr. Wiggins is at present in the custody of the county jail for killing H. Smitz with intent to murder him," said Mr. Gubb.

"Oh, then — then it's all settled," said the banker. "They've proved it on him. I thought they would. Well, I suppose you've got to do your little bit of detecting just the same. Got to air the camphor out of the false hair, eh?"

The banker waved a cheerful hand at P. Gubb and passed into his banking institution.

Detective Gubb, cordially greeted by his many friends and admirers, passed on down the main street, and by the time he reached the street that led to the river he was followed by a large and growing group intent on the pleasant occupation of watching a detective detect.

As Mr. Gubb walked toward the river, other citizens joined the group, but all kept a respectful distance behind him. When Mr. Gubb reached River Street and his false mustache fell off, the interest of the audience stopped short three paces behind him and stood until he had rescued the mustache and once more placed its wires in his nostrils. Then, when he moved forward again, they too moved forward. Never, perhaps, in the history of crime was a detective favored with a more respectful gallery.

On the edge of the river, Mr. Gubb found Long Sam Fliggis, the mussel dredger, seated on an empty tar-barrel with his own audience ranged before him listening while he told, for the fortieth time, the story of his finding of the body of H. Smitz. As Philo Gubb approached, Long Sam ceased speaking, and his audience and Mr. Gubb's gallery merged into one great circle which respectfully looked and listened while Mr. Gubb questioned the mussel dredger.

"Suicide?" said Long Sam scoffingly. "Why, he wan't no more a suicide than I am right now. He was murdered or wan't nothin'! I've dredged up some suicides in my day, and some of 'em had stones tied to 'em, to make sure they'd sink, and some thought they'd sink without no ballast, but nary one of 'em ever sewed himself into a bag, and I give my word," he said positively, "that Hen Smitz could n't have sewed himself into that burlap bag unless some one done the sewing. Then the feller that did it was an assistant-suicide, and the way

HE WAS FOLLOWED BY A LARGE AND GROWING GROUP INTENT ON WATCHING

A DETECTIVE DETECT

I look at it is that an assistant-suicide is jest the same as a murderer."

The crowd murmured approval, but Mr. Gubb held up his hand for silence.

"In certain kinds of burlap bags it is possibly probable a man could sew himself into it," said Mr. Gubb, and the crowd, seeing the logic of the remark applauded gently but feelingly.

"You ain't seen the way he was sewed up," said Long Sam, "or you would n't talk like that."

"I have n't yet took a look," admitted Mr. Gubb, "but I aim so to do immediately after I find a clue onto which to work up my case. An A-1 deteckative can't set forth to work until he has a clue, that being a rule of the game."

"What kind of a clue was you lookin' for?" asked Long Sam. "What's a clue, anyway?"

"A clue," said P. Gubb, "is almost anything connected with the late lamented, but generally something that nobody but a deteckative would think had anything to do with anything whatsoever. Not infrequently often it is a button."

"Well, I've got no button except them that is sewed onto me," said Long Sam, "but if this here sackneedle will do any good —"

He brought from his pocket the point of a heavy sack-needle and laid it in Philo Gubb's palm. Mr. Gubb looked at it carefully. In the eye of the needle still remained a few inches of twine.

"I cut that off 'n the burlap he was sewed up in,"

volunteered Long Sam, "I thought I'd keep it as a sort of nice little souvenir. I'd like it back again when you don't need it for a clue no more."

"Certainly sure," agreed Mr. Gubb, and he examined the needle carefully.

There are two kinds of sack-needles in general use. In both, the point of the needle is curved to facilitate pushing it into and out of a closely filled sack; in both, the curved portion is somewhat flattened so that the thumb and finger may secure a firm grasp to pull the needle through; but in one style the eye is at the end of the shaft while in the other it is near the point. This needle was like neither; the eye was midway of the shaft; the needle was pointed at each end and the curved portions were not flattened. Mr. Gubb noticed another thing — the twine was not the ordinary loosely twisted hemp twine, but a hard, smooth cotton cord, like carpet warp.

"Thank you," said Mr. Gubb, "and now I will go elsewhere to investigate to a further extent, and it is not necessarily imperative that everybody should accompany along with me if they don't want to."

But everybody did want to, it seemed. Long Sam and his audience joined Mr. Gubb's gallery and, with a dozen or so newcomers, they followed Mr. Gubb at a decent distance as he walked toward the plant of the Brownson Packing Company, which stood on the riverbank some two blocks away.

It was here Henry Smitz had worked. Six or eight buildings of various sizes, the largest of which stood immediately on the river's edge, together with the "yards" or pens, all enclosed by a high board fence, constituted the plant of the packing company, and as Mr. Gubb appeared at the gate the watchman there stood aside to let him enter.

"Good-morning, Mr. Gubb," he said pleasantly. "I been sort of expecting you. Always right on the job when there's crime being done, ain't you? You'll find Merkel and Brill and Jokosky and the rest of Wiggins's crew in the main building, and I guess they'll tell you just what they told the police. They hate it, but what else can they say? It's the truth."

"What is the truth?" asked Mr. Gubb.

"That Wiggins was dead sore at Hen Smitz," said the watchman. "That Wiggins told Hen he'd do for him if he lost them their jobs like he said he would. That's the truth."

Mr. Gubb — his admiring followers were halted at the gate by the watchman — entered the large building and inquired his way to Mr. Wiggins's department. He found it on the side of the building toward the river and on the ground floor. On one side the vast room led into the refrigerating room of the company; on the other it opened upon a long but narrow dock that ran the width of the building.

Along the outer edge of the dock were tied two barges, and into these barges some of Wiggins's crew were dumping mutton — not legs of mutton but entire sheep, neatly sewed in burlap. The large room was the packing and shipping room, and the work of Wiggins's crew was that of sewing the slaughtered and refrigerated sheep carcasses in burlap for shipment. Bales of burlap stood against one wall; strands of hemp twine ready for the needle hung from pegs in the wall and the posts that supported the floor above. The contiguity of the refrigerating room gave the room a pleasantly cool atmosphere.

Mr. Gubb glanced sharply around. Here was the burlap, here were needles, here was twine. Yonder was the river into which Hen Smitz had been thrown. He glanced across the narrow dock at the blue river. As his eye returned he noticed one of the men carefully sweeping the dock with a broom — sweeping fragments of glass into the river. As the men in the room watched him curiously, Mr. Gubb picked up a piece of burlap and put it in his pocket, wrapped a strand of twine around his finger and pocketed the twine, examined the needles stuck in improvised needle-holders made by boring gimlet holes in the wall, and then walked to the dock and picked up one of the pieces of glass.

"Clues," he remarked, and gave his attention to the work of questioning the men.

Although manifestly reluctant, they honestly admitted that Wiggins had more than once threatened Hen Smitz — that he hated Hen Smitz with the hatred of a man who has been threatened with the loss of his job. Mr. Gubb learned that Hen Smitz

had been the foreman for the entire building — a
sort of autocrat with, as Wiggins's crew informed
him, an easy job. He had only to see that the crews
in the building turned out more work this year than
they did last year. "'Ficiency" had been his motto,
they said, and they hated "'Ficiency."

Mr. Gubb's gallery was awaiting him at the gate,
and its members were in a heated discussion as to
what Mr. Gubb had been doing. They ceased at
once when he appeared and fell in behind him as he
walked away from the packing house and toward
the undertaking establishment of Mr. Holworthy
Bartman, on the main street. Here, joining the
curious group already assembled, the gallery was
forced to wait while Mr. Gubb entered. His task
was an unpleasant but necessary one. He must visit
the little "morgue" at the back of Mr. Bartman's
establishment.

The body of poor Hen Smitz had not yet been removed from the bag in which it had been found, and
it was to the bag Mr. Gubb gave his closest attention. The bag — in order that the body might be
identified — had not been ripped, but had been cut,
and not a stitch had been severed. It did not take
Mr. Gubb a moment to see that Hen Smitz had not
been sewed in a bag at all. He had been sewed
in burlap — burlap "yard goods," to use a shop-
keeper's term — and it was burlap identical with
that used by Mr. Wiggins and his crew. It was
no loose bag of burlap — but a close-fitting wrap-

ping of burlap; a cocoon of burlap that had been drawn tight around the body, as burlap is drawn tight around the carcass of sheep for shipment, like a mummy's wrappings.

It would have been utterly impossible for Hen Smitz to have sewed himself into the casing, not only because it bound his arms tight to his sides, but because the burlap was lapped over and sewed from the outside. This, once and for all, ended the suicide theory. The question was: Who was the murderer?

As Philo Gubb turned away from the bier, Undertaker Bartman entered the morgue.

"The crowd outside is getting impatient, Mr. Gubb," he said in his soft, undertakery voice. "It is getting on toward their lunch hour, and they want to crowd into my front office to find out what you've learned. I'm afraid they'll break my plate-glass windows, they're pushing so hard against them. I don't want to hurry you, but if you would go out and tell them Wiggins is the murderer they'll go away. Of course there's no doubt about Wiggins being the murderer, since he has admitted he asked the stock-keeper for the electric-light bulb."

"What bulb?" asked Philo Gubb.

"The electric-light bulb we found sewed inside this burlap when we sliced it open," said Bartman. "Matter of fact, we found it in Hen's hand. O'Toole took it for a clue and I guess it fixes the murder on Wiggins beyond all doubt. The stock-keeper says Wiggins got it from him."

346

"And what does Wiggins remark on that subject?" asked Mr. Gubb.

"Not a word," said Bartman. "His lawyer told him not to open his mouth, and he won't. Listen to that crowd out there!"

"I will attend to that crowd right presently," said P. Gubb, sternly. "What I should wish to know now is why Mister Wiggins went and sewed an electric-light bulb in with the corpse for."

"In the first place," said Mr. Bartman, "he did n't sew it in with any corpse, because Hen Smitz was n't a corpse when he was sewed in that burlap, unless Wiggins drowned him first, for Dr. Mortimer says Hen Smitz died of drowning; and in the second place, if you had a live man to sew in burlap, and had to hold him while you sewed him, you 'd be liable to sew anything in with him.

"My idea is that Wiggins and some of his crew jumped on Hen Smitz and threw him down and some of them held him while the others sewed him in. My idea is that Wiggins got that electric-light bulb to replace one that had burned out, and that he met Hen Smitz and had words with him, and they clinched, and Hen Smitz grabbed the bulb, and then the others came, and they sewed him into the burlap and dumped him into the river.

"So all you 've got to do is to go out and tell that crowd that Wiggins did it and that you 'll let them know who helped him as soon as you find out. And you better do it before they break my windows."

PHILO GUBB, THE DETECTIVE

Detective Gubb turned and went out of the morgue. As he left the undertaker's establishment the crowd gave a slight cheer, but Mr. Gubb walked hurriedly toward the jail. He found Policeman O'Toole there and questioned him about the bulb; and O'Toole, proud to be the center of so large and interested a gathering of his fellow citizens, pulled the bulb from his pocket and handed it to Mr. Gubb, while he repeated in more detail the facts given by Mr. Bartman. Mr. Gubb looked at the bulb.

"I presume to suppose," he said, "that Mr. Wiggins asked the stock-keeper for a new bulb to replace one that was burned out?"

"You're right," said O'Toole. "Why?"

"For the reason that this bulb is a burned-out bulb," said Mr. Gubb.

And so it was. The inner surface of the bulb was darkened slightly, and the filament of carbon was severed. O'Toole took the bulb and examined it curiously.

"That's odd, ain't it?" he said.

"It might so seem to the non-deteckative mind," said Mr. Gubb, "but to the deteckative mind, nothing is odd."

"No, no, this ain't so odd, either," said O'Toole, "for whether Hen Smitz grabbed the bulb before Wiggins changed the new one for the old one, or after he changed it, don't make so much difference, when you come to think of it."

"To the deteckative mind," said Mr. Gubb, "it

makes the difference that this ain't the bulb you thought it was, and hence consequently it ain't the bulb Mister Wiggins got from the stock-keeper."

Mr. Gubb started away. The crowd followed him. He did not go in search of the original bulb at once. He returned first to his room, where he changed his undertaker disguise for Number Six, that of a blue woolen-shirted laboring-man with a long brown beard. Then he led the way back to the packing house.

Again the crowd was halted at the gate, but again P. Gubb passed inside, and he found the stock-keeper eating his luncheon out of a tin pail. The stock-keeper was perfectly willing to talk.

"It was like this," said the stock-keeper. "We've been working overtime in some departments down here, and Wiggins and his crew had to work over-time the night Hen Smitz was murdered. Hen and Wiggins was at outs, or anyway I heard Hen tell Wiggins he'd better be hunting another job because he wouldn't have this one long, and Wiggins told Hen that if he lost his job he'd murder him — Wiggins would murder Hen, that is. I didn't think it was much of anything but loose talk at the time. But Hen was working overtime too. He'd been working nights up in that little room of his on the second floor for quite some time, and this night Wiggins come to me and he says Hen had asked him for a fresh thirty-two-candle-power bulb. So I give it to Wiggins, and then I went home. And, come to find out, Wiggins sewed that bulb up with Hen."

"Perhaps maybe you have sack-needles like this into your stock-room," said P. Gubb, producing the needle Long Sam had given him. The stock-keeper took the needle and examined it carefully.

"Never had any like that," he said.

"Now, if," said Philo Gubb, — "if the bulb that was sewed up into the burlap with Henry Smitz wasn't a new bulb, and if Mr. Wiggins had given the new bulb to Henry, and if Henry had changed the new bulb for an old one, where would he have changed it at?"

"Up in his room, where he was always tinkering at that machine of his," said the stock-keeper.

"Could I have the pleasure of taking a look into that there room for a moment of time?" asked Mr. Gubb.

The stock-keeper arose, returned the remnants of his luncheon to his dinner-pail and led the way up the stairs. He opened the door of the room Henry Smitz had used as a work-room, and P. Gubb walked in. The room was in some confusion, but, except in one or two particulars, no more than a work-room is apt to be. A rather cumbrous machine — the invention on which Henry Smitz had been working — stood as the murdered man had left it, all its levers, wheels, arms, and cogs intact. A chair, tipped over, lay on the floor. A roll of burlap stood on a roller by the machine. Looking up, Mr. Gubb saw, on the ceiling, the lighting fixture of the room, and in it was a clean, shining thirty-two-candle-power bulb. Where another similar bulb might have been in the other socket was a plug from which an insulated wire, evidently to furnish power, ran to the small motor connected with the machine on which Henry Smitz had been working.

The stock-keeper was the first to speak.

"Hello!" he said. "Somebody broke that window!" And it was true. Somebody had not only broken the window, but had broken every pane and the sash itself. But Mr. Gubb was not interested in this. He was gazing at the electric bulb and thinking of Part Two, Lesson Six of the Course of Twelve Lessons — "How to Identify by Finger-Prints, with General Remarks on the Bertillon System." He looked about for some means of reaching the bulb above his head. His eye lit on the fallen chair. By placing the chair upright and placing one foot on the frame of Henry Smitz's machine and the other on the chair-back, he could reach the bulb. He righted the chair and stepped onto its seat. He put one foot on the frame of Henry Smitz's machine; very carefully he put the other foot on the top of the chair-back. He reached upward and unscrewed the bulb.

The stock-keeper saw the chair totter. He sprang forward to steady it, but he was too late. Philo Gubb, grasping the air, fell on the broad, level board that formed the middle part of Henry Smitz's machine.

The effect was instantaneous. The cogs and wheels of the machine began to revolve rapidly. Two strong, steel arms flopped down and held Detective Gubb to the table, clamping his arms to his side. The roll of burlap unrolled, and as it unrolled, the loose end was seized and slipped under Mr. Gubb and wrapped around him and drawn taut, bundling him as a sheep's carcass is bundled. An arm reached down and back and forth, with a sewing motion, and passed from Mr. Gubb's head to his feet. As it reached his feet a knife sliced the burlap in which he was wrapped from the burlap on the roll.

And then a most surprising thing happened. As if the board on which he lay had been a catapult, it suddenly and unexpectedly raised Philo Gubb and tossed him through the open window. The stock-keeper heard a muffled scream and then a great splash, but when he ran to the window, the great paper-hanger detective had disappeared in the bosom of the Mississippi.

Like Henry Smitz he had tried to reach the ceiling by standing on the chair-back; like Henry Smitz he had fallen upon the newly invented burlaping and loading machine; like Henry Smitz he had been wrapped and thrown through the window into the river; but, unlike Henry Smitz, he had not been sewn into the burlap, because Philo Gubb had the double-pointed shuttle-action needle in his pocket.

Page Seventeen of Lesson Eleven of the Rising

PHILO GUBB'S GREATEST CASE

Sun Detective Agency's Correspondence School of Detecting's Course of Twelve Lessons, says: —

In cases of extreme difficulty of solution it is well for the detective to reënact as nearly as possible the probable action of the crime.

Mr. Philo Gubb had done so. He had also proved that a man may be sewn in a sack and drowned in a river without committing willful suicide or being the victim of foul play.

THE END